Praise for
Sophia Money-Coutts

'So funny. And the sex is amazing!'
Jilly Cooper

'Hilariously funny – I couldn't put it down'
Beth O'Leary

'As fun and fizzy as a chilled glass of Prosecco'
Daily Express

'Fast and furious, funny and fresh'
Daily Mail

'Howlingly funny'
The Sunday Times

'I started reading this book on the 3.48 from Waterloo
and by 4.15 I was crying with laughter. Brilliant'
Sarah Morgan

'Wonderfully rude'
Red

'Fizzy, fun and some seriously saucy shenanigans'
Mail on Sunday

'Perfect for fans of Jilly Cooper and *Bridget Jones*'
HELLO!

'Fizzes with joy'
Metro

'Surprisingly saucy and distractingly funny'
Grazia

i

Sophia Money-Coutts is a journalist and author who spent five years studying the British aristocracy while working as Features Director at *Tatler*. Prior to that she worked as a writer and an editor for the *Evening Standard* and the *Daily Mail* in London, and *The National* in Abu Dhabi. She's a columnist for *The Sunday Telegraph* and the *Evening Standard* and often appears on radio and television channels talking about important topics such as Prince Harry's wedding and the etiquette of the threesome. *What Happens Now?* is her second novel.

Also by
Sophia Money-Coutts

The Plus One

What Happens Now?

SOPHIA MONEY-COUTTS

ONE PLACE. MANY STORIES

HQ
An imprint of HarperCollins*Publishers* Ltd
1 London Bridge Street
London SE1 9GF

This edition 2020

1

First published in Great Britain by
HQ, an imprint of HarperCollins*Publishers* Ltd 2019

ISBN: 978-0-00-828854-9

MIX
Paper from
responsible sources
FSC™ C007454

This book is produced from independently certified FSC™ paper to ensure responsible forest management.

For more information visit: www.harpercollins.co.uk/green

Printed and bound in Great Britain by
CPI Group (UK) Ltd, Croydon, CR0 4YY

To all parents, whatever shape they come in.

PROLOGUE

I WASN'T SURE I had enough wee for the stick. I pressed my bladder through my jeans with my fingertips, holding the pregnancy test in the other hand. Not bursting but it would have to do. I peeled off the top of the foil packet, balanced the stick on the top of the loo roll and unzipped my flies. I sat down and reached back for the stick.

Looking down at my thighs, I realized I was sitting too far forward on the loo seat, so I shuffled my bottom backwards and widened my knees until there was enough space to reach my hand underneath me, trying to avoid grazing the loo bowl with my knuckles. Christ, this was unsanitary. There must be better ways.

I narrowed my eyes at the bath in front of me and wondered if it would be easier to step into that, crouch down and wee on the stick in the bath, letting it trickle out down the plughole. No worse than weeing in the shower, right?

I shook my head. I was in my parents' bathroom. Couldn't do a pregnancy test by pissing on a stick in my mum's bath. She loved that bath. She spent hours in it wearing her frilly bath hat, shouting at Radio Norfolk.

I frowned down into the dark space between my legs again

where the stick was poised in mid-air, ready for action. What a simple bit of plastic to deliver such potentially life-changing news. It was the shape of the vape my friend Clem carried round with him everywhere, loaded with lemon sherbert-flavoured liquid.

'Why lemon sherbert?' I'd asked him once. He'd shrugged and said he just liked sweets.

I shook my head again as if to try and physically dispel thoughts of Clem and lemon sherbert. Concentrate, Lil. The stick. Wee on the stick. Get on with it. But I couldn't. At this, the most important moment of my bladder's life so far, it had stage fright. Funny how, when you really concentrate on weeing, you can't. And yet normally, when you sit yourself down what, six, seven, eight times a day, out it comes, no trouble.

I sighed. The other problem was I wasn't sure where to hold the stick in order to catch maximum wee. I shifted my hand slightly towards the front. Was that a good place? Maybe. But if it came out as more of a trickle than a jet it would need to be in the middle.

'Oi,' came Jess's voice from outside the bathroom door. I'd locked it because I knew she'd come in otherwise. 'Have you done it yet?'

'Shhhh,' I hissed back. 'No. I haven't. And pressure from you won't help.'

Jess went quiet for a few seconds, then I heard her whistling from outside the door.

'Why are you whistling?'

She stopped. 'It makes horses pee when you're riding them.'

'I'm not a horse.' Although it gave me an idea. With my left hand, I reached across for the bathroom sink and twisted the hot tap, then held my hand underneath the warm water.

It worked instantly. I started weeing and moved the stick into prime position, sort of between the front and the middle. Please could I not be pregnant, I thought, my eyes fixated on the stick as I felt warm wetness on my fingers. Brilliant, I'd weed on my own hand. Please, please, please could this not be positive. I was thirty-one, single, barely able to afford my rent. I had a life plan. Well, a vague life plan. This was not it.

I finished and jiggled up and down on the loo seat, trying not to drop the stick. Then I turned off the hot tap with my left hand and tugged off a few sheets of loo roll. I retrieved the stick, resisted the urge to tap it on the section of loo seat in front of me like a teaspoon on the side of a teacup – ting, ting, ting! – and wiped myself.

I looked at the test in my right hand, feeling as if I'd swallowed a jar of butterflies, before gently dropping it on a pile of Mum's *History Today* magazines and pulling up my jeans. I picked up the stick without looking at it and unlocked the bathroom door.

Jess was standing there, picking at her cuticles like a nervous father outside the delivery room.

'Show me,' she said instantly, holding her hand out for the test. 'What's it say?'

Come on, Lil, I told myself, stomach still churning, look down. Get it over and done with and then you can go to the pub with Jess and have a drink to celebrate. After that, no more sex. Never again. Not worth it. Not worth the hassle and the drama and this panic attack over the infinitesimally small chance you might be pregnant. I'd take a vow of celibacy and get a cat. I'd become a priest. I'd move to somewhere in the Far East, become a Buddhist and renounce all physical desires. I'd convert to asexualism. Just please, please, please, God, if there is one, if you are there, I know I'm always asking you things and swearing I'll never ask again, but this time I really mean it. I promise I'll never ask anything trivial again if you grant me this one tiny wish: please can I not be pregnant.

I looked down at the stick.

'Fucccccccccck,' I said, looking at it, holding it out for Jess. No question about it, there were two little purple lines. 'I'm pregnant.'

CHAPTER ONE

I'D RATHER HAVE EATEN my own foot than go on a date that night. The whole thing was Jess's idea. She said I needed to 'get back in the saddle'. Hateful expression. I didn't feel like doing any sort of riding, thank you very much. But she'd insisted I download a dating app called Kindling, which is why I was now sitting on the bus, so nervous it felt like even my earlobes were sweating, on the way to some pub in Vauxhall to meet someone called Max. We hadn't been messaging for very long so I knew almost nothing about him. Only that he was thirty-four, had dark curly hair and seemed less alarming than some of the other creatures I'd scrolled through – no, no, no, maybe, no, no, definitely not, you're the sort of pervert who'd have a foot fetish, no, no, YES. Hello, handsome, stubbly man who looks like a cross between a Jane Austen hero and Jack Sparrow the pirate. That was Max.

He'd asked me out a couple of days after matching, saying he didn't believe in 'beating around the bush'. I liked his straightforwardness. No messing about. No dick pics. Just, 'Fancy a drink?' I figured it was better to meet and see whether you got on with someone rather than message for several weeks and paint a madly romantic picture of them in your head, then meet up and realize you'd got it wrong and in real life they were a psychopath.

So, even though Max's question made me want to throw up with nerves, I'd agreed. A tiny, minuscule part of me knew Jess was right, knew that I had to make an effort. Otherwise I'd never get over Jake, the one I used to think was The One before he broke my heart into seventy thousand pieces and turned me into a cynic who had bitter and self-pitying thoughts whenever I saw a couple holding hands on the Tube.

Jake and I had split six months earlier. He split up with me, I should say, if we're being totally accurate. It was after eight years together, having met at uni. Various friends had started getting engaged and, all right, I'd very occasionally allowed myself to think about what shape diamond Jake might buy for an engagement ring. But only once or twice, tops. Maybe three times. Tragic, I know, but in the absence of a ring I was happy with Jake. I just wanted us – married or not. And I thought he did too. We used to fall asleep making sure we were touching one another every night. My arm over his chest or our feet touching. Or holding hands. And if one of us woke in the night and we'd moved apart, we'd reach out for the other one so we could feel them there again. It was real. I knew it.

Well, some clairvoyant I was. Six months ago, Jake came home from his office to our flat in Angel and told me that he felt 'too settled'. That he wanted more excitement. And as I sat at the kitchen table, crying, wondering whether I should offer to dress up as a sexy nun or be more enthusiastic about anal sex, he told me he was moving out to go and live with his friend Dave. It felt so sudden that I could only sit at the kitchen table weeping while Jake packed and left ten minutes later with the overnight bag I'd bought him from John Lewis for his last birthday. With hindsight, not the sexiest purchase. But he'd said he loved it. It had a separate compartment for his wash bag. Practical, no?

The Dave thing turned out to be a front for the fact that Jake had been shagging a 24-year-old called India from his office. Jess and I had devoted hours (whole days, probably), to stalking her on all forms of social media. On Instagram, she was a blonde party girl who never seemed to wear a bra; on LinkedIn, her profile picture showed a more serious India, smiling in a collared shirt, blonde hair tied back in a smooth ponytail. It was also via LinkedIn that Jess and I discovered she'd only been working at Jake's law firm for two months before he left me.

'Quick work,' I'd slurred, pissed, lying belly down on the floor of Jess's bedroom where we were stalking her on my laptop one evening.

The next day, I'd got an email from Jake.

Lil, you can see who's been looking at your profile on LinkedIn. I'm not sure this is healthy. Please leave Indy out of it.

Indy indeed. I'd thrown my phone on the floor in a rage and smashed the screen. But my fury was helpful. Anger was more motivational than sadness. Sadness sat in my stomach like a stone and made me cry; anger made me want to get up and do something. I decided I needed to move out of the flat I'd shared with Jake and find another room somewhere. I'd start again. Optimistically, I bought a book about Buddhism and tried a meditation I found on Spotify, half-hoping to wake up cured the following day.

I didn't wake up cured. But I knew I had to give it time. The oldest cliché there was and the most irritating, depressing thing anyone can say to you when you're in the depths of a break-up, staring at your phone, longing to message them. Or for them to message you. But the time thing was true. Annoyingly.

Six months later, I was living in a flat in Brixton on a street just behind McDonald's. My flatmates were an Aussie couple called Riley and Grace – he was a personal trainer, she was a yoga teacher – who made genuinely extraordinary noises when they had sex. I'd joked to Jess that Attenborough should study them ('And now the male climbs on top of the female'), but they were lovely when they had all their clothes on, and my room was cheap. Plus, India had made her Instagram profile private which meant I couldn't stalk her any more. Probably better for all of us that way.

So, here I was, on the bus chugging towards Vauxhall for this date with Mystery Max, sweat patches blossoming in the armpits of my new Zara shirt. I'd gone shopping earlier that day for an outfit because my wardrobe was full of sensible work dresses and it felt like the last time I went on a first date women wore bonnets and floor-length gowns. And although the shops seemed to be full of clothes designed for thin hippies

– sequinned flares in a size 8, anyone? – I'd eventually found a pair of black jeans that made my legs look less like chicken drumsticks, and a silky black shirt which gave me exactly the right amount of cleavage. Not too Simon Cowell. Just a hint, so long as I was wearing my old padded bra which hoiked my small to average-sized breasts up so high I could practically lick my own nipples.

While showering, I'd had a brief moral battle with myself about whether to shave my legs or not. I didn't want to go on this date feeling like a rugby player, but there would be no sex because the thought of sleeping with someone other than Jake still terrified me, so what was the point? Plus, I hadn't bothered for so long my razor was rusty. Can you get tetanus from using a rusty razor? My Google search history was littered with such quandaries: 'sharp stabbing pain under ribs cancer?' Or 'walk 20,000 steps a day lose weight?'

In the end, I'd used Grace's nice new pink razor and shaved because I thought it was sloppy preparation not to. Like going into battle without armour. I felt a twinge of guilt at blunting her razor on my legs – it was like scything though a jungle with a machete – but I figured certain household items like this could be co-opted in an emergency. I'd told myself the same that morning when I stole the batteries from the flat's Sky remote for my vibrator. This was an emergency, I decided as I'd sat on my bed, solemnly removing the triple AAAs from one device and sliding them into the other. But I'd also realized this was a new low and that I should probably go out and at least flirt with a human being again. I couldn't rely on my vibrator all the time. What if I got so used to it that no man could ever make me come again? That happens. I read about it once in a magazine.

I felt my stomach spasm again as we pulled into Vauxhall bus station. It was mostly nerves, I hoped, but Jess's twin brother Clem, a haphazard cook, had made us curry the night before at their place and I'd spent much of that morning on the loo, trying to ignore the grunting coming from Grace and Riley's bedroom. I reached into my bag to check I'd brought my Imodium with me. I'd taken one just before leaving the flat but figured I should bring the packet. Just in case. Got to be prepared. The packet was there, safely zipped from sight in my bag's side pocket. Then I looked at my phone. Missed call from Mum which could 100 pc wait. A message from Max asking what I wanted to drink.

Vodka and tonic please! I texted him back, annoyed at myself for using an exclamation mark – so perky! – but worried I sounded too demanding otherwise.

The bus doors hissed as they opened and my heart sped up at the anxiety. Jesus, come on, Lil. It's a date, not an induction into a cult. You can do this. Literally thousands of people go on first dates every day. And they weren't all total disasters. They couldn't be. Otherwise the human race would die out. It was going to be fine. One or two drinks in the pub with a man, like a normal person. Or at least as much like a normal person as I could manage. I wiped my clammy palms on my jeans as I stepped down from the bus into the sticky evening air.

I continued chiding myself as I walked towards the pub.

You're going to be fine. What did that Spotify meditation say? Breathe. Smile. Imagine your higher self, whatever that was. Ignore your stomach, the Imodium will kick in soon. I pushed open the pub door and was immediately hit by noise from clusters of people ordering at the bar and others laughing at tables. For the billionth time that day I wondered if there was anything worse than a first date. Waterboarding?

Then I saw him wave from a table by the window. Max.

Oh.

My.

Days.

Was this a joke? Some kind of set-up?

He was so good-looking, so obviously, absurdly handsome, that I felt instantly more nervous. I'd always been someone who'd appreciated classically good-looking men from a distance. Sure, that man at the bar, or the party, or the wedding might be so hot he was almost beautiful – Superman jaw, wide shoulders, big smile – but he was never going to go for me, so I wasn't going to consider him. It was self-defence – I had mousy hair that fell to my shoulders and frizzed out at the ends, and a nose with a weird bobble. I often squinted at women I saw on Instagram – perfect fringes, matt skin, flicky eyeliner – and wondered if I could ever be one of them. But whenever I tried to do flicky eyeliner, my hand wobbled and the line went all watery.

Jess once told me my best attribute was my height since I was only a couple of inches off six foot. But ask a man what he looks for in a woman and none of them reply 'a giantess with a nose like a bicycle horn.' The handsome ones were out of reach, I'd long known, and yet here was a man so mesmerizing I could barely look at him without blushing. He was trying to mouth something at me from the table. What was it? I squinted at him to try and guess what he was saying, then regretted it. Don't squint at the handsome man, Lil.

'Hi!' I mouthed back at him. Maybe he was short, I thought, as I pushed my way through other people. Maybe that was the problem. That was why he was single. Face like a gladiator, legs like a hobbit. That had to be it.

He stood as I approached. Not short. He was several inches taller than me. Well over six foot, for sure. In jeans and a dark blue shirt which was undone to reveal a perfect triangle of chest. Not hanging loose to his navel like a dancer from *Strictly*. Not buttoned to the top, which was too East End hipster. Couldn't see his shoes. And shoes were crucial. But so far, so excellent.

'Lil, hello,' he said, leaning forward over the table to kiss me on the cheek. He smelt good. Course he did. Woody. I pulled back but he went in for a kiss on the other cheek. A two-kisser. We brushed cheeks on the other side and then both laughed awkwardly.

'I got you a vodka,' he said, nodding at two glasses on the table. He sounded posh, a low drawl like James Bond.

'Thanks,' I said, trying to slip off my leather jacket in a manner which didn't reveal my sweaty underarms.

'Good to meet you,' he said, once I'd sat down, lifting his glass towards mine.

'You too,' I replied, raising my glass slowly, still trying to keep my right arm clamped. I grinned shyly at him and my mind went blank. Suddenly, it was as if I'd lost the power of speech. I'd gone mute while all around us people laughed and talked normally.

'This is an all right location for you because you're in Brixton, right?' he said.

I had a sip of my vodka and nodded. What can I ask him? *Come on, Lil, think of something otherwise you might die of awkwardness.*

'Where are you again?' I asked.

'Hampstead?' he replied, as if it was a question.

I nodded again.

'Cool,' I said, having another sip of my drink. Quite a big sip. 'You been there long?'

'Yeah,' he replied, 'a few years. I love it. Got the park. Can get out of London easily. It's great.' He had a sip of his drink. 'You?'

I frowned at him. 'Huh?'

'Have you been in Brixton long?'

'Oh right, sorry, er, no. Not really. Like, six months.'

'Where were you before?'

'Angel?'

He nodded.

We both had another mouthful of our drinks.

'And you said you were a teacher?'

'Mmm,' I replied. 'Five-year-olds. I love them most days, want to kill them on others.' *Why are you threatening child murder on a date, Lil?*

He smiled. He had good teeth. White. And the vibe of a man who owned and, crucially, used dental floss. 'You must be unbelievably patient,' he went on. 'I have a couple of godchildren who I love, but I get to hand them back again after a couple of hours.'

I laughed. People always said that about teachers, that we must be 'patient'. But children were easier to handle and less complicated than most adults I knew.

'What about you though?' I asked him. 'How come you're always jet-setting? Are you a spy?' *Well done, a joke! That's more like it, this sounds more like an actual conversation two human beings would have.*

Max laughed. 'No, I'd make a terrible spy. Very bad at keeping secrets. But I travel a lot because I'm a climber.'

I frowned. 'A climber? Like… of mountains?'

'Exactly. Mostly mountains. Walls when I'm in London. Not many mountains in the city.'

'Wow,' I said. 'Cool. I didn't know it could be a job.'

He laughed. 'I carry rich Americans up Swiss mountains to pay the bills, then go off and climb elsewhere for myself.'

'Like where?'

He shrugged. 'Wherever. Europe. America. Himalayas. I'm about to go to Pakistan to try and climb a mountain there.'

'Pakistan? Wow, amazing,' I said. I worried I sounded vacuous. But I didn't know much about climbing. And if you handed me a map and asked me to stick a pin in Pakistan I wasn't absolutely sure I could. I taught my 5-year-olds basic reading and writing skills. Not geography.

My phone lit up on the table. A message from Jess.

'Sorry,' I said, sliding it into my bag, feeling quite grateful that the screen hadn't flashed up again with 'Mum calling'.

Max shook his head. 'No problem.'

'Just a mate checking up on me,' I said, rolling my eyes at him.

'That you're not on a date with a crazy?' he teased. His tanned forehead had lines running across it and smaller lines at the corners of his eyes which crinkled when he smiled. A modern-day Robinson Crusoe who'd clearly spent more time outside than cooped up in an office.

'Something like that.'

He nodded and ran a hand through his hair. Then he grimaced at me. 'I'm sorry. First dates are awkward, aren't they?'

I grinned sheepishly. 'I thought it was just me. But… yeah, they are. You do many of them?' Then I cursed myself for letting that slip out. I didn't want to sound like I was trying to suss his intentions so early.

He shrugged, unfazed. 'Not millions. I'm away a lot. Don't do much dating in the mountains. You?'

I shook my head. 'Nope. Not a huge… dater.' I could feel the vodka loosening my hang-ups. 'This is my first date since a break-up, actually, so I may… er… I may be a bit rusty.'

I looked down, fingers encircling my sweating glass on the table during the awkward silence that followed. It was dumb to mention Jake, so I wondered how long it would take me to get to Jess's from the pub. If I jumped on the Tube to Hammersmith I could probably be there in forty minutes.

Buy a bottle of wine from Nisa on the walk to the house, order a Deliveroo. Perfect. It wouldn't be a wasted night. And I could take this bra off and let my breasts settle back down at their usual altitude.

I looked up again at Max across the table, his mouth in a lopsided smile.

'What?' I asked, narrowing my eyes at him.

'Then we're in the same boat, you and me.'

'What do you mean?'

'I broke up with someone not very long ago.' His smile fell and he looked suddenly serious. 'Although, to be fair, it was more a mutual decision in the end.'

'Ohhhhh,' I said slowly. 'Brutal, huh?'

He shrugged. 'All part of life's rich tapestry.'

'Why d'you break up?'

He shrugged again. 'I wasn't around much. She wanted to settle down. Get married, children, that sort of thing.'

'And you… didn't?' I said it carefully. Again, I didn't want him to think I was trying to work out his potential as a baby-daddy. For him to think I was on some sort of husband-hunt myself.

'No. Well, not no. Just… not yet. Things to do. Places to see.'

'Mountains to climb?'

'Something like that,' he said, smiling and leaning towards me. 'What about you?'

I frowned. 'What do you mean?'

'Well, if we're having a joint Jeremy Kyle session, how come you broke up?'

'Oh.' I grimaced at him. 'We'd been going out for eight years. Living together. I thought it was going one way, he… didn't. So that was that.'

I picked up my glass and was raising it to my mouth when Max laughed.

'What?' I said, defensively. I still found it hard to articulate my feelings about the break-up. I went over it in my head all the time. Over and over again. Over things I could have done differently. Over moments that I realized should have given me a clue. Over Jake's increasing reluctance to hang out with my friends. Over his late nights in the office. But I felt like even Jess had heard enough now so I kept quiet about it unless prompted.

Max shook his head and waved a hand at my expression. 'I'm not laughing at you. I'm laughing at us. Sitting here, nursing our drinks like we're at a wake. Come on, let's have another drink and cheer up.'

I laughed back. 'OK, but my round.'

Max shook his head again as he stood up. 'No. Absolutely not. Same again?'

'Yep, please.'

'Grand. And when I get back, no more talk about break-ups. This is supposed to be a date, not a counselling session. Deal?'

'Deal.'

I watched him push his way back to the bar and touched my right cheek with the back of my fingers. It was warm. We were one drink in, the point at which I'd envisaged one of us making excuses – 'Good to meet you,' awkward kiss goodbye, never message one another again – but I didn't want to escape to Jess's house. I wanted to stay here talking to Max. Initial awkwardness over, I could sense that I liked him. Sitting here, chatting, I could feel a spark of excitement at exploring someone new, at finding out all those first things about someone. I hadn't felt that for a long time. Years, if I was honest. The excitement of finding out about one another dissipated early with Jake and lapsed into something more comfortable. This Saturday night already felt more exciting than most of our relationship. Or maybe that was the vodka.

'I took the liberty of buying some crisps,' Max said, returning to the table a few minutes later with a drink in each hand and two packets in the crook of his arm. 'And also, here's a menu.' He put the drinks down, dropped the crisps (one ready salted, one salt and vinegar – promising taste in crisps), pulled two menus out from underneath his elbow and handed me one. 'You hungry?'

I'd been too nervous to eat much all day. Too adrenalin-y at the thought of the date. Plus there was my dodgy stomach issue. All of which probably accounted for why I felt a bit pissed already.

'Yep,' I replied.

'Great,' he said, sitting down. 'Me too. Although I warn you, I'm greedy. It's all freeze-dried food on expeditions. So if I'm out, I go a bit mad.'

With hindsight, the second bottle of wine was probably what did it. We'd ordered food – actual steak for him, tuna steak for me, then shared cheese – and stayed at the pub until closing. One bottle of red wine, then another. Conversation had meandered more easily from travels to where we grew up. When I told him about being raised by two eccentric academics in Norfolk, he laughed.

'No way!' he said, grinning at me. 'Mine live just over the border in Suffolk. I'll drive up and we can go for a walk along the beach.'

'Which beach?' I asked, trying to stay outwardly cool while all my internal organs were cheering. A walk on the beach meant there had to be at least one more date. I envisaged us strolling along Brancaster, my hair blowing in the wind in a manner which left me looking tousled and sexy rather than a woman who'd recently escaped the local asylum. Perhaps we'd hold hands. Perhaps we'd have sex in the sand dunes! Calm down, Lil, I told myself, this is a hypothetical situation.

'I don't know the beaches of Norfolk,' went on Max, doing his lopsided smile again. 'You'll have to show me.'

My stomach flipped so hard this time I was nearly sick on the table, but I managed to claw it back. 'Sure,' I said, trying to keep my voice steady. 'Do you go home much then?'

Max puffed out his cheeks as he exhaled. 'Not as much as I'd like, but then I'm away a lot. You?'

I nodded. 'Yeah, quite a bit. It's home. And I went back for a while after, er, the break-up and everything.'

Max took one of my hands from my lap in his and shook his head, looking at me with a mock-serious expression. 'Nope, I told you, no exes. We're having a good time. Let's not ruin it.'

'OK, deal,' I said, feeling his fingers curled over mine, hoping that my palms didn't start sweating again.

And it was nice. More than nice. It was wonderful, actually, sitting, gently flirting with one another. It was the kind of date you never wanted to end, and I tried to bottle every minute in my head (after the first half hour was over), so I could go over it again and again the next day. To luxuriate in the pleasure at having met someone who made me feel this giddy. I'd always inwardly cursed any of my girlfriends when they talked excitedly about meeting someone new and having 'a spark'. I often wanted to suggest they save it for a soppy card and not subject the rest of us to their Hallmark ideas of romance. But there was… something here. I felt it.

'Can I kiss you?' Max said, shortly afterwards, having shifted closer to me when the waitress took our plates away. I nodded, even though I was worried that I had red wine teeth and a tongue that tasted of cheese. He gently reached out and put his hand behind my head, pulling me to him. His beard tickled my chin. It was softer than I'd expected. And you know that kiss in *The Notebook*? On that boat jetty in the rain? In my head, the kiss with Max looked a bit like *The Notebook* kiss. A proper, steamy, full-on-the-mouth snog. In reality, it probably looked a good deal less romantic, given all the vodka and wine. But I didn't care. Look at me! I was out on a Saturday night kissing a man like a normal person instead of crying on my sofa! I pulled back after few moments, though, aware that we were in a public space and people might be trying to enjoy their dinner around us.

'You want to get out of here?' he said, his hand still on the back of my head.

'Sure. To where?'

'My place?'

I didn't hesitate, even though this was a man I'd known for less than five hours. I just had a sense that it would be all right. Murderers have eyes that are too close together and matted hair. Or no hair. Max had thick hair that I wanted to run my hands through, and a collared shirt. Murderers didn't wear collared shirts.

'Cool,' I replied.

As we stood on the pavement outside the pub minutes later, I felt less confident, as if I was about to lose my virginity again. I could just about remember which bit went where. But what if Max was into something weird? What if he wanted me to talk dirty? I couldn't do that first time. I didn't even know his surname. Or, what if he wanted me to put my finger in his bottom? I wasn't into that.

'Lil?' Max was standing by a black cab, holding the door open for me.

'Oh great, sorry, was just… thinking,' I said, jumping in the taxi.

'Hampstead, please,' Max said to the driver. 'East Heath Road.'

The cabbie pulled out and I fell back against the seat as Max put a hand on my leg. It made my stomach flip again. I don't want to say 'I felt something inside me stir,' because that would be embarrassing. But I did feel something I hadn't for several months, or longer, if I was honest with myself, as happiness unfurled itself underneath my ribcage. I put my hand over Max's and gently ran my fingers over it. Then he drew me in for another kiss, more urgent than the last, his mouth pressing hard against mine as he ran his hand up my thigh.

'I'm glad I messaged you,' he said, pulling back, but remaining inches from my face.

'Me too,' I said back. I nearly added 'Just please don't murder me,' but I decided it would kill the vibe.

★

We got out on of the cab in front of a huge white house. Enormous. It was a mansion. I counted the windows. It was four storeys high, set back from the road slightly with a path leading to the front door.

'Jeeeeeeesus. How big is your house?' I said, looking up at it.

He laughed as he pulled his keys out of his pocket. 'It's not mine.'

'Huh?'

'I mean it's not all mine. It's flats.' He opened the front door and walked me through a carpeted hall to another door. 'This is my bit,' he said, unlocking that door and standing aside for me to walk in first.

It opened into a bright white corridor with a dark wooden floor. A neat row of shoes and boots was lined up underneath a full-length mirror at the end of it. It was huge. Who knew climbing was such a lucrative career option?

'This way,' said Max, closing his front door behind me.

'Um… can I quickly go to the bathroom?' I said. I was desperate to pee and still worrying about my breath. I'd been desperate to pee all taxi journey but didn't want to say anything. I figured 'I need a wee,' fell into the 'List of bodily functions you cannot talk about on a first date.'

'Course,' said Max, turning round and pointing. 'That door there.'

'Great, two seconds,' I said.

I sat down in the bathroom and frowned as I tried to gauge how my digestive system was feeling. Fine, I decided. A big relief. I ripped off a square of loo paper and ran it across my teeth to de-fuzz them. It was a lacklustre attempt at freshening up but I didn't have any gum. I pulled my jeans up and inspected myself in the mirror. Weird how you can start off the night feeling like Brigitte Bardot and check yourself a few hours later to see a creature from a Stephen King novel staring back. I washed my hands and ran a damp index finger under both eyes to remove the smudged mascara, then reached into my bag for my bronzer to try and make my skin look less like I was attending my own funeral.

When I opened the loo door I heard classical music, so I walked in the music's direction, pausing to look at a photograph of Max, framed in his hall. It was a close-up of his face, clearly somewhere cold because his beard was frozen, and he had a hood pulled tightly around his head. His eyes looked almost turquoise against the ice.

I followed the music and pushed another door open to find

him standing in the kitchen, opening a bottle of red wine. I say kitchen, it was an enormous kitchen and living room in one: metallic kitchen cupboards and counters up one end, sofas in front of a floor-to-ceiling window at the other end.

'Drink?' he asked, raising the bottle at me.

'Go on then,' I said. 'What's one more?' He laughed as I walked towards the big window and put my hands to the dark to try and see out. My breath frosted the glass.

'It's the heath,' Max said, suddenly behind me. 'The most sensational views. It's why I moved here. Wilderness in the middle of the city.'

'Poetic,' I said, taking the glass and grinning at him.

'Cheeky,' he said, looking at me. 'I like it.' Then he leant forward and kissed me again, so I stumbled back against the window shutter behind me and red wine sloshed over the rim of my glass.

'Oh shit, sorry,' I said, rubbing the wood with my foot. 'I don't want to stain your floorboards.'

'Fuck the floorboards,' said Max, taking my wine glass and putting it down on a glass coffee table. Fuck the floorboards! It was the sexiest thing anyone had said to me for years. In my recent adventures on Kindling, a few men had tried heroically bad pick-up lines. 'Hey, sexy,' was one. Seriously? Another tried 'You look a lot like my next girlfriend.' Bless. But Max hadn't said anything moronic, clearly saving his best lines for now. He took my hand and led me to the sofa, pulling me down with him as he sat.

He kissed softly, his beard prickling my lower lip, his tongue gently pushing at mine. And then it became more urgent, his lips pushing against mine while one of his hands ran up my neck and into my hair. Jake and I hardly ever kissed like this towards the end of our relationship. I'd assumed it was because we were both mindful of morning breath, politely avoiding one another's mouths. But I'd also worried that it showed how much passion had leaked from our relationship.

I sighed like a hormonally deranged teenager and ran my right hand up the back of his shirt. Here we go, it was all coming back to me. Moaning softly again into his mouth, I pushed my hand through his hair, although I froze when one of my fingers caught a knot and he inhaled sharply.

'Sorry,' I squeaked.

But he pulled back his head and grinned at me, one of his hands still in my hair, his eyes centimetres from mine. 'I'll live.'

Then he stood up and held his hand out for mine. So I got up and Max led me from the sofa to his bedroom next door. It had another huge window facing the same direction, into the inky darkness of the park.

He kicked off his shoes beside an antique chest of drawers, and went to the window to fold its shutters. I slipped my shoes off and sat on his bed. Then he walked towards me and pushed me back against the mattress.

Weirdly, as I leant back, I realized my anxieties had vanished. I was in the flat of an improbably handsome man who I could sense I liked already. I was about to have sex with him but, as Max leant over me, his groin against mine, my fears about it were quelled.

He carried on kissing me while expertly undoing the buttons of my shirt with one hand. Then, when he reached the last shirt button, he carried on southwards, flicking open the button of my jeans and pulling the zip down.

'Take them off for me,' he said, nodding at my jeans before he stood up at the end of his bed and reached for the bottom of his shirt. He removed it over his head in one go to reveal the kind of body I'd only ever seen in pictures. Not grotesquely muscled and smooth. We're not talking *Love Island*. But perfectly defined, with a light covering of dark hair across his chest, which tapered down towards his stomach.

He started undoing his flies, while keeping his eyes on me.

'Off,' he instructed again, inclining his head towards me. I was less cool here, trying to get my shirt off but flailing my arms around as if competing in an Olympic butterfly heat. Then I peeled my jeans down my legs, arching my back and making a sort of bridge like you do in yoga. Incredibly, Max didn't seem turned off by this. His eyes stayed on me the whole time until my legs were finally free, when he leant down to pull his jeans off in one easy motion. No underwear, I noticed, which I was kind of into. Macho, no? Although you have to hope the jeans are washed regularly.

I didn't want to drop my gaze and immediately look at his penis. I'm too coy. So as Max knelt back on the bed and lowered his body above mine, I stared at his face. He started kissing me again, running the side of his hand across my nipples and down my body. I could feel his erection against my thigh and then, suddenly, he rolled himself on top of me and started kissing the hollow between my breasts and down my stomach. Thank GOD I'd had a whip round and tidied myself up earlier instead of doing that thing where I deliberately left it looking like an overgrown allotment so I couldn't go home with him.

He worked his way south until his head was between my legs and he was very lightly flicking my clit with his tongue. I looked down a couple of times to check his head was there and this was actually happening. A tiny thought bubble had formed in my mind: Is there any way I can take a photo to preserve this moment where a stupendously handsome climber with a body like a classical statue is going down on me? Jess had once knowledgeably told me that handsome guys were bad in bed because they didn't have to try so hard. But I wasn't at all sure I believed her, right at this moment. Max knew exactly the right pressure and where I wanted to be touched, so I wasn't lying there thinking, 'Down a bit, up a bit.'

I arched my back again and exhaled loudly as he carried on flicking his tongue over me, and then gently pushed a finger into me at the same time. I could feel an intense heat growing, spreading across my belly, and I rolled my hips in time with his tongue but just before I came, he stopped and pulled himself up. 'Uh-uh, not yet.'

WHAT?

Maybe that was his problem. Maybe he was a sadist.

'I'm going to grab a condom,' he said, kneeling up on the bed.

I shook my head. 'It's OK, I'm on the pill,' I said quickly. I couldn't bear to delay this moment, a moment which felt like it should be in a film it was so perfect, with a basic discussion about contraception.

It's often this way when you're having sex with someone new, right? You're hardly going to raise the matter in advance at the pub because you don't necessarily know you're going to have sex with them.

'Excuse me, I know we're only on our second round, but do you mind if we have a quick chat about contraception so it's not awkward later?'

I don't think so.

So the subject is left until you're rolling around together, often pissed. But this never feels like the right moment to have a big discussion either. Unromantic. It breaks the rhythm. So you mumble at one another about it being 'all right' or needing to 'be careful'. Irresponsible, I know, but in that second, I was so seduced by the surprisingly erotic turn of my evening that I didn't want anything to ruin it. I wanted to experience the kind of sex I'd read about and watched onscreen, but never quite managed myself. No pauses. No awkward fumbling with a fiddly plastic packet. No carpet oyster afterwards. Nobody ever steps on a squishy, cold, carpet oyster in the movies.

So the condom was ignored and Max carried on, putting his hands under each of my bum cheeks and pulling me to the edge of his bed, before lifting my legs up so each was resting on his shoulders. Then, slowly, so slowly, he pushed himself into me.

'Fuccccccck,' I said, as he carried on thrusting in and out of me, unhurriedly, as if he was teasing me. I wasn't sure it was the most flattering position in the world. I glanced down at my stomach and the rolls had all bunched together so they looked like packet ham. Plus my legs were over my head; my feet were, in fact, dangerously close to his head and I worried they might smell. But it felt so good, and Max was staring at me so intensely, that I forgot about my feet.

After a few minutes, he then pulled out and turned me lengthways across his bed. I tried to shift position as gracefully as possible. Never sexy to be thrashing around on top of a duvet like a dolphin, but Max had a knack of sweeping me around effortlessly so I was suddenly underneath him and we were doing it missionary, his head buried in my shoulder as he kissed my neck.

I rocked with him, running my nails down his back as we kissed properly again, mouths wide, tongues pushing against one another. Ha! All those worries about forgetting how to do it, I thought. Not a problem. Look at us go. Look at me having sex with this beautiful man. I moved my nails down over his bottom and then up across his back again. I am a modern, single woman, enjoying myself, being all liberated, enjoying being back on the dating scene again. It's a Saturday night and instead of getting drunk with Jess, I'm having sex with Max. No more stalking Jake on social media. No more moping over old selfies of us. No more tears on a Sunday evening. I am free! I can do whatever I want! I am—

Suddenly, Max pulled out and, reaching underneath my back with one of his muscly arms, flipped me on to my stomach. I tried to look over my shoulder at him in what I hoped was a smouldering way, although I knew my eye make-up had probably smudged again so I looked like Noel Fielding. Max was on his knees behind me, but lowered his head to kiss my left shoulder, then my right shoulder, then, slowly, he kissed his way down my spine. His beard gently tickled my back and I sighed into my pillow. Then the kissing stopped and I was pulled backwards by my legs, Max's hands underneath my thighs. My bottom was now on the end of the bed, my knees on the carpet.

'Give me your hands,' he said, so I lifted my arms from under my head and moved them behind me.

'Here, put them here,' he said, putting one hand on each of my butt cheeks and spreading them apart slightly. There I was, lying on my chest, with my hands on my bottom as if I was about to do a naked version of the Macarena.

Max then buried his head in my crease, starting to flick up and down with his tongue again, harder this time. It felt so good that I didn't even worry about what my bottom looked like at that angle. I just wanted him to carry on, harder, faster, harder, faster, harder, faster, until that hot feeling of being on the cusp of exploding again and I came, moaning into the pillow.

'That was amazing,' I whispered, looking over my shoulder.

'Good,' he replied, and then, within seconds, he was lying on top of me, having pushed his cock into me again. His forearms were on the bed and he moved back and forth, breathing loudly and more urgently until he too made a sort of roar and flopped down on my back.

I silently congratulated myself for the performance then wondered how long I had to lie there underneath him before trying to move. I needed a wee.

He kissed my neck and rolled off a few moments later.

'I'm just going to nip to the bathroom,' I said, sitting up on the edge of the bed.

'That one,' said Max, inclining his head towards a doorway besides his wardrobe.

'Thanks,' I said. Strange how you could suddenly go into polite mode when moments ago someone was licking your bottom.

I sat down on the loo in his bathroom – grey marble and black and white photos of mountains on the walls – and tried to wee. It took ages. Come on, Lil, he'll think you're doing something revolting in here if you don't hurry up. Finally, I weed. Then I wiped, stood up and looked at my face in the mirror. My cheeks were flushed, my lips pink. I reached for the Colgate, lying beside the basin, and dabbed it on my forefinger. Then I ran the finger over my teeth and gums, turned on the tap, palmed a pool of water into my mouth and swilled it around.

I tiptoed back towards his bed and got into it, glancing across at him as I lay down. He was lying on his back, one arm bent above his head on his pillow, but rolled on to his side as soon as I was lying down.

'Head up,' he instructed, so I lifted it and he put one arm underneath it and wrapped the other over me. Spooning someone you'd met only hours earlier seemed weirdly intimate. Even more intimate than them licking your bottom. But it was the perfect end to this most perfect night, and I fell asleep without even a second of neurosis that I shouldn't have gone home with him on the first date.

★

The only thing was, when I woke up in the morning, Max wasn't there. I lifted my head to survey his room, listening for clues. Ouuuuuuuuchhhhhh, my head. It felt as if my brain had grown too big for my skull overnight. Throb, throb, throb. I tried to ignore the pain and listen for any noise in the flat. But the place was silent. What time was it? I looked on the floor for my bag. No bag. I must have left it in the sitting room. Then I spotted a clock on his bedside table: 8.23 a.m. Early for a Sunday. I sat up in bed.

The floor of Max's room looked like a battlefield, various items of discarded clothing lying on the carpet like wounded soldiers. My knickers, my bra, my shirt, my jeans, all at different spots. I swung my legs out and reached for my knickers, pulled them on and then tiptoed to listen at his bathroom door. Nope. Nothing. I retrieved my clothes from their various locations, put everything on and opened his bedroom door a fraction to the hall to see if I could hear a kettle or a radio out there. Still nothing. I found my way back to the living room but he wasn't there either. Then I saw a note on the kitchen counter.

L, SORRY TO ABANDON YOU, JUST GOT A FEW WORK THINGS TO DO. BUT MAKE YOURSELF A CUP OF TEA AND GREAT TO MEET. M.

I stood at the kitchen counter analysing it. Analysing every word. Analysing every letter. No kiss after the M, was my first thought. And did 'great to meet!' feel a bit corporate? I don't want to harp on about the bottom thing, but 'great to meet!' felt like something you said after meeting someone at a middle-management awayday, not what you said after putting your tongue in – I quickly counted in my head – three of their orifices. And who had work this early on a Sunday morning? But he'd also called me 'L', which seemed sweet. A bit intimate. L&M, we'd be, if we were a couple. As in 'Shall we have L&M round for dinner?' or 'I wonder if L&M are free this weekend?'

I ordered myself to stop. What was I doing, standing barefoot in a stranger's kitchen, wondering about what we'd be called if we were a couple? That was nuts. I needed a cup of tea and thirty-seven glasses of water, plus toast. And some Nurofen. And some more water. Lots more water. My mouth felt like something had died in it. But I didn't want a cup of tea in Max's flat. I wanted to get out of there and into my own space where I could go over the evening in my head, or at least the bits I could remember.

I folded the note up and slid it into my pocket, grabbed my bag off the sofa and went back to the bedroom. I resisted the urge to poke around his room too much – what if he was watching, somehow? – so made the bed and then took my bag into his bathroom to sort out my face. It was predictably terrible. Dry flaky skin. Faintly bloodshot eyes. Probably a good thing Max wasn't there. I'd seen better-looking animals when I took my class to London Zoo.

A few minutes later I let myself out, praying silently that I didn't bump into a neighbour. I made it to the front door of his building when I realized I didn't know how to get home. What line was Hampstead on? I felt for my phone in my bag and retrieved it. Uh-ohhhhh. Eight missed calls from Jess and a mad number of WhatsApps. I scrolled through them. The gist, basically, was had I been murdered.

Are you dead? Please don't be dead read her penultimate message.

Then the last one, sent at midnight: **If you're just shagging and not dead, then I might kill you myself when you surface. LET ME KNOW YOU'RE ALL RIGHT xxxxx.**

I was about to open Citymapper and work out how long it would take me to get home when my phone started buzzing in my hand. It was Jess.

'Hi,' I croaked into the phone.

'Oh thank God, you're not dead,' she said, deadpan.

'No,' I replied. 'Not quite. But I feel like I might die soon.'

'Did you stay with him?'

Christ. I wasn't up to this before a cup of tea. It was like being on the phone to MI5.

'Yup.'

Jess whooped down the phone. 'String up the bunting, let the bells ring out. I need to see you immediately.'

I sighed on the pavement. Had anyone in history ever needed a sugary tea more than I did at that very moment? 'I'm about to go home, love, think I need a bath and piece of toast. What are you doing later?'

'No, forget later. Where are you? Why don't you come over now and I'll cook us breakfast while you have a bath here. I can hear Clem clanking downstairs in the kitchen.'

She was in one of her determined moods. No point in arguing. I didn't have the energy. And maybe it would be better to go debrief with Jess. To be fed and watered by someone else and go home afterwards. Grace and Riley were probably making the flat walls shake this morning anyway.

'OK,' I replied. 'I'm… in Hampstead… somewhere. Fuck knows how I get down to you. But give me, say, forty-five minutes?'

'Amazing,' said Jess. 'I'll go to Nisa and get some juice.'

★

It took me an hour to cross London. Jess and Clem lived in a tall, thin house on the north side of the river near Chiswick. Theirs was one of those red-brick houses that overlook the Thames, with big windows surrounded by climbing ivy; a road

ran in front of the house and beyond that there was a little
private garden which sloped down to the river. Most of the
houses along this stretch were immaculate, the sort of homes
lived in by rich hedge-funders or app millionaires. They had
wisteria climbing up their walls, roses twisting over the railings and painted signs on their gates with grand names like
Heron House and River View. Dog walkers strolled up and
down the road, peering nosily into the bay windows, trying
to gawp at the owners.

Jess and Clem's house was different. Chaotic was the word
I'd use, but I mean it affectionately. It was just as big as all the
others – three storeys, plus an attic room in the roof which
Jess – a portrait artist – had turned into her studio when she
and Clem moved in. But if you were a dog walker wandering
past their place, you might have assumed it had been taken over
by squatters. The paint was peeling off the window frames, the
path to their front door was uneven because several bricks had
mysteriously disappeared and moss had long since covered the
others. There was no painted sign on their railings – which
were rusting – just a number: 19. Although the '9' had swung
upside down so it looked a bit like it was number 16 Chiswick
Mall.

Clem and Jess couldn't afford to patch it up. They couldn't
have afforded to live there at all, but they'd inherited their
house from their grandmother, Blanche. She's dead now but
she was a famous concert pianist, who had a daughter with
an Italian conductor in the 1960s. The daughter was Jess and
Clem's mum, Nicoletta, who'd inherited the conductor's fiery

tendencies and just about managed to get her two children safely to adulthood before abandoning London a decade or so ago for an apartment in Rome.

By the time I knocked on their door that morning, I was practically hallucinating about tea.

'Here she is,' said Jess, as she opened the door in her dressing gown. She stood back and squinted at me. 'I can tell you've had sex.'

'What?' I rasped, standing on the step but leaning on the door frame. 'You can't possibly tell that.'

'I can,' she said, standing aside as I went in. 'You look shattered. And you have sex hair.' She waggled a finger in small circles at my head and then closed the door behind me. 'Plus I can smell it.'

'You're a bloodhound, are you?' I said, heading towards the kitchen. 'That's gross, by the way.'

'I have a very sensitive nose. Tea?'

I nodded and pulled out a seat at the kitchen table, then sat down and put my arms on the table in front of me, laying my face on top of them. 'Where's Clem gone?'

'Out walking.'

Clem was a terrible musician who had to supplement his creative endeavours by dog-walking. He'd gone through various musical stages since leaving uni. The guitar phase. The drumming phase. Even, at one particularly bad moment, an accordion phase. Now he was into his electronic phase and was working on his 'first single'. He'd been working on his 'first single' a while and, lately, this seemed to mean a lot of sitting in his bedroom, enormous headphones on, tapping away at his laptop. Whenever he felt an artistic block, which was frequently, he sought refuge in the kitchen, hacking about with knives and experimenting with strange bits of meat the butcher on Chiswick High Road had persuaded him to buy. Offal, if you were unlucky. I remembered a vile liver tagliatelle; he was roughly as good at cooking as he was at music.

On the upside, he was the most popular dog-walker in the area, not only because he was so charming, but also because he had a boyish face that appealed to women of a certain age. He was tall and blond but had soft, pink cheeks that looked like they'd never needed to be shaved and he was always dishevelled. Mismatched socks, shirts fastened with the wrong buttons, tufty hair poking up like straw from the head of a scarecrow. But he came off as endearing, rather than useless, and so he had successfully, if unintentionally, cornered the local bored wives market. They scrabbled to sign their dogs up with him and then appeared in very pink lipstick and tight lycra at the house each morning to drop off their pugs and French bulldogs.

Jess busied herself with mugs and milk while I remained with my head on the kitchen table, gazing at the TV in the corner where a politician whose name I should know was droning on about some scandal in the Sunday papers.

'Walt was upstairs,' Jess went on, 'but I've sent him home.'

Walt was an art dealer – full name Walter de Winter – who Jess had been dating for the past couple of months. Very English and very posh, he always wore corduroys and was 'too fumbly' in bed, Jess had told me a few weeks ago. But he took her to exhibitions and discussed painters with her.

'Oh sorry,' I said, sitting up. 'I didn't mean to crash your Sunday morning.'

Jess shrugged in her dressing gown. 'Don't be ridiculous. I want to know everything.' Then she lowered her voice. 'And I can't spend all day with him again. Yesterday afternoon was too much but I'll tell you about that in a minute. You first.'

I wondered where to start. 'OK, so we met at the pub, and it was total agony to begin with.'

'Why?'

'Just sticky. Couldn't think of anything to say so made small talk about where we lived until a couple of drinks in.'

'What happened then? Do you want sugar?'

'Two please. And then it just got a bit easier. Talking, I mean. Then our respective relationship history came up.'

She spun around from the kettle on the sideboard and raised her eyebrows at me. 'Did it now?'

'I didn't bang on about it. Promise. And he mentioned his ex as well so we were equal.'

'OK, go on.'

I sat up from the table and leant back against my chair. 'And then... we just stayed there getting more and more pissed, basically.'

'Aaaaaaand?'

'Then he suggested going back to his place.'

'Aaaaaaaaaand?'

'And then, well, we had sex.'

Jess put a mug down in front of me so hard that tea spilled over the edges on to the table. 'I'm not cooking you breakfast for that pathetic recap. Come on, more details.'

I heard the front door close in the hall and Clem appeared in the kitchen in his dog-walking kit: ancient green Barbour with plastic bags bursting from one pocket and a whistle hanging around his neck. 'Lil, top of the morning.' He bent down and kissed my head. 'Bit early for you, isn't it?'

'Shhhh, Clem, she's telling me about her date and she's just got to the sex,' said Jess.

'Excellent,' said Clem. 'Can I join in? Is the kettle on?'

'It's just boiled,' said Jess. 'And I'm making bacon. Want some?'

'Yes please.'

'It was sort of… athletic,' I started. 'Because he's a climber.'

'A climber?' said Clem. 'What does he climb?'

'Be quiet, Clem. He's climbing Lil right now,' said Jess, peeling rashers of bacon from a packet and laying them in a frying pan.

'He sort of threw me around. Was quite… dominant. One minute I was underneath him, the next he was behind me.' I stopped and thought. 'It was like having sex with the Jolly Green Giant.'

Jess threw her head back and laughed. 'Ha, I'm so jealous. Did he have a jolly green penis?'

Clem sat down heavily at the table. 'Girls, it is the Sabbath, you know.'

'Never mind Jesus, Clem,' said Jess, then she looked back at me. 'How have you left it?'

'OK, this is the thing,' I said. 'When I woke up this morning, he was gone.'

'Gone?' they chorused.

'Mmm. As in, gone from bed. His bed. Vanished. And I found a note in his kitchen that said he had "work".'

'Have you got the note?' said Jess.

'Yes, Miss Marple,' I said, leaning forward in my chair and sliding it from my jeans pocket. 'Here you go.'

She smoothed it on the table and read it silently.

'But yeah, I would like to see him again,' I said, while Jess read. 'It was the ideal date, after the first bit. We chatted for hours in the pub. And I did vaguely wonder whether I should play hard to get and not go to his place, but it just felt so natural, that I thought, why not?'

Jess nodded while still looking at the note. 'I'm not sure rules like that matter any more.'

'I'm always thrilled if a girl comes home with me on a first date,' added Clem.

'Well that's the other thing,' I said. 'I know it was just a first date, but it felt like there was more to it than that. That there was something, you know?'

Jess looked up at me from the note. 'Well it's not Shakespeare. But it's sweet. Polite. Good manners. Have you texted him?'

'No, obviously not. I can hardly form proper sentences this morning, let alone compose a message.'

'OK, let's have breakfast and then think about it. You need to be casual yet sexy. Clem, you're on toast duty. And can you get the ketchup out? And put the kettle on again. We all need more tea.'

'Some people call Sunday the day of rest,' he said. But he stood up anyway, winking at me as he did.

★

An hour or so later, plates smeared with egg yolk and baked bean juice, Jess held her hand out and asked for my phone.

'OK, but can you not send anything without checking first?' I said, passing it over the table.

'Obviously I won't. But I'm very good at this.'

I narrowed my eyes at her.

'I am!' she insisted. 'Aren't I, Clem? Didn't I help you with whatshecalled last week? Milly? Philly? Jilly?'

'Tilly,' corrected Clem, who always had someone on the go. Mostly petite blonde girls who he wooed intently with Spotify playlists and by taking them for romantic walks along the river. They often disappeared shortly after he cooked for them, but Clem remained stoically unaffected and simply moved on, as if he were a Labrador looking ahead to its next breakfast.

'Yes, Tilly, exactly,' went on Jess. 'How long is she going to last, by the way? I had to help her with the front door because she couldn't work out how to open it.'

'She's very sweet and the door was probably double-locked,' said Clem, 'and anyway, at least she's not boring. I had to hide in my bedroom last week because Walt was loitering downstairs and I couldn't face another conversation about his latest artist. And he leaves terrible skid marks in the loo, if you hadn't noticed.'

'Clem!' said Jess. The house echoed with cries of 'Clem!' several times a day. 'At least he's got a brain.'

'Enough!' I said, interrupting them before they really got going. 'Can we write this message?' I nodded at my phone in Jess's hands. 'What about "Thanks for last night, had a lovely time. Hope the head's feeling all right this morning." With one kiss?'

Jess looked disgusted. 'You can't say "had a lovely time". That's what you'd say to a great-aunt who'd taken you out for tea and scones. And not the head thing either.'

'Why?'

'Because it's feeble, that's why.'

I sat back in my seat and thought. Funny how much energy we can all expend on a few words in messages like these. Hours, potentially, to write a message that was designed to sound as if it had been composed casually in a few seconds.

And that was when I saw him, while I was gazing blankly at the news again. I didn't take it in for a few moments. I just stared at the screen, thinking the dark hair looked familiar. Then I realized. It was him. It was Max.

But WHAT? What the hell was Max doing on television? Why was he sitting in the news studio talking to the news presenter? I looked at the time. Just after midday. I'd left his apartment basically three hours ago and he was now in front of me on the screen. I felt like I was dreaming. Maybe I was dreaming? Maybe I was still asleep and this was all made up. But it didn't seem like a dream. I wiggled my fingers in front of me. They were definitely my real fingers. And a fresh bout of bickering between Jess and Clem over the washing up was also quite loud and real, which is why I couldn't hear what Max was saying.

'It's your turn,' Jess said, reaching for our plates.

'Guys…' I tried to interrupt, eyes remaining on the TV.

'Absolutely not,' said Clem. 'I did it last night.'

'Shhhhh, don't fight in front of guests,' said Jess.

'Calm down, it's just Lil,' he replied.

'Guys, stop it,' I said, louder, so they both looked at me.

'What?' said Jess.

'It's Max, it's the guy, he's… he's there… he's on TV.' I nodded my head at the television and they both turned to it. 'Can you turn it up a bit, Clem?'

'British explorer Max Rushbrooke aims to be the first man to scale…' Jess started reading from the screen but stopped at a complicated name.

'Muchu Chhish,' said Clem. 'In Pakistan, I think.' Then he swivelled round in his seat to look at me. 'But, Lil, that's Max Rushbrooke, the explorer. You went on a date last night with Max Rushbrooke?' He sounded offensively surprised.

'Technically she didn't just go on a date with him. She shagged him,' said Jess, who'd stopped gathering plates and was also staring at the screen. 'But who is he? How do you know about him, Clem?'

'Shhhhh, guys, seriously, can we just watch for a second?'

I nodded at the television again and gestured at Clem to turn the volume up.

'It's a daunting expedition. My most ambitious challenge to date,' said Max, 'but I've dreamt about this mountain my whole life. Ever since I was a small boy.'

'How confident are you about succeeding?' said the presenter, a blonde woman who was wearing quite a tight, red dress and straining towards Max.

Max looked seriously at her, his eyebrows knitting together. 'Pretty confident. I wouldn't do it otherwise. We just have to keep our fingers crossed for a weather window.'

'And when do you leave?'

'We fly from London next week, and then it's about a week to base camp where we'll be acclimatizing for a few weeks. Then hopefully starting the climb shortly after that, hopefully mid-October,' Max replied.

'Well we'll be rooting for you, and thank you very much for coming in,' said the presenter, still gurning at him.

'Not at all,' said Max. 'Thank you for having me.'

They smiled at one another again before the presenter swung back to face the camera. 'That was Max Rushbrooke talking about his upcoming expedition to climb Muchu Chhish, one of the highest unconquered mountains in the world. So best of luck to him, and next we're going to Adam for the weather.'

I put my hands to my cheeks and shook my head in disbelief. 'I mean,' I started saying, 'I had no idea. He just said he was a climber.' And then I thought about his flat. 'But it makes more sense now. He had photos of himself in climbing kit and pictures of mountains everywhere.'

'I'm confused,' said Jess. 'Clem, how do you know about him?'

'Guys, come on, he's pretty well-known,' said Clem, frowning as if exasperated by our lack of expertise about explorers, remote control still in his hand.

'No?' he said, to our blank faces. 'He's a sort of Bear Grylls. I think they've climbed together, actually. And I've read about his expeditions before. Max's, I mean. Can't remember what the last one was…' He stopped and frowned. 'Somewhere in Tibet. And I think he comes from quite a posh family. His dad's a cousin of the Queen or something.'

'Well I've never heard of him,' said Jess. 'But he's hot. Lil, this is amazing. I'm going to google him.' She picked up her phone. 'OK, M… A… X… Rushbrooke,' she said as she tapped. 'Fuck! He's got his own Wikipedia page. Lil, you've shagged someone with a Wikipedia page!'

'Modern romance,' I said, getting up to peer over her shoulder. Annoyingly, a little part of me was pleased by this, but there was no way in hell I would openly admit that. 'Let's have a look.'

'"Max Rushbrooke is an English mountaineer and guide,"' Jess read. '"He is one of Britain's leading high-altitude climbers and has summited Mount Everest ten times. He was born in 1985" – so he's…'

'Thirty-four,' I said. 'I knew that already. It said that on his profile.'

'Went to Eton College then… Er, didn't go to uni. Went to Sandhurst. Oh my God, with Prince William. Then it just lists loads of expeditions.'

'There was some Everest disaster a few years back,' said Clem authoritatively from the other side of the table. 'Bad weather and they got stuck. He might have nearly died. I think they all nearly died.'

'Shhhhh, Clem,' Jess went on, flapping her hand at him. 'Lil, listen to this bit. "His older brother Arundel died in a skiing accident in France in 2002…"'

'Oh shit, he didn't mention anything.'

'But listen to this,' went on Jess, still staring at the computer screen. '"His older brother Arundel died in a skiing accident in France in 2002, which makes Max the heir to his father, the 17th Viscount Rushbrooke. The family seat is Little Clench Hall in Suffolk and their estimated wealth is around £135 million."' She looked up at me. 'Lil, he's a trillionaire! Did he not mention any of this?'

'No, course not! What would he have said? "Hello, Lil, nice to meet you. I'm Max. My brother died when I was younger which makes me a viscount as well as a famous mountaineer and, oh, did I mention I am also very rich?" I paused. 'I think I like him more because he didn't talk about it.'

'Technically, he's not a viscount yet,' said Jess. 'But he will be.' And then she added, quickly, as if all her words were trying to overtake one another, 'Oh my God, imagine, you could be a viscountess.'

'Jess, come onnnnnnn. We haven't even sent that message,' I

said, reaching for my own phone to look Max up on Instagram. Bingo. There he was. Blue tick, 64.2k followers. I scrolled through his photos. Mostly him on mountains – in France, in Canada, in Switzerland. Max on the top of Everest last August, shards of ice in his beard.

'There's some stuff here about his ex-girlfriend,' went on Jess, and then she put on a high-pitched posh voice. 'Lady Primrose Percy and Max Rushbrooke are believed to have dated for several years.' She looked up at me. 'Did he talk about her?'

'Briefly, only when we discussed exes.'

'Look, here's a picture of them,' said Jess, squinting at her screen. 'She's got quite a long nose. And a big forehead. I don't think we have to worry about her.'

'Show me.'

She held up her phone. Lady Primrose was pretty. Jess was exaggerating about the nose. And blonde and smiley. It was a picture of them taken at a party. Max had his arm around her waist, she was tanned and wearing a strapless top that showed her collarbones. She looked quite thin, irritatingly.

'Mmm,' I said, as Jess lowered her phone again. 'He didn't actually mention her by name but she must have been the one he was talking about. But then he said our date wasn't a therapy session and we had to discuss something else.'

'We need to compose that message right now,' said Jess, firmly. 'Clem, do the plates. Lil and I really need to think about this. Oh this is thrilling. Imagine how furious Jake would be if he knew.'

Jake. I hadn't thought about him since the day before, which meant he hadn't taken up any head space for nearly twenty-four hours. Practically a record.

Jess insisted that she take my phone back again and concentrated on the message while I sat at the table, still reeling from this discovery, and Clem wearily picked up our plates and slid them into the sink. The news shouldn't change how I felt about Max, I knew, but part of me couldn't help but feel even more impressed by him. Why was sleeping with someone even slightly famous such a thrill? Did that make me a bad person?

Jess was quiet for a few moments while tapping.

'What are you saying? Jess?'

She ignored me.

'JESS?'

She looked up. 'Cool it. All I've said is "Gorgeous Max, what a night. Looking forward to the next one. Dot, dot, dot." And then two kisses. Little ones. Bit more casual than one big kiss. Less premeditated.'

I shook my head. 'I'm not saying that, give it back. I can't say "looking forward to the next one". It makes me sound mad. Even more psycho than calling him "gorgeous Max". I hate the word gorgeous. Come on, give it back.'

Jess sighed. 'Here you go. But it's too late. I've sent it.'

'WHAT? Jess, you promised.'

'I did no such thing. And come on, Lil, men need encouragement like that. They can be very slow otherwise.'

'Oh, thank you very much,' interjected Clem, from the sink.

I checked my phone. Two grey WhatsApp ticks. She had sent it.

'Fuck. Jess. That isn't cool. Clem, what do you think about that message?'

He turned his head to look at us. 'Honestly, girls, Churchill wrote some of his greatest speeches with less fuss than this. I'm sure it's fine.'

I winced with embarrassment and stared at my phone screen, willing the message to come back. Could I send another message to him, explaining the first to lessen this intense embarrassment? Or did that look even weirder? Was it even possible to sound weirder? I wasn't sure.

'I wish you hadn't,' I muttered. But I could never get cross at Jess.

'What were you going to tell me about Walt anyway?' I asked her, deciding to change the subject and remembering what Jess had said earlier.

She frowned at me.

'You know. You said you'd tell me something. About Walt. About yesterday.'

'Ohhhh.' She nodded in recognition. 'Yes. He said he'd bought us tickets for a weekend in Paris.'

'That's sweet of him. Isn't it?'

'Incredibly sweet, that's the trouble.' Jess bit her lip and looked guilty. 'A man tells you he's bought tickets for a romantic weekend in Paris and your heart should leap right out of your chest. I should be rushing off to buy sexy knickers and thinking about all the oysters and the shagging.'

'And you're not?'

She shook her head. 'Not really. Not at all, in fact. My first thought was "Ooooh, Paris. I wonder if I'll meet any hot men."'

'Not ideal,' I agreed.

'Anyway, it's not for a few weeks. So I was sort of non-committal about it. But I felt so guilty I said I'd go to this exhibition opening at his gallery on Friday. You free? Will you come with me? Then we can stand in a corner and get pissed and decide what I should do.'

'Think so,' I said, looking at my calendar on my phone. 'Yup, I am.' My week looked bare, but I was hoping that one of the nights might be a second date with Max. Or at least I'd been hoping that before Jess sent the world's most embarrassing message.

★

I didn't get home until about nineish and the ticks beside the message were still grey. I was trying to stay breezy but that clearly meant he was ignoring it. Who didn't check their phone for seven hours? Even Mum looked at hers more often than that. Max had definitely seen it. I just had to hope that they'd go blue and he'd send something back later that evening. I imagined he would, he didn't seem like the kind of guy to just ignore a message, however embarrassing it was. Good manners to reply, right?

I found Grace and Riley doing yoga in the living room on their mats, laid out in front of the TV.

'Hi, guys,' I said, dropping my bag on the kitchen counter.

'What time d'you call this, missy?' said Riley, remaining twisted in his pose, his head hanging down between his legs.

'D'you shag him?' added Grace, in the same position.

I paused and then laughed. 'Yes.'

They both cheered from their mats.

'Good work,' said Riley, admiringly. 'Grace only gave me a gobby on our first date.'

Grace reached out and smacked him on the leg. 'You're a pig.'

'What's a gob— actually, do you know what? Never mind,' I said, knowing that I'd regret asking him.

'It's a blowie,' clarified Riley.

'Mmmm. I guessed,' I said, opening the fridge to see if it had anything promising in it. I'd been eating biscuits all day at Jess and Clem's but I still had a little gap for a snack. A piece of toast, maybe. My forty-seventh cup of sugary tea that day.

'Oh, darl, you seen the Sky remote?' said Grace, standing up on her mat and frowning. 'We can't find it anywhere.'

I felt a stab of guilt, knowing it was in my bedside drawer, lying next to my vibrator. But shook my head and reminded myself to smuggle it back into the living room.

'Sorry,' I said, trying to look innocent, before excusing myself for a bath, saying I was desperate for an early night.

I left my phone on the bath mat so I could see if it blinked with a message. It didn't. But just after 10 p.m., I got an alarming email from my boss, Miss Montague, St Lancelot's headmistress.

Dear Miss Bailey, started the email. There was a school rule that all staff call one another by their surnames, which most of us ignored so long as we weren't within earshot of Miss Montague. Please could you come to my office at 7.30 a.m. tomorrow morning for a meeting.

I felt instantly guilty. One week into the school year and I'd already done something wrong. What could it be? Mothers were always emailing the school on Sunday evenings having spent all weekend brooding over something spectacularly minor – a lost sock, a quibble about the school's internet policy, was the cottage pie served at lunch last Thursday made with antibiotic-free beef? There was no matter too trivial for a St Lancelot mother. I set my alarm for 6.15 a.m. and went to sleep with my phone on vibrate on my other pillow. But by the time I drifted off, Max still hadn't messaged.

CHAPTER TWO

THE SITUATION ON MONDAY morning remained unchanged. The ticks were still grey, two little daggers beside that preposterous message. But I forced myself out of bed and tried to summon up some optimism in the shower. Dating had changed since I'd started going out with Jake, I knew. People didn't reply immediately any more. Probably I'd get a message that day. And if not that day, because he might be busy doing whatever explorers did during office hours, then I'd hear from him that evening. I was sure of it. Nobody left a message unread for longer than that. It was rude. I elbowed my way on to the Tube at Brixton feeling hopeful about Max, but slightly less so about my meeting with Miss Montague.

I knocked on her door at precisely 7.29 a.m. She was a woman who appreciated punctuality and the school ran as if it were a military academy.

'Come in,' came the crisp, English voice.

She was sitting at her desk looking as she did every day – stern, in a blue skirt suit, collared shirt, a pearl in each ear sitting underneath a rigid hairstyle which I'd always figured was inspired by that unlikely style icon, Princess Anne.

'Morning,' I said, hovering just inside the door. Pasta, Miss

Montague's dachshund, lay dozing on his side in a patch of early sun beaming through the window.

'Miss Bailey, good morning. Do have a seat.'

I sat. She looked over her glasses at me from behind her desk and leant forward, the chair creaking as she did. 'It's a sensitive situation, which is why I'm telling you now before I mention it to the other members of staff.'

I raised my eyebrows at her and spoke slowly. 'O-O-O-K-K-K-K.'

'It's a late entry to the school year. Coming into your class. Roman Walker.' She paused and looked at me expectantly.

'O-O-O-K-K-K-K,' I said again. It sounded familiar but I couldn't quite place him. St Lancelot's had various celebrity sons – of royalty, of musicians, of artists, of tech billionaires, of politicians. Who'd called their son Roman?

'As in, Luke Walker's son, Roman.'

'Oh. Right.' The mists cleared and I realized who she was talking about. Luke Walker, the premiership footballer. His son. This was a huge deal. No wonder Miss Montague had called it sensitive. There had been a rumour that we'd get Prince George a few years ago, an exhausting period of time when Miss Montague was especially warlike and had made all members of staff practise their curtsy or bow ahead of the anticipated Royal visit. But then they'd picked Thomas's in Clapham and we'd all calmed down again.

'Probably a blessing,' my favourite colleague Steph had said in the playground shortly afterwards. 'Imagine what the mothers would wear if he was here, poor little bugger.'

'Why's Roman coming here now?' I asked Miss Montague. Term had already started. It didn't make sense.

Miss Montague opened her mouth but remained silent for a few moments as if working out how to explain. 'Spot of trouble at Holland Gate. I gather there was a... dalliance between Mr Walker and a teacher. And apparently the governors there felt it best that Roman be moved.'

'To here?'

'Well, to somewhere different,' said Miss Montague, smoothly. 'It's all extremely last-minute and I've spent the weekend arranging it. But he'll be joining your class this morning, so could you make sure everyone welcomes him and be aware of the... sensitivity?'

'Yes, course.'

'No need to do anything differently. Do reading this morning and see how he gets on. If there are any problems, please inform me.'

'Sure,' I nodded. 'And should I, er, meet the, er, Walkers at any point this week? Like the others...' All class teachers had met their new parents just before the new school year had started, to talk them through the syllabus and what would be expected of their sons. I'd spent an evening in August shaking hands with my new parents and lecturing them about mobile phone policy.

This year, I had eight boys in my class, including the son of a Tory MP, the son of a Russian steel magnate (the father had the menacing air of a man who ate his victims for breakfast; the mother looked eleven years old); a Greek prince, and a sweetheart called Vikram whose family had just moved from Delhi to London. His mother was so concerned about Vikram settling in that she'd asked if they could send his nanny to sit at the back of the classroom, so I'd had to say gently she couldn't.

Miss Montague shook her head, the helmet of hair unmoving. 'The Walkers aren't coming in for now. I'm going to liaise with them directly. It does of course mean there may be more media interest in us. But the usual rules apply – nobody is to talk to any press and if anyone approaches you please direct them to me.' Her eyes burned into me like a female huntress on safari.

'OK, no problem,' I said.

'Marvellous, I'll see you for staff meeting in a second then,' said Miss Montague.

I nodded and stood up, relieved I wasn't in trouble.

Because I'd come in so early, the staffroom was empty when I arrived, so I dropped my bag on a chair and went straight for the coffee machine in the corner. I liked being in early. It gave me time to swallow at least two coffees before the kids started sliding up to the school gates on their scooters.

St Lancelot's wasn't huge compared to some of its rivals in Knightsbridge and Battersea, but it was generally considered the most exclusive boys' school in London (as Miss Montague told us almost daily), with just over five hundred boys aged from four to thirteen. It occupied the site of a Gothic red-brick building between Chelsea and Pimlico which had once been a hospital but was converted into the school after the Second World War by a zealous army captain. Captain Bower, he was called. I had a sip of coffee and glanced at the portrait of him in army khakis hanging up in the staffroom. He had a moustache and was covered in medals. He had also studied Classics at Oxford and so the school motto – *moniti meliora sequamur* – was engraved in stone over the main entrance.

During my interview for the job five years earlier, Miss Montague, Captain Bower's granddaughter, had begun by asking whether I knew what the motto meant. Hadn't a clue.

She'd peered at me over her desk and replied: 'After instruction, let us move on to pursue higher things.'

'Oh I see,' I'd answered politely.

'It's a line from Virgil's Aeniad. I expect you've read it,' she said, and I'd nodded vaguely into my coffee cup.

I hadn't.

'It's fitting,' went on Miss Montague, 'because we teach a great many pupils who are destined for public life. Both here and abroad. Do you feel capable of shaping these young minds, Miss Bailey?'

I'd said yes, obviously, but five years on, I sometimes wondered whether these young minds should be destined for public life. Just ahead of the last general election, a Year 2 called Theodore had marched up to me in the playground during lunch and asked who I'd be voting for.

'Errr,' I'd started, unsure what to reply. We weren't supposed to foist our own politics on the pupils. 'The thing is, Theodore, some people think it's rude to ask that question.'

Theodore had looked nonplussed at this. 'My daddy says everyone who doesn't vote Conservative is an idiot.'

I was so surprised I didn't have time to answer before Theodore had turned round and swaggered off to canvass elsewhere in the playground.

'Don't worry about him,' said Steph, standing next to me and keeping an eye on the future prime ministers and despots pushing one another off the climbing frame. 'His dad's a minister. Minister for sheep or something.'

Being a teacher at school is much the same as being a kid at school. You need mates. Allies. Steph was one of my closest allies. She taught Year 8, the 12-year-olds, and I loved her for her no-nonsense attitude – she didn't take lip from the kids or grumbles from the parents. Outspoken and somewhere in her mid-forties (I'd never dared ask), she lived in Surbiton where her own kids were at the local school and where her husband, Tim, worked as a GP.

'Morning, love,' she said, coming through the staffroom door laden with bags, red in the face and with wisps of hair sticking to her forehead.

'Hiya. Coffee?' I replied, still hovering beside the kettle.

'Mmm, please,' said Steph. 'Victoria was a fucking night-mare this morning.'

I spooned some Nescafé into the least grimy cup I could find on the tray and poured hot water over the top. It often sounded more like a working men's club than a staffroom in here, although Miss Montague took a dim view of swearing among her staff. She took a dim view of many things – beards, the internet, staff on their mobile phones, parents who picked their boys up late, parents who dropped their boys off too early, parents who took their boys out of school before the holidays for skiing in Val d'Isère, and parents who threw their son's birthday party at Claridge's.

'Fuck knows where all my lesson plans are this morning. I thought I had them but couldn't find them anywhere on the train so I'm going to have to print them all off again,' added Steph, collapsing on a chair next to her bags and bending down to take off her trainers. 'I hate the bastard Anglo-Saxons.'

I put the coffee on the table next to her.

'Ta, love. How was your weekend?'

'Good.' Then I paused and lowered my voice. 'I had that date on Saturday night.'

'Oh my giddy aunt,' said Steph, looking up from untying her trainers, cheeks puce from the effort. 'Tell me everything.'

Other staff members were drifting in and hanging their coats up. 'Morning, Renée,' I said, waving at the art teacher, then I lowered my voice again. 'It was… nice.'

'Nice?' shrieked Steph. 'Lilian, love, I'm an old married woman who gets her leg over once a year. You've got to do better than nice.'

'All right all right. It was better than nice. Lovely. Will that do?'

'So you shagged him?' she said, narrowing her eyes at me. 'A proper shag?'

'Shhhh!' I inclined my head towards the door, which Miss Montague had just drifted through, like a battleship coming into port.

'Hiya, Mrs M,' said Steph, who'd taught at St Lancelot's for over a decade and was one of the few members of staff who could get away with referring to her as such.

'Good morning,' said Miss Montague, loudly, so everyone heard.

We dutifully murmured mornings back and looked round the room for seats. Every Monday morning we had a staff meeting. Sometimes the meetings were five minutes; sometimes they were twenty. The trick was to grab a seat as fast as possible, because if you had to stand throughout the meeting the chances were Miss Montague would catch your eye when she was after a volunteer for something – cleaning out the guinea pig cage or taking that week's Lego Club.

As Miss Montague made her way to the front of the room, colleagues parting for her and Pasta to waddle their way through, I reached into my pocket to check my phone – nope, still nothing from Max. And because I was momentarily distracted, I missed the spare seats, so I had to hover awkwardly behind Steph's chair.

'Undivided attention, please, everyone. There's a serious matter I need to bring to your attention,' said Miss Montague, standing underneath the painting of Captain Bower. He looked like he'd been a stern, imperial chap and I imagine that was where she'd inherited her authority from. If Stalin and Joan of Arc had had a lovechild, it would have been exactly like Miss Montague.

Her face darkened as if ahead of a storm. 'Joel Glassman in Year 6 arrived at school in a Range Rover last week,' she announced.

Steph glanced up at me and frowned. I shrugged. What was the problem? Most of the school arrived in a Range Rover every day. Dmitri, the Russian in my class, arrived in a blacked-out one each morning, and only jumped down, clutching his schoolbag, once a security guard from the front of the car had opened a back door for him. He had two security guards, actually, who he referred to as his uncles. 'Uncle Boris' and 'Uncle Sasha'. Burly, with necks thicker than their heads, I still hadn't worked out which was which but one of them had winked at me during the first week of term and I'm afraid to say I did feel a frisson of excitement.

'I don't mean a normal Range Rover,' went on Miss Montague, her voice louder and more menacing, as if she was a party leader building to a crescendo. 'What I am talking about is one of those electric, toy Range Rovers.' She said the word 'toy' with absolute disgust. 'Joel had been given it for his birthday and decided to drive it to school, accompanied by the nanny, but we simply don't have room in the scooter park for electric vehicles. So I've had words with Mr and Mrs Glassman but I would like you all to keep a vigilant eye on the situation and alert me if you see this happening again.'

The toadiest teachers – mostly the language department – all nodded back dutifully before Miss Montague moved on.

'I've also had an email from Lady Fitzalan over the week-end. She and her husband are divorcing so can whoever is little Rupert's form teacher – ah, Miss Cookson, yes, there you are – can you keep an eye on him, please?'

Steph sighed heavily in her seat and I saw Mike slip through the staffroom door. He was our other ally. Head of music.

'Good of you to join us, Mr Abbey,' said Miss Montague.

'Ah yes, um, sorry,' he said. 'Tube was terrible.'

'But of course it was,' she said, blinking at him with a deadpan expression. 'And could I remind you all that it's our Harvest Festival in few weeks so if you could talk to your forms about it that would be appreciated. An email will be going out to all parents this week.' We all nodded dutifully while I caught Mike's eye and smiled. He was always charged with assembly rehearsals for the Harvest Festival and, for several weeks last year, arrived at the pub after work humming songs with titles like 'A Very Happy Vegetable'.

'Finally, could I have a volunteer for someone to help Mrs O'Raraty with Harry Potter Club on Wednesday afternoon?'

Mike winked back at me and I stifled a laugh with my hand, turning it into a cough. He was always late and the Tube was always the excuse but the truth was that he was hung-over and slept through his snooze button. This meant he always looked crumpled – creased shirt, scuffed shoes, curls of hair springing out from his head at odd angles, as if he'd slept on it while wet. I winked back.

'Miss Bailey, how kind of you to volunteer,' said Miss Montague from the front. 'Please could you liaise directly with Mrs O'Raraty as to what she needs you to do.'

Shit.

I nodded.

'And that's everything from me. So I suggest we all get on with our day. Unless there's anything else?' said Miss

Montague, gazing out at her teachers like Napoleon about to send troops into battle.

Silence.

'Very good,' she said, and the room started moving again.

Mike hurried over to Steph and me. A pillow crease was still imprinted on his cheek.

'Either of you got any Nurofen? My head feels like it's about to fall off and I've got to give a Year 6 his French horn lesson,' he said.

'No, sorry,' I said.

'Go see Matron,' said Steph. 'She'll have some.'

'She told me off last week. Said it wasn't her job to hand out painkillers like sweets. Mad old bag.'

'Well you'll have to have a coffee and get on with it then. Come on, let's get going. The sooner we start the sooner it's over,' said Steph, getting to her feet.

*

Roman took the number of my class to nine. Small class sizes at St Lancelot's was one of the reasons that parents paid £8,420 a term (extras and uniform not included) for their sons to come here. It meant that the pupils were supposedly lavished with attention by the teachers and our teaching assistants, although my teaching assistant this year was a dim 18-year-old called Fergus who got the job because Miss Montague is his aunt and he apparently needed to 'get something on his CV' during his gap year.

Only one week into the school year, I had mentally relegated Fergus to the same level of intelligence and ability as the 5-year-olds. He arrived late every morning, made more mess at the art table than any of the boys, constantly checked his phone in the classroom (phones were forbidden there, 'only visible in the staffroom' was the rule) and took extremely long loo breaks.

Still, the boys were mostly cherubic (it was like teaching a litter of puppies every day), and Fergus's uselessness hadn't mattered a great deal. Yet.

The four British boys sounded as if they could have stepped straight from the pages of an Oscar Wilde play – George, Arthur, Cosmo and Phineas (although I'd got off lightly because Steph had a Ptolemy in her class this year). Plus Dmitri the son of the Russians; Achilles, the Greek prince; Hunter, the son of two Americans who wanted him to go to Harvard, and Vikram, who hadn't acclimatized to London yet and had arrived at school every morning, his teeth chattering, wearing three coats.

Because the classes were so tiny at St Lancelot's, the parents (or nannies, or bodyguards) of the boys brought them to their classrooms every morning, instead of dropping them at the gate. Or to Nelson, as my classroom was called, since Captain Bower had named them all after British military heroes. Other class names included Wellington, Marlborough, Kitchener and Steph taught Allenby, Year 8.

A couple of years ago, one mother had said this was distasteful and launched an impassioned discussion about the classroom names on Mumsnet. But when this came to Miss Montague's attention, she sent an email to all parents saying if they didn't like the school traditions, they were welcome to take their sons elsewhere. Nobody did. Nobody ever gave up a place at St Lancelot's because their boys were guaranteed to go on to Eton, Harrow, St Paul's or Westminster. Really, wherever the parents wanted.

That morning, the boys started arriving as usual from around 8.30.

'Hi, George, did you have a nice weekend? Pop your bag on your desk.'

'Hunter, hello, I could hear you coming down the corridor. Did you have magic beans for breakfast?'

'Vikram, quick, come inside and warm up.' This went on for a few minutes as I waved to various nannies.

Then Roman appeared in the doorway, or at least who I took to be Roman because I didn't recognize him. I squatted down and held my hand out. 'Hello, you must be Roman.' He frowned at my hand and didn't take it.

'I'm not allowed to talk to strangers,' he said, kicking the heel of his shoe repeatedly against the carpet.

'Roman!' said a woman hurrying in behind him in suede ankle boots and sunglasses. 'I'm so sorry, I think he's nervous.'

'Of course,' I said, standing up. 'You must be Mrs Walker.'

She nodded and we shook hands. 'Miss Bailey?'

'Exactly.' She looked like many of the other St Lancelot mothers – expensive. She had a yellow diamond the size of a raspberry on her right hand and long, shiny hair which I suspected wasn't all her own.

'Great. Can we just have a word…' She gestured to the corner of the classroom away from the door.

'Sure, er, Fergus?' He had just arrived, wafting cigarette smoke around the classroom. 'Can you man the door?'

'Yah, no problem,' he replied.

In the corner, Mrs Walker talked in a hushed voice: 'I just wanted to triple-check the privacy issue. I know Miss Montague said there's a strict no mobile phone policy. It's just that I don't want any photos of Roman to leak and we can't move him again.'

'Not a problem,' I said smoothly. 'I'm sure Miss Montague has already told you but we have several high-profile pupils here and security is our first priority.'

'Fabulous,' she said. 'OK, gotta run. Bye, sweetie. Be good.' And without even kissing her son goodbye, she trotted out on her suede boots.

I turned back to Roman and smiled brightly. 'Let's get you to your desk.'

*

By Wednesday, not only had I not heard from Max (even though the ticks had finally gone blue), I'd also got thrush. I realized this while sitting in the staff loos that lunchtime because my vagina felt like it was on fire, and not in a good way. Terrific, I thought grimly, standing and pulling my knickers up. I'd have to nip to Boots for some Canesten. I absolutely couldn't teach anything about the Pyramids this afternoon with this level of itchiness going on in my pants.

When I got to Boots, there was a queue of people taking for ever to discuss their Nicorette and their sleeping problems. And then, finally, when I got to the front of the queue, the pharmacist seemed deaf.

'Could I have some Canesten please?' I said quietly. Almost a whisper.

'I'm sorry, dear?' said the elderly man in his lab coat, leaning towards me.

'Some Canesten,' I hissed, slightly louder. I pointed behind him at the boxes of it.

'Oh, right you are,' he said, turning round to look. Then, bellowing so that everyone in Boots could hear, he said: 'The Canesten Combi or just the cream? Or just the pill?'

'The combi,' I whispered, glancing over my shoulder to see a snake of people behind me. I hoped they were all buying embarrassing items too. I hoped they were all buying Anusol for their piles.

'Here you go,' he said, slowly picking a box, slowly turning back to the till, slowly scanning it. 'Would you like a bag?'

'No thanks,' I said, snatching it and shoving it into my pocket.

I went straight back to the staff bathrooms, pulled my knickers down again – Christ, the INTENSE itchiness – unscrewed the lid on the little tube and rubbed it in. 'Aaaaaaah,' I sighed audibly as I felt the cream's soothing effect immediately kick in, forgetting that there was someone in the cubicle next to me.

When I stepped outside the cubicle to wash my hands, it transpired that the person in the cubicle next to me was Miss Montague. I quickly dropped the Canesten back into my pocket.

'Hello,' I squeaked, our eyes meeting in the mirror in front of us.

'Afternoon, Miss Bailey,' she said, raising her eyebrows at me. 'Everything all right?'

'Mmm, all good.'

But the cream still hadn't helped much by the time Harry Potter Club rolled round at 4.30 that afternoon, so I spent an hour trying to help boys of varying ages try to design their own broomstick while crossing my legs back and forth to try and take the pressure off things down there.

*

I didn't have time to go home between school and Walt's exhibition on Friday evening so I had to go straight there. I hate doing that. For a night out, I feel like you need to go home, wash your hair, put on a clean pair of pants and reapply make-up to transform into weekend mode. I wanted to get drunk tonight. I was in that sort of mood.

Max was clearly not going to text, which made me sad. And gloomy about my dating antennae. I knew we'd had a good time. A great time. So I didn't understand the silence. Maybe it was the shagging him on the first date thing? Maybe the old rules did still apply? Depressing.

I caught the Tube to Green Park and walked down Piccadilly towards a pub in Shepherd's Market to meet Jess. In the evening dusk, the former red-light district still had a raffish air. Several pubs, a few cramped restaurants with tables that over-spilled to the pavement outside and the unmistakable whiff of London drains.

I saw her standing outside the pub, a bottle of wine in a cooler between her feet. She was smiling and chatting to a tall man in a black polo neck and a leather jacket. One of the art crowd, I decided, walking towards them. Either that or a trained assassin.

'Hiya,' I said, giving her a hug.

'Hi, babe, here you go,' she said, picking up an empty glass at her feet and filling it with wine. 'And meet Alexi. He's coming to the party too. Alexi, this is Lil. My best pal. Knows literally nothing about art. No offence, love.'

'None taken,' I said, reaching for the wine glass from her.

'Lil, sensational to meet you,' said Alexi, whereupon I went for a handshake and he went for a kiss on the cheek, so we did both and I then pulled back, awkwardly.

I thought sensational was over-egging it a bit. Was he high?

'How do you guys know each other?' I asked, before tipping back my wine glass. Ah, that first mouthful on a Friday evening.

'We don't,' said Jess. 'I met him at the bar and we realized we were both going to the opening.' She smiled at Alexi and reached behind her neck to pull her hair over one shoulder. Oh dear. I recognized that flush on her face. She fancied this tall, dark stranger who was wearing a polo neck even though it was a balmy Friday evening in September. I glanced from Jess to Alexi. She and I had very different taste. Jess was into beautiful men – slim, delicate, arty men. The sorts you saw drifting about Rome or Florence in drainpipe jeans, who existed on tiny coffees and rolled cigarettes. Not for me. I'd never fancied a man with skinnier thighs than me.

'Rrrrright,' I said, slowly. 'And Alexi, how do you know Walt?'

'Old friend from art school,' he said, scratching his chin.

'You're an artist?'

He shook his head. 'A collector.'

As Jess said, I knew little about art. If you asked me, most Picassos looked like they'd been drawn by a 4-year-old with a packet of Crayola. But collecting meant Alexi had money, no? Rubbish collecting was a job. Art collecting was less of a job, more a hobby for rich people.

'What sort of thing do you collect?'

Alexi shrugged in his leather jacket. 'I'm interested in young artists, but it can be any medium. Paint, graphics, installations. So long as I feel something towards it. A reaction. Something visceral, you know?' At this, he curled his right hand into a fist and held it up to his chest, beating it against his heart.

'Mmm,' I replied vaguely into my glass of wine. I went to gallery openings every now and then with Jess and the only thing I felt at them was hunger because there was always plenty of wine but no snacks.

'I think you'll love this show,' Jess said to Alexi, eyelashes fluttering like a baby gazelle's. Christ. I wondered if she'd told Alexi she knew Walt because she was dating him.

Alexi smiled back at her. 'I'm excited about seeing it.'

I felt like a pawn in a game of foreplay. 'What is it?' I asked. 'I mean, who's the exhibition by?'

'A young artist called Daniel,' said Jess. 'From the Ukraine. So his work is quite intense. Twisted.'

'He uses light to show darkness and darkness to show light,' added Alexi.

'Exactly,' said Jess, gazing at Alexi with such admiration it was as if he'd just announced he'd discovered the secret to everlasting life.

'Sounds cheerful.'

'Oh, come on, misery guts,' said Jess, digging me in the ribs with an elbow. 'I take it no word from you-know-who then?'

'Nope,' I said, grimacing at her. 'But it's all right. Onwards and sideways, as Mum says.'

'He's an idiot, in that case, and there'll be millions more,' said Jess, before turning to Alexi. 'Lil had a date last weekend but he hasn't texted her.'

I wasn't sure I wanted Alexi knowing about my love life, but too late.

'Lil, I can't believe it,' said Alexi, smoothly. 'I'm sorry. You liked him?'

I sighed. 'Yeah. He was interesting. And it was my first date in ages. But I reckon if you haven't heard from someone in five days that's probably a bad sign, right? You're a man. If

you guys want to see someone again you let them know, no?'
I hoped my tone didn't come across as desperate.

Alexi looked thoughtful for a moment. 'Normally, yes. But
without knowing the details it's quite hard to say. Sometimes
we can be just as complicated as women.'

'Fiiiiiinally, a man who admits it,' said Jess, laughing.

Oh God. If there was one thing that Jess liked more than
a skinny man who was into art and tight trousers, it was a
complicated, skinny man.

'What about you, Alexi?' I said. 'You single?'

'Ha.' He grimaced and ran a hand through his hair. 'It's
complicated for me, too.'

Course it was. This was a disaster. Poor, innocent Walt,
I thought, who was probably this second pouring wine into
plastic cups and brushing down his neatly ironed chinos ahead
of the opening. He didn't stand a chance.

★

Walt's gallery was a few minutes away on a little street off
Piccadilly. 'Walter de Winter' said a sign hanging outside it.
By the time we arrived, people were already overflowing on
to the pavement outside the gallery, under the sign, plastic
cups of white wine in hand. It looked like a circus gathering.
A woman with bright purple hair stood talking to a man in a
tartan jacket with a large dog asleep at his feet. Behind them
was a man wearing a cravat over a T-shirt and a panama hat,
deep in conversation with a lady who'd come dressed entirely

in black lace. One man, standing with his back to us, had the world 'REAL' tattooed across his neck.

'Alexi!' shouted someone, so he said he'd come and find us in a minute and slunk his way through the crowd.

'Let's find Walt,' said Jess, so I followed her inside the gallery where I spotted him, just as I'd suspected, in chinos, a sensible blazer and suede loafers, standing in front of a large canvas, gesturing to a lady with cherry-coloured lipstick beside him. We snuck up behind him and stood silently, not wanting to interrupt.

The canvas was entirely black, so far as I could see. As black as a blackboard. It was like looking out through a window into the night. No colour whatsoever.

'And you can see here,' said Walt, sweeping his hand across the bottom left-hand corner of the canvas. 'He intensifies the drama. There's a sense of heightened emotions, of fury, of anger and despair which is juxtaposed with here, where the mood changes.' Walt stopped and waved his hand towards the top of the canvas, which was exactly as black as the lower half. 'It's calmer, it's lighter, there's less chaos. So really what he's revealing is a true picture of mental anguish. Black and violent at times, but at other moments, far less disturbed.'

The lady with the vibrant lipstick nodded. 'Hmmm,' she said. 'Eeet ees fascinating.' And then she squinted at a small label beside the canvas. 'Let me haff a look at the others and decide, but I like thees very much.'

'Absolutely, take your time. Would you like another drink?' said Walt, gesturing at her empty glass.

She shook her head and handed him her glass as if he was a waiter. 'Marvellous,' he said. 'Like I said, take your time.'

She wobbled off on her heels and Walt turned to us, his face beaming at the sight of Jess.

'Hello, you two. Wonderful you could both come. Have you got drinks?' He leant forward to kiss Jess, then me.

'Nope, only just got here,' said Jess. 'We met your friend Alexi in the pub beforehand.'

'Oh, Alexi's here, that's tremendous news,' said Walt. 'I should go and say hello, but will you two be all right?'

'Yes, yes, course, go and mingle. Chat up the punters,' said Jess. 'Don't worry about us.'

He kissed her on the cheek again and headed towards the door as Jess reached for two glasses of wine from a passing waiter.

She gave one to me and I raised my eyebrows at her.

'What?'

'Don't what me. Poor Walt. I saw the way you were looking at Alexi.'

Jess bit her lip. 'Oh, Lil. Trouble is, Walt's too nice. I mean, look at him!' We turned to watch Walt through the front of the gallery where he was clasping Alexi in a hug. Then Walt released him and stood gesticulating madly with his hands, grinning like a madman.

'I get it,' I said, turning back to her. 'He's nice but...'

'Too nice,' said Jess. 'In no way do I want to rip that blazer off his back. And Alexi is more my type.'

We looked back through the window. Alexi was rolling a cigarette while Walt held his packet of tobacco.

'Yeah, he looks dangerous.'

'Right?' she said, grinning at me. And then her face fell. 'Oh, but I'm sorry about Max. He's not good enough. And I reckon explorers must be selfish fuckers anyway. All that time at extreme temperatures. Can't be good for you.'

'I guess,' I said, shrugging. 'It's just weird because I thought we really got on. But, I'm fine. Honestly.'

'Tosser,' said Jess. 'Come on, let's have another drink. Then I want to talk to Alexi again.' She glanced back through the window at him.

'Oi,' I said, waving my hand in front of her face. 'Focus. Come on, why don't you tell me about these terrible paintings?'

*

Waking up the next morning, I knew something bad had happened. I could sense it. I opened my eyes and felt a few moments of bewilderment as my brain groped for information. Why this lurking sense of guilt?

I reached out my hand for my bedside table. And at least my phone was in its usual… Oh. No, it wasn't. Fuck. Where was my phone? Why wasn't it charging on my bedside table? Astonishing, the panic this can induce in a fully-grown woman. No phone! I sat bolt upright in my bed and saw my phone lying on my bed beside my pillow. And then I remembered what I'd done. I remembered why there was something niggling at me. A little voice in my head that was whispering 'Shame.' A sinking feeling. Already half-knowing what I'd see, I opened WhatsApp. Yep, well done, Lil. I'd sent Max a message last night at… 2.03 a.m. Brilliant.

I read it back, feeling sick.

The message started 'Just to say,' which was a bad beginning because it already sounded hectoring. People start sentences with 'Just to say' when they're annoyed about something but are trying to sound laid back about it.

'Just to say, I think you're a dick.'

'Just to say, I never liked your mother in the first place.'

'Just to say, I hate you and I never want to see you again.'

My intention at 2.03 a.m. was clearly to sound calm. And yet, the underlying vibe was fury. *Just to say, last Saturday was my first date in six months,* I'd written, which made me groan out loud in bed because it managed to sound cross and tragic at the same time. Quite a skill, that.

I read on, my stomach sinking further at each word. *Just to say, last Saturday was my first date in six months. Which was kind of a big deal for me. And I know you're busy climbing mountains or whatever but I think it's polite to reply to messages from people you've shagged. X*

FUCK'S SAKE, LIL, TELL IT TO A THERAPIST. TELL IT TO JESS. TELL IT TO GRACE. TELL IT TO THE MAN WHO SERVES YOU COFFEE IN THE PORTUGUESE CAFE. JUST DON'T TELL IT TO MAX.

The single 'X' was a hilariously mental touch too. The subtext, basically, was 'I'm furious and want to rant at you, but I'm also going to try and sound normal by rounding off this message as if we're mates.'

There was no reply, obviously. And he'd read it at... 7.22 this morning. I rolled over on to my front and screamed into my pillow. That was it. I'd disgraced myself. I'd become one of those people you worry about becoming. We knew it was in all of us, this propensity to be a psycho, but the trick was to try and stop it slipping out. To maintain the façade of sanity until you'd been with someone for, what, six months? A year? Only then could you start absolutely losing it over things – their inability to pick up socks, their stubble shavings scattered across the basin like iron filings, when they liked a random girl's photo on Instagram.

What you absolutely shouldn't do is hint at any sort of lunacy after one date. Not that there would be another date with Max. I knew that for sure now. I wouldn't blame him if he stayed safely up that unpronounceable mountain. And somehow, this pitiful scenario felt worse because Max was famous. As if he'd be sitting round the campfire or wherever they sat on the mountains, joking about it with his climbing pals. He probably had this all the time, groupies sending him desperate messages.

I roared into my pillow again. How had this happened? We'd been at the gallery for a couple of hours, I remembered that. Then we went to a pub round the corner. Then? I supposed I'd had one too many glasses of wine. Oh dear, oh dear, oh dear. I was livid with myself. And I felt a hot sense of shame sweep through me. I was literally never having sex again.

CHAPTER THREE

IT WAS THREE WEEKS later, on the train home to Norfolk, that I developed an inkling. Or maybe the word 'inkling' is too strong. It suggests that I knew what was coming, which I didn't, despite what certain people claimed later. But it was on the train that the possibility presented itself in my head and, milliseconds later, my body responded by convulsing with fear. Shit. What if? Nah, couldn't be. And yet? What if?

It was all thanks to Jess, who'd decided to come home with me for the weekend because she said she wanted to escape London for the 'wilds' of the country. This seemed ambitious considering we were off to stay in my parents' semi in Castleton, but Jess had overly romantic ideas about life. She was late to Liverpool Street that Saturday morning so I picked up our tickets and dithered for ten minutes in Caffè Nero wondering whether I could stomach a Danish. I felt sick, which was weird, because I hadn't been out drinking last night. I stood in front of the glass cabinet frowning to myself. What did I have for supper? I remembered. My 'special' pesto pasta – pasta, couple of spoonfuls of pesto and a few peas – the 'special' element of this gourmet dinner – lobbed in from a bag in the freezer so I could tell myself I was getting one of my five a day. But it didn't contain anything sinister, so why did I feel vommy, as if saliva was pooling at the back of my throat?

'Can I have an Americano please? Medium?' I said to the woman behind the till. She wordlessly nodded at the card machine in front of me.

I reached down for the purse in my bag and stood up again, but had to put a hand on the counter to steady myself. I felt like I'd been out until 3 a.m. doing parkour in the streets, yet all I'd done was eat my pasta on the sofa with Grace and Riley while we watched a weird Netflix documentary they'd chosen about dolphins. Did you know that dolphins masturbate? I didn't. Male dolphins wrap wriggling eels around their penises apparently and that does it for them. Isn't that odd? It made me think quite differently about ever wanting to swim with dolphins. Each to their own but I prefer a vibrator. Although even that had felt like too much work last night, so after the documentary finished I'd dragged myself into bed and, before I could hear any of Grace and Riley's own mating rituals, fallen asleep.

I picked up my coffee from the end of the counter just as my phone rang in my coat pocket.

'Morning, darling, I'm here,' said Jess.

'Hi. Just grabbing a coffee in Nero. But we should maybe hurry up because…' I pulled my phone away from my ear to check the time, 'we've only got eight minutes so our platform should be up.'

'Amazing, I'm desperate for a coffee. Wait there and I'll come find you,' said Jess, ignoring my mention of the train. In the eleven years I'd known her, she'd never been early, or on time, to anything. 'Sorry, Italian blood,' she'd say, shrugging, and not sounding remotely sorry whenever she arrived at the pub half an hour late.

I hovered at the door of Caffè Nero, scanning the station for a familiar blonde head. There she was, not moving with any sense of urgency, rolling along in a leather jacket with a red canvas bag hanging over her shoulder. She waved as she got closer.

'Hello, my heart. Let me get this coffee. What an adventure, I can't wait to see your parents, it's been FOR EVER.'

'Could I have a cappuccino please? Large?' she asked the Caffè Nero lady, before turning back to me, grinning.

'Guess what?' she said.

I narrowed my eyes at her and took a swig of my coffee. 'Er, dunno. Give me a clue.'

'OK. How do I look this morning?'

I scrutinized her face. It was a face I knew almost as well as my own. Unfairly small nose, wide mouth, brown eyes which were generally thick with black liner, hair, well, generally all over the place but today it was pulled over one shoulder in a plait.

I shrugged. 'Had your eyebrows done?'

She shook her head. 'Guess again.'

'Cappuccino,' grunted the coffee lady, putting Jess's cup down at the end of the counter.

'Come on,' I said, checking the time on my phone again. 'We've got to go. Can't stand round playing Guess Who?. Tell me on the train.'

Since it was early Saturday morning, the train was empty. One middle-aged man in a rugby shirt sitting at a table, reading his paper.

'This one?' I said, gesturing at a free table opposite him.

Jess nodded and sat. 'OK, since you're not going to guess it, I'll tell you,' she said. 'Are you listening?'

'Yup,' I said, sniffing my coffee. I wasn't even sure I could drink it. I felt like swallowing anything would make me gag.

'Lil?'

'Mmmm,' I said, lifting the paper cup towards my mouth.

'Did you hear me? I just said I think I'm in love.'

'What?' I put the cup back down on the table and frowned at her. 'With Walt?'

Jess quickly shook her head. 'No. No, not Walt. I've had to let him go. I'm talking about Alexi.'

'Who's Al— Ohhhhh. That guy from the exhibition?'

'Exactly,' said Jess. 'We've been texting ever since that night and I saw him again last night. And he's amazing, Lil. Like, properly amazing. Funny and clever and he's into art and—'

'Hang on,' I said, holding my hands up in front of me as if stopping traffic. 'We need to go back to the start. You met him on that Friday but you only saw him again last night? And now you're in love with him?'

'I know, I know. It's mad. But he was travelling after the exhibition. In America. And then he got back on Thursday so he came over last night. That's why I was asking about my face. I only got about two hours' sleep and I probably look like hell.'

'No no, you don't at all.' She didn't. She hadn't bothered to remove last night's eye make-up so it was smudged, but she looked kittenish, like a 1960s model. Whenever I slept in my make-up I woke up looking like Miss Havisham.

'I know I've said this before but I think he's maybe… well, I just have a good feeling about this, Lil. You know when you know? Or you know when people say "you know when you know"? I think I know.'

I hate that saying. I thought I'd known with Jake and then look what happened. I didn't know at all. And then I thought about Max. Ha, Max! Another thing I was wrong about. He'd seemed a nice one on our date but then off he'd scarpered, up that mountain quicker than Ranulph fucking Fiennes on speed.

'Lil?'

Obviously I did not say any of this to Jess, who was radiating such excitement that I felt I had to be enthusiastic.

'Exciting! Although poor old Walt. But how come I'm only hearing about this now?'

Jess looked guilty, pulling one side of her mouth into a grimace. 'I didn't want to say anything until I saw you because I just thought it might be mean, given the Max thing. I'm actually still so cross with him that I don't even like saying his name. I never want to say it again.'

I laughed. 'Thanks, love, but never mind about him,' I said. 'Tell me about last night. What did you do? How was the…' I glanced across the aisle to the table with the man reading his paper, then I lowered my voice and turned back to Jess. 'S-e-x?'

'Why are you spelling it?'

'Because…' I flicked my head towards the table.

Jess rolled her eyes. 'You're so paranoid. And we didn't have sex because I've got my period, which was annoying.'

I heard the man rustle his papers as Jess rattled on: 'But we did everything else, then we just lay there for hours chatting. About my work, about his work, about my family and where he comes from. He's got an aunt who lives in Liguria too. Isn't that spooky?'

I listened to her while holding my cup in the air. It was when she mentioned her period that my brain clicked, as if in a film scene, like a police detective who has a brainwave in his car while eating a doughnut. My period. Where was my period? Shit. I was due this week. I'd finished a packet of the pill last week, hadn't I? I picked up my phone and scrolled through my apps for my calendar. I opened it and counted by drumming my fingers on the table. Thumb, two, three, four, five.

'What you doing?' said Lex.

'Counting,' I said, still looking down at my phone screen.

'Counting what?'

I took a breath and paused before going on. 'I'm late.'

'Huh?' Jess leant towards me to look at the calendar. 'Ohhhhhh. You mean period late?'

'Mmm.'

'You should have got it when?'

'Er, like, Tuesday. Wednesday latest.'

'OK, Tuesday,' went on Jess. 'And it's now Saturday. But you're never normally regular, right?'

I thought back. I'd had my first period when I was thirteen. I went to the girls' loos during lunch break and was astonished to see rust in my pants. Why was I rusting? But then I'd wiped myself, seen blood all over the tissue and nearly screamed over the cubicles that I was dying, only to realize this must be the great moment of womanhood that my mother had told me about. I'd felt so pleased with myself. A grown-up! A woman! I couldn't wait to get home and share the news. Mum embraced me with a hug when I told her, and, later that evening, I found a box of tampons and a copy of *The Female Eunuch* on my bed with the corner turned down on a particular page, a sentence underlined in faint pencil: If you think you are emancipated, you might consider the idea of tasting your own menstrual blood – if it makes you sick, you've a long way to go, baby. That didn't seem a very sanitary idea to me. I'd ignored it and tucked the book underneath *The Worst Witch* on my bedside table.

Over dinner that night at the kitchen table, Mum had advised how to insert a tampon, waving her index finger in the air by way of demonstration. 'You have to angle it towards your back, darling.' I studied the leaflet in the box while sitting on the loo afterwards, musing that tampons looked like cocktail sausages with string, and when I finally succeeded getting one in there, it felt like a milestone. Not dissimilar to when I later passed my driving test. Just a bit messier.

It only took a few more periods for me to realize it wasn't a great development. All those sanitary products, all that leaking, the pain, and all that paranoia about suddenly dying from Toxic Shock Syndrome if you slept with a tampon in.

It was now eighteen years on and, what's eighteen times twelve? I did the sums in my head: 18 times 12 equals 216. I was now roughly 216 periods into my life but I couldn't single any of them out. They'd all blended in my head, a boring hiccup that punctuated every month. Sometimes three days, sometimes five days. But mine were never late because I'd been on the pill for years. Ever since Jake and I started going out. Give or take a day, I knew when it would arrive. I knew when my stomach would bloat like a barrel and I'd start crying at adverts for donkey sanctuaries. I knew when to stock up on Feminax Express because the pain felt like my uterus was about to fall out of my vagina.

I'd thought about coming off the pill when Jake and I broke up, about giving my body a break, but decided to carry on just in case. So where was my freaking period?

I shook my head. 'No, I'm always regular. I'm still taking the pill. But does that happen sometimes, that you sort of miss a period? If you've been taking it for years?' I looked hopefully at Jess.

'I don't really know, love. Maybe?' Jess didn't believe in contraceptives. She insisted that she knew where she was in her cycle, then made them pull out and hoped for the best. 'Or maybe it was so light you didn't even notice it?' she suggested.

That seemed unlikely. Quite hard to miss a whole period, right? I was always amazed at those headlines you sometimes saw: 'Woman who didn't know she was pregnant gives birth in a motorway service station!'

I put my right hand over my left boob, then my right one.

They felt a tiny bit sensitive, like I was about to get my period. But it was so late. I wondered if I should google it, and then decided against it. Google would only tell me I was 100 per cent pregnant. Or I had some form of cancer. Then I looked at my coffee again.

'I don't feel great either this morning,' I said to Jess. 'Like, a bit sick. But I can't be… can I? It doesn't make sense.'

'I'm sure it's fine,' she said, reassuringly. And then slightly less reassuringly, 'But maybe we should get a test just to make sure? So you don't worry?'

I nodded and looked across at the man with his newspaper, who briefly met my eye and then looked back down. Poor man. He presumably thought he was catching a peaceful Saturday morning train with the paper only to find he was trapped in his very own live version of *Loose Women*.

*

We walked straight to Boots from King's Lynn station, praying that I didn't see anyone I knew. One of Mum's t'ai chi women asking questions about my love life, that was all I needed. But we reached Boots unscathed, and I grabbed a £4.99 Boots own brand test despite Jess's grumbling that I should get a more expensive one.

'All I'm going to do is wee on it. I don't think it matters whether I have the Rolls Royce test or the Skoda version,' I told her. 'Let's just get it and go.'

'Do you want a bag?' asked the lady behind the till as I paid.

'Nah, it's all right thanks,' I said, stuffing the box down the side of my overnight bag.

When we got home ten minutes later, I pushed open the front door to a familiar smell – the sweet, fruity tang of boiling jam. Mum was always making jam for local markets and selling it for good causes – women's charities, animal charities, children's charities. Distressed llamas of North Norfolk, that sort of thing. She loved a cause.

'Hi,' I shouted loudly into the hall, dropping my bag at the foot of the stairs and waving at Jess to follow me through to the kitchen.

Mum, standing with her back to us at the oven, whirled around with a wooden spoon in her hand. She was wearing her favourite apron – 'There are no soggy bottoms in my kitchen' slogan on the front – and a pair of glasses that had steamed up.

'Hello, my ducks,' she said, reaching for her glasses with her free hand and taking them off. 'Give us a hug.'

She reached for me first, wooden spoon going over one shoulder, then Jess. Drops of jam fell to the lino.

'How was the journey? Do you want a cup of tea? Dennis is at the football. Won't be home till sixish, so I'm making a batch of this for the market tomorrow. Look, sit down, sit down.' Mum always talked quickly, imparting information in bursts as if we only had a limited number of seconds left on this planet and she had to get it all out.

Mum met Dennis in the early 1990s while she was teaching students and working on her PhD (about the role of the Victorian prostitute) at Norwich University. She'd already had me by then since my biological father was a guitarist called Adrian, who Mum had a brief fling with while studying for her undergraduate degree at Manchester a few years before. Dennis appeared on the scene when I was four. He was a military historian in the same faculty at Norwich, and moved into our lives overnight. Sometimes, Mum would refer to a period of her life 'BD', which meant 'Before Dennis', but I didn't remember that time. Dennis was the man who taught me to swim one summer off Holkham beach. Dennis was the man who taught me to recite the dates of famous battles – the Siege of Thessalonica, Verdun, Barbarossa – like other children reeled off nursery rhymes. Dennis was the man who smelled like his writing shed in our garden, of strong coffee and old history books.

Mum had explained the situation to me with a biology lesson not long after she met Dennis. As I sat in the bath one evening, she drew a picture in the fogged-up bathroom window of a pair of ovaries, a womb and a single sperm. She explained the facts of life with huge enthusiasm and talked about how she'd made me with another man, not Dennis.

'But can Dennis be my daddy?' I'd apparently asked her, having digested the drawing on the window in silence for some minutes.

I didn't remember this conversation. It became one of those memories I formed in my head from Mum recounting it to me when I was older. She often used the story about the biological drawings to embarrass me as a teenager. But the upshot of that bath-time chat was Dennis became my father in everything but name. Not stepfather, because he and Mum never married, but also because calling Dennis a 'step' felt disloyal. He was more than that to me. He was everything. Adrian, a stranger I'd never met and knew nothing about, was technically my father, but Dennis was my dad.

He and Mum had bought the house in Castleton a couple of years on and had taught at Norwich ever since, combining academic life with their social crusades. These days, subjects they felt strongly about included but were not limited to: the demise of the Labour Party, the lack of education funding, the lack of NHS funding, Andrew Marr, the bus service in their area of Norfolk and the price of milk in the Tesco Express.

Both he and Mum were now sixty and retained the zeal and energy of Russian revolutionaries. That's why I was called Lil, or Lilian technically, after one of Mum's favourite suffragettes, Lilian Lenton. She was a flinty-eyed woman who, in a black and white picture taken in 1955, looked like a witch. But she'd been part of the suffragist movement during the pre-First World War years, committing arson, going on hunger strike and escaping prison so many times she was nicknamed the 'tiny Pimpernel'.

Mum put the spoon down beside the cooker and gathered up a pile of papers in her hands, moving them from the table to the wooden dresser underneath the kitchen window. Gerald the tortoise was eating a piece of lettuce under a kitchen chair.

'I'll put the kettle on,' I said. 'Jess – tea?'

She nodded at me. 'Yep, please. What you making?'

'Well,' said Mum, a note of uncertainty in her voice. 'I picked some plums from the farm this week, so it's supposed to be plum jam. But…' she stopped and peered into the pan, 'I'm not sure it's going to set properly. So it might be plum sauce, at this rate.'

'Delicious,' said Jess.

'Mmmm,' said Mum, still peering into the pan, before she spun around again. 'But forget the jam. How are you both?'

'Jess has exciting news actually,' I said, keen to deflect attention from me.

'Oh yes?' said Mum.

'I think I'm in love,' said Jess, a faraway smile on her face.

'Oh that is exciting,' said Mum, stirring the plums. 'Who with?' Mum loved a romance. If I ever came home from school when I was younger and even mentioned a boy's name, she'd start asking about who he was and did he want to come over for tea.

'He's a Russian art collector, called Alexi. I only met him recently. Lil was there, actually, so it's super quick but we spent all last night together and just…' Jess exhaled loudly, 'I think he's the dream.'

I'd gone through this process several times with Jess. Complete and utter obsession with a man for a few weeks, couldn't think about anything else, mentioned his name every other sentence, fantasized about their future life and how many children they'd have until it was nearly intolerable for the rest of us. If falling in love was like being high, it was as if Jess had taken several drugs simultaneously.

I'd felt that high briefly when I started going out with Jake, but then it mellowed into something more sedate, less manic. I longed for that thrill again. That buzz of clicking with someone and wanting to spend every minute with them, of dreading the moment you had to leave them even if it was for a night. Of falling into a gloom if you weren't going to see them for a few days. That was love, right? It made idiots of us all, but it was also the most intoxicating feeling in the world.

Which is why whenever Jess declared she'd fallen in love, part of me felt jealous. How did she manage it? How did she fall in love and find someone who fell in love with her back, when I couldn't even get a reply on WhatsApp? I didn't want to feel bitter towards my best friend, but it seemed a tiny bit unfair. Although her latest story kept Mum distracted for half an hour, before she said she had to nip into town to drop off the jam at the village hall for the market in the morning.

★

That's how I ended up standing outside Mum and Dennis's bathroom, having handed the damp, positive pregnancy stick to Jess. I didn't do the second test. We've all seen films where the woman has the bladder of a horse and does 193 pregnancy tests, simply unable to believe that it's positive. But firstly, I didn't have any wee left, and secondly, it was like I kind of knew.

I didn't *know* know. I wasn't telepathic. But from the moment on the train when I realized I was late, I suspected.

I still hoped I wasn't pregnant with a strange man's baby, but a little voice inside my brain told me I was. I put a hand on my stomach. I was pregnant with the baby of a man I'd met once. I was carrying a bundle of cells, half of which technically belonged to someone else. It felt freakishly intimate. What was one normally left with after a first date? A bad case of thrush? A string of embarrassing, flirty WhatsApp messages which stop immediately the morning after when you both realize it wasn't meant to be? I remembered Jimmy Day in biology lessons at school once asking Mrs Martin if it was true that semen survived for three days. Mrs Martin had looked at him with the unfazed expression of a long-serving biology teacher and said yes, spermatozoa could indeed survive for up to seventy-two hours, or even longer in the correct, 'hospitable environment'.

Jimmy had sniggered and gone round for weeks afterwards asking confused girls if their stomachs were 'hospitable environments'. I don't know what happened to Jimmy. I suspect he hadn't gone off to work in Silicon Valley or find the solution to world peace.

While leaning against the bathroom doorframe, I felt Jess's hand on my arm.

'You all right?'

I nodded slowly and looked at the test in her hand. 'Yeah, but shall we get rid of that and go for a walk before they get back?'

'Good plan,' said Jess.

I took the stick back from Jess and went to the kitchen,

where I grabbed a Co-op bag from under the sink and bundled it in there.

We walked for five minutes, straight to the pub, via a bin just outside the village shop where I chucked the plastic bag.

'What d'you want?' said Jess, once inside the Fox and Cushion, as I looked around for a table.

I opened my mouth to say 'vodka and tonic' and then stopped. Jess read my mind. 'I think you need one.'

I shook my head. 'Nope. Just… lemonade?'

I found a table in the corner, bench along the back, rickety wooden chair on the other side of it. I sat. My brain was flitting about like a sparrow, unable to settle on any thought for more than a few seconds.

In your twenties, maybe in your teens, did you ever play that game with your girlfriends: what would you do if you got pregnant? Jess and I would discuss it at uni from time to time, together with our three flatmates – Nats, Lucy and Bells – as we lay on the sofa watching *Ready, Steady, Cook*, still in our tracksuit bottoms, still hung-over from the night before. Probably one of us had had a scare, or forgotten to take our pill, and the answer had always seemed obvious. 'Get rid of it,' we would agree, before discussing whether it was a red tomato or green pepper day. We could just about afford to keep ourselves in pasta and have enough money left over for tequila in Edinburgh nightclubs. The thought of a baby was laughable. Not for us. We had plans. We were going to graduate, get jobs, work and have children at a blurry date in the future. That was how it would go.

When we got to our mid–twenties, nearer thirty, the question came up again in cheap Italian restaurants in London where we met for catch–up dinners. Breadsticks. Bottles of chianti that made your teeth furry. Bowls of spaghetti, or tricolore salads for the ones who were on diets. By that point, I'd been going out with Jake for a few years. The others had boyfriends too. Apart from Jess, who always had someone but was about to move on to a different victim.

The game had become trickier by this stage, more of a moral maze. If we'd got pregnant with our boyfriends, what would we do? There were still dozens of reasons not to: lack of money, I wanted to spend more years teaching, I remained too young, I wanted to get married first, I wasn't even sure that I could keep a baby alive. What if I dropped my imaginary baby on its head and it fell on that soft bit where its skull hasn't fused yet? That seemed like the kind of thing I would do.

But the idea of being pregnant was less terrifying than it had been at uni. I was in a long-term relationship with Jake, I wanted to have children with him one day anyway, he had a job which could just about support us. Plus, what if I got pregnant, then aborted it, then found out I couldn't have any more? We decided at these dinners that it would depend on the circumstances and we wouldn't necessarily 'get rid of it'. Then we'd order another bottle of wine and merrily move on to another topic – some new TV drama, our mothers, how much we hated our bosses, whether one of us should get a pixie cut or would it make our face look fat?

A few years on, people started getting married and having babies anyway and the game was forgotten. Everyone started changing their Facebook profile pictures to them on their wedding day, like a badge of honour. There was Nats being showered with confetti as she came out of church. Lucy sitting in the back of a posh car, beaming through the window. Bells on her new husband's shoulders, the dress bunched up around her hips, while we all waved sparklers around her. My profile picture remained just me, on the beach in Norfolk, a picture taken by Dennis a few years ago.

Jess came back from the bar, a white wine in one hand, lemonade in the other.

'Right,' she said, sitting down and raising her eyebrows at me, 'what you going to do?'

I shrugged. 'Honestly, I don't know.'

'Did you miss a day? Or take it at a different time?'

I shook my head. The packet lived on my bedside table and I always took it when I woke up in the morning.

'They say it's like 99 per cent effective, right?' went on Jess. 'So I guess that means one woman in a hundred will get pregnant. Or maybe the odds are a bit better than that. But still, some people will get pregnant.'

I nodded, still stunned. And then I remembered my stomach the day of the date. The morning spent gurning on the loo. The Imodium I'd had to take.

'Fuck, Jess, I think the pill didn't work.'

'Well we know that,' she said, as if I was an idiot, before having a mouthful of her wine.

'No, I mean I had a bad stomach that day, before the date. After dinner with you guys, after Clem's curry.'

Jess clapped a hand to her mouth and then removed it to speak. 'Yes. I barely ate any but Clem was sick, I think. Or he had something wrong with his stomach. I remember being kept awake half the night with him thundering into the bathroom.'

She fell silent while I puffed out my cheeks and exhaled. 'Crap.'

'Literally,' said Jess.

I curled my mouth in a half-hearted attempt to laugh but I couldn't manage it. I was too stunned to summon up any fury towards Clem.

'OK, let's look at the options,' went on Jess. 'You could go to the doctor, for one thing. It's very early, get it all sorted. Done. Never think of it again.'

I nodded. That felt like the sensible option. The option that I, Lilian Bailey, thirty-one, single, with a job that only just covered rent, bills and lunchtime sandwiches, should take. I wasn't sure how to go about 'sorting' it – did one make an appointment at the GP? It couldn't be that bad. I'd feel a bit sad. But perhaps it would just be like a bad period? But still, better a bad period than giving birth to a small human in nine months' time that then sucked the life out of me for the following eighteen years and probably beyond. That would be a VERY bad period.

'Or,' went on Jess, 'you could have it.'

I yelped with laughter and waited for her to go on. But she didn't.

'What?' she said, frowning at me.

'Is that it? I was waiting for more options.'

'I can't think of anything else.'

'Well I can't have it, can I? I don't even know where I'd start with that.' I stuck my little finger and my thumb out and put my hand to my ear. 'Hi, is that Max the famous explorer? Great, hello, Max, it's me, Lil. I'm the one you shagged and then ghosted. Just to let you know that I'm knocked up and keeping it. Hope that's OK. Byeeee.' I put my hand down again.

'Where is he anyway?' said Jess.

'Max?'

'No, Father Christmas. Yes! Obviously Max. You look at his blog?'

I thought about saying no but Jess would see through that. I'd developed an irritating habit of checking Max's blog every couple of days, usually just when I'd got into bed and I was absent-mindedly scrolling on my phone. A couple of days ago he was still at base camp eating porridge from a packet for breakfast but hoping to start his ascent the next day.

'Yep,' I admitted. 'Starting his climb, the last I knew.'

'So it's not as if you could tell him anyway.'

I shook my head. 'Not very easily.'

At no point during this conversation did I want to say the 'a' word. I wasn't particularly squeamish. It just sounded so brutal, so charged. Soldiers aborted missions, NASA aborted rocket launches. Babies didn't belong in the same category as soldiers and rockets.

'It's only a dot, you know,' said Jess. 'It's not an actual baby. You wouldn't be able to even see it.'

'I know,' I replied quickly. 'It's just that… I've never thought about it. I mean, I know other people have done it. I know it doesn't have to be a big deal. I know it's our choice. I just… didn't ever think I'd be in this situation.'

'I've had one before,' said Jess, reaching for her glass again.

'What? When?'

'Few years ago. D'you remember Leo? The one who always wore that terrible hat?'

'Inspector Gadget?' He was an art student Jess had dated years ago and who we'd so nicknamed because he was tall and thin, and always arrived at the pub in a black trilby, and then kept it on all night. I remember once asking Jess if the hat remained on in bed.

'Ha, yes. I'd forgotten we called him that. But yeah, it happened back then. Not really sure how. Condom must have broken or something. I never actually knew how it happened. I just realized a few weeks later, like you.'

'How old were we?'

'Liiiiike… twenty-five, maybe? I was never going to keep it. So I told him, Leo, and I said what I wanted to do, which was fine, I think he was relieved, but he kind of disappeared after that. It was all a bit awkward.'

I tried to think back to that time. I must have been with Jake, living in Angel. 'Why didn't you tell me?'

She shrugged. 'It was so early. Same as you. And there was no way in hell I was going to have his baby.'

'Where did you go for it?'

'Clinic somewhere near Warren Street.'

'Expensive?'

'No, no, it's free. NHS.'

'Actually?'

She nodded. 'Yeah. I just took a couple of pills. Felt grim for about a week, so I stayed in bed. Clem brought me endless cups of sugary tea and diabolical soup he kept making.

'So, do you think you'll do it?' she went on, after a brief pause. 'The same thing, I mean?'

I stared at the lemonade, untouched, on the table in front of me. 'There are a million reasons not to do this. Not to...' I still couldn't say the 'a' word. 'Not to have it. Right?'

She nodded.

'But also, I'm thirty-one, not twenty-one,' I went on. 'And I know I want children at some stage. Not necessarily like this but this has happened and there's a tiny, tiny voice in my head which is sort of saying "why not?"'

It felt a relief to say this out loud. In the bathroom, I'd felt paralysed by the news, like a frozen computer with the rainbow wheel spinning. It was as if a big, flashing sign was going off in my head – 'YOU'RE PREGNANT, YOU'RE PREGNANT' – and I couldn't analyse the thought any further.

An hour or so on, the immediate shock having receded, I could think more rationally about it. Sure, the situation was a monumental mistake but what was I going to do about it? Become unpregnant again, or have a baby?

'Tell you what,' said Jess, suddenly, reaching for her bag.

'We're going to write a list. Pros and cons.' She smoothed out the back of a receipt with the side of her hand and then retrieved a Biro.

'What's that receipt from?'

She turned it over. 'Nisa,' she said simply. 'Hummus, milk, wine, bar of Dairy Milk.'

'I mean, I think the fact we're writing this list on the back of that gives you some indication of how suitable either of us are to be parents.'

She ignored me. 'Never mind that,' she continued, drawing a line down the middle of the paper. On the left side, in her neat, loopy handwriting, she wrote 'pros', on the right 'cons'.

'OK, let's do the positives first,' she said. 'You want a baby someday, right?'

I nodded. She wrote 'want baby one day' in green pen underneath the pros, then looked up at me. 'What else?'

'Er… it's a life,' I said. 'And what if this is my one chance? What if I got rid of it and then I couldn't have another one for some reason?'

She nodded again and wrote 'might be only chance' in the left-hand column. I wasn't sure whether to laugh or cry at that bit.

'What about "could dress it up in amusing fancy dress outfits"?' I joked.

'I'm not putting that.'

'OK, um…' I was struggling to think of any more. 'What about my age, and the fact that I'm responsible enough to have a baby now? Like, it wouldn't be such a big deal to have one, unlike if this had happened, say, ten years ago.'

Jess lowered her Biro again and wrote 'old enough'.

'OK, can we do the negatives because I've got loads of those,' I continued. 'I can't afford it, it would be a massive upheaval, where would I live, I might have to do it on my own...'

'You don't know that.'

I shot her a sardonic look. 'Oh yeah, great father material, Mr Explorer out there currently cramponing his way up an ice-shelf.'

'Point taken,' said Jess, writing 'questionable father mate-rial'.

'I'd be tired all the time, I'd have sore nipples, I'd never be able to have a lie-in again, I'd have to tell both my mother and Miss Montague and I'm not sure which would be worse. Er...'

'The world is overpopulated already?' she volunteered.

'Put that down,' I said emphatically, gesturing at the receipt. 'Oh, and if I did do it on my own, it means I'd never meet anyone else.'

'That's not true,' said Jess, looking up at me. 'Look at your mum and Dennis.'

'Alright,' I said, feeling a pang of guilt on their behalf. 'But probably no more dating for a bit, given that birth leaves your vagina like a war zone.'

'I'll allow it but I think you're being melodramatic,' she said, bending her head to the list again. The column on the right was full, the column on the left was much shorter.

★

Mum was sitting at the kitchen table reading the papers when we got back, but she stopped as soon as she saw us and took her reading glasses off.

'Right, you two, a word.'

I frowned at her. This was all I needed. A lecture about something.

'What?' I said.

She turned and picked something up from the dresser behind her, then turned back to us. Fucccccccccck. It was the pregnancy test box.

'Whose is this?'

I opened my mouth to start explaining but Jess jumped in before I could say anything.

'It's mine, sorry, Jackie. That's embarrassing. I, er, had to do it earlier.'

Mum looked confused. 'But you've only had one date.'

Jess nodded. 'Yup, I know, last night, but this was for something before. Just being paranoid. It's fine. I'm not pregnant. But I just, er, thought I should check.'

Mum squinted at Jess as if she was trying to gauge whether she was telling the truth, then her face relaxed again and she laughed, waggling the box at her in the air. 'Jess, my darling, you should take more care. A whole generation of women didn't campaign for their contraceptive rights for nothing, you know.'

'Nope, I know, point taken,' said Jess, sliding a quick glance at me.

'That's a relief,' said Mum, turning away from the table again and throwing the box in the bin. 'I was worried for a second. Now, supper's in the oven but I fancy a drink. Glass of white?'

Jess nodded but I cried off on the pretext of a headache. Then Dennis arrived home.

'Hi,' I said, hugging him and burying my face in his collar. It smelled so comforting that I welled up, and had to blink several times before letting him go so nobody saw.

'Hiya, love, welcome home.'

'Thanks,' I said, finally releasing him and standing back. 'How was the game?'

'A shitshow,' he said. 'Dylan let a goal in in the eighty-third minute so we're another three points down. But there we go. How are you lot?'

'Good,' I said, trying to smile as convincingly as possible.

'Hiya,' said Jess, reaching forward to hug him. 'It's been ages.'

'It has,' said Dennis. 'How's life, Jess? How are the portraits?'

'We were about to open a bottle of wine, Den, so let's do that and then we can chat pleasantries afterwards,' said Mum, as she untied her apron and slung it over the kitchen door.

'All right, all right, I'm just going to get these boots off,' he said, grinning at me and Jess as he sat down on a kitchen chair. 'I don't know, girls, sometimes it's like living with Genghis Khan.'

'You wish,' said Mum.

★

Tell you what's a fun game if you're a woman aged between twenty and forty-five and you can't sleep: fertility maths. I woke just after 2 a.m. and calculated my odds while listening to Jess snore. Let's say the average woman gets twenty-two years of perky ovaries and tip-top fertility. That's twenty-two years roughly between the age of eighteen to forty, although actually your average woman is at her baby-pushing prime between the age of twenty and twenty-four. I know this because I googled it while lying there.

So, a twenty-two year window in which to have children, although some women have more, some women have fewer and some women have no window at all.

But I clearly could get pregnant because I was pregnant now. So I had a window. But I was already over a decade into it, and I only had nine years left. Sounds a lot, right? Plenty can happen in nine years. Wars. Entire US presidencies. Political movements. It's a big time span.

Except when it comes to periods. If I had nine years of fertility left, that only meant 117 periods. Or, to put it another way, 117 shots at getting pregnant. And suddenly, boiled down to this precise figure, it didn't seem that many. Especially when technically (because I googled this too), the average woman's fertility tails off after the age of thirty-five. Which meant I really only had four years of happy ovaries left, which is fifty-two periods, or fifty-two chances of getting pregnant.

It's not that many. You'd get better odds on horses in William Hill.

Say I got rid of this baby and then wanted to meet someone

else and have a baby with them. That might take a year, but let's err on the side of caution and give it eighteen months on the basis I had severely impaired flirting skills. Then we had to fall in love. Give it another year. I was slovenly. I left dirty knickers on my bedroom floor and old razors in the shower that went rusty. It might take him a while to see my endearing qualities. So that took us to two and a half years from now. Which would make me nearly thirty-four. Which meant I'd only have one good year of fertility left. Twelve periods. Twelve chances of getting pregnant.

Lying there that night, this is what it felt like it came down to. I had this baby now, or I didn't have it, and in the best-case scenario, I might meet someone in a year or so and get knocked up within twelve months. I know there are options. IVF, sperm donors, surrogates, adoption. Not having children, that was also an option. But as I sweated in bed, my heart beating under my duvet, I drummed my fingers on my chest doing my fertility maths. Having this baby felt mad, but giving it up felt like a risky roll of the dice.

★

Jess and I didn't discuss it much the next day. Largely because we were hanging with my parents – helping Mum sell twenty-three jars of plum jam at the market in the morning (this meant the Norwich Donkey Sanctuary got £57.50, so she was thrilled), before going for a walk with them along Snettisham beach after lunch.

'How's your love life anyway?' Mum asked me, after Jess had taken several pictures of the shoreline and explained she was sending them to Alexi.

I looked down at my feet crunching along the shingle. Should I even mention Max? Mention having been on a date? I used to tell them everything about my relationship with Jake – every time we had an argument, if he was promoted or having trouble at work, when we'd decided to move in together. Dennis had come down to London to help paint our bedroom once we'd found the flat in Angel, and at least once a month Jake and I had caught the train to spend the weekend with my parents, doing this very walk. We'd been a happy foursome. But I worried that if I mentioned Max now, then a jumble of words about being pregnant would tumble from my mouth and I wasn't ready for that yet. My brain was still whirring with the news. I couldn't handle extra opinions about what I should do.

'No updates on that front, sorry,' I said, still staring at my feet so Mum couldn't catch my eye.

Mum tutted. Then she turned to look at Jess. 'Jess, don't you have some nice friends?' she asked.

'Jacks,' interrupted Dennis, putting an arm round my back, 'I don't think Lil needs to be interrogated on her Sunday afternoon.'

'I wasn't interrogating, I was just… wondering what was happening, that's all.'

'I'm sure when there's something to tell, she'll tell us. Right, pet?' said Dennis, grinning conspiratorially at me in the way we both did whenever Mum went off on one of her rants.

'Yeah, course,' I said, reaching up for his hand on my shoulder and squeezing it.

Later, on the Sunday evening train back to London, Jess asked me how I was feeling as she slung our bags on the rack above our heads.

'Not sure,' I said, wincing at her. Because I still didn't know. 'Am I ready to have a baby or not?' felt much too serious a question for this juncture of the week, given that most Sunday evenings I normally asked myself, 'Thai or Indian?'

CHAPTER FOUR

IN THE END, MY decision came about quicker than expected because I woke the following morning with a sharp pain – neep, neep, neep – pulsing just above my left hip. As I lay in bed, I put my fingers to the area, half-expecting to feel a lump throbbing there. But it felt normal. I lifted up my T-shirt and inspected it. Nothing. So I did what we all do in the circumstances but know that we shouldn't, and I googled a spaghetti sentence of words – 'sharp pain throb lower stomach pregnant'.

Google threw up millions of results that predicted everything from indigestion to sudden death. But after scrolling through several pages, pressing my stomach with my fingers every now and then as if to gauge how bad the pain was, I knew I should go to the doctor.

'If you are pregnant and have a throbbing in one side of your lower abdomen and are experiencing pain,' said one alarming website, **'this may be an indication of an ectopic pregnancy and you should immediately contact your GP.'**

Obviously I assumed straight away this was what I had, even though I didn't know what an ectopic pregnancy was. I opened another tab and searched that too.

'**An ectopic pregnancy is when a fertilized egg implants itself outside of the womb, usually in one of the fallopian tubes,**' said the NHS website.

Made sense. I was pregnant with the foetus of a climber; perhaps it was simply trying to make its way up my insides.

Aiiiiiiich. I winced again as the pain stabbed at me. I emailed Miss Montague apologizing but saying I had an 'urgent' medical issue and could Mrs Peers, the Year 2 teacher, possibly include my boys in her class for the morning. Then I googled NHS walk-in centres. I was almost never ill – a handy quality in a teacher – so hadn't bothered registering with a GP since moving to Brixton. And I didn't want to cross the whole of London to my old GP in Angel. But apparently I could walk into St Thomas's and be seen there. I was getting dressed and worrying it was going to involve hours sitting in a waiting room, wasting precious classroom time, when the pain stabbed at me again.

★

I took a ticket when I arrived at St Thomas's and watched the numbers tick up while cradling a lukewarm coffee. It was 10.15 by the time I was called. My class would be reading, I thought, glancing at my watch as I got up from my seat. Poor Mrs Peers, I felt guilty foisting my class on her. It meant she'd have to go through twice the number of reading books and look after Fergus at the same time.

'Hello,' said a smiling man with glasses in a blue shirt sitting at a desk in Room 11, then he looked at his computer. 'So you're… Lilian?'

'Yep,' I said, as I sat down in a plastic chair beside the desk.

'I'm Dr Coleman, how can I help?'

My eyes welled up and spilled over, so tears rolled down my cheeks and into my lap. I guess it was the endless worrying, the back-and-forth in my head, the constant 'what should I do?' The situation felt overwhelming. I hadn't meant any of this. All I'd wanted was to go out and try not to think about Jake, to have a nice time, to reassure myself I was a functioning part of the human race.

'Sorry,' I said, groping in my bag for a tissue or paper napkin.

'Here,' said the doctor. I looked up to see him holding out a box of Kleenex.

'Thank you,' I said, but it was through a thick nose so it came out more 'Dank do.'

'Dorry,' I added.

'Not at all,' he said, still sitting calmly in his seat, waiting for me to explain.

'The thing is, I'm pregnant,' I said, 'and I woke up this morning with a pain here.' I leant back in my seat and hitched my jumper up a couple of inches, pointing at my skin.

He nodded and looked serious.

'How many weeks pregnant are you?'

'Not many, I just did a test on the weekend.'

He turned and tapped at his computer. 'When was the first day of your last period?'

'Er…' I thought. It had been the first day back that term because I remember nearly crying with various mothers as they dropped their boys off, and having to pull myself together. 'Third of September.'

He tapped at his keyboard again. 'Which makes you… six weeks pregnant.'

I nodded dumbly. I'd never really paid much attention to friends or colleagues before when they talked about how pregnant they were. I'd overheard just such a conversation last week in the staffroom between two members of the science department – Mrs Hassan and Miss Cran. Miss Cran was pregnant, and she'd been telling Mrs Hassan that she was just in her second trimester.

'That's the lovely bit,' Mrs Hassan had replied. 'You're over the worst. It is all very much downhill from here.'

I remember thinking, quietly in the corner, that this couldn't possibly be true given that Miss Cran would eventually have to push something the size of a bowling ball from between her legs.

'Can I ask you a few more details about this pain?' said Dr Coleman.

'Sure,' I said, fiddling with the damp tissue in my fingers. 'When did it start?'

'Er, this morning. It was there when I woke up.'

'OK,' he said, tapping at his computer again. He had a soothing manner. I felt like I could have waltzed in here showing symptoms of the bubonic plague, leaky pustules all over my face, and Dr Coleman would have sat me down and talked me serenely through it.

'And how often are you feeling this pain?'

'Um, it sort of… comes and goes. Like I'll feel it sort of throbbing for a few seconds, then it stops again.'

'For how long?'

'Er, maybe ten or fifteen minutes or so.'

'And then the pain comes back again?'

'Yep.'

'Fine,' said Dr Coleman. 'What I'd like to do is a quick examination, but I think you should have an internal scan as well. That's in a different wing.'

'Oh right, OK. Do you know how long it'll take?' I glanced at my watch. I was still worrying about my class. If St Lancelot's parents got a whiff of their form teacher being off sick they emailed Miss Montague and demanded to know if this was going to set their son back from getting into Oxford.

'They tend to be quite busy over there so it might not be for a couple of hours,' said Dr Coleman. 'Is that going to be all right today?'

'Yeah, think so,' I said. 'I'd rather, er, get it sorted. I've told my boss I'm not in this morning anyway, so…' I trailed off.

After Dr Coleman examined me – fingers so cold it was like being felt up by the White Witch – he sent me to Radiology in another wing.

I navigated the maze-like corridors of St Thomas's, down a corridor, down a lift, past one reception, outside to another building, down another corridor and finally found it. I gave my name to a middle-aged woman with orange hair sitting behind the reception desk, found a spare seat underneath a poster about flu jabs and retrieved my phone to text Jess.

Slight drama, am waiting for scan at hospital, St Thomas's. The one in Waterloo. You about? Xxxx I felt guilty, I didn't want to disturb her if she had a sitting, but I wouldn't mind having someone with me. I'd decided I wasn't going to tell my parents anything until this whole issue was sorted, however it was sorted.

On the one hand, Mum might be fine with the news. She'd marched on pro-life protests in the 1970s, she written letters to her MP about women's representation (or lack of it) in parliament and begging for more money for state nurseries in the area. She persuaded Ted the local pub landlord to allow her to throw an 'I'm with Her' fund-raising quiz for Hillary Clinton when she was running for president. She got Mrs Nibley to stop stocking *The Sun* in the local newsagent when they refused to back down on their Page Three girls (for two weeks, before Mrs Nibley snuck it back in again). After launching a petition online, Mum once took it upon herself to clean up the Edith Cavell statue outside Norwich Cathedral because she said it was covered with bird shit and 'a disgrace' to her name. She'd written dozens of papers on the women's liberation movement. Basically, she'd devoted her whole career to women's rights. But I couldn't help feeling that her daughter being suddenly pregnant after a one-night stand would cause consternation, as if I hadn't been looking after my own rights carefully enough.

In the week that I turned sixteen, Mum had made an

appointment for me at the GP surgery in King's Lynn, so I could get a prescription for the pill. I was mortified, sitting in the surgery, meekly asking the doctor for a prescription even though I didn't actually have sex for another two years. But Mum wanted me to be protected, so I thought it was what I should do. I went along with it.

I felt another jab of pain and winced. I was grateful, in a way. An ectopic pregnancy felt like fate. It meant that the decision had been made for me. It was less of a moral battle. For my own safety, I'd have to go through with the 'a' procedure, job done, everything would go back to normal.

But perhaps no more dating. I'd take up a hobby instead. People did that, didn't they? They became champion knitters or bakers. They learnt a new language or started climbing. No, definitely not climbing. But perhaps I should sign up for a marathon? People always seemed to be doing marathons. The staffroom was always full of talk about split times and energy gels. Mr Matthews, a Year 7 teacher, did a Tough Mudder the other weekend and we hadn't heard the end of it. It was like he'd given birth.

'Lilian Bailey?' came a voice from across the waiting room. I looked up to see a nurse holding a clipboard, so I stood.

'Follow me please,' she said with a curt nod.

I followed her into another small room where there was a petite woman in a white doctor's coat sitting at the desk, who beamed at me when I walked in.

'Lilian?'

'Yes, hi.'

'Hello, I'm Dr Stagg.'

'Hi,' I repeated, smiling back nervously.

'So you've been sent here for a transvaginal ultrasound?'

Jesus, that sounded like something from a horror film. 'Dr Coleman just said some sort of scan?' I'd been imagining one of those scans I'd seen on TV, when a nurse squirts jelly over a woman's pregnant stomach and rubs it in with what looks like an epilator.

'Yes, that's right. I've got your notes here,' said Dr Stagg, looking at the computer screen. 'So you're… six weeks pregnant and having pain in your left lower abdomen, is that right?'

'Yes.'

'Which means it has to be an internal scan, with an ultrasound wand.'

'Oh. Right. OK. Is it… painful?'

'No worse than a smear test.'

I hated smear tests – the cold, smeary speculum, the pinching sensation of it being opened up inside you, the uncomfortable scratching as the doctor took a swab. Astonishing that we'd put a man on the moon, but women still had to have their insides examined by something that looked like it was used on witches in the Middle Ages.

'So if you wouldn't mind taking your bottom half off and lying on this bed, I'll have a look,' said Dr Stagg. 'Would it be all right if some medical students oversee my examination today?'

Oh, even better. A whole team of people looking at my vagina. Woohooo, party in Dr Stagg's office, everyone in to gawp at Lil's private parts.

'No. No, that's fine,' I squeaked.

Down my jeans came again, and I took off my oldest knickers, a faded black pair from M&S with fraying elastic round the waist. Then I lay back on the bed and spread one of those ridiculous paper blankets over my stomach and thighs. Not much point in a modesty blanket when a whole team of people was about to inspect my uterus.

'Come in,' I heard Dr Stagg say from behind the curtain and then, moments later, the door open.

The door closed again and she started up, 'Morning, everyone…'

Everyone? How many were there?

She went on, 'We have a 31-year-old patient today who is six weeks pregnant and has presented with a pain in her left lower abdomen. A recurring pain which started this morning, so I'm going to examine her with an ultrasound wand.'

The curtain was whipped back and I looked sideways at six or seven faces. 'Morning,' I said. A Chinese student with a shaved head smiled back. Nobody spoke. Apart from Dr Stagg, who reached towards a white machine at the end of my bed and picked up a giant dildo.

'Girish, will you stand here and hold this please,' she said to a student with a round face and the whisper of a moustache on his upper lip. Girish stepped tentatively towards Dr Stagg.

'No no, behind me, this way,' she said, gesturing with her head.

Girish moved and dutifully took the dildo. Next, Dr Stagg ripped a small packet open and rolled a condom down the dildo, then reached for a tube of KY Jelly and rubbed some of that over the condom.

'Thanks, Girish, I'll take that back. Now, Lilian, this might be a liiiittttttle cold going in, but I'll try and be as gentle as possible.'

I held my breath as I felt Dr Stagg's fingers find the right place and she slowly pushed the wand inside me.

'That all right?' she said from the other end.

'Uh-huh,' I said, in a high-pitched voice. I kept my gaze on the ceiling. I absolutely did not want to catch the eye of any of the medical students.

Dr Stagg was quiet for a few moments, and I could feel the wand turning inside me while she pressed on my stomach with her fingers. I wasn't sure what the procedure was from here. Perhaps they'd send me to yet another department to collect those pills you have to take. I wasn't sure if I could face going back to school if I had to start taking the pills, but I felt guilty. I'd told the boys we'd be drawing scarecrows as part of the Harvest Festival plans this afternoon.

'OK, Lilian, it's relatively good news,' said Dr Stagg, after a few moments, still twisting the wand. 'If you look here, on the screen, you can see a cyst on your left ovary. Not big. Not small but not huge. Not threatening.' She tapped at a black space on the screen which looked like a mushroom.

'Oh. But where's my ovary?' I said.

'Here,' she said, pointing to small grey area.

'And then here,' she went on, turning the wand again, 'is your baby.'

I raised one hand over my mouth. There, on the screen, was what looked like a broad bean, lying at the bottom of my womb as if slung in a hammock. I could see the outline of a head and, below that, a little oblong body. It was a proper shape. A small human shape. My vision went blurry and I welled up again. It was a little person. The tears spilled over and down my cheeks again.

'Congratulations,' said Dr Stagg, turning to smile at me from the other end of the bed. 'There's nothing to worry about, it's all perfectly healthy.'

'So it's not ectopic?' I checked, through my tears.

She shook her head. 'No. We'll need to keep an eye on this cyst but it's very normal. I'm just going to measure it, but plenty of women get them and most just go away in their own time.'

'Dank do,' I said, smiling.

'And can you see that,' said Dr Stagg, dragging the computer cursor towards a tiny flashing dot in the middle of the broad bean.

I nodded.

'That's your baby's heartbeat.'

If this was a film, classical music would start playing now and they'd zoom in on my face, gazing at the screen, tears streaming down my cheeks and meeting under my chin before falling on to my jumper. Nose running down my upper lip. Eyes puffing. It wasn't a pretty sight. They'd make me much less repulsive in the movie.

But it was then, looking at that tiny, flickering heartbeat, that I knew I couldn't get rid of that bean. There it was, sitting happily inside me, as if it had just put its feet up after a long day at work. How could I abort that? I'd seen it now, it was too late to consider any other option. The worries about money, living arrangements, being single and about a million other preoccupations all faded. It could sleep in a drawer in my bedroom. I'd make it work, somehow. I had to.

Dr Stagg dismissed the medical students and said she'd give me a few moments to get dressed. When I sat back in the chair beside her desk, I'd never felt so sure about anything in my life. Or anxious. Or excited. Or terrified. Or alarmed about what size my nipples would swell to. I'd seen friends breastfeed their babies and their nipples were the size and colour of conkers. But I was still certain that this was the right thing to do.

'And everything's all right? The... cyst won't hurt the baby?' I asked. Suddenly I cared more about this bean slung in my stomach than anything I ever had before. I felt a rush of protectiveness. I lost my Tamagotchi once on a school trip to Legoland, I was about thirteen, and I cried the whole way back to Norfolk on the bus. But this new emotion felt primal, fierce. I wanted to bubble-wrap my abdomen to protect it. I wanted to immediately google everything that I should be doing to look after that miniature heartbeat. I needed some of those vitamins I always saw adverts for on the Tube, illustrated by pictures of women with glossy hair cradling their stomachs like Demi Moore.

Dr Stagg reassured me and slid a pamphlet about the first trimester across her desk. (Embarrassing confession: until this moment, I never understood what people meant when they talked about trimesters. It seemed a strange, complicated pregnancy time scale. Dr Stagg explained to me that it's actually incredibly simple – your first three months of pregnancy are your first trimester, your second three months are your second trimester, and your final three months are your third trimester. From the Latin for 'three', obviously. Good job I am a teacher and in charge of young minds.)

I checked the time as I left the Radiology department. It was just after twelve. If I jumped on the Tube across the river, I could be at school in half an hour, I reckoned. But I needed a cup of tea first.

My phone vibrated in my pocket as I stood in the queue of a nearby coffee shop. It was Jess. Scan??? Call me when you can. Xxxxx

I quickly tapped a reply back. *All OK, heading into school in a minute. You around later for supper or not?*

Yes!!! she texted. Fancy pasta or something? Will make Clem cook.

I grimaced at the thought, but texted back that I'd get to the house around five.

★

My class were allowed out every day at 3.20, ten minutes before the other years. It was a system designed to ensure that the smallest boys were reunited with their nanny or parent (or bodyguard) before the bigger boys ran into the playground and bowled them over like skittles. I went out that afternoon desperate to hand everyone over as quickly as possible so I could talk to Steph, but sadly the playground gods weren't smiling on me.

'Hi, Miss Bailey, I'm Monica, Hunter's mother,' said a woman with an American accent and eyebrows that didn't move. She was smiling at me, but I recognized it as a dangerous smile. The sort of smile a mafia boss would make before gunning someone down. She was also dressed head-to-toe in lycra, the expensive sort that you didn't work out in. Leggings that cost several hundred pounds, a silver bomber jacket zipped to reveal a hint of cleavage, embroidered Gucci sneakers.

'Hello, yes, we met, at the introduction in August. How are you? Bye, Achilles.' I was trying to wave off the right children with the right person at the same time while talking to her.

'Good thanks. I just have a little concern I wanted to talk to you about.'

'OK, go for it,' I said, still smiling. You had to keep smiling and not show them any weakness, otherwise they thought they had the upper hand and this sort of 'little concern' was usually about a lost button or a missing Pokémon card. 'Bye, George. See you tomorrow.'

'It's just that Hunter came home on Friday and said he'd had apple crumble for dessert.'

'Yup, that was the pudding for lunch. Is that… a problem?' I said, waving off Arthur as he took the hand of his nanny.

She winced at me. 'It's just way too much refined sugar.

Hunter doesn't respond well to sugar. I'd really rather he didn't have desserts like that.'

'OK, no problem,' I said, trying to stay calm. 'I can put him on the allergies list, so that he has a green placemat and chef knows not to give him pudding?'

Any boy who had an allergy, to nuts, to gluten, to dairy, was given a separate coloured placemat at lunch and then Len, the chef, knew not to give them certain things. Poor Len, he'd tried rabbit sausages on them a couple of months back and there was a near-riot the following day when various mothers demanded to talk to Miss Montague.

Hunter's mother winced again. 'I'd prefer he wasn't singled out like that. Would you mind just keeping an eye on the desserts menu and making sure he doesn't have anything with too much sugar in it? He could just have an apple. But not a banana, their sugar content is off the scale.'

'Sure,' I said, just for ease, so she gave me a patronizing smile and slid off with Hunter. I put a hand over my stomach, praying to myself that I wouldn't be that kind of mother as I left the playground, all my boys ticked off, and went to the staffroom to find Steph. Being protective was one thing; thinking that bananas were evil fruits, intent on bamboozling us all with their hidden sugar content, was quite another.

★

I didn't tell Jess about my decision until I arrived for dinner later that night. Since Clem was cooking, I ate a Twirl on the

Tube, jolting along the District Line to Chiswick and arriving at No. 19 just as he did, lumbered with shopping.

'Hello, Lil,' he said, leaning forward to kiss me as he opened the door. 'How are we?'

I wasn't sure how to answer that, not knowing if Jess had mentioned anything to Clem about the aftermath of my date with Max.

'Er, bit of a strange couple of days,' I began, before deciding that I might as well tell him. 'So I found out that I'm pregnant…'

Clem looked instantly horrified. 'With a baby?' he asked.

'As opposed to…?'

He frowned. 'I don't know. A big lunch?'

'A baby,' I confirmed, 'although it's hardly even that right now. Just a tiny speck.'

Clem remained rooted on the doorstep, frozen as if in shock. 'But I mean, how has this happened?' he asked eventually.

'The traditional way,' I said, deadpan. 'I had sex with a man and, well, here we are. But don't worry. It's OK. It's an accident and I was in shock, but now I've decided I'm happy about it. And it's Max's baby, by the way. Max Rushbrooke.'

Clem couldn't even answer this. His mouth just fell open, gaping like a goldfish.

'Come on, let's go in,' I said. 'Chilly out here.'

'Yes, of course,' said Clem, coming to his senses. 'Course, after you.' He stood aside while I went in.

'It's quite a lot to take in,' he said behind me. 'All I've done this week is walk a terrier called Alan along the towpath and go to Tesco. But you're all right?'

'Yeah, think so,' I said. 'Millions of people have babies, and they seem to manage.'

'That is true,' he said solemnly. 'But this news calls for a nutritious supper. I was thinking risotto?'

'Delicious,' I replied, with as much confidence as I could. I didn't mention his curry, the curry that had potentially got me pregnant. Clem was so sensitive that he'd only blame himself and immediately do something dramatic like proposing by way of apology.

He flicked on the TV in the corner and started humming as he put various items of shopping in the fridge.

'I'm going to go find Jess,' I said to his back.

'Right-o,' he said, and carried on humming.

I dragged myself up the house's four flights of wooden stairs that shrank at each level so, by the time you reached the stairs that led to the attic, you had to collapse your head into your shoulders like a tortoise to squeeze up there.

'Hi, darling,' said Jess, giving me a hug. She looked very painterly today – bare feet, baggy jeans which were rolled up at the ankles, a T-shirt which was presumably once white but now looked like a Jackson Pollock and she had, somehow, managed to get streaks of green paint not only across both her forearms but also on her cheeks, like a tribal chieftain. 'How you feeling? What's the latest?'

She pushed a wisp of hair back from her face with her forearm and looked expectantly at me.

'I'm keeping it,' I said, grinning at her.

She clapped her hands to her cheeks and opened her mouth at the same time. 'Serious?'

I nodded.

'Oh my God I'm going to cry, come here.' Jess held out her arms for another hug and I worried momentarily about getting green paint on my work dress and then told myself to stop being so uptight. I'd be too fat for it soon anyway.

'I can't believe this, love, I'm so proud of you,' she mumbled into my ear.

'Really?' I said, standing back and looking at her. 'Because I'm shitting myself.'

She put her hands on my shoulders. 'Lilian Bailey, this is a happy, grown-up decision. We're not teenagers. We've got this.'

I nodded back again, boosted – as always – by her unwavering confidence that everything would work out. 'Yeah, I feel like it's the right call,' I said. 'Right?'

Telling Clem and Jess my decision felt unreal, as if I was having one of those alarming dreams that I was pregnant and that I'd soon wake up and feel a wave of relief that, actually, it was another Thursday morning, I wasn't pregnant, and I needed to get into the shower, shave my armpits and prepare for a day of combat with the 5-year-olds. The only difference now was that I didn't want to wake up. I wanted to stay pregnant.

'Course it's the right call,' Jess said. 'Totally and absolutely. A baby, Lil! I'm so excited I'm going to have a drink to celebrate. Want anything? I might have some juice or something in here. Or tea?'

She moved towards the small fridge in her studio that she'd told Clem she needed to store milk for her tea during the day, but which actually contained several bottles of whatever white wine was on offer from Nisa.

'No no, I'm good, thanks,' I said, lowering myself on to the sofa under her window. 'Clem's started making supper downstairs. Risotto, apparently.'

'I'm not sure you should eat anything he makes for the next few months,' she said, unscrewing a bottle.

She poured a glass and then came and sat down on the other end of the sofa. 'So when are you going to tell Max?'

I shook my head slowly. 'I don't know. Or even how to tell him. He's in Pakistan. What do I do? Send an email? Send a message? Send an aubergine emoji and then a few baby ones?'

'Did you see the piece in the paper about him today?' She raised her eyebrows at me over her glass.

'What? No! Where?' I sounded instantly shrill.

'*Standard*, brought a copy back in case you missed it. Hang on, hold this.' She handed me her wine and leant over the side of the sofa, then retrieved the paper from her bag and started leafing through the pages.

'Look,' she said, stabbing a finger at a photo of Max in full climbing kit, grinning out at us.

'**BRITISH CLIMBER STARTS DARING ASCENT**,' said the headline. I reached for the paper but Jess started reading out loud.

'"Record-breaking British climber Max Rushbrooke, 34,

was today expected to start his ascent up…'" she paused. 'Well, whatever that stupid mountain's called.'

'Muchu Chhish,' I said. I'd been on his blog too many times.

Jess continued: '"Widely considered one of the highest unclimbed mountains in the world, its peak stands at 7,453 metres above the valleys of Pakistan. Poor weather and ava-lanches this season have forced many climbers to abandon their ascents in the region, but Rushbrooke has been waiting at base camp in…'" She paused again. 'I can't pronounce that either.'

'Never mind the names, what's it say?'

'"Acclimatizing at base camp in this unpronounceable place, waiting for a weather window,"' went on Jess, '"Rushbrooke and his team have decided to tackle their climb by spending the night at 5,700 metres on a plateau halfway up the mountain rather than making one day-long push for the summit."'

'Then there's a quote from him,' she said, before putting on a posh voice. '""The weather hasn't been ideal and our chances of success are not high,' Rushbrooke said via satellite phone on Sunday evening. 'But we haven't come this far to give up.'"'

'Is that the end?'

'Nope, one more bit,' she said. '"In 2001, a Dutch expedi-tion attempted to summit Muchu Chhish without success. In 2010, one of America's best climbers, Ethan Butler, died while attempting a nearby summit. Details were unclear but it appeared that Butler was unroped when he fell through a cornice."'

'That's it? That's the end?' I said.

She nodded and chucked the paper on the studio floor.

I sighed and handed back her wine glass. 'OK, I know I need to tell him, but I just need to work out how. And when. Can you get WhatsApps when you're hanging off a mountain thousands of metres up?'

Jess bit her lower lip and then looked at me. 'We could construct a message over supper?'

I thought back to the 'Gorgeous Max' text she'd sent him after my date.

'Maybe,' I said lightly, then changed the subject. 'How you doing anyway?'

She swallowed a mouthful of wine and nodded towards a canvas beside the sofa. 'Good. I've been working on this one all afternoon but I can't get the mouth.' A woman in a green dress with a lopsided smile looked back at us, a small dog asleep in her lap.

'Who is she?'

'Lady somebody or other. Her dog weed all over the floor last week so I poured white spirit over it but I think you can still smell it. Can you?' She nodded her head towards a damp patch on the floorboards by the window. I sniffed, but all I could detect was paint.

'What's happening with Alexi? When you next seeing him?'

She smiled bashfully. 'Oh, Lil, honestly, he's amazing. He's in Hong Kong so I'm not sure,' she said, glancing over her shoulder at a clock above the door. 'But we've spoken and texted like a million times and he's just—'

'Lil! Jess! Guys!' Shouts from Clem downstairs interrupted us.

'What is it?' Jess turned her head to shout at the studio door before looking back at me 'Honestly, if he's burned supper I'm going to ban him from that kitchen.'

There were sudden thuds on the stairs and Clem appeared, stooping under the low roof but panting and looking panicked.

'Guys,' he said breathlessly, 'it's on the news. I've just seen it. Lil, Max Rushbrooke's gone missing on his climb. They don't know where he is. They've lost contact.'

CHAPTER FIVE

THAT WAS A VERY long week. Issues like apple crumble and burned risotto paled into insignificance as I surreptitiously kept refreshing the news on my phone in my classroom.

'I thought we weren't allowed our phones, Miss Bailey,' Roman said one afternoon, sidling up to my desk when I thought they were all quietly drawing. I'd told him it was a family emergency and could he sit back down immediately. He walked very slowly back to his desk, glancing over his shoulder as he went. Poor Roman. I reminded myself that it wasn't his fault, that he presumably had a tricky home life. But he'd already become a handful. He'd shoved poor Vikram off his chair at the art station earlier that morning and I'd had to have words.

I looked back to my phone screen. According to the news stories, Max had left base camp with his sherpa, aiming to spend the first night at a hut at 5700m to help them acclimatize. His team on the ground, back at base camp, lost contact with him the following day as the cloud lowered over Muchu Chhish and the temperature dropped. The day after I found out he'd gone missing, the *Evening Standard* had a quote from a man called Lawrence Edwards, his operations manager:

'We haven't heard anything since midday yesterday, and I am concerned, given the weather conditions. Max is an experienced and skilled climber but when this sort of weather comes in at these kinds of altitudes, it's man against nature.'

Then the article reiterated everything I already knew – the mountain was unconquered, it had killed climbers before, and also that Pakistan was refusing to send out air rescue services because the weather was too bad. In 'such dire conditions', according to Lawrence, even ground rescue had been ruled out.

One of the BBC pieces online included a line about Max's parents. 'The explorer's parents, Viscount and Viscountess Rushbrooke, declined to comment.'

No wonder. Imagine being called up by a reporter and asked to comment on your missing son. Then I remembered Max's brother Arundel, the one who'd died as a teenager. Could there be anything sadder, losing one child and then facing the loss of another? Reading it, I'd instinctively put a hand on my stomach and then felt silly. Was I making a huge, irresponsible mistake, having this baby, if it didn't even have a father? I thought about my own situation. Mum had once told me that Adrian, my biological father, wore round glasses and looked 'a bit' like John Lennon, so whenever I'd tried to imagine Adrian, it was as John Lennon. But I didn't imagine him that often and it had never occurred to me to look for him. I didn't need to because I'd always had Dennis – devoted, generous Dennis was the one who let me help him in the garden; who always made bad fart jokes and took me to Norwich games; who once pulled a funny face at me from the audience the year I played the star role in *The Princess Who Never Smiled* at school. I laughed so much on stage he'd got a ticking off afterwards from Mrs Gaunt, the form teacher. I'd never, not for a single second, felt that I'd suffered from not knowing my biological father. But what if my baby had no father at all?

By the weekend, there was still no news so most of the papers had got bored and moved on. Apart from the *Mail*, which had an interview with his ex-girlfriend. '**MY FEARS FOR MISSING MAX**,' said the headline, over a picture of Lady Primrose Percy looking sad, sitting on a beige sofa, her blonde hair falling around her beige jersey. A beige dog – some sort of handbag dog – sat at her feet.

'**We broke up earlier this year because the demands of Max's climbing and my career were getting too difficult,**' she said. She was a milliner, apparently, with a studio in Notting Hill.

Lady Primrose went on: '**But his disappearance has made me realize how much I miss him.**'

Then there was stuff about her childhood, about how she and Max had been friends since they were teenagers because her family was also from Suffolk, about how they'd got together (at the Royal wedding, apparently, since Max and Prince William had been mates at Sandhurst and Lady Primrose was mates with Kate from boarding school), and about how Primrose was 'praying' for his safe return.

'**I know Max. He's the most determined man I've ever met. We just have to keep our fingers crossed that he'll be home soon.**'

I sighed and shut my laptop. I'd been lying in bed all morning feeling sick, my laptop propped up on a pillow as I scrolled through news articles and climbing blogs, reading other climbers theorize about what might have happened. It was all bad. He might not have been roped on, or he might have slipped on an ice shelf. Some said he shouldn't have been there at all, that he was an 'arrogant risk-taker who gives climbers a bad name'.

My flatmate Grace, who I'd told I was pregnant, kept coming in with cups of fresh ginger tea. By 5 p.m. that evening, I had three half-drunk mugs on my bedside table.

'Thanks, love,' I said, when she reappeared with mug number four.

'No worries, darl,' she said, sitting on the edge of my bed. 'Can I get you anything else? You should eat.'

Riley's head appeared from behind my bedroom door like a Jack-in-the-box. 'I've been reading,' he said, 'and you need to stay hydrated and keep your protein levels high. So what I was thinking is an avocado smoothie, and I'll chuck a load of blueberries and walnuts in there too.'

The thought of drinking a smoothie made by Riley which included avocados and nuts made me flinch. I shook my head and smiled weakly at him.

'I'm good, but thank you, both. I'm going to watch something on Netflix, have an early night.'

'OK, but we're here,' said Grace, squeezing my feet through the duvet. 'Just holler if you need.'

'Thanks,' I said again, and was about to flick back to my computer when my phone started vibrating on my bedside table. Mum.

I picked up: 'Hi, Mum.'

'Hello, you sound awful. You all right?'

I heaved myself higher up on the pillows behind me. I still didn't want to tell my parents yet. I would. Course I would, but I thought it would be better face to face so they both heard it at the same time.

'Yep. Just… doing some work at home.' It was the same tactic I used with mothers at school. Remain calm and breezy at all times. 'How are you guys?'

'All fine up here. Den's working on the Battle of Okinawa in the shed. I was just ringing to chat about Christmas. When do you think you'll be home, love?'

I hadn't thought that far ahead. Normally, school broke up in the second week of December, then there was a staff party and I spent a day or so sorting the classroom and Christmas shopping before heading to Norfolk. I did a quick calculation in my head. If I was nearly seven weeks now, I'd be… around fourteen weeks by then.

'I imagine the usual, sort of a few days before. If that's all right?'

'Yes, fine, fine, I'm just trying to plan so I can give my dates to Derek.'

Every year, Mum took part in the local pantomime. Derek was a local director who, several decades ago, had once had a play in the West End. He approached Castleton's annual panto-mime with the same zeal – auditions, a strict rehearsal schedule, then three performances over Christmas. I normally went to the first one; Dennis, sweetly supportive, went to all three.

'Oh course, what's it going to be this year?'

'*Snow White.* Derek says he's hoping we might get Stephen to make a cameo.' She meant Stephen Fry, who lived outside King's Lynn and so was a local celebrity. Mum met him once at a charity cake sale and had referred to him as 'Stephen' ever since.

I suddenly felt another wave of sick reverberate through me. 'Mum, I might have to get back to this marking. Can we speak next week?'

'Right you are, darling, you do that.'

I dropped my phone on my duvet and felt a stab of guilt at keeping such a big secret from them both. But I just had to hang on until I felt better, stronger. Until I was standing in the kitchen at home in front of both Mum and Dennis, and I could reassure them that I felt fine, that the situation was under control and they were going to have a bouncing grandbaby. I just needed to get rid of this morning sickness first. Although calling it morning sickness was a joke: all-day-and-all-night-fucking-sickness was more like it.

★

On Monday evening I went to the Antelope with Steph and Mike. It was a pub several streets away from school where we drank after work because it was cheaper than the other Chelsea pubs. Also because, apart from Mr Herbert the caretaker, none of our colleagues bothered with it. The tables were sticky and the stale air smelled of cigarettes smoked 100 years ago, but we were safe to bitch about the rest of the staffroom there.

Steph was fussing about mock common entrance exams, Mike was tutting over the music for the Christmas concert. I was relieved to have finished the afternoon activity I'd devised, called 'What I want to be when I grow up'. Phineas said he wanted to be a dragon-keeper, which was suitably imaginative. But Cosmo had declared he was going to be a YouTuber and Roman said he wanted to be a footballer, 'like my dad,' which alarmed me.

There hadn't been any more news about Max and I'd read a blog last night which said there was 'almost no chance' they'd be found alive. I'd got nineteen minutes of sleep as a result. I didn't know what to believe.

Steph, as ever, was straight to the point: 'Look, Lil, you're having this baby whether he's here or not. Right?'

I nodded.

'And I know it's a tough situation and you didn't ask for this, but you have made a decision. So you've just got to plan for you.'

I had a mouthful of lemonade and nodded again. I knew from my relationship with Dennis that being a parent was about more than biology, but Max's disappearance had added another layer of complication to this scenario. Would I have made this decision if I knew I had to have a baby on my own? I wasn't so sure.

Mike opened his mouth but then stopped and looked pained, as if he had indigestion.

'What?' I asked, frowning at him.

'The thing is,' he ventured, 'even if he was here, what do you want? Do you want to be together?'

I put my hands to my face and groaned. 'I don't know,' I mumbled into my palms. 'No, because he ghosted me after our date.' Then I dropped my hands and winced. 'But also a tiny bit of me says yes because… well, I did like him.' I'd hardly even admitted this to myself, let alone out loud. It felt weak, confessing that I still liked him even though he vanished and never texted me back. I wanted to be Beyoncé, all independent woman. But I was up and down like a barometer. Determined to hate him in the morning; checking the headlines with a thumping heart that afternoon.

Mike looked at me with a mock stern expression. 'He's got to be better than that walking testicle you call your ex.'

'Mike!' warned Steph.

'Oh, come on, he is,' said Mike, before looking at the empty glasses on our table. 'Another one?'

★

It was on Friday afternoon that I heard about Max. Or, rather, I didn't hear, I was told, breathlessly, by Mike. I'd been teaching the boys about castles that morning so they were sitting at their desks, drawing their own versions. Phineas had announced loudly that his grandfather lived in a castle 'with a drawbridge and a moat and peacocks and EVERYTHING, Miss Bailey,' so I'd told him to pipe down and just draw.

Shortly afterwards, Mike appeared at the classroom door, knocking madly on it like a human woodpecker.

I gestured at him with my hand to come in.

'What's up?' I said, immediately alarmed. His hair was even wilder than usual and he was panting.

'They've found Max.'

I held my fists up to my cheeks. 'Oh my God.'

'No no,' said Mike, still heavy breathing. 'He's alive. They've found him alive, he's on his way back to base camp.'

'Oh my God,' I repeated, sitting down at my desk. I felt a wave of relief followed, fairly quickly, by a knot of fear. Max was alive: good. But that meant he would be coming home and I'd have to tell him: bad. Or, not bad exactly, just fucking terrifying. Even more terrifying than the time I'd told Mum I was leaving the state sector for a job at a private school. And that was pretty bad.

'Is Mr Moorhouse your boyfriend, Miss Bailey?' said Roman, looking at Mike.

I ignored him.

Mike was now leaning with one hand on my desk. 'Sorry to burst in, I thought you'd want to know.'

'Yes, course, thank you.'

'Do you want Mr Moorhouse to be your boyfriend?' continued Roman, watching Mike and me.

'Can you concentrate on your castle please?' I turned back to Mike. 'Did they say anything else? Are there any more details?'

'I didn't see, I just saw it come up as breaking news. On their website. So I ran straight here. Christ, I'm unfit.'

But Roman wasn't done yet. 'Why aren't you married, Miss Bailey?'

Mike looked at Roman and then back to me. 'I'm gonna go,' he said, before muttering at me, 'otherwise I'll throttle that one and be in all the papers.'

'OK, and thanks again.'

'You're welcome, see you later.'

I then made Fergus rotate around the desks checking the castles while I sat at my desk, subtly trying to read the BBC piece. Max had been found alive by a drone, and was suffering frostbite and 'minor' injuries and was being flown from base camp to Islamabad for hospital checks, but wasn't thought to be seriously injured.

There was nothing from him in the piece but another quote from his operations manager. '**It's been a tense ten days but I'd like to thank the operations team at Muchu Chhish base camp for all their work. Max is a tough and strong-willed man, but he knows how fortunate he was to be found. He'll be making a statement as soon as he's cleared from hospital.**'

I put my phone into the desk drawer and puffed out my cheeks. Alright, so he'd just had a near-death experience and probably didn't feel his absolute shiniest, but I did now need to let Max know about this baby situation. No more delays. Except the thought of confessing made me wish I was the one stranded on a remote Pakistani mountain.

★

How do you start a message telling someone you've met once that you're having their baby?

I opened Notes in my phone. It felt safer than typing directly into WhatsApp – what if I wrote half the message and then accidentally sent it? And then Max realized that not only was a strange woman having his baby, but she was also the kind of incredible moron who couldn't even compose a text message? Disaster. So, Notes it was. I sat at the café table and blinked at my blank screen.

I'd come to the local Portuguese place a few streets away from the flat. I often did this if I had to mark spelling books on the weekends or when Grace and Riley were going at it in the flat and I needed to escape before I perforated my own eardrums. It was run by a grumpy man I'd nicknamed Manuel. He was always short-staffed so the coffee took ages, and if you dared ask for anything on top of a coffee – a croissant, say, or a biscuit – he always forgot it. Because it had nice wooden tables and did babychinos (was I going to become the kind of woman who ordered babychinos?), it was normally overrun with middle-class mothers discussing oat milk.

Although it wasn't even nine today so the mothers hadn't started appearing. On Saturdays, the dads generally came first anyway, despatched to go and get pain au chocolat with one or several children attached to them like baby monkeys. Then parents started appearing together with their kids and the place got busier and hotter and noisier until I decided the flat would be relatively peaceful in comparison and retreated home again. But for now, it was quiet, so I had to crack on. Come on, Lil, get it together.

I looked back at my phone.

Hey, Max, I typed. Then I deleted it. Too casual. Like, 'Hey, dude, what's up? You've had a pretty shocking couple of weeks but have I got news for you!'

Shit. If I couldn't even manage a greeting I shouldn't be having a baby in the first place.

Max, hello, I typed, and then squinted at it. There, that sounded all right.

I forged on.

Hope you're well, I wrote. Then I deleted it. I couldn't write that to a man who was missing in the Pakistani mountains a few days ago.

I sighed. In my head, messaging the news to Max had seemed the simplest option. A short but informative message with the bare facts, telling him I was around to speak whenever he wanted. He still hadn't made any kind of statement about being found, or updated his blog, so I didn't even know if he was still in Pakistan but I knew I had to break this news to him.

The actual writing of this message felt almost impossible, though. A simple explanation – 'I'm pregnant with your baby' – looked too stark, typed in front of me. I felt a jumble of emotions about being pregnant, about finding myself in this situation, but I knew I was already falling in love with my baby. Every fibre of me knew that having her was the right thing to do, as sure as left is left and right is right. But Max couldn't possibly have that connection. I flicked off Notes and googled the distance between Brixton and Pakistan. It was 3,747 miles. Max was 3,747 miles away and about to get a life-changing message from someone he barely knew. This dot inside me wouldn't necessarily be a baby to him. She'd be a disaster. An accident he regretted as soon as he knew of her existence.

I sighed and went back to Notes, wishing I could imbue the words with the positivity I felt, and the only thing I could do was be honest.

Max, hello. I don't really know how to start this message. And I've worried about messaging you but I wasn't sure how to get hold of you otherwise. It's Lil, by the way, we had a date in September, at the pub in Vauxhall.

I stopped typing and read it back, cringing. But I had to make who I was as clear as possible. What if he'd been dating loads of women? Or he'd never saved my number in the first place? Or in case his brain had been starved of oxygen in Pakistan and he needed help remembering? I knew that happened. I'd seen Ben Fogle on *The One Show* when he got back from Everest, saying he wasn't the same for several weeks after getting home.

Concentrate, Lil. What's Ben Fogle doing popping into your head at a moment like this?

I looked back at my screen.

Anyway, I typed, *I realized a few weeks afterwards that I was pregnant. And the baby is yours. And I wasn't sure what to do. But then I had a scan and I've decided to keep her. And you can be involved or not, it's up to you. I don't want you to feel obliged in any way. But I wanted to let you know.*

I sat back and reread it, chewing the cuticle on my thumb. There wasn't much else to say.

I hope you're all right after everything, I added. *I'm around to speak at any point.*

What should I sign off with? I settled for just 'L'. Then I added a kiss afterwards. 'Lx'. Then I took the kiss off again. But just 'L' on its own looked too curt. I re-added the kiss.

It was fine. Not too long, not too short, got the message across. Job done.

With a sick feeling churning in my stomach, I copied the message from Notes and went into WhatsApp. I scrolled down to find Max's name. I moaned quietly when I saw the last message I'd sent, the message I'd sent at 2.03 a.m., berating him for not texting me after we slept together.

Ah well, I thought, pasting my message in and feeling a sudden burst of bravery. At least he'd have to reply to this one.

I held my breath and clicked on the little green arrow. There. Sent. I felt as if I was about to throw up all over the café, but I couldn't tell if it was morning sickness or nerves.

Manuel appeared at my table, looking pointedly at my coffee. 'Want another one?' I'd faffed about with the message for so long that the place had started filling up and I guessed he wanted the table back.

'It's all right,' I said. 'I'm off.'

He grunted, picked up my empty cup and gave the table a cursory wipe with a tea towel, flicking several croissant flakes into the air. That was another thing about this place – I reckoned the boys' bathrooms at school were probably more hygienic.

★

I walked back to the flat feeling my heart thudding underneath my coat. I wrapped my hand around my phone in my pocket, half of me desperate to look and see if he'd read it and messaged back; half of me too worried to look, wanting to fling my phone in the bin. Maybe he'd ring as soon as he saw it? I climbed the stairs to our front door. Shit, what if he tried to video call? I'd scraped my hair back with an elastic and wasn't wearing a speck of make-up.

It was quiet in the flat, thankfully, so I went to my room and sat on my bed. Then I pulled my phone out of my pocket and looked at it with one eye closed. A WhatsApp! OK, deep breath, Lil, try not to throw up your coffee all over your feet. I unlocked my phone and pulled the message down.

Not Max.

It was from Mum, a photo she'd sent of Ginger the cat asleep under the kitchen table, her back against Gerald the tortoise. Then she'd sent a string of heart-eye emojis. I mean, sweet, but really not NOW, Mum. I ignored it and clicked on Max's name. Blue ticks.

BLUE TICKS.

He'd read it.

And then I saw he was online, instantly clicked off WhatsApp and threw my phone on the bed, as if it was scalding and had burned me. I closed my eyes briefly and sighed. Had anyone ever been this feeble? I breathed deeply several times and then slowly tiptoed my fingers across my duvet back towards my phone.

Come on. Come on, come on, come on. You're going

to have a baby with this man. You should be able to read a message from him.

I opened WhatsApp. **Max typing...** it said. I sat on my bed, frozen, and held my breath, although he seemed to be taking such a long time with typing that I finally had to exhale.

Max typing... stayed there for several minutes. It reminded me of playing chess, waiting for my opponent to move. Dennis had taught me to play when I was about five, insisting that it was an 'important lesson in warfare', even though we lived in a rural Norfolk village, not Tudor Britain.

But then **Max typing...** disappeared a few minutes later, and I frowned. Huh? I leant forward and rested my arms on my knees, phone still in my hand. He'd got the message, then started replying, then stopped replying and had now seemingly gone offline.

My brain raced, trying to work out what that meant. Max couldn't ignore this message, surely? Even if you were a heartless cad who never replied to girls' messages after taking them out on whirlwind dates, you still had to reply to a message like this, right? This was the message you really couldn't ignore. So why the silence?

*

I didn't hear from him for three days. I went to Jess and Clem's one evening for supper but became so short-tempered at Jess banging on and on about Alexi that I feigned exhaustion and came home early. I felt bitter. And unsupportive. But I found myself annoyed by her relentless wittering about him – about

Alexi's art, his obsession with Francis Bacon, his selfless-
ness in bed (apparently he'd made her come four times the
other night). I couldn't tell if I was just being bitter because
I felt as sexy as a genital wart. My best pal was high on love
chemicals while I was waking up sick every day, pregnant
with a stranger's child. And I kept checking WhatsApp to
see if it said 'Max typing...' at any point again, but it didn't.
He'd been online a couple of times, I could see when he was
online. But still, no reply.

Initially I'd told myself he needed a couple of hours of
thinking time, to allow the news to sink in before coming
back to me. But when he didn't respond that first night, or
the next, or the next, my mood changed. I went from jittery
confidence that he'd obviously get in touch, to fury and
disbelief that he could ignore such a message. I wasn't just a
date angling for another drink. I was pregnant with his baby.
Seriously, seriously, could any man ignore that?

It was during morning break on Tuesday that my phone
vibrated in my pocket, while standing on the steps with
Steph, overseeing the carnage happening in the playground
beneath us.

'Ludo Tollemache, will you give Ned back his shoe
immediately?' shouted Steph, as one of Year 4 tore round
the AstroTurf waving a loafer in the air, leaving another one
hopping by the swings.

I slid my phone halfway out of my pocket and glanced
down at it. A WhatsApp. I opened it, braced for it to be
another picture of the animals from Mum. Unless it was

Ginger the cat doing something extraordinary with Gerald the tortoise – tap-dancing, reading him a book – I wasn't in the mood.

Then I saw it was Max.

'Oh my God,' I said faintly, feeling suddenly winded. I could see the first line of the message, so tapped it with my thumb to read the whole thing.

Lil, it started, I fail to see how this has happened. As far as I remember, and I do remember this, you said we were 'OK'. I appreciate that two people are traditionally involved when one of them gets pregnant, but I did check with you. Forgive me for being short, but I'm genuinely at a loss as to what to say. I will be back in London in a couple of weeks so I suggest we meet then to discuss the situation and for a paternity test. I'll ring you.

'Lil? Lil? LIL?' I heard Steph saying beside me, and then I felt her hand on my back. 'You all right, love?'

I nodded. 'Yeah. No, I'm fine, it's all good, I'm fine, I just need…' I was garbling, still looking at the message, trying to process it. A paternity test. I felt so naive. I'd guessed Max might be shocked and angry. I'd understood that he probably wasn't going to ring me up and say, 'Darling! Great news, let's get married.' But I hadn't ever considered that he would demand a test, that he'd doubt the baby was his. The Max I remembered from our date didn't sound anything like the Max in this message – so cold.

'You don't look all right. You look almost green. Come on, love, look, perch here,' Steph instructed, stepping aside so I could sit on one of the playground steps.

'It's fine,' I repeated, lowering myself down. 'I just, er, just got a message from Max. I told him on the weekend and I hadn't heard anything and he's just…'

I trailed off as Steph bellowed at the boys again. 'LUDO TOLLEMACHE, I'M WARNING YOU.'

Then she looked down at me. 'He's just what, love?'

I wasn't sure how to phrase it. 'He's not very happy,' I told her. 'He doesn't believe me. He wants a paternity test. Look.' I help my phone up for her to see.

'Budge up,' said Steph, so I moved closer to the railings and made space for her bottom. She then took my phone. 'Left my glasses inside,' she said, holding it an inch from her face.

'Hmmmm,' she said, handing it back to me a few moments later. 'On the bright side, at least he knows.'

I nodded slowly.

'And he says he'll be in touch.'

'Yeah,' I said, staring blankly at the AstroTurf in front of the steps. One of the boys could have been throttling another with his stripy tie and I'm not sure I'd have noticed.

'And what does a paternity test matter, really?' went on Steph. 'It'll prove it's his. Maybe it's better that way. No doubt. He'll have to accept it then, no wriggling out of it. JEREMY HUNTER, PUT YOUR TONGUE AWAY PLEASE, NOBODY WANTS TO SEE THAT.'

I puffed out my cheeks and exhaled. 'Yeah,' I said, and then I nodded again, feeling a small slither of comfort at Steph's words. 'Yeah,' I repeated, 'you're right, at least this way he has no doubt. And I can explain, when I see him, that it was a total accident, no?'

'Exactly,' said Steph, before putting a hand on mine and adopting a more sympathetic tone. 'It wasn't going to be straightforward, this, Lil love. But let's look on the bright side. Hopefully this is the trickiest bit, before you both get everything straightened out.'

'Uh-huh,' I mumbled, my mind still reeling. Paternity tests felt like the kind of drama that happened in TV soaps, not my life. I sat silently beside Steph for a few moments while the boys carried on shouting like small Bravehearts, before she heaved herself up on the railings and said it was time to marshal them inside.

CHAPTER SIX

I WAS DISTRACTED (a tiny bit) over the next few weeks by the build-up to Christmas at school. The end of the Christmas term was one of the best things about working at a school. Alright, every single boy had a weeping nose and jersey cuffs lined with shiny snot, as if snails had crawled up them, because 5-year-old boys were incapable of using tissues. But their excitement about Christmas generally started towards mid-November and doubled-down every morning when we opened another window of the class advent calendar.

There was also much chatter about their Christmas holidays.

'We've got to go to the Maldives again this year, Miss Bailey,' said Roman, full of sorrow one morning when we opened another window of the calendar.

'We're going to Antigua,' piped up Dmitri.

'I'm going to the sea shells,' shouted Oscar.

'Well you're all very lucky. I'm going to Norfolk to stay with my parents,' I said, trying to inject a modicum of humility into the classroom.

Although it wasn't just the boys who were obsessing about the less holy side of Christmas. The subject of presents came up the following week while sitting in the Antelope. Steph and Mike were playing the annual game of who would get the most absurd present from which parent. The Christmas present bandwagon at St Lancelot's was legendary among staff. Diptyque candles, Jo Malone bath oil, Fortnum hampers and bottles of champagne were the least of it. On the last day of term, it wasn't unusual to see nannies or parents arrive at drop-off with blue Smythson bags containing personalized diaries or handbags. Or Brora bags stuffed with cashmere scarves. Cartier and Rolex bags were also whispered about in the staffroom, as if all the members of staff were trying to work out what they'd get from the world's most extravagant lucky dip.

I knew a couple of staff members who'd given parents their home address for cases of wine to be delivered (fearing Miss Montague's wrath if they took delivery of these at school). Holiday villas and vouchers for spa weekends were also common. A couple of Christmases ago, Miss Allen, the drama teacher, was given an early Banksy sketch. Last year, rumour had it that Mrs Hassan had flown to Venice for the weekend on a private jet, courtesy of a pharmaceutical billionaire whose son was in her class.

Steph was usually one of the biggest beneficiaries since her boys were going through common entrance exams and the parents would have given her anything – one of their cars, one of their houses, one of their internal organs – if they thought it meant their son would get preferential treatment.

That was also the evening Max called.

'Uh-ohhhhh,' I said to the others, who had moved on from

presents and were now bickering over who'd get most pissed at the staff Christmas party. 'Guys, it's him.'

They went silent and looked at me. I stared at the phone, vibrating on the table.

'Well go on, don't just look at it, answer it,' chided Steph.

I picked up.

'Max, hi,' I said stiffly.

'Lil?' I don't know why he asked that as if it was a question. Who else would it be?

'Hi,' I repeated.

Mike mouthed something across the table at me that I couldn't make out so I swivelled in my seat, away from them, and faced the bar.

'I'm back,' he said, 'in London, I mean.'

'Right, OK, cool...' I replied, before rolling my eyes at myself. Why did I say 'cool'? I wanted to sound aloof and mature, not like a 14-year-old on their first date.

Then there was a brief pause before Max spoke again.

'When would work for you to meet up?' He sounded clipped. Formal. As if he was arranging a business meeting.

I thought. School broke up on Thursday the following week and the staff party was the same evening. But I could probably do Thursday afternoon. I was supposed to be clearing out the classroom and going Christmas shopping for my parents. I hadn't bought a single present, as usual. But I probably wouldn't mind a break from the shops after a couple of hours.

'Next Thursday afternoon any good?' I suggested, trying to match his practical tone and not let my voice get too nervous.

It did a weird, squeaky thing when I got nervous. Jess said it was like talking to a bat.

'Fine, where works for you?'

'Around Chelsea?' I suggested. 'I've got various things at school I need to sort out that day. And I've got my twelve-week scan at St Thomas's the next day if you…' I trailed off as my voice started getting really quite bat-like.

'Let's discuss that next week,' he said, unemotionally. 'But Chelsea's fine. Any particular place?'

I thought again. I didn't want to run the risk of bumping into any other staff members, so here was about as discreet a place as any.

'Er, it sounds a bit odd, but do you mind meeting in a pub called the Antelope? Just off Sloane Street? It's just quiet, there'll be space, away from the shoppers.'

'Not a problem. See you there at four?'

'Yes,' I squeaked, before lowering my voice. 'I mean yes, that suits me. See you then.'

We said goodbye and I dropped my phone into my bag, before spinning round to face Steph and Mike.

'I can't believe you're meeting him here,' said Mike. 'I am so coming. I'm going to wear a flat cap and sit at the bar pretending to read the paper.'

'If you even think about it,' I said.

'Course he won't,' said Steph, shooting him a warning look. 'Was that all right?'

I wrinkled my nose at her. 'Not really. He sounded like one

of those automated messages.' I put on a robotic voice. 'Hello, I have an important message about your home insurance.'

Mike laughed and Steph winced. 'Oh, pet,' she said. 'But good to have a plan.'

'A battle plan,' said Mike.

'No, not a battle plan,' corrected Steph, quickly. 'Just a plan.'

I smiled gratefully at them both and opened the calendar on my phone. 'Drink with Max,' I typed into next Thursday. And then I changed 'drink' to 'meeting'. I nodded to myself as I saved it and put my phone down. If Max was going to talk like a businessman with a stick up his bottom, then I would be just as standoffish.

*

By the following Thursday, I was freaking out about what to wear. If left unaided, 5-year-olds will always put their plimsolls on the wrong feet. But by the time you get to thirty-one, you generally understand how to get dressed, right? I had various sensible* (*boring) dresses for work, mostly grey or navy. I had two pairs of favourite jeans which I wore on the weekends. I had various tops that lay dormant in my drawers, mostly from Topshop and Zara, that I'd bought on a whim when I'd wanted to try something that was briefly fashionable – a smocked shirt, leopard print, a blue pussy-bow blouse. The blouse was a real low-point. But I generally wore jeans with a couple of old jumpers which I liked because I could pull the sleeves over my hands, a habit I'd never grown out of.

Thursday morning was one of those moments when I wished my wardrobe was more expansive. What was the right outfit to meet my baby-daddy? Urgh, grim word, it made me feel like a Kardashian. I frowned while rifling through my hanging cupboard, as if something I'd never seen would leap out at me.

Then I opened the bottom drawer instead. Jeans. Would have to be jeans with a shirt. Maybe I had something I'd forgotten about which would fit. Because that was the other problem. I was just over three months pregnant and, when naked in front of the bathroom mirror, I looked like I'd just swallowed an enormous Sunday lunch. Roast, pudding and cheese. I was starting to feel like sausage-meat squeezed into its skin.

Also, nobody tells you about the gas when you're pregnant. My farting was incredible. I'd genuinely impressed myself a couple of times. Shortly before the end of term, while the boys were doing worksheets and Fergus and I were circling the classroom, I accidentally let one slip while I was crouching down next to poor Cosmo, and Roman loudly accused him of farting, which made Cosmo cry. I obviously didn't confess, I just told Roman to be quiet and carry on counting hedgehogs. But the smell was properly evil. It made my eyes water. While thumbing through my wardrobe, I silently prayed that this wouldn't be a problem in the pub with Max.

Finally, I settled for jeans and a pink Zara jersey and stuffed them into a tote bag. Then I pulled on a boring work dress and set off for the Tube station.

Since it was the last day of term, the boys only had to tidy their desks. Then I took down the various paintings from the classroom wall and handed them out before putting on *The Snowman* so they could all sit quietly on the beanbags to kill time before final assembly.

'Chop-chop,' I said, trying to get them to stand straight in a line. It was like herding ants.

When it was pick-up time, I parcelled them out to the waiting nannies, who had mostly arrived at the playground holding bags for me. I took them as gracefully as I could, trying to stop myself from immediately untying the thick ribbon to scrabble through them all.

'Thank you, and happy Christmas, Dimitri!'

'Happy Christmas, Achilles, thank you. And happy Christmas, Vikram!' and so on until they'd all gone and I could stagger back upstairs to the classroom and inspect the bags.

They included a fragrance diffuser from Harrods that smelled like oranges (thank you, Cosmo's parents); a pair of Hermès leather gloves from Hunter's parents; a jar of marmalade from George's parents and a tin of something that looked like shoe polish from Dmitri. No, not shoe polish, I realized, turning the tin over. It was caviar. A 125g tin of beluga caviar from Fortnum and Mason which apparently cost £843. I googled it while sitting there. Then I looked up how to eat it and Google told me with toast. Spreading something so expensive on a slice of Hovis seemed extravagant, but I'd take it home for Christmas for Mum and Dennis. I squinted at the tin in my hand. Could I persuade them it was a present from me? Nah, they'd never fall for that.

It was while rifling through the bags like a burglar that my phone buzzed on my desk. Jess.

'Hi, doll,' she said, when I picked up. 'All good for the scan tomorrow?'

'Yup, think so. Thanks for coming. If we just meet at St Thomas's main reception at midday, is that OK?'

'Course,' she said.

'Allllso,' I said slowly, 'I'm seeing Max this afternoon.'

'Shit, love, of course, how you feeling?'

'All right.' This was a lie. I felt as if I needed the loo VERY urgently every time I thought about the meeting that afternoon, but I was trying to be outwardly confident.

'Mmm,' she said. 'OK, good luck. Will you let me know how it goes?'

'Course.' Then I heard a man's voice down the phone.

'Who's that?' I said to her. 'Alexi?'

'Yes,' she said, before giggling. 'He's trying to get me to come back to bed and I'm ignoring him.'

'When can we hang out?' I said. If friendship is a pie chart, then I felt like the baby and I were taking up four-fifths of the pie at the moment and Jess was only one-fifth. I felt guilty. However irritating people are when they fall in love, I knew I needed to be more supportive.

'Tomorrow night,' she said. 'I'm bringing him.'

'What's tom...' Fuccccccccccck. I suddenly remembered. It was our uni Christmas party. It happened every year on the last weekend before Christmas. A big group of us from Edinburgh, whoever was around, gathered together in a pub, all wearing Christmas jerseys. Last year, Jake and I were still together and we'd worn matching Mr and Mrs Snowman ones.

'Shit, do you reckon Jake will be there?' I'd been so preoccupied that I'd totally forgotten about the party.

'Dunno, love. I mean, probably?'

'Shit,' I said again, 'I'd totally forgotten. But great about Alexi though, can I hide in a corner with you guys?'

'Obviously. There'll only be about three people that I want to talk to anyway.'

'OK, deal. But right, you go back to bed. I'll see you tomorrow.'

'But report back on how later goes?'

'Yup, will do.'

Next, I packed the tinsel and paper angels from my classroom into a box and carried it down to Mr Herbert's room. The school caretaker never came into the staffroom. He had his own, separate 'office' (more like a shed) just to the side of the playground.

'Here you go, Mr Herbert,' I said, knocking on the door with my free hand.

He came to the door in his sandy-coloured coat, grunted and took the box from me. Mr Herbert wasn't a big conversationalist.

'OK, thanks then,' I said. 'See you later at the party?'

He grunted again. Or it could have been a laugh.

That done, I headed out into the Christmas shopping crowds in Chelsea. I always did this, left my shopping right up until a few days before going home and then bought completely the wrong presents. Out I went, into the throng with everyone else picking up things on shelves and looking at them with wide-eyed terror, then panic-buying L'Occitane gift sets. No offence to L'Occitane, but nobody ever deliberately set out to buy a gift set of soap and hand cream, did they?

I knew what I wanted to give Dennis this year. It was a quick trip to the bookshop tucked off the King's Road to get a new biography of Stalin's favourite general which Mr Hooper, the history teacher, had recommended for him. Mum was trickier. She'd say 'don't get me anything', but she didn't mean this. I walked the length of the King's Road looking for inspiration but nothing, so walked back again and ducked into Peter Jones and finally decided on a set of four Frida Kahlo side plates.

It was while browsing in the make-up area that my eye fell on a sign at a make-up counter that said 'Get party ready in 20 minutes.' I looked at the time. It was only just 3.15, so I had ages before I needed to get to the pub and my face could probably do with a touch-up before meeting Max and the party later on.

With hindsight, this was not my best idea. But I'd been walking all afternoon and I wanted to look less ragged. I wanted to feel less like a dumpy pregnant woman who could hardly get her jeans done up, and more together. More polished. More like Lady Primrose Percy. It wasn't a date with Max, obviously, but for some reason I still wanted to impress him. I wanted to arrive at the Antelope feeling confident enough to stand up to him if he was difficult. Composed enough to tell him I could do this on my own, without him, if that's what he wanted.

'Hello,' I said to a lady wearing electric-blue eyeshadow standing behind the counter. 'Can I get my make-up done?' I pointed at the sign.

'Absolutely,' she said. 'It's twenty pounds but redeemable against our products.'

'No problem,' I said. I hadn't realized that it cost anything but I decided it would be embarrassing to back out. I'd just buy a new mascara.

She gestured at a stool and I sat down, shopping bags at my feet.

'You been buying last-minute presents?' she said, rubbing cotton pads that smelt of roses across my face.

'Mmm,' I said, trying not to breathe on her.

'Now,' she said, standing back and looking at my face. 'What look are we going for?'

'So I've got my work party later,' I said, 'but I've got a meeting with, er, well, never mind. I've just got a meeting this afternoon and I need to look confident. Sort of… brave.'

She nodded. 'Got it. I think what we need here is perfect skin and a bit of a smoky eye?'

'Perfect, thank you.'

Because I was so preoccupied about meeting Max, I wasn't paying attention as she worked on my face. If I had, I might have noticed that she was using a dazzling array of creams, powders, pencils and brushes. As it was, I was just happy to sit there with my face being touched while I obsessed about how Max and I would greet one another. I wasn't sure how to greet someone you've only met once but who is now the father of your child. A kiss on the cheek? Two kisses? A hug? A high five? Maybe nothing would be less awkward. If I got there early, I could be sitting at a table and just wave across it when he arrived.

'That's you done,' said the lady, sounding pleased with herself, while standing back and squinting at her canvas, so I turned on my stool to look in a mirror.

Shitting hell. It was like Cher in her disco phase. Eyes thick with kohl, some sort of silvery eyeshadow and very defined pink cheekbones.

'Oh!' I said.

'D'you like it?' she asked. 'I thought you needed a bit of sparkle for your party.'

'Mmm,' I said vaguely, glancing at my watch. Ten to four. I didn't have time to put my face back to normal. I needed to get to the pub.

'So that's £20 or you can buy one of the products,' she said.

'Oh, yup. Course. Um, could I have the mascara?' I asked. I figured that was the least offensive item she'd used on me.

'Course you can,' she said, reaching into a cupboard. 'Although the mascara's £24 so you'll need to make up the difference.'

'Right, OK,' I said, reaching for my wallet. Essentially I'd paid £4 to go to this meeting with Max as if a child had finger-painted my face.

★

I kept glancing at myself in shop windows as I hurried to the pub. The pace was making me hot, so I knew I'd arrive and sit down, only to instantly start sweating so my make-up would run down my face. Brilliant.

Max wasn't there when I arrived, so I hurried to our table at the back and was piling my coat and shopping bags on a chair when I heard a voice behind me.

'Lil?'

I turned round. It was him, looking thinner than I remembered him. But more tanned. His beard had blond, bleached flecks in it.

'Hi, hello, sorry just trying to sort myself out.' I could feel a bead of sweat gathering on my upper lip.

'Hello,' he said stiffly, and there was a momentary pause before we both went for an excruciating half-hug.

I quickly wiped my upper lip as we pulled back so he didn't see.

'Please ignore my face,' I started gabbling. 'I've got my Christmas party later and the make-up lady in… Actually, you really don't need the whole story.'

'Would you like a drink?'

'Oh. Yes, please. Um, a lemonade?'

'OK, I'll just…' He inclined his head in the direction of the bar. He was nervous, I realized.

'Course, go for it.'

He went off and I sat down, remembering our first date

when I arrived and he already had a vodka waiting for me. If anything, I thought, glancing at his back, he looked even more handsome. Rugged. Perhaps it was because he was a returning hero and he had an extra allure of glamour about him. I felt a flutter – annoyingly – as soon as I'd seen him.

He came back to the table with my lemonade and a cup of tea, the cup and saucer looking dainty in his hands.

'No drink drink?' I asked, and then kicked myself.

'No,' he said. 'It takes a while to get used to alcohol again. After altitude.'

'Oh, right. Course.' Definitely no jokes, Lil. 'It's, er, good that you're back safely,' I added, wanting to strike a conciliatory tone.

'Thank you,' he replied, staring at his tea before looking up at me. 'Listen, I, er… I'm… I mean I don't… I don't know where to start, to be honest. I'm confused, I suppose,' he said, going on before I had a chance to answer, 'because I know we did what we did and I take full responsibility, but I offered to, er,' – he lowered his voice – 'get a condom, and you told me it was all right.'

I nodded quickly. 'It was. I mean, it should have been. I was on the pill.' I was struck by the ludicrousness of the situation, of sitting in a pub discussing such intimate bodily details about my life with a stranger, a famous stranger, and I almost laughed. But fortunately didn't.

'But then how? How did this happen, Lil?' He stared at me intensely, leaning forwards and resting his forearms on the table.

'It just does sometimes.' I sounded defensive. 'I'd been on the pill for, like, fifteen years and it had always been fine. But it's not 100 per cent. Nothing is.'

Max glanced down at his tea again. 'I've got to ask, and I'm sorry but… it was definitely an accident, right? It wasn't—'

I interrupted him. 'Deliberate, you mean?'

He nodded slowly, looking at me.

'I promise,' I said. 'I swear. Trust me, getting pregnant with a stranger on a first date wasn't one of my life goals.'

'And you decided to keep it without even consulting me?'

'No,' I said firmly. 'I mean yes, but you were halfway up a mountain, thousands of miles away. Well, three thousand and forty… actually, never mind.' I glanced down at my hands in my lap and exhaled, reminding myself to sound calm. Channel Miss Montague, Lil. Confidence. Then I looked up at him again. 'So, yes, I did decide to keep her while you were away but I'd been thinking about it for days.'

'Days!' said Max, shaking his head. 'Are you joking? Days to decide something that completely changes other people's lives?'

'It wasn't an easy choice,' I said, stressing every word. 'And then I had to have a scan for…' I didn't want to say the word 'cyst' to him. 'I had to have a scan and I saw the heartbeat. And that was when I decided. You can't imagine the feeling. You haven't seen it. But it changed everything. You can come tomorrow for my twelve-week scan if you like, it's midday.'

'Yes, you mentioned,' he said. 'I did some research and we can have our blood taken at St Thomas's genetics centre.

I didn't reply.

'For the paternity test,' he went on.

'Fine,' I said coolly.

He sat back in his seat and ran a hand through his hair. 'Jesus.' Then he sighed and looked at me, eyes burning. 'So you found out you were pregnant, then you had a scan and then decided you really wanted to do this on your own?'

'I didn't want to do this on my own because I didn't want to be pregnant in the first place. But it's happened,' I said, trying to keep my voice steady. 'And what I wanted to say today is you can be involved or not. Obviously it was a surprise, a big surprise, but I took the decision to keep it for me, while understanding that you might not want the same thing. I get it if you don't want to be involved, I just… keeping it felt like the right thing to do.'

'The right thing for who?' said Max, loudly enough for the barman to glance over at our table. 'Seriously, how can bringing a child into the world possibly be a good idea when we've only met once?'

'It's the right thing for the baby,' I insisted. 'You don't have to be involved.'

He shook his head again and I felt a surge of anger inside me. He wasn't listening to anything I said.

'But don't you want a normal family?' he asked.

'What's normal?' I said, throwing my hands up in the air. 'My parents certainly aren't. I bet yours aren't.' I wasn't about to admit that I'd googled them. 'Loads of women do this nowadays.'

'What? Get pregnant deliberately and decide to have a baby with a man they don't know?'

I felt as if I'd been punched in the throat.

'I told you it wasn't deliberate,' I said, my voice suddenly thick. Tears, that was all I needed. Tears dissolving the eye make-up that mad woman had plastered me with, so I'd be sitting here, opposite Max, looking like a sad clown.

'I'm sorry,' he said, handing me a napkin from his saucer. 'I didn't mean to upset you. But you've got to see it from my perspective. I meet someone from a dating app, we sleep together, I go away and come back to her telling me she's pregnant. I feel like...' He paused and clenched his fists on the table. 'I feel like I've been robbed. Robbed of the kind of future I want. Robbed of how I wanted it to be. Robbed of the chance to be a father because this isn't the way, Lil, this isn't the right way at all. You haven't given me any option. That's why I have to insist on a paternity test. You must see that?' He sounded almost pleading.

'You haven't been robbed,' I said, shaking my head and blinking through my tears. 'I didn't mean for it to happen. It just has. I've always wanted the same – having a family, together, not like this.' My voice had gone bat-like again. 'But life doesn't always unfold the way we think it will. And I'm sorry if you don't want this, but I do.'

I blew my nose on his napkin and then realized I didn't want to be sitting there weeping. It felt like Max had already decided he didn't want to be involved, and the hostility I could sense across the table made me protective of my baby, as if she'd somehow be able to hear this argument over her future.

'Actually,' I went on, 'do you know what? Don't worry

about it. I'm going. Come tomorrow or don't. But I can do this without you.'

I wanted to be on my own. I felt naive, and desperately sad. Sadder than I had at any point since I found out I was pregnant. I'd played out what felt like a billion scenarios of this meeting with Max in my head but none of them had left me feeling this stupid, this accused. I'd even let myself wonder if he'd come back and suggest we go on a few more dates, see how it went. I screwed my eyes shut in embarrassment for a second, as I turned to pick up my shopping bags.

'Lil, wait…' He grabbed my left arm.

But with as much dignity as I could muster with a face that looked like it was melting, while carrying my Frida side plates and a heavy book about a Russian military general, I shook off his arm and made for the door. I couldn't sit there any longer and be interrogated as if I'd done something wrong.

*

I hailed a black cab and went straight to Brixton. An extravagance but I couldn't get the Tube looking like this and I just wanted to get home. I'd been too optimistic about Max, about his reaction. I'd assumed things about him without even really knowing him. I'd imagined he might be stunned by the news. I'd considered the possibility that he might be suspicious of me. But I hadn't thought he'd be so angry or flare up, growling at me across the table like that. I choked as more tears slid down my cheeks.

'Is it a man?' said the driver, looking at me in his rear-view mirror.

I sniffed and blinked back at him.

'I can always tell,' he went on. 'There's plenty more, love.'

'Thank you,' I said, blowing my nose on the damp napkin I was still clutching. I didn't want to get into a debate with him about what was appropriate to ask and not to ask when you have a teary woman in the back of your cab. Say what you like about Uber, but the drivers were less chatty.

I WhatsApped Steph when I got home. *Meeting with Max a disaster so might skip the party, will you forgive me?*

She replied almost immediately. **Course pet, but you all right?**

Not really, I texted back, *but I'll live. I just want a bath.*

I'd always loved the school Christmas party because it was like being a teenager again. Held in the assembly hall, it always included terrible wine, sausage rolls and someone (normally a member of the science department) who overdid it and had to go home early. But obviously I couldn't drink this year and I wanted to avoid everyone. Plus, I thought, looking in the bathroom mirror, my face looked extraordinary – eyes so puffy I could hardly see out of them and ten kilos of kohl smeared down my cheeks.

★

I woke the next day and reached for my phone. I'd wondered if Max would have sent me anything by way of apology or saying he'd be there later. Nope, nothing. But I had a WhatsApp from Jess asking how the meeting went and a short video from Mike of him and Steph on the dance floor at the party. 'We miss yooooooou,' he shouted over a backdrop of Slade.

Missed you back, any gossip? I texted him. Then swung myself out of bed, wrapped myself in a towel and had a shower. I looked down at my belly while the water ran over it. I'd downloaded an app called Pregnancy Tracker which emailed me jaunty, daily updates about pregnancy. Apparently, at this stage, she was the size of a 'small plum'. But this seemed unfair when I looked at my stomach, because it felt more swollen than that. It felt like I'd swallowed a cantaloupe instead of a plum. Was that normal? Although the app had also informed me this morning that my baby could now move her arms and legs individually, which made me smile. A proper little person dancing about in there.

I walked to St Thomas's. It was a grey walk of pubs and petrol stations until Vauxhall, but then I could snake up the river. I arrived at the hospital with forty-five minutes to spare, but that was no bad thing since I was supposed to drink enough water before the scan to ensure I had a full bladder.

Am here but no hurry, in Costa, I texted Jess, and then leafed through a battered copy of *Metro* before she arrived half an hour or so later.

'Hi, love,' she said, giving me a hug.

'I'm so glad you're here,' I said, hugging her tightly back, feeling weirdly emotional at seeing a familiar face. Then I burst into tears again.

'Hey, hey. What's the matter?' she said.

I hadn't told her anything about the meeting with Max last night because I couldn't face going into it. So it all came out now, in between sobs.

'OK,' said Jess afterwards. 'He's in shock. And being a bit of a wanker. What a surprise, another man who's a dickhead.' An elderly woman in Costa jumped in her seat and turned to glare at us.

Jess didn't even notice. 'But listen, Lil, you were going to have this baby even before Max came back, even before he went missing. You don't need him. You made this decision before he knew. And course you're not on your own because I'm here.'

I smiled as I wiped my cheeks with a napkin. 'Thanks.'

'You're very welcome. Now tell me where we're going. This is exciting. Do you think they'll assume we're lesbians?'

Given that Jess had come to the hospital in her painting dungarees, I thought this was reasonably likely.

Thankfully, the appointment was on time because by midday my bladder was so full I had to walk into the sonographer's office with bandy legs, swaggering like a cowboy.

Dr Papadakis was a small man with a round face and neatly brushed hair who definitely thought Jess and I were together.

'And this is your partner, yes?' he said, smiling at Jess, as we both sat next to his desk and he asked me various medical questions.

'No no,' I said quickly. 'Friend. No partner.'

'All right. And do you have any elf problems?' went on Dr Papadakis.

I frowned at him. Elf problems? Problems with elves? I wondered if he was making a joke about Christmas.

'Um, no no. No problem with elves,' I said, still confused.

'No art issues?'

'He means health,' muttered Jess, 'and heart.'

'Ohhhh,' I said, 'yeah, a cyst on my left ovary. But they say it's fine, that it shouldn't be a problem?'

Dr Papadakis shrugged. 'It should not be a problem so long as you feel good? No complainings?'

'Nope,' I shook my head again, 'no complainings.'

'OK, that is the very best of news. And now if you don't mind getting up on this bed behind me, we will see the baby.'

I heaved myself slowly on to the bed, anxious that my bladder would burst over Dr Papadakis's floor and make a mess. Then he gave me some tissue paper and, as if playing a game of charades, demonstrated how to tuck the tissue paper into my knickers.

'It is because of the gel,' he said solemnly. 'To protect against the gel.'

I tucked the tissue paper into my knickers and pulled up my jumper.

Dr Papadakis squeezed gel that was so cold on to my stomach that I gasped. He reached for the scanning device and rubbed the cold gel across my belly, dangerously close to my bladder. If I was a spy who fell into enemy hands and they used this method to try and make me talk, I'd have given up every state secret.

And then, suddenly, on the screen, was the bean. A bigger bean than before, but still fairly bean shaped. 'Jess, look!'

After a few moments of staring, I turned my head to see she'd welled up.

'Pretty amazing, right?'

She nodded and wiped her face with her fingers. 'Incredible,' she whispered.

'And here, these are the arms and these, they are the legs,' said Dr Papadakis. He zoomed in. 'And look, this is her nose.'

'It's a girl?' I said quickly. Ever since finding out I was pregnant, I'd felt I was carrying a girl. Bad morning sickness can mean it's a girl, my app had told me.

'No, my apology.' Dr Papadakis paused and squinted at the screen. 'I cannot yet tell. It is too early. You want to have the sex?'

'No thank you,' I said. Even though I had my suspicions, I wanted to wait. 'I want to keep it a surprise.'

He smiled. 'I like that. I think it is better not to have the sex.'

From the corner of my eye, I could see Jess shaking with laughter.

'I am now going to take a few measurements,' he said, clicking on the screen. 'Just to check everything is 'elfy, but it looks perfect. And by my estimations you are due in June, around June ten.'

'Great.' Then I turned my head to Jess and muttered between gritted teeth, 'Stop it.'

'Sorry, I think it's partly a reaction to how surreal this is. That's your baby, Lil,' she said, sounding awed. 'Look at her. She looks like ET.'

'Jess!'

'What? ET is a nice alien.'

I rolled my eyes. 'I suppose. But you think it's a girl too?'

'Well, I'm not a trained medical professional but it's got to be. The last thing we need on this planet is another man.'

Then came a knock on the door. A nurse poked her head round it. 'Sorry to disturb, Dr Papadakis, but we've got Dad here.'

My first thought was that she was talking about her own dad, which I thought was strange of her. What was this nurse doing bringing her dad into my scan appointment? Then I realized she didn't mean her father and assumed it was Dennis, but what was he doing here? He didn't even know I was pregnant. Then Max appeared from behind the door, and I was so shocked that I couldn't think what to say. I just blinked at him several times while Dr Papadakis kept clicking away on the screen.

Then I panicked that he might be able to see the odd stray pube poking up from behind the tissue paper.

'Hi,' he said finally, still standing awkwardly half in the room, half out.

'Hi,' I said back.

'This is your father?' said Dr Papadakis, looking over his shoulder, a frown wrinkling his forehead.

'No, no, this is the baby's father,' I said.

'Oh, welcome, welcome, come in. How do you say it in English. The more, the happier.'

'Merrier,' I corrected, although I wasn't sure it applied in this case.

'Hi,' he said to Jess, holding out his hand. 'I'm Max.'

'Jess, and I guessed,' she said, leaving his hand hanging in the air for a second before shaking it. She stood up and looked pointedly at me. 'I'm going to step outside and leave you to it.'

Max moved aside as she left.

'Sit if you like?' I said, gesturing at the empty chair.

He sat and we watched while Dr Papadakis kept clicking away. He seemed blissfully ignorant of any awkwardness. 'And this is your baby's art,' he said, pointing to a small flashing area.

'He means heart,' I said from the side of my mouth to Max.

He didn't reply so I looked at him. He was staring at the screen.

'Max? You all right?'

'I'm fine,' he said, nodding, still gazing at it. 'I never really imagined… It's so weird, seeing it. I never thought…' He trailed off.

We both looked at the screen for several moments in silence. I felt something akin to relief, not only that he'd come but also at his tone. It wasn't accusing. He sounded softer, less angry. I glanced briefly across at him from the bed and his expression was much like mine at my first scan – stunned into silence by a little flickering beat.

'Can you tell… I mean, do you know if it's a boy or a girl yet?' said Max, his eyes sliding from the screen to Dr Papadakis.

Dr Papadakis glanced at me and then back to Max. 'I spoke to your wife, before you arrive, and she says you don't want to know.'

'Not wife,' I said quickly, practically shouting it so Dr Papadakis flinched in his seat. 'Just, er, friend.'

I turned my head towards Max. 'I thought kind of better to keep it a surprise?' A little bit of me wanted to say, 'Plus you only just showed up to the party,' but I figured that might ruin things.

'Oh. Sure, that makes sense,' he said.

I half-smiled back at him. He seemed a different person today, more like the Max on our first date. It almost made me feel wistful. Could there be anything more exciting than going through this with someone you love?

'OK, that is all done and everything is looking good, so your next scan is at twenty weeks,' said Dr Papadakis. 'You can get dressed. Here is some paper towel for the gel.'

'Thank you,' I said, glancing at Max, trying to shield him from the sight of me wiping the gloop from my knicker line. Then I zipped up my jeans and swung my legs down. Max was staring determinedly at the floor.

'I present to you the photograph,' said Dr Papadakis, holding it towards us. I hesitated, not wanting to grab it.

'You have it,' said Max.

'Sure?'

'I can do two?' ventured Dr Papadakis.

'Not if it's any trouble?' replied Max.

'Pffff,' said Dr Papadakis, tossing one hand in the air. 'Course it is no trouble. We have to do it all the time. People want them for the grandparents, the aunties, the cousin, the cat. Is easy.' We stood while he printed another before handing it to Max, then we said goodbye to him and stepped outside the room.

'I think it's this way,' I said, inclining my head down the corridor towards the waiting area.

Max nodded but then stopped suddenly, as if he couldn't walk and talk at the same time. 'Would you have time for a coffee?'

'Now?'

'Er, yeah.' I suddenly remembered the genetics centre. 'But what about the blood test?'

'Could we just have a coffee first?'

'Yeah, OK, let me just have a quick word with Jess.'

I was also desperate for a pee. If I didn't pee there was going to be the kind of accident that normally happened in my classroom.

'Meet you downstairs, at the Costa?' I said to him. 'It's just by the main entrance.'

He nodded and carried on through the waiting area while I walked over to Jess.

She looked up from her seat as I approached. 'All I can say is that your baby's going to be incredibly beautiful.'

I laughed. 'A giant with curly dark hair?'

'Yeah. I hate him but he's gorgeous, Lil. I quite want to be pregnant with his baby.'

I winced at her. 'He's said did I want to grab a coffee so do you mind if I do that? Sorry, I feel like a bad friend dumping you, but I figure we should talk.'

'Course,' she said, closing her book.

'OK, amazing, I'll ring you later. And thank you again for coming, you're the best.'

'Don't be silly, I wouldn't have missed that for anything. Or that comedy doctor.'

We hugged and then I hobbled to the nearest loo. I have never been so grateful to get there. Oh, that blissful feeling when you've been so desperate to go you think your bladder might pop inside you like a balloon (I've always wondered if this could happen inside the body, but never wanted to google it), and then you finally find a bathroom. Better than sex.

★

Max insisted on queuing at Costa while I stayed at the table, as if I suddenly couldn't stand for longer than five minutes. I sat staring at the scan picture – it was as if I were ferrying a cartoon around inside me. Big head, smaller body with a round stomach like a tennis ball, two little legs waving in the air. Jess was right, she did look a bit like ET.

He came back with two teas. Then he exhaled loudly. 'Right, OK, so can we start again? I'm sorry for yesterday.'

I blinked at him from across the table and tried to resist giving in. Don't wilt immediately, Lil, just because he's there in front of you, smelling like a sexy lumberjack.

'I don't get it,' I said eventually. 'I didn't expect you to be here or to want to come. Or… I kind of don't understand. You're all right with this all of a sudden?'

Max paused and frowned. 'I don't know,' he said finally.

'I don't know what to think, but I guess just as you said you knew it was the right thing to keep this baby, I knew this morning that it was the right thing to come today.'

I fished the tea bag out of my cup and dropped it in the lid. 'The thing I was most upset about yesterday was you thinking this was deliberate,' I said. 'It really, really wasn't. I know this is an incredibly weird situation, but I really did mean it about you not having to be involved. If you don't want to, that's fine.'

Max sat back in his seat and glanced at the table next to us where a male nurse in scrubs sat drinking from a paper cup.

'I think I basically just need some time, to think, to get my head straight,' said Max, after a few moments. 'It's been a weird month. A weird few months. The build-up to the climb, the climb, this, my parents…'

'You've told them about this?' Given that I was still waiting to tell my own when I arrived home for Christmas, I felt a fresh wave of guilt.

'No. Christ no,' replied Max. 'I'm trying to figure out how to do that at the moment.'

'Will they be… angry?'

'Not sure,' he said, after another long pause. 'I have a strained relationship with them. My brother died when I was younger, when I was a teenager. It was an accident. He was skiing too fast in France and hit his head, basically. But my parents hate what I do in the mountains as a result. They don't understand why I need to go near them.'

'I'm sorry,' I muttered, pretending I didn't know all this already from my extensive internet trawls.

He shook his head at me. 'It's all right. Del, that was his name… well, Arundel, but he shortened it… he loved it up there. Any altitude, any peak. So that's why I do what I do, I guess. I feel closest to him when I'm on a mountain. I couldn't imagine sitting at a desk or doing some boring City job. I never wanted to be cooped up but my father wants me to move home to Suffolk. There's this… house.'

Again, I tried to look innocent, as if this was all entirely new information.

'Anyway,' Max added, looking glum, 'he wants me to take over.'

'But you don't?'

'Not now, no.' Then he paused and sighed. 'I don't know. Maybe I'm too selfish.' Then he winced at me. 'I didn't mean to ignore you, by the way. Afterwards. I didn't reply to your messages, and I'm sorry. It wasn't… on purpose. It was just so hectic, planning the climb and focusing everything on that. And I'm honestly not much of a dater. My ex and I, we hadn't split that long ago.'

'It's all right,' I said, grateful for the apology but shrugging. 'Kind of irrelevant now.'

'Yeah,' he said, nodding slowly, before going on, 'Listen, I'm an explorer. I'm bad at emotion. A therapist would probably tell you I was repressed from school.' He paused and rolled his eyes at me. 'It might take me a while to figure this all out. But I don't want you to feel like you're totally alone.'

It felt like a small concession. 'But what about the paternity test?'

A cloud of something like shame crossed Max's face. 'I'm sorry, I guess it was maybe the shock. I don't think… I mean, well, I guess…' His eyes fell to the table, and then back up at me again.

'Listen…' I said, 'why don't we just do it? Then you'll know. You'll know for sure.' I could hardly believe I was the one pushing for this, but it suddenly mattered to me that there was no doubt in Max's mind. I wanted him to know that this baby was his.

He reached forward to fiddle with the plastic lid from my cup. 'I'm sorry,' he said again, flicking his eyes up to me. 'I know it seems like an asshole thing to demand. But if you don't mind and don't have to rush off anywhere?'

I shook my head. 'It's OK. Let's do it while we're here. It won't take long, right?'

'No, don't think so,' he said, dropping the lid and reaching for his phone. 'I can't remember what they said, hang on.'

He tapped at his phone and we sat in silence. Here I was, sitting like Humpty Dumpty opposite a man I barely knew, about to go and have a test to prove I was carrying his baby. But our conversation had given me a small burst of optimism. He wanted to be involved. We just had to figure out what that involvement looked like.

'Sorry,' he said, putting his phone down on the table. 'I've banged on about myself and I haven't even asked how you're feeling. If you're all right? Can you, er, feel anything yet?'

'No, not really. I'm a bit tired but otherwise fine. I did feel sick but that's gone.'

'But being sick is fine, right?' he asked, frowning. 'That's normal?'

'Yeah,' I said, smiling at him. 'Yeah, totally normal.'

'OK,' he said, nodding as if reassuring himself.

'Are you going away again?' I asked. I tried to sound as casual as I could, like a hairdresser asking if he was going anywhere nice for his holidays.

'No, not for a while. I need to be here. Well, between here and Suffolk anyway.'

'And are you all right?'

'Me? What do you mean?' Max looked confused, as if nobody had ever asked him that.

'Well, you know, after the climb and everything.'

He hunched up his shoulders, his cup of tea between both hands. 'I think so,' he said, after a short pause. 'I didn't think we'd make it back but we did. And I'm still glad I tried.' Then he looked up at me with a grin. 'I'll climb it the next time.'

'You're joking?'

He shrugged. 'It was just bad weather, we were unlucky. I could have got there.'

'You guys,' I said, shaking my head. 'You're mad.' I was relieved to be talking to him about something other than pregnancy, having a different conversation with him. It felt almost normal.

'We are pretty mad,' he admitted. 'But since I'm in London for a bit, I guess maybe we should hang out?'

I must have frowned since he quickly corrected himself. 'I mean, get to know one another. Since we don't, really.'

'As friends?' I blurted. Whoops, I wanted to poke myself in the eye with the little spoon in front of me. I wasn't sure what I felt towards Max by this point, but I certainly didn't want to scare him away.

Max looked embarrassed. 'Um, yeah… I mean… I don't know what… or how things will—'

'Sorry,' I said, interrupting and waving my hands to stop his stuttering. 'Don't worry. We'll work things out as we go along, right?'

He smiled gratefully back. 'Good plan.'

'OK, cool,' I said, before glancing at a clock on the wall behind his head, 'but I need to get home by three, so shall we head?'

★

As hospital appointments go, it was fairly quick. The genetics centre was in another building, up another lift and along another squeaky corridor, but once there we were seen straight away.

Max and I sat next to one another in the waiting area, each filling out a form. I ticked the various boxes. No history of heart disease. Not a smoker. Number of alcohol units a week: 0, sadly.

We were then ushered into a small clinic room by a large nurse called Abigail.

'Oh dear, I am afraid I am too fat and there's not much room in here,' she said, laughing, while pushing a trolley on wheels into the corner and opening a drawer to pull out several plastic packets. I winced and looked away. Wasn't good with needles. I'd cried so much over my BCG that Dennis had to come and collect me from school and I only stopped crying when he bought me a paper bag of strawberry Millions on the way home.

'Who first?' said Abigail, smiling brightly at us.

'Lil,' said Max, stepping back. 'After you.'

I sat down on the chair beside the trolley and rolled up my sleeve, then rested my forearm in the plastic trough on the armrest.

'OK, my darling, here we go,' said Abigail. She leant so close while tightening a tourniquet round my arm that I could see individual hairs curling at the nape of her neck and a little gold crucifix on a chain swung towards my face. Then Abigail picked up a plastic packet and tore the back of it off. I looked towards the other wall.

'You all right?' said Max.

'Fine,' I said, in a tight voice, 'just not going to look.'

'Deep breath and then there'll be a leeeeettle scratch,' said Abigail, and I held my breath as I felt the prick in my skin.

'There we go,' she said, seconds later. I looked back at my arm, the puncture already covered with a plaster. 'Good girl.'

Max and I swapped places and Abigail took his blood. I stood to his side so I couldn't see the needle again.

'All done, my beauties,' said Abigail, sticking a plaster on his arm. 'If you could just take this back up to the reception.'

'Terrific, thank you,' said Max, taking a sheet of paper from her.

Back in the waiting area, I sat down again and pretended to look at my phone while Max sorted the paperwork.

'Let's go,' he said, spinning round from the desk.

'When do we get the results?' I asked, as he held the door to the lino corridor open for me.

'Normally takes ten working days, but they said because it's Christmas it might not be until the new year.'

We reached the lift and he hit the down button. I didn't reply. I was busy wondering if Joseph the Carpenter would have asked for a paternity test from Mary. It would have been more understandable in their situation. At least I wasn't trying to claim my baby was the son of God. I glanced across at Max as we travelled down in the lift and wondered if I could make a joke about it, but decided probably not. Too soon.

Once back outside the hospital's main entrance, we turned to face one another.

'So, happy Christmas, I guess,' I said, feeling awkward. How to say goodbye after this afternoon? I felt as if I'd undergone an emotional assault course, suddenly desperate to get home and have a snooze before the uni drinks that evening.

'Yeah,' nodded Max, smiling back. 'Happy Christmas, Lil.'

He leant forward and, for half a second, I panicked that he was lunging, but he just kissed me softly on both cheeks. 'See you in January.'

★

Later that afternoon, I woke from an accidental afternoon nap with that groggy sensation of not quite knowing what decade it was or my own name, but hauled out my Mrs Snowman jumper from the drawer underneath my bed and made it to the pub in Notting Hill an hour later.

I walked in nervously, relieved to see Jake hadn't arrived yet, then spotted Jess at the bar, her back to me.

'Hello, wife,' I said, going up and putting a hand on her shoulder.

She spun to face me. 'Hi, my love, I want to hear all about this afternoon but quickly, what you having? I've been standing waiting for them to take my order for so long I might die of old age.'

'Er,' I looked behind the bar, 'usual please, a lemonade.'

'OK, you take this,' she said, nodding at a bottle of red wine the barman had just put down in front of us, 'I'll bring ours and the glasses.'

'Where's Alexi?'

'Stuck with some work thing, so he's going to text when he's on his way.'

I followed Jess to a table in the back of the pub where our old Edinburgh flatmates sat – Nats, Bells and Lucy. We'd lived together for the final two years of uni and been an inseparable fivesome. It was only in recent years that we'd split into two groups because Nats, Bells and Lucy got married and overnight became more grown up. They threw dinner parties with linen napkins and different glasses for red and white wine, for example, while Jess and I continued to eat crisps and drink cheap house wine in pubs.

We all hugged and did the usual – 'it's been for ever,' 'where have you been?', 'how are you?' while Jess poured the wine.

'Nats, how's Rosie?' I asked, relieved that I remembered her one-year-old's name. At a certain point, when you reached the tipping point on the seesaw, when more of your friends are married than not and little bald babies start sprouting on social media like mushrooms, it becomes quite hard to remember all their names.

Nats rattled on about Rosie for a few minutes then Jess started talking about Alexi. 'So we met at an exhibition,' she told the others, 'and there was just something about him. Wasn't there, Lil? She was there,' she explained to the others.

'Yep,' I said, nodding. 'I could tell the second I saw you guys chatting.'

'He travels the whole time for work so he's away a lot but, yeah, I'm just happy. Oh, and he's taking me to Venice for New Year. I forgot to tell you that earlier,' she said, looking at me.

'Oooooh, romantic,' said Bells, in a comedy voice. 'What if he gets down on one knee?'

Jess grinned and shook her head. 'No way, not yet.'

'Would you say yes though?'

She bit her lip while thinking. 'I mean, it would be crazy. But probably. I guess, at this stage, we don't mess around, right? We're grown-ups. We know more about what we want than, say, ten years ago when we were drinking apple sours in Voltaire.'

'Grim, don't mention that place,' said Lucy, pretending to shudder. It was the Edinburgh nightclub where we spent our student loans and I believed you could get an STD from the loo seats. Someone always drank too much, someone always threw up, someone always cried. All the hallmarks of a top student night.

'Anyway, what about you, Lil?' went on Luce. 'What's going on? How's school?'

'Finally broken up,' I said, 'but they're mostly sweet this year. Apart from Luke Walker's son Roman, who's a little brute.'

'Shut up, he's in your class?' said Bells.

Shit, I wasn't thinking. She was a journalist for *The Sun*.

'Yes, but I'm not telling you anything else about him, so don't even think about it,' I said, narrowing my eyes at her.

'Boooooooring,' she said, hitting me on the arm.

'And I suppose the other vague bit of news I've got is that I'm pregnant,' I said.

Bells, Nats and Lucy froze. Jess laughed.

'And that is exactly the reaction I was hoping for,' I said, having a sip of lemonade.

'Wow,' said Bells, 'I mean, congratulations!'

'Thanks,' I said.

'I can't believe I haven't seen you for this long. I didn't even realize you were dating again,' said Nats. 'But... I mean... shit. Clearly you are. Which is great. Just, who is he?'

'This is the funny part,' I said.

Jess laughed again and the other three frowned at me.

'What d'you mean?' said Lucy.

'I'm not actually with anyone. It was a one-night stand.'

'Fuuuuuuuck,' said Bells.

'Jesus,' said Nats. 'Are you in touch? Does he know?'

'He does now. But I didn't tell him for a couple of weeks because I wasn't sure what to do.'

'How pregnant are we talking?' said Lucy.

'Just over 12 weeks, had my scan today.'

'And all good?' said Nats.

I nodded and smiled. Then reached into my bag for the photo and held it up. 'Guys, meet ET.'

'Lilian Bailey, you cannot call your baby ET,' said Nats, reaching for the photo.

'What is wrong with everyone?' said Jess. 'He was a nice alien.'

Nats ignored her and carried on. 'Look at it, Lil, I can't get over this. Did the father, whatever he's called, did he go to the scan?'

I looked at Jess. 'No, just my life partner here.'

'How come?' said both Nats and Lucy, frowning at me. 'Is he not OK with it?'

I wondered how honest to be. But they were close girl-friends and I didn't see that it had to be any great secret.

'OK, if I tell you guys something, can we keep it between us? Bells, I'm looking at you. This is honestly to go no further.'

'Course,' said Lucy.

'Bells, promise?'

'Yes, obviously, get on with it, it feels like you're about to say it's Prince William,' she said.

'Not him, although weirdly I think they're mates, but

it's that explorer, the one who went missing recently, Max Rushbrooke.'

Bells, needless to say, was the first to reply: 'Holy fucking Christ.'

Then Luce: 'You KIDDING me?'

Then Nats: 'Who's he?'

'Nats, please try and read the news,' said Bells. 'He's that one who got lost in Pakistan last month, went missing on a climb. But then he was found and all was fine blah blah blah. But hang on, if he's been larking about in the Pakistani mountains, how come he's got time to be getting people pregnant in London?'

'It was just before he went.'

'How d'you meet?'

'Dating app.'

'Oh no, am sorry, guys, Alexi can't make it,' said Jess suddenly, looking at her phone.

'How come?' I said.

'Not sure, some deal,' she said, sliding her bottom lip over her top one and looking at me.

I grimaced back at her. 'I'm sorry, love.'

'Would another bottle help?' asked Bells.

'Yeah, go on then,' said Jess, although she looked sad.

'You've got Venice,' I told her, as Bells stood up. 'Think about that.'

She nodded and smiled. Then I looked across at the door just as Jake came in, and behind him, I assumed, India. Tiny, like a human doll, with blonde hair cascading in that annoyingly deliberate way, half tucked into her coat collar, half flowing over it.

'Oh look,' I said to the others at the table, inclining my head towards them so they knew what I meant.

Jake and Indy went straight to the bar.

'How are things with you guys?' said Lucy, turning back to me.

'Dunno. Haven't seen him since he left.'

'You going to tell him?'

'About ET?'

'About your baby, yes.'

I looked across at the bar where he was standing with his arm round Indy, and they were laughing together at something the barman said. 'Not sure yet.'

'Lil,' warned Jess.

'Just joking,' I said. 'You know I'm not brave enough to cause a scene.'

We carried on chatting at our table, the odd person from uni coming up to say hi and then drifting away again. I explained more about Max, about our meeting yesterday and then the scan and the blood test today. What a twenty-four hours.

'I guess he thought you'd spurgled him,' said Bells.

'What?' I snapped.

'Spurgled,' she repeated. 'It means sperm burgling. He thinks you're a spurgler.'

'Gross, can you stop saying that word?'

'It's on Urban Dictionary,' she went on, tapping at her

phone and then reading from it. '"To be sperm burgled – to become intentionally inseminated without the consent or knowledge of the poor bloke involved in the intercourse."'

I sighed. 'It's not true though.'

'We know that,' said Bells, 'we know you. But he doesn't necessarily. Happens to celebrities all the time. It's supposedly what happened to Boris Becker with that woman in the cupboard. She gave him a blow-job and then she threw it up inside her. Couple of months later she tells him she's pregnant.'

'Seriously?' said Nats. 'What did you call it again?'

'Spurgling,' Bells said again, with authority. 'Or baby-trapping. Entrapment. It all means the same thing. Like Liz Hurley too; that's what she was accused of by that billionaire.'

'Well I haven't done that,' I said forcefully. 'It was an accident.'

'So what are you going to do?' said Lucy. 'With him, I mean?'

I shrugged. 'Work it out as we go along, apparently.'

'So you're not together?'

I shook my head. 'Uh-uh. It kind of complicates things, I guess, going from date one to pregnant.'

'Oh, love,' said Nats, putting her hand on mine. 'I'm sorry, what a nightmare. Except it's not obviously,' she added quickly, 'because you're having a baby. But just let us know what we can do to help?'

'Thanks, team,' I said, smiling gratefully at them.

They decided to order yet another bottle and we moved on to different topics. The jokes were mostly about husbands instead of boyfriends but otherwise we could have been back in Edinburgh. It was comforting. We could not see each other for ten years, but then meet up and fall straight back into the same stories: 'Do you remember the time that Jess got stuck in the bathroom at that guy's flat and they had to call the fireman?'

By eleven, though, I was tired and sober while the rest of them started singing carols at the table, so I figured it was time to slope home. But before I left I wanted to say hello to Jake, who was sitting across the pub at a different table with another group from uni, mostly his old football team. Even if it was just a hello, I wanted to say something. It felt childishly hostile to ignore him.

I hugged the girls and promised to keep them updated. 'Happy Christmas, my love,' I said to Jess. 'We'll speak.'

'Course, and look after ET. I'm excited about next year when we can dress her like an elf.'

I left them singing 'Silent Night', braced myself and walked up to Jake's table.

'Hey,' I said, waving lamely at him.

They were all roaring with laughter which suddenly stopped and Jake stood up, squeezing round the table towards me. He had his Mr Snowman jersey on too and I was a *tiny bit* tickled to see the beginnings of a belly underneath it. Not that I could talk.

'Nice jumper,' I said, as he kissed me hello. So strange, he smelt the same. The memory of it took me back to our bedroom in Angel.

'Thanks,' he said, 'someone with excellent taste got it for me. How you doing?'

'I'm great,' I said, smiling as broadly as I could. 'Going home tomorrow. Pantomime, Norwich game, the usual.'

'Course, what is it this year?'

'*Snow White*,' I said. 'Mum's Grumpy.'

He threw back his head. 'Ha, amazing.'

'How are you?'

'Yeah, good.' And then he suddenly turned back to the table, 'Sorry, Lil, this is Indy, Indy, this is Lil.'

She stayed sitting at the table but held out a hand. 'Hi,' she said. 'Nice to meet you.' Although her face betrayed her because she didn't look like it was nice at all. Her expression looked like she'd just smelled drains.

'Hi,' I said back, shaking her hand. 'Really good to meet you.' I was lying too. I'd rather have hung out with Putin.

'Listen, I was just on my way home, so I'll leave you guys to it,' I said. 'Just wanted to say hi, and happy Christmas.'

Jake leant in towards me and gave me a hug. 'Happy Christmas.' My cheek on his shoulder, I inhaled and smelled him again. But then we pulled back.

'See you, guys,' I said, turning towards the door again. It wasn't the right time to tell him about ET. That could wait. Or maybe he didn't need to know. Maybe we'd moved beyond that. When should you stop telling your ex about milestones in your life? When did they just become another person you used to know? On the Tube home, I realized maybe Jake and I had got to that point already.

I didn't sleep because I lay in bed thinking about that word, spurgle. Then I looked up Bells's definition of it on my phone.

It led me down an internet wormhole. First, a long piece titled 'Confessions from women who baby-trapped'. Their stories varied – some worried their boyfriends were about to leave them, others wanted to ensnare a rich baby-daddy, one woman pierced holes in a condom to get pregnant and persuade the man in question to leave his wife, another lied about being on the pill and got pregnant so he'd propose. The final story made me shudder. It was by a woman called Veronica, who said, 'He told me he'd always be there for me if I got pregnant, so I did in order that I'd never lose him.'

I found myself scrolling down a long thread in a forum on another tab, in answer to a post originally started by a mother who feared her 22-year-old son had been trapped by a one-night stand and was worrying about the legal implications. She'd told him she was on the pill, apparently. The comments under this weren't helpful.

'Babies are a well-known side effect of having sex,' snarked someone called Mrs Pestilence.

'I was the child born in a similar situation when the father didn't want one. My mother said she was on the pill. It's truly shit not to be wanted and my life has been very difficult because of it,' wrote another.

'Women are allowed to choose a way out of pregnancy. Men are expected to suck it up without a word of concern,' said Aquafresh16.

I read and read. There were fifteen pages of comments on this one post, mostly criticizing the woman's son for trusting that his one-night stand was telling the truth about being on the pill and slamming them both for being so 'irresponsible', 'immature' and 'stupid'.

Was that what Max thought? I wondered, finally forcing myself to put down my phone and try to sleep. Did he really think I'd been so calculating? And would other people think that too?

CHAPTER SEVEN

I CAUGHT THE 10.11 from Liverpool Street the next morning, relieved to be escaping London. Generally, we're all relieved to finish work for Christmas, right? We've had weeks of drinking, of enforced merriment with colleagues, and paper hats and dry turkey. Diets have gone out the window. Everyone has a cold. It is acceptable to have pigs-in-blankets for breakfast. We can't remember the last time we woke without a hangover.

This year was different for me, obviously, but I could see the evidence everywhere at the train station that we'd reached those final, desperate few days before Christmas. People looked like the 'before' version of themselves – pale, bloated, sniffing. Travellers clutched their coffee as if the cup contained immortality instead of a flat white. The Boots' windows were decorated with tinsel and huge posters for First Defence. Shoppers were panic buying presents in Hotel Chocolat.

The train journey home felt like the first moment of peace all week. With my hands circling a cup of tea, I gazed through the window at London vanishing behind me and and plotted how to tell my parents. I had to. No excuses. I'd promised myself I'd tell them over Christmas, once I'd had my scan and knew that my baby had the right number of ears and legs. I wondered whether to present it as a Christmas miracle.

'Hey, guys, guess what? Mary's not the only one who's knocked up this Christmas!'

'Hey, guys, have I got a present for you this year!'

In the end, I blurted it out just before we had lunch later that day when Dennis tried to pour me a glass of wine.

'But it's Christmas,' he said, as I put my hand over the rim of the glass. 'You feeling all right?'

'Ha ha, very funny,' I said, feeling a rush of adrenalin as I knew what I was about to say. 'I'm not really drinking, actually, because I'm pregnant.'

Mum, retrieving the plates from the oven, put them down on the side with a loud crash. Dennis froze, as if playing his own game of musical statues, wine bottle tilted over his glass.

'What?' said Mum.

I gritted my teeth and pulled a face. 'Yeah. Sorry. Bit of a shock. But I thought I should tell you now. Surprise!'

Dennis put the bottle down.

'Pull a chair out, Den, quick, before you have a turn,' said Mum, fanning herself with an oven glove. 'Lil, love, how has this happened? I'm not judging,' she said, holding one hand in the air, 'I just didn't know you were... planning anything.'

'I wasn't,' I said, 'that's the thing. It was an accident.'

'With who?' said Mum, in a high-pitched voice.

'Nobody you know. Well, nobody I really know, to be fair. A one-night thing.'

'Oh my God,' said Dennis, lowering himself on a kitchen chair.

'But it's fine, and I'm happy, and I had my twelve-week scan yesterday and the baby's perfect,' I said. 'So please don't worry that this is a disaster because it's really not. Actually, look...'

I pulled out the photo of ET from my bag, which was already starting to look crumpled and had smudgy fingerprints on it.

Mum took the photo and put a hand to her mouth. 'Oh, Lil, look at him. Den, look. Oh, you need your reading glasses. No stay there, I'll get them. Where are they?'

She disappeared to the living room and Dennis reached for my hand.

'But you're all right?' he asked, cocking his head at me, as if trying to see through my skull and into my brain.

'Totally, I promise. I'm just sorry to give you guys a shock.'

Mum bustled back in. 'Here you go, they're dirty, you need to give them a clean.'

'Give them here.' Dennis put the glasses on and Mum passed him the picture.

'Looks just like you,' he said, inspecting it and then peering up at me over the top of his glasses.

I laughed. 'A prawn with a big head?'

'Something like that,' he said, winking at me and handing back the picture.

'But who is this mystery father?' went on Mum.

'He's an explorer, called Max.' I couldn't face going into his background now. I wasn't sure they'd approve. 'Mum, I called you the week afterwards actually, do you remember? Saying I'd met someone but he hadn't messaged?'

'Oh yes,' said Mum, before narrowing her eyes at me. 'I thought you said that was a one-off thing?'

'Well it was,' I said. 'Or that was what I thought, anyway.'

She put her hands on her hips and glared. 'Lilian Bailey, did I teach you nothing about looking after yourself?'

'Yes, and I was on the pill,' I interjected quickly. 'But somehow it still happened.'

Her glare remained.

'Look, I'm thirty-one, not seventeen. This isn't a catastrophe. I've got to sort out where I'll live and I haven't told school yet. But it's not like women don't do this on their own these days.'

Mum and Dennis exchanged a look.

'I know it's not conventional, but when have we been conventional?' As I said this, my eye fell upon the picture Mum had put up above the kitchen table when I was eight and had gone to World Book Day at school dressed as Virginia Woolf, with talcum powder in my hair to make it grey. It had been Mum's idea since she wanted me to go as a 'strong' woman, but I'd felt silly when everyone else arrived as Matilda and Tinkerbell.

'Fair enough,' she said. And then her voice cracked as she welled up. 'Oh, let's have another look at that picture. I'm going to be a grandma!'

Dennis looked up at me from the table. 'Lil, love, if you're happy, we're happy.' And then he nodded at my stomach. 'I just hope he's going to be a Norwich City fan.'

'I have a weird feeling it's going to be a girl.'

'All right, well, I hope she's going to be a Norwich City

fan,' he said. 'Third generation,' he added, beaming at me. And I couldn't quite tell, but it looked like Dennis's eyes were swimming behind his glasses.

★

The first performance of Mum's pantomime was that night so she walked over to the village hall after lunch for a final rehearsal and hair and make-up.

'You can just go as you are, surely, if you're playing Grumpy?' said Dennis, one of his less good jokes.

He and I went for a quick drink in the Fox and Cushion before this grand opening night. It was one of our rituals. We'd done this ever since I was little. I used to have a Coke while Dennis had his pint and he taught me how to flip beer mats on the edge of the bar. It was the first place I'd ever tasted beer, one Christmas when I was about seven or eight and Dennis let me have a sip of his. I'd spat it straight back into his glass.

'Hiya, Ted,' I said, as I climbed on to a bar stool. Ted was the landlord, a village institution and gargantuan man who'd run the pub as long as I could remember, possibly since Victorian times.

'Welcome home, Lil, what you having?'

'Lemonade, please.'

'And a pint of Beeston, Ted,' said Dennis. 'And give us one of the programmes, will you?'

Ted handed Dennis a *Snow White* programme from a pile at the side of the bar; Dennis handed it to me.

I ran my eye down the cast list. Stephen Fry, unsurprisingly, did not feature but I lolled where it said 'Grumpy – Jackie Bailey.'

'So you're all right then?' said Dennis, lowering his pint glass and smacking his lips.

Ah, I was in for one of Dennis's life chats. Bless him, we had these, usually in the pub when he sensed I had something to talk about. Mum was good at brusque, no-nonsense advice. But if she gave me any guidance, I had to take it otherwise she grumbled for several days that I never listened to anything she said. Dennis was better at gentle discussions, at prodding me in the right direction but not forcing me there.

'I'm great,' I told him emphatically. 'It was… a shock. And I don't know how things will pan out but…'

'How do you want them to pan out?' he asked.

'Er, honestly? I don't quite know. I want him to be involved in ET's life. She's half his. I want her to know her father… Not that DNA means everything, obviously,' I said quickly, looking sheepishly at Dennis.

'Do you like him?'

'Romantically?'

Dennis shrugged. 'Maybe, but also, as a person. As the future father of your child. As someone who will be in your life in some way for ever now.' He lifted his pint again. 'Or, at least for the next eighteen years or so.'

I blew out my cheeks, trying to weigh it up. 'I think so. As a person, I mean. I had a sense about him when we first met. Like, there was something about him that I recognized.

I don't mean physically. I'd never seen him before in my life. But it was like there was something about him that I sort of… got, that I felt like I understood, d'you know what I mean?'

Dennis nodded over his glass.

'Although then he went climbing and disappeared,' I added.

I'd filled Mum and Dennis in about who Max was, and what he did, after lunch. Mum's left-wing sensibilities bridled on discovery that he was the son of a viscount, but then I'd googled a picture of him to show her and she'd stopped saying Britain should have had a revolution, 'like they did in France,' and gushed about how handsome Max was instead.

'But he came to the scan and wants to help?' asked Dennis.

'Yeah,' I said, before repeating it. 'Yeah. It was obviously a shock for him too. But we've said we're going to work it out as we go along.'

'That sounds very sensible.'

'And if disaster strikes, well, Mum did this first bit on her own, with me, I mean. Before you came along and saved us.' I grinned at him again.

'You're never on your own, love, you've got us,' he said, squeezing my hand.

'Luckily,' I said, squeezing it back.

Half an hour later, the village hall was filling up. Dennis and I had bagged seats on the aisle – 'You might need to nip out and spend a penny.' The atmosphere, if not quite as electric as if we were at an opening night on the West End, was still upbeat, the smell of mulled cider wafting about because Ted's son, Al, had set up a stall at the back flogging it in paper cups.

Then it was showtime and the village hall curtain was drawn back. It was the start of proper Christmas for me, this amateur performance. The scenery was made of cardboard, the beards from cotton wool and there was always at least one person who forgot their lines. But Dennis and I always cried with laughter.

One year the production was *Peter Pan*. I can't remember who Mum played, I was about six, but Tinkerbell had instructed all those who believed in fairies to stand up on their chairs and turn round three times, sprinkling fairy dust around us. Dennis stood on his chair immediately, pulling me up with him, and we turned round three times while spraying fairy dust together. I remember laughing so much I thought I might faint.

Mum's lines made us howl with laughter that night. Dressed in a brown felt waistcoat and shorts, with white tights and buckled shoes and a pointy brown hat, she trudged about the stage looking furious, moaning about having porridge for breakfast 'again', refused to get into the bathtub, until the other dwarves dunked her, and at one point blamed the wicked stepmother for 'austerity cuts' with a knowing wink to the audience. Classic Mum.

*

I woke on Christmas Day in the same single bed I'd slept in since I was about three. And my room hadn't changed much since I left for uni. It still contained a single bed, a chest of drawers covered in stickers, a lava lamp I asked for on my fifteenth birthday, a poster of Leonardo di Caprio from *Titanic*, a bookshelf which contained everything from *Charlotte's Web* and *Pippi Longstocking* to my uni books, withered, heavenly annotated copies of *Beowulf* and *Paradise Lost* among them. All of these childhood mementoes made it quite an odd place to masturbate. Plus, my parent's bedroom was on the other side of the bathroom, which was sandwiched between our rooms. But I was feeling more sexually frustrated than I could remember. Sorry, not very holy. But I was.

The books said this could happen. After the hideousness of the first three months, you have a surge of hormones. But whereas most pregnant women could roll over and tap their other half on the shoulder, I was on my own and would have to look after myself. Plus, I'd left my vibrator at home (unfestive to pack your vibrator for the Christmas holidays at your parents'), so I was going to have to do it the manual way. A happy-Christmas-to-me present.

I lay there wondering what to fantasize about. Then I thought of Max, of the night we'd gone back to his place, of the drawn-out slowness of it, the way he had moved me around his bed. Except I was getting ahead of myself, I couldn't think about the actual sex bit yet because this normally took a while. I needed more build-up. In an effort to inject a bit of excitement into our sex life, Jake and I once watched porn together on his laptop in bed. But he'd chosen a clip which was mostly close-ups of a guy ramming this woman with his veiny penis on very nasty bed linen. The poor woman was trying to sound grateful but she couldn't have been, given what he was doing to her. Plus, he'd looked a bit like Mr Hooper at school and Mr Hooper absolutely did not do it for me.

I moved my hand between my legs and thought about Max in the pub, the moment he'd looked at me and said, 'Can I kiss you?' And then he'd leant forward, reached for the back of my head and pulled me in towards him. There, that was it, I gently worked my finger around my clit, feeling a slight tingle.

I carried on thinking about sitting in the pub, kissing him, his beard tickling my chin, one hand in my hair, the other on my thigh. I pressed harder with my finger, and faster, and started grinding my hips into my mattress.

Then, all of a sudden, we were back in Max's house, because you can do that in fantasies, you don't have to worry about practicalities like whether you got the Tube or a taxi. We were on his sofa and I was straddling him, my knees either side of his thighs. We were fully clothed but he started to unbutton my shirt. Aaaah, that felt gooooooood.

I suddenly heard the click of the bathroom light and the extractor fan whirr. Then came the sound of basin taps running and Mum humming. Fuck's sake. That was not part of my fantasy. I pulled my hand up briefly to reach for the earplugs on my bedside table and put them in.

Back to it.

I was straddling Max as he unbuttoned my shirt, slowly, and then he pulled my bra down, a bit roughly, but not so roughly that he damaged the nice bra, and then he started sucking each nipple in turn while I threw my head back and gasped. Yep, this was doing the trick. My finger sped up again, and ran down to where I could feel myself getting wetter, and then back up as I imagined Max and I were suddenly in the same position but naked on this sofa – again, something you could do with fantasies, the mechanics of undressing were less awkward and clothes could melt away – and we were rocking together while he still flicked his tongue over my erect nipples. Fucccck, my body pressed back hard against my finger and then—

'All yours, Den, but I'd give it a couple of minutes,' I heard Mum shout, through my earplugs.

Jesus CHRIST.

I screwed my eyes shut even harder and tried to maintain the image of me on top of Max. Rocking, riding, heavy breathing. He put his hands around and held my arse while we kissed. 'You're so wet,' he whispered in my ear. 'You wanted this, didn't you, you needed this, you wanted me inside you.'

Again, in real life, Max was a posh boy and didn't talk like that. But in my head he had the accent of an Etonian and the vocabulary of a docker, and it was pushing me closer and closer. My finger was now rubbing my clit so hard and so fast that my forearm was aching, but I knew I was seconds away.

'Dirty, dirty girl,' Max said again in my ear.

Then I heard Dennis shout outside the bathroom. 'Pop the kettle on, Jacks. I'll be ten minutes.'

Brief pause.

'Maybe fifteen.'

And then the bathroom door closed and the buzz of the extractor fan started up again.

Fuck's SAKE. I stopped all activity under the duvet. This was hopeless. I couldn't do this while Dennis was sitting on the loo on the other side of the wall. It would have to wait.

*

'Happy Christmas, darling,' said Mum when I appeared downstairs a few minutes later in tracksuit bottoms and my old dressing gown. I hugged her and quickly washed my hands at the kitchen sink since Dennis was still occupying the bathroom and, traditionally, on Christmas morning at home we had smoked salmon and eggs on toast and I didn't want to be sharing slices of toast with mucky fingers. Mum had Radio 4 on in the background and the sound of a choir singing 'Once in Royal David's City' was competing with the sound of the kettle.

'We've got to have that caviar, too,' I reminded her, as Mum took the salmon out of the fridge.

'Oh yes!' she said. 'How exciting.' She fished about in the back of the fridge and brought out a tin that said Kitekat on it.

'That's Ginger's food.'

She squinted at it. 'Right you are, hang on.' Then she brought out the caviar. 'We should wait for Dennis. I don't know what's taking him so long upstairs.'

I didn't answer. I was worrying about whether I was allowed caviar in the first place. Sushi was banned, I knew, but what about fish eggs?

'I'm not sure I'm allowed it,' I said, picking up my phone to google it.

'**Can pregnant women eat caviar,**' I typed.

'Oh yeah, it's fine if it's pasteurized,' I said, reading from my phone.

'Come on then, let's crack it open. Where is that man? DEN, HURRY UP, WE'RE OPENING THE CAVIAR.'

I heard footsteps above the kitchen which meant Dennis was on the move. He appeared a few moments later in the same jersey he always wore on Christmas Day – a woolly jumper from the Eighties, with white mountains and green pine trees knitted across it.

'Look, it's the Virgin Mary,' he said, greeting me with arms wide for a hug.

'Happy Christmas,' I said, folding into him.

'Happy Christmas pet,' he replied. 'Now then, where's this caviar?'

'I'm opening it,' said Mum, 'Lil's setting the table, Den you make the coffee. Oh, and open that champagne in the fridge.'

We did our separate jobs and sat down a few minutes later, the caviar in the middle of the table as if a sacrifical offering.

'How do we eat it?' said Dennis.

'I think just with a spoon,' Mum replied, eyeing the tin nervously. 'Lil, you first.'

I scooped at the tin with a teaspoon. The consistency was softer than I expected, like running a teaspoon through a tub of Lurpak. Then I sniffed my spoon. 'Fishy,' I said, frowning at it. The little black eggs looked like slimy poppy seeds glued together on the tip of the spoon. 'Here goes,' I said, before trying it.

The taste was overpoweringly fishy at first, but then it changed and became more delicate in my mouth. Buttery and rich. I wanted another spoon instantly but Mum had the tin.

'It's quite nice, isn't it?' she said, before licking her teeth. 'I'm not sure I'd pay thousands of pounds for it, but it's perfectly pleasant.'

'Nah, not for me,' said Dennis, having tried a minuscule nibble off the end of his spoon.

I had a couple more mouthfuls but was then defeated by the richness.

'We'll give the rest to Ginger,' said Mum. Which is how our cat ended up eating £843 worth of beluga caviar out of a bowl that said 'Feed me or the goldfish gets it.'

The rest of our day passed as usual. Mum refused to go to church because she didn't believe. Not that I believed either but Dennis liked going for the carols so I always went with him. Castleton's church, St Mary's, was tiny, and cold, so you had to arrive early if you wanted to sit in a pew instead of a dusty, fold-out chair at the back. I sang self-consciously through the carols and shook hands with Vicar Peter afterwards, feeling guilty that, as usual, I had forgotten to bring anything for the collection plate.

Then it was presents. Mum clapped with joy at her Frida Kahlo side plates; Dennis kissed me on the head after opening his book and said it was exactly what he wanted.

I got a blue herringbone blanket for my bed in Brixton and

a new biography of Maya Angelou from Mum and Dennis, a bottle of posh olive oil from Ginger, bubble bath from Gerald and a keyring in the shape of a chicken from the chickens.

'That's very clever of them, how did they know I needed one?' I asked Mum, grinning.

'My chickens are highly intelligent,' she replied.

The major surprise of the day was that I got a message from Max. All right, it didn't say much – **Happy Christmas Lil, hope you and the small person are well X** – but it felt significant that he was thinking about me on Christmas Day, a day when you only bothered getting in touch with people you properly cared about.

I hadn't braved sending anything to Max because a Christmas Day message seemed too intimate. I'd tried to imagine him at home in Suffolk, in the huge house I'd seen on Google. I'd wondered if he and his parents sat at a long dining room table, like in *Beauty and the Beast*; Max on one side, his mum and dad at each end, a few candlesticks down the middle. My own Christmas was quite different. I spent the remainder of the evening on the sofa composing a reply to him while Dennis grumbled about the new *Star Wars* film on telly. I wrote out six different versions in Notes (again) so I didn't accidentally send any of them, and finally decided that I should be brief, but throw in a joke.

Happy Christmas! Hope you've had a lovely day. I've eaten so much I feel eight months' pregnant instead of three. Xxx

On an even less festive note, Jess WhatsApped me pictures of all the underwear she'd bought for her New Year's eve flit to Venice with Alexi, including a lacy black bra which had cut-out holes you poked your nipples through. I looked down at my own chest, bursting from my T-shirt bra, and made a mental note to go maternity shopping when I got back to London.

★

The days between Christmas and New Year blurred as I ate 76,000 further calories, caught up with old primary school friends in the pub, went for walks along the beach with Mum and to a Norwich game with Dennis. Mum had never been interested in the football so I'd always gone instead. The bottom drawer in my old bedroom contained all my old shirts in Canary colours, green and yellow, and one of my earliest memories was Dennis buying me hot chocolate from a man who used to push a trolley about the perimeter of the pitch, pouring it from an urn.

'Are we ever going to meet this Max?' he asked me, on the way back from the game. We'd lost 4–1 to Hull, so I knew Dennis wanted something else to think about.

'Course you are,' I said, although I wasn't sure when. It felt like I was doing life backwards, having a baby with a man I barely knew, who hadn't met my family.

I'd always assumed, in a blithe, unthinking way, I'd have children. I couldn't envisage them, but when younger, I'd assumed that at some hazy point in the future I'd meet someone and do everything I'd watched my friends do. Date someone for a couple of years, move into a house with nice lamps. Go on a hot holiday somewhere – Italy? South Africa? – and pretend to be surprised when he proposed. Girls often did that. 'I literally had no idea!' they'd swear afterwards, even though in their engagement photo on Instagram – mouths wide as pies – they had perfectly manicured nails which suggested pre-meditated planning.

Anyway, I'd do all that (but be less nauseating about it), then hopefully have a baby. Maybe two of them. Siblings like Jess and Clem seemed to have an invisible bond that I longed for. I put a hand on ET and looked out of the car window at the navy sky, the light disappearing on the horizon. Was having her by myself just history repeating itself? A pattern which I was predisposed to follow?

'What are our resolutions then?' Mum asked a couple of nights later, on New Year's Eve. We were in the pub. We always came to the pub on New Year's Eve and stayed until about five minutes after midnight then tottered home. Although I wasn't sure I'd make it to midnight this year.

'I'm going to finish writing my bloody book,' said Dennis. 'And Norwich are going to come top of the league.'

'That's a wish, Den, not a resolution,' snapped Mum.

'I know, but we can do things we're hoping for too, can't we?'

'All right, in that case I want to get better at my t'ai chi and have a woman president in America. Lil?'

'Er, to have this baby and for everything to be all right?'

'Course it's going to be all right,' said Dennis, putting his arm round my shoulders.

Jess texted me just after midnight, a selfie of her and Alexi holding champagne flutes in Venice.

I sent back a selfie of me and my main man (Dennis) in the pub.

CHAPTER EIGHT

AT LEAST, BACK IN London, I had some privacy. After returning from Norfolk for the holidays, my vibrator was getting way more action than my phone and I'd bought two packets of batteries which lived in the drawer next to it so I never ran out. I'd glanced down at myself a couple of nights ago while in action and felt depressed. I looked like a masturbating space hopper.

There was no hiding my stomach any more. Or my tits, which now entered a room a few minutes before the rest of me. My new shape meant I had to confess to Miss Montague, which I did the day before the boys came back to school to avoid any staffroom rumours. I emailed her to make an appointment and she told me to come in at 3 p.m. I dressed in the loosest shirt I had, over my stretchiest jeans, and spent as much time on my make-up as if I was going on a date. I wanted to look as if I was fully in control.

'Come in,' she said, when I knocked on her door that afternoon.

I pushed open the door and put on my broadest smile. 'Happy New Year.'

She was writing something at her desk so didn't look up.

'Forgive me if I don't say it back,' she snapped, still scribbling. 'I find it tiring having to say "Happy New Year" ninety-six times a day for the first half of January, so I don't.'

'Very sensible,' I said, sitting down on the chair in front of her desk.

'Now,' she continued, in the same, clipped tone, 'what can I help you with?'

'Well it might come as a bit of a surprise,' I started, 'but I'm pregnant.'

Miss Montague blinked at me twice and frowned. Then she tried what I suspect was meant to be a smile but came out more like a grimace. 'That is a surprise. Congratulations.'

'Thank you,' I said.

'I didn't know you were…' And then her face suddenly darkened. 'Miss Bailey, it's not one of the fathers, is it?' Then she gasped. 'Goodness, it's not Mr Walker?'

I bit my cheeks to stop myself from laughing. 'No, no. It's, um, no, not Mr Walker.'

'Of course, employers aren't really allowed to ask such details, but as you know I feel it's my duty to be informed about St Lancelot's staff,' she went on smoothly.

'Mmm, course,' I said, nodding.

'So have you a vague plan as to when you might go on maternity leave?'

'Well I'm nearly sixteen weeks now. Due in June. So I thought I'd try and get as close to the end of May as I could.'

Miss Montague nodded. 'Fine. And was there anything else?'

'Er, nope, no I think that's all my news.'

'My nephew's doing well, I take it?'

'Fergus? Oh, er, yes,' I said, with as much enthusiasm as I could, considering Fergus had the IQ of a butternut squash. 'He's doing a great job.'

'Marvellous. I'll see you tomorrow then.'

I laughed to myself as I left school and caught the 137 home. Mr Walker indeed. I couldn't wait to tell Steph.

★

The week that term started, I also told my boys that I was having a baby, then immediately regretted it because their reaction was even more confused than Miss Montague's.

'But how did the baby get in you, Miss Bailey?' asked George, while they were sitting on the carpet in front of me. 'Did you have to eat it?'

'No, George,' I said, trying not to laugh, 'I did not eat my baby.' Then I stopped and thought. Sex ed was technically not in my remit. Poor Mr Knight had to deal with that in Year 7, showing the boys a video clip that looked like it was from the 1970s. Last year, he'd come into the staffroom at break with a condom sticking to the back of his trousers because he'd taken several packets in for the boys to feel, only for them to start flicking them around the classroom like rubber bands.

So, no, technically I was not supposed to broach the facts-of-life talk. But I wasn't sure how to properly answer George and I've always thought it was misleading to tell children that 'storks' brought babies. I was a teacher because I wanted them to learn, not be muddled by untruths.

'Who here has a pet?' I suddenly asked them.

Five little hands went up in front of me.

'Achilles, what do you have?'

'We have a snake called Boris,' he said.

Shit. I'd forgotten Achilles had a snake. I'd been hoping for a dog or a cat. Snakes were harder. They laid eggs.

'OK,' I went on, 'let's not worry about Boris for a moment. Phineas, what do you have at home?'

'Magic,' he said. 'He's a spaniel. He's two.'

Great, I could work with a spaniel.

'OK, and do you remember when Magic was a puppy?'

He nodded. 'Yes, and Mum got cross because he ate our shoes.'

'That was naughty of him. But OK, Magic would grow in his mother's tummy, a bit like my baby is growing in mine.'

'And then he came out through her bottom,' said Phineas, authoritatively. 'There were lots of puppies that came out through her bottom and we went to see them all and I chose Magic.'

'Mmm,' I said, wondering how long I had left until it was 3.20. 'Yes, that's true, dogs have lots of puppies whereas people normally only have one baby. Or maybe two.'

'How many babies have you got?' said Phineas.

'I've got one. And it will come out in about five months.'

'Did you do a naked cuddle, Miss Bailey?' piped up Oscar. 'My mum said she had a naked cuddle with my dad and that's how she had Molly.' Molly was his sister.

'Exactly,' I said, relieved. 'I had a naked cuddle and now I have this baby.'

'But you're not married so who did you do your naked cuddle with?' went on Oscar, frowning.

I glanced behind me at the classroom clock. It was 3.04 p.m.

'With a friend,' I said. 'Sometimes you can have a naked cuddle with a friend and you have a baby then too.'

Oscar turned his head and looked at George doubtfully, sitting next to him. 'Can daddies do naked cuddles with other daddies?'

'Er, they can if they want,' I said carefully. 'But you don't get a baby in your tummy that way.'

'I know two daddies who have a baby,' said Roman.

'Sometimes two daddies have a baby and sometimes two mummies have a baby. That's fine. But only a mummy can make a baby in her tummy. Right, shall we carry on reading *Mister Magnolia*?' I said briskly.

*

Fortunately, the boys were distracted from the topic of babies by a trip to the Natural History Museum later that week. We were doing a project on the dinosaurs this term, which meant multiple pieces of health and safety paperwork and multiple emails to the parents reminding them that the boys could each come with a maximum of £10 spending money – 'no more'. Then, multiple emails back from certain mothers demanding to know what was in the packed lunches.

To my astonishment, Fergus (the other 'responsible adult' on the trip) arrived on time that Friday morning. 'I love the Natural History Museum,' he said, as we chivvied the boys into the minibus. He'd dressed like a Tory poster boy for the outing – brown corduroy trousers, brown lace-up brogues with a fawn-coloured jersey, and a thin green mac. 'Aunt Venetia used to take me as a half-term treat and we'd have sticky buns in the café afterwards.' He suddenly looked embarrassed, as if he'd spilled state secrets about Miss Montague.

'Cute,' I replied, before leaning into the back of the bus where I could hear squabbling about seats. 'Right, boys, belts on, please. Roman, sit down. No, I don't care if you want to sit by the window. It's not a long journey. Sit there and buckle up. Otherwise nobody's going at all and we can all stay in the classroom. Who wants that?'

Silence.

'Thought not.'

I stepped up into a front seat and Fergus clambered in next to me as Mr Herbert slid the back door closed.

'I need a wee,' shouted Arthur from the back, less than twenty seconds after we pulled out from school.

An hour or so on, the boys sat (relatively) peacefully in the corner of one hall filling in work sheets.

'Miss Bailey, what did the dinosaurs sleep on?' asked George, frowning over his sheet.

'I think that's a question for Mr Lawrence,' I said, looking at the assistant who was taking us around the museum.

Mr Lawrence pushed his glasses up his nose and launched

into a speech about dinosaur sleep habits. I let my mind wander to Max and whether to message him. I'd been mulling this over all week. The paternity test must be back by now, but I didn't want to chase him, as if I was nervous about the results. And yet he'd said 'let's hang out', so should I message him? Or wait for him to get in touch with me first?

My angst about whether to message Max first or not reminded me of when you start dating someone. You worry about every message you send (too many emojis? Too many exclamation marks? Too many kisses? Not enough kisses?). You worry about what to wear when you next see them, about every item of clothing, from shoes to socks and knickers. You spend nineteen hours doing your hair and make-up, even if it's to make you look like you haven't got any make-up on in the first place. You worry about what to say when you see them. Were you funny enough? Interesting enough? Why did you make that weird sex joke?

Also, according to my app, ET was now the size of a turnip. I'd felt her moving for the first time in the bath that week and whooped with pleasure to myself. At least I thought I'd felt her. It didn't feel like much of a kick, more of a bubbling as if I had indigestion. I wanted to share details like these with Max, but I wasn't sure where the line was with 'co-parents', particularly co-parents that you had a teeny-tiny crush on because they looked like someone you'd see on a billboard advertising tighty whities. Tell him all my bodily functions or not?

I didn't know where to pitch it. I didn't want to sound too

coupley – 'Guess what, our baby moved!' But I didn't want to sound too remote either – 'Hi, Max, just to let you know the baby moved last week which felt a bit like trapped wind and she's now the size of a root vegetable. Hope you're well.' That sounded weird.

I sighed. Fuck's sake, Lil. Just do it. So, while the boys continued colouring in, I typed out a message.

Hey Max, just wanted to let you know all's good and I felt her moving around last week. It was amazing! And she's now the size of a turnip, although hopefully she won't look like one! X

I clicked send and then we had lunch in the picnic area downstairs, before we spent an hour weighing fossils, the boys sitting on benches at a round table. At one stage, Mr Lawrence produced what is technically called a coprolite, or fossilized dinosaur poo. The boys immediately stopped chattering as they gazed at it, awed into silence.

'Can we sniff it?' said George, a few moments later.

'Sure you can,' said Mr Lawrence, holding the fossil out.

'No pushing,' I said, as they jostled for prime sniffing position.

'It doesn't smell like poo,' said George, wrinkling his nose.

'That's because it's 220 million years old,' said Mr Lawrence.

'That is so old,' said Phineas. 'My dad is only forty-two.'

We had to get back to school for the usual pick-up time so I gave everyone a ten-minute warning before we left that afternoon. They all needed it, so Fergus and I took turns to ferry them in and out. We couldn't have the minibus that afternoon since it was taking Year 8 to swimming, so as another part of today's educational experience we were getting the Tube one stop from South Kensington to Sloane Square.

'Right, boys, into pairs, line up. Are we all OK? Arthur, where's your coat?'

It took a while until they were neatly lined up but finally, we were in formation and walked, slowly, along the underpass to the station.

I was at the front, leading Achilles and Dmitri, each holding plastic dinosaurs they'd bought in the gift shop, discussing which one would win in a fight. Fergus was at the back chivvying along Roman and Vikram.

I stopped and turned round as we approached the station. 'Boys, you need to follow me very carefully. I don't want to lose anybody. Can you all keep hold of one another's hands. Roman? I can see you. Vikram's hand please. Fergus? Fergus?' He was looking at his phone while poor Vikram strained his neck, trying to dodge Roman waving his new T-rex in his face. It roared when you hit a button and Roman hit it again and again, swiping Vikram's nose with its claw.

'Fergus!' I hissed, trying not to give other Tube passengers the impression of a teacher on the verge of a breakdown.

'Yeah?' Fergus looked up at me.

'Can you keep an eye on those two?'

He slid his phone into his pocket with a martyred air, as if he was a teenager, and I turned back round to marshal them through the disabled gate. 'Come on, that's it. Oscar, concentrate. Left, right, left, right.'

We snaked in line down the steps to the platform.

'OK, boys, we want this side. The train will be here in…' I squinted up at the ticker, 'one minute. George, don't do that. Leave Oscar's hair alone please. Roman, I'm warning you, if you won't keep hold of Vikram's hand you'll have to hold mine.'

Sulkily, Roman put his T-rex under one arm and took Vikram's hand.

I looked down the line as the train approached and put my arm out as a barrier. 'Stay back, boys. And can everyone wait for other people to get off the train please before you get on. ROMAN, that's it, I've warned you. Fergus? Fergus? Seriously, can you keep an eye on Roman? Just put your fucking phone away for one minute and concentrate? Can you keep hold of Roman?'

'MISS BAILEY, YOU SAID FUCK,' jeered Roman, jumping around and waving his dinosaur again. 'FUCK FUCK FUCK FUCK FUCK.'

I didn't want to shout at him as passengers spilled off the Tube, pushing roughly as they freed themselves from the mass of bodies inside the carriage. It was heaving. I looked up at the sign. The next Tube was in two minutes. We'd have to wait for that, I couldn't force the boys on here. Especially with Roman shrieking like a small escapee from a lunatic asylum. Who were all these people on the Tube at 3 p.m. on a Tuesday afternoon? Why weren't they at work? I could sense the furious mood that came from low blood-sugar, making me want to kill someone. Possibly myself.

'Fergus, we'll have to wait,' I said, looking into the carriage again. 'We'll get the next one, it's too full. Boys, we need to hang on for another two minutes, for the next train. Everyone all right?'

'I need a wee,' said Arthur.

'Oh Arthur, can you hang on until we get back to school? It shouldn't be too long.'

The doors started beeping, signalling they were about to close.

'OK, everyone, stand back as the train goes again.'

'I really need a wee,' said Arthur. He'd clamped his knees together and was jiggling on the spot.

'I promise we'll be back to school in…' I looked at my watch and crouched down, 'about fifteen minutes. Maybe less. All right?'

It was while I was worrying about Arthur's bladder issues that I missed what was happening at the other end of the line.

'Miss Bailey! Miss Bailey,' said Fergus, suddenly high-pitched and hysterical.

'What?' I said, standing up.

He pointed at the Tube door in front of him and I saw Roman on the other side waving his T-rex through the window as the train started pulling away.

Shit. Shit, shit, shit, shit, shit. SHIT.

'He let go of my hand and jumped,' said Fergus. 'I'm sorry. I'm sorry.'

I momentarily froze, unsure of what to do. Scream? Shout? I watched the end of the Tube disappear into the tunnel.

'Stay here, watch them,' I said to Fergus, before running

down the platform to a thin, bald man wearing an orange high-vis vest.

'Excuse me, one of my class just jumped on that train, without us. Can you stop it?'

He shook his head. 'I'll radio,' he said quickly, ducking into the booth behind us and picking up a walkie-talkie. Then he stuck his head out again. 'Can you describe him for me?'

'Fair hair, in a green jumper, called Roman. With a dinosaur. A toy one. He's five,' I said. I could feel my heart pounding against my breastbone.

The man nodded and spoke into the walkie-talkie. I stood there watching him, quite helpless. And furious with both Roman and Fergus. But most of all terrified. And responsible. They were all my responsibility. Please please please could he be caught at Sloane Square. Please could he be safe. And please, please, please could I not be fired.

I glanced back at the gaggle of boys. Arthur was crying. Fergus was looking anxiously in my direction.

The high-vis man poked his head out again. 'There's someone on the platform at Sloane Square, they'll hold the train.'

'But what if they can't find him? Or what if he gets off and disappears?'

'Is he your son, madam?'

'No, no, he's my pupil. I'm a teacher.'

He squinted at me slightly, as if trying to weigh up my suitability to be in charge of other people's children. Then he glanced at my stomach, so I instinctively put a hand on it.

'Don't worry. They'll find him. S'not the first time this has happened here.'

I nodded and then we stood there waiting while I willed his walkie-talkie to crackle with news.

As another Tube pulled into the platform, I glanced back at Fergus who had shuffled the boys away from the edge of the platform.

Then the high-vis man ducked into his cabin. His nasal voice came over the tannoy system. 'Please stand back to allow others off the train first. This is the District Line train to Upminster, all stations to Upminster.'

More minutes ticked by as the Tube shunted out. If Roman was safe, I swore I would never complain about him in the Antelope again.

I walked back to Fergus and the other boys while waiting.

'I'm so sorry,' Fergus kept saying. 'He just let go and jumped on before I knew what was happening. I'm so sorry. Aunt Venetia's going to murder me.'

'It's all right,' I said, trying to stay calm in front of the other eight. 'Boys, we've just got to wait while that nice man over there – see him? In the orange jacket? – he's finding Roman and then we can go back to school. Is everybody all right?'

'I still need a wee,' said Arthur, tearfully.

I put a hand on his head. 'I'm sorry, sweetheart. But I promise we'll be back soon.' The others stayed quiet, silenced because they knew something serious had happened.

But then I glanced back towards the cabin where my saviour in orange suddenly gave me the thumbs up. The relief! I wanted to run up and propose to him, declare my immediate love and suggest we run away together.

'They've got him, madam,' he said, as he walked towards us. 'Platform two at Sloane Square. They'll keep him there so if you lot get the next train it'll get you to the same place.'

'I'm so grateful,' I said. 'I can't thank you enough. Really. You're my hero. I'm so, so grateful.'

He blushed in response. 'Not to worry, madam. These things happen.'

Did they? Colleagues at St Lancelot's often moaned about individual boys in the safety of the staffroom, but I'd never heard of anybody losing one of them.

On the Tube back to Sloane Square, while obsessively counting the boys' heads, I felt woefully incompetent. If I couldn't keep a 5-year-old safe, how was I going to manage with a baby?

★

Roman was crying on the platform, the T-rex dangling from his fingers, while another man in a high-vis jacket was standing beside him. 'Thank you,' I said to him, trying to look suitably grateful as I took Roman's free hand.

'I'm sorry,' I said, crouching down and brushing his hair of out his eyes. 'Are you OK?'

He nodded, but tears continued rolling down his cheeks and dropping on to his blazer.

'Come on, trouble, let's go back to school because it's home time. Who's picking you up today?'

'I d-d-d-don't know,' he said, through his tears. 'I think it's maybe AJ.' He was one of the Walkers' security team, a former soldier-turned-bodyguard who looked like a human bullfrog. Neck as wide as his head and stocky legs.

'All right, let's go back and find him, then home. OK?' I looked at the others. 'Fergus, can you hold Vikram's hand and I'll take Roman. Then we're nearly there, come on, troops.'

While we walked back, nine pairs of little legs suddenly flagging after a long day, I weighed up my options.

With hindsight I should have told Miss Montague immediately, as soon as I'd handed the boys back that afternoon. But I didn't. I wanted to get home and eat ten pieces of toast on the sofa. I hadn't heard back from Max and, although waiting to hear from him was a familiar feeling, it made me tetchy. I thought our day at the hospital before Christmas had shown he wanted to take this seriously.

'Fergus, can we discuss this tomorrow?' I said, once everybody had gone.

He nodded but still looked stricken.

'I'm not cross with you. It was an accident.'

'OK. Sorry again,' he said. I left him standing in the classroom, still wearing his mac.

★

By the following morning, there was still no reply from Max and I'd slept badly, finding myself awake and blinking at the ceiling at 4 a.m., rehearsing how to explain the incident to

Miss Montague. In the end, I was beaten to it by Miss Bowen, the school secretary, who sidled up as I stood beside the kettle in the staffroom and said Miss Montague wanted to have a word in her office.

Being summoned to head's office as a grown-up was much the same as being summoned as a child. Instant clammy palms. I left the staffroom and wiped them on my dress before knocking on her door.

'Come!'

'Er, morning,' I said, entering Miss Montague's office and sitting down.

'Miss Bailey,' she said, putting her pen down and eyeballing me. I tried to gauge how serious she looked. Pretty serious. But that could just be her usual face. She didn't do carefree. She did severe prison guard.

'Now,' she said, 'could you tell me about yesterday's trip to the museum?'

'Is this about Roman on the journey back to school?' I asked.

'It is indeed.'

I sighed. 'I'm sorry,' I said. 'I'm so sorry. It was an accident. It happened within seconds, one minute he was on the platform, the next he'd jumped on the train. He'd been pretty disruptive all day. He's just... not easy.'

'Why didn't you report this when you got back here?'

I rolled my lower lip through my teeth. 'Sorry, again, I know I should have done but it was a long day and...' I didn't think explaining that I was waiting for a WhatsApp message from my baby-daddy would elicit much sympathy.

Miss Montague blinked at me. 'Well I've had Mrs Walker on the telephone already this morning,' she went on. 'Roman was tremendously upset last night and now it transpires some-one filmed the whole scene on their phone.'

'What?' I said, raising my voice.

'Someone at the station recognized him. Or at least heard you saying his name. And they've got a video they're threaten-ing to sell to the papers.'

'Jesus.'

'Unfortunately he can't help us. I believe Mr and Mrs Walker are planning to buy the video themselves to stop this going any further, but I need to be seen to be doing something.'

'Like what?'

'I think for the time being it's best if you go home.'

'WHAT? What about the boys?'

'Mrs Peers can manage for a few days.'

'No, Miss Montague, please. Nobody was harmed, it was an accident. Can I talk to Mrs Walker? If I explain that it wasn't actually—'

She shook her head. 'I'm sorry, Miss Bailey, but temporary suspension is all I can suggest right now to stop this going any further.'

I closed my eyes and sighed in my seat. Suspended.

'If it's temporary do you know how long I—'

'I will to speak to the Walkers in person,' said Miss Montague. 'But until then there's nothing else I can do. I've got the reputation of the school to think about.'

I left her office feeling three millimetres tall. Suspended. A bad teacher. Irresponsible. The shame of it made me want to disappear. Like a small, tearful child myself, I decided that I wanted to go home for a hug from Dennis and advice from Mum. I slunk into the staffroom to collect my bag, and decided I'd go to Brixton and pack a bag, then head to Liverpool Street for the train.

It was while trudging to the Tube, trying not to cry, that my phone rang. Max. I looked at it in my hand for a couple of seconds before picking up.

'Hi.' My voice had gone tight.

'Hello,' he said, breezily, 'sorry I haven't called back since your message. Mad day running around yesterday. But I wanted to call you to say, er, firstly the test results have just come back. The doctor called me. And they, er, prove everything. So I wanted to let you know.'

'OK,' I said. While Max had been talking, I'd ducked into an alleyway next to the station to lean up against a wall. Tears were sliding down my cheeks but I didn't want to let on that anything was wrong.

'I also wanted to say do you fancy meeting up in the next week or so?' Max rattled on. 'I meant to call you before now actually, but everything's been crazy with work and there's talk of a book after the climbing disaster so I'm trying to plan the next steps and... Lil?'

'No, no, I'm here, and that'd be great,' I said, through a thickening nose.

He twigged instantly. 'What's wrong? You all right?'

'Yup,' I said. 'I've just got a cold.' I sniffed down the phone and wiped my damp chin with my thumb.

'Hey,' said Max, more softly, 'what's up?'

Which is when I let out a sob and the whole story unravelled as I stood in that alleyway. The trip. Losing Roman. The video of him. Suspension. Going home to Norfolk. Max listened patiently. Calmly. Not interrupting.

'Why don't I take you?' he said, once I'd stopped burbling down the line.

I sniffed again. 'Huh?'

'I'll drive you up,' Max said, simply. 'I was going to Suffolk tomorrow anyway. So I might as well take you back to your parents' and then I'll head on to mine. Easy. Just tell me where to come and find you now.'

'No, Max, it's fine, I can get the train, it's easy. Honestly, that's so kind of you but I don't need to be driven. I just need to get home and pack a bag and then—'

'I know you don't need me to,' he said, 'but I'd like to. Seriously. Just tell me where to collect you and I can be there in…' He paused. 'Probably an hour, depending on traffic. Fucking London traffic. This is why I want to live in the hills like Bilbo Baggins.'

'OK,' I said, suddenly laughing so a snot bubble briefly formed over my nostril, before bursting. 'I mean, thank you.' I gave him my Brixton address and got on the Tube hoping that my face would look less swollen by the time he arrived.

Knights in shining armour don't exist, I told myself as I jolted south on the Victoria Line. Don't get silly about this.

He's only doing you a favour, saving you the cost of a £37.50 ticket to King's Lynn.

Yet amidst the guilt I felt at losing Roman and the drama of this morning, I couldn't help but feel comforted by the idea of seeing him.

CHAPTER NINE

THE FLAT DOORBELL RANG just over an hour later and I walked downstairs nervously, bag over my shoulder. I'd packed in such a blur it felt like I was taking two pairs of knickers and three mismatching shoes with me, but at least I'd managed to have a shower and redo my face before he arrived.

'Your chauffeur, madam,' he said, as I opened the front door. Max, standing there smiling in jeans and a sheepskin coat, like something from a Belstaff advert, looked so incongruous amidst the empty Big Mac boxes and green wheelie bins in the street that I didn't answer immediately.

'You OK?' he said, suddenly frowning.

'Yes, yes, sorry, I'm fine. Thank you for this. I honestly could have got the train…'

'Don't be absurd,' he said, holding out his arm. 'Come on, hand over your bag and we can get going.'

I slid the strap off my shoulder and handed it to him. With his free hand, he opened the passenger door of a huge black 4x4 right outside the door. 'Hop in.'

'Nice wheels,' I said, climbing up into it. The car looked like something you see playboys cruise around Knightsbridge.

Tinted windows, leather seats, a dashboard with a mad number of buttons.

'They sponsor me,' he said, almost apologetically. 'So it's one of the perks.' He shut my door and put my bag in the back, then walked round to his side. I quickly glanced at myself in the wing mirror. The bobble on the end of my nose was still pink, but I was hoping that Max would concentrate on the road.

'Right then,' he said, as he shook off his jacket and threw it in the back behind his seat. 'Let's get going.' He looked over his shoulder and pulled out.

'Should be two and a half hours from here. Maybe three. You comfortable?' he asked, glancing across at me. I was looking down, fiddling with the seat belt, wondering whether it was a bad idea to run it across my stomach.

'Yup,' I said, deciding to smooth it under my bump. 'All good. And thank you again.'

'No more gratitude. I was going home anyway and I wanted to see you, so it's a perfect solution. Sorry about work,' he added, quickly. 'Although it seems a bit over the top, if the boy's safe and no harm's been done?'

I rested my head back against the seat and sighed. 'Yeah. But if there's this video then the school's got to be seen to be doing something. The irony is I'm not sure the Walkers even care that much about their son. I've only met his mother once.'

'Jeez,' said Max, shaking his head. 'Why bother having children unless you're going to be involved?'

I looked across at him and raised my eyebrows.

'What?' he said, glancing at me and then back to the road.

I didn't reply, just put my hands either side of my stomach and carried on looking pointedly at him.

Max laughed. 'All right. But I don't understand people who seem to have children for the sake of it, just doing it at a certain stage just because everyone else is doing it.'

'You didn't want children?' I asked, alarmed.

'No no, I do want them. I always have,' he said. 'But because of my own childhood, and then Del's accident, I wanted to do it right. I suppose that's why I reacted so badly at the beginning of all... this.'

'What was wrong with your childhood?' I asked, 'before your brother, I mean?'

Whoops. I hadn't meant to blunder into such delicate emotional territory like an elephant. Too late.

Max paused for a few beats, as if he was trying to frame his answer. 'I don't know how much you know about my family,' he said eventually.

I blushed, thinking about my internet search history. If Max ever saw it I'd have to emigrate to the moon. Mental note: delete search history on both phone and laptop.

'Not much,' I replied, in a high-pitched voice, grateful that we were sitting side by side and he couldn't see my flushed cheeks.

'OK, there's this big house in Suffolk,' he said. 'And other houses and some land...' He trailed off, as if embarrassed. 'It sounds idyllic, and it was, kind of. Then Del had the accident and died, and my mother went to pieces and stayed in her bedroom for months, and my father couldn't handle it so spent all his time outdoors. I sort of got stuck in the middle. I hated boarding school, but after Del had gone I hated being at home more.'

'What are they like now? Your parents, I mean?'

Max laughed again, but it wasn't a happy laugh. It was mocking. 'The same. Mum's essentially a recluse, Dad's become this furious old man, angry at everything in the world.'

'But you go back?'

'Of course,' he said, 'although it's partly out of guilt because I'm away so much. But it's still home. And I'll have to go back at some point and take over.' He paused as we pulled up at a red light. 'So that's why I was determined, when it came to my children, that it was all perfect for them.' He glanced across at me. 'You know, marriage, then babies.'

'Who says that's perfect?'

'It's less dysfunctional, surely?' said Max. 'Anyway, enough about me, what about you?'

'What d'you mean?'

'Well, you seem pretty sorted, capable, level-headed. Your parents did something right.'

'Ha. Yeah, really sorted. Pregnant and possibly out of a job.'

'When you put it like that,' he said, smiling across at me again. 'But seriously, when we first met I remember thinking you seemed like someone who had her shit together. You've got a job doing something you love, you're intelligent, you're funny, you stand up for yourself. It may not feel like it but you seem pretty tough.'

'Thanks,' I said, in a small voice. I'd always been bad at taking a compliment. 'I, er, kind of thought the same about you.'

'That I was tough?' Max frowned at me, surprised.

'Well, not only that,' I said, trying to work out how honest I dared be with him. 'I guess I thought you were clever and you made me laugh, and you were pretty charming. Until I woke up the next morning and you'd vanished.' I said this through a grin, whereupon Max lifted a hand from the steering wheel.

'I admit that wasn't great,' he said.

'Heartbreaker,' I shot back, teasing.

'Not at all,' he said, serious again. 'I was in a relationship for a few years, then I went on a date with you, and now here we are. I suppose I had a period of dating, before then, when I went off the rails slightly.' He looked at me as if he was trying to gauge how much he could admit, too. 'It was just after I left the army, and I don't think I'd ever dealt with all the Del stuff properly. But then I started going out with Prim, that's my ex, and she kind of saved me.'

I stared through the windscreen, feeling awkward at the mention of her name.

'Sorry,' said Max, 'is it weird, discussing all this?'

'No,' I said, realizing it was quite the opposite. It felt bonding, a relief. 'But what do you mean she saved you?'

Max sighed as he pulled out into the fast lane, overtaking a red car in front of us with a 'Princess on board' sticker.

'I'm forbidding us to ever have one of those,' he said, nodding his head at it.

'OK, deal,' I said, stupidly pleased that he'd said 'us', although I also quite wanted him to get back to the Primrose question.

'I'd been partying too much and behaving badly,' he went on. 'But then Prim and I got together, although our parents are friends so I'd known her for ever, and she helped me get sorted. Work out that I really wanted to climb. She supported me while I started out.'

'How come you broke up? If it was good?'

He sighed again. 'It was good, at first. But I don't think it was ever great. I thought it would work back then. It seemed the right relationship, you know? She was the kind of person I thought I should be with. My parents approved of her, we had the same friends, that kind of stuff. But looking back now, it wasn't right. For me, anyway.'

'What about her?'

I looked at him as he winced. 'It was different for her, I think,' he said. 'She wanted to get married, do all that. Which is why I knew I had to break up with her, eventually. There were... complications. It took a while. But, yeah, then we broke up, and I downloaded Kindling because that's what you do, right? Then I met you.'

He laughed again, as if self-conscious. 'Sorry, that was probably a bit full-on.'

'No, it's not. I get it. If I look back at me and Jake, that's my ex, it wasn't that dissimilar. I thought it was everything at the time, but now I realize it wasn't. That we're different people.'

'How did it end?'

'Badly. He cheated on me with someone from his office.'

'Ouch, I'm sorry, what a dick,' said Max, before looking across at me. 'Want me to beat him up?'

'Nah, it's fine. I think we're beyond that.'

'You still in touch?'

'Nope, although I did see him just before Christmas, but super briefly. Just to say hi to.' Then I paused before trying to put on my casual voice. 'What about you and Primrose? You guys still speak?'

'Errr…' started Max. His voice sounded slightly strained. 'She got back in touch when I came home from Pakistan but other than that, not really.'

I nodded slowly. Moments of this conversation did feel awkward, as if we were treading on one another's shadows. But more of me felt pleased to be sitting here talking openly about our pasts. It felt like the kind of conversation you might have on a second or third date as you tentatively sussed the other person out. And if we'd been in a bar, not a car. And if I wasn't on my way home having been suspended from my job. And if I wasn't going to share a baby with him in a few months' time.

'Co-parent,' I reminded myself, as we stormed up the M11.

'What?' said Max, frowning at me.

Shit, I thought I'd said it in my head.

'Nothing,' I said quickly. 'Just, er, my parents. They're looking forward to meeting you.' I'd texted Mum while I was packing, saying I was coming home after work but it was all fine, I'd explain when I got there. I'd added that Max was driving me, which meant Mum had completely ignored the work details and texted me back with a line of party popper emojis, saying that she'd get a new jar of jam out for tea.

'Great,' said Max, before looking at me with a grin. 'Mums love me.'

'Oh my God, you are full of yourself,' I said, laughing and hitting him on the arm.

'Kidding!' he said, still grinning. 'I'm just hoping your dad doesn't murder me.'

'He won't, and technically he's not my dad. Mum had a fling at uni and I was the result, but she only got together with Dennis a few years on. Although Dennis kind of is my dad, in everything but name.'

'Blimey,' said Max. 'But OK. Right. Dennis and…'

'Jackie,' I said.

'OK, Dennis and Jackie,' he repeated. 'Got it. Do you know your real dad then?'

'Nope,' I said, 'some guitarist called Adrian.'

Max glanced at me again, smiling. 'Families huh?'

'Exactly,' I replied. 'See? Nothing's perfect.'

*

The time between Max turning off his car and Mum appearing outside the house was roughly one and a half seconds. She must have been listening for us, an ear pressed to the front door.

'Hi, Mum,' I said, giving her a hug.

'Oh my love, come here,' she said, giving me a hug so tight I could hardly breathe. 'I've put the kettle on.'

'Thanks,' I said, stepping back and gasping for air like a free-diver who's just surfaced. 'And, er, Mum, this is Max.'

'How do you do?' said Max, stepping from behind me and holding out his hand.

'I do very well, thank you,' said Mum, shaking it. 'Would you like a cup of tea?'

'Love one,' Max replied.

The kitchen was the usual shambles. Ginger, who normally hated all men apart from Dennis, wound her way around Max's legs while, in the corner, Gerald the tortoise sucked on a piece of melon.

'Have a seat, Max,' said Mum, picking up a pile of paper and redistributing it to the dresser where there were already several other piles of papers.

Dennis appeared from the garden shed. 'Lil!' he cried, opening his arms. 'Welcome back, darling, tell us everything.'

'Hiya,' I said, hugging him, before introducing him to Max.

'Max, very good to meet you,' said Dennis. 'I've read about you, of course. Very brave. Very brave indeed.'

'Oh, thank you very much, sir,' said Max. I thought 'sir' was ladling it on a bit thick. It wasn't 1849. But Dennis went pink with pleasure.

'Well, yes, exceptionally brave, really very heroic,' carried on Dennis, suddenly busying himself with the papers on the dresser.

'I made some scones,' said Mum, carrying a plate to the

table. Then she retrieved several mugs from the cupboard. 'Mind they don't have Ginger's hairs in them, they get everywhere,' she said, handing one to Max.

He blew into his mug. 'All clear,' he said, smiling at Mum, who turned pink herself. My parents, honestly. Social revolutionaries until presented with a dashing member of the aristocracy, and then they fell over themselves.

Dennis sat while Mum continued piling the table with a pot of tea, with butter, with knives and plates, with her jar of blackberry jam which tasted too sharp because she hadn't used enough preserving sugar but Max said was the best blackberry jam he'd ever had.

He asked serious questions about Dennis's books and Mum's latest paper – 'Evolutionary feminism in late-Victorian women's poetry'.

'That sounds fascinating,' said Max, with what seemed like genuine enthusiasm. 'What made you pick that?'

From time to time I squinted at him and tried to gauge if he was just being polite, if he was humouring them. But he seemed quite at home in this ramshackle kitchen, eating his fourth scone, while talking to Mum about Christina Rossetti.

They, in turn, asked Max about Suffolk and his Pakistan expedition. Nobody raised the topic of ET, the little elephant in the room.

Although Mum did suddenly remember that I shouldn't be here in the first place.

'What's happened at school then?' she said, looking at me.

'Long story,' I said, sighing, before explaining the school trip and the Tube journey as succinctly as I could.

'But it seems very unfair to blame you,' said Max, once I'd finished updating Mum and Dennis. 'Fungus should be the one copping it, if you ask me.'

I twisted one side of my mouth into a grimace. 'Yeah, but I was responsible overall, so I do get it.'

'Well I'm just happy we've got you home again,' said Dennis, beaming at me from across the table. He never could get cross with me.

After an hour or so, Max tipped his mug back and emptied it again. 'Right,' he said, lowering it back to the table. 'I should get going.'

'If I were you,' said Dennis, standing up and taking Max's empty mug, 'I'd take the Thetford road and dodge Norwich because it can be bloody murder at this time of day.'

'Got it,' said Max, smiling and holding out his hand to shake with Dennis, whereupon he pulled him into a hug and they did that manly thing of clapping one another on the back.

'Give us a hug then,' said Mum, hovering behind Dennis. 'And please come again. Whenever you like. We're always here. She doesn't come home nearly enough so thank you for bringing her back.'

'All right, all right,' I said, 'let poor Max go before it's Christmas again.'

Mum and Dennis stayed in the kitchen while I said goodbye to Max back outside.

'Thank you,' I said. 'For the drive, and this.' It had been

a curious day. I should have felt glum at my suspension and depressed by retreating back to my single bedroom in my parents' house. But I didn't. I felt buoyed by spending more time with Max. Scooping me up, rescuing me in that gangster car of his and bringing me home, revealed a protective side I hadn't seen before. Instead of feeling worried about the next few months, the journey up here – and tea – had made me feel more hopeful that we'd find our way through this.

'You're welcome,' he said. Then he grinned. 'It was selfishly motivated anyway.'

'What do you mean?' I asked.

'Well, since I've met your parents, how do you feel about maybe meeting mine?'

★

I spent most of that weekend at home, scrolling through teaching jobs online and wondering whether, if all else failed, I could work in Manuel's coffee shop in Brixton. Steph texted to see if I was all right. Mike sent an articulate message about Roman's parents: Walkers? More like wankers. Jess texted to check that I'd be back in London for her birthday party in a couple of weeks. *Hope so love*, I replied. But I hadn't heard anything further from Miss Montague so I didn't know how long 'temporary suspension' might last. I was in limbo in the meantime, washing my pants every other day and occasionally breaking off from job-hunting to read a pregnancy book Mum had given me with the cheerful title 'Pregnant and Alone'.

'But she's got us, Jacks,' Dennis had said when he spied the book lying on the sofa. 'And Max, of course,' he'd added hurriedly. 'I did like him,' he added, for the fifty-second time since our tea in the kitchen.

A couple of mornings later, Dennis and I dropped into the local post office to buy the papers. 'Oh Lilian, you look… well!' said Mrs Nibley, noticing my belly.

'That's because I'm pregnant,' I said, smiling broadly at her.

Mrs Nibley's eyes flicked to my left hand and then back to my face, confusion lining her forehead.

'I haven't got married,' I went on, 'it was an accident.'

'Just *The Times*, please, Mrs Nibley,' said Dennis, loudly. 'How are you anyway? All well?

'Poor Mrs Nibley, I'm not sure she's up to scratch with modern parenting,' he said afterwards, as we walked back towards the house.

'Sorry. I wasn't sure if you and Mum had told anyone.'

'You don't have to apologize to me. Or anyone, for that matter. I can't wait to be a grandpa. I can't wait to trundle that little person about the village and take her into Mrs Nibley to buy sweets and generally spoil her rotten. Morning, Howard,' he said, raising his hand at a neighbour across the road from us with his fat Labrador waddling beside him on a lead.

Then he lowered his voice. 'But you know what some people round here are like. More judgemental. If you saw Mrs Nibley without her clothes on she'd probably have scales all over her back.'

'Yeurrrrgh, please.'

'You know what I mean,' he went on. 'There's a way of telling certain people up here. And your mum and I thought it was your news to tell, anyway.'

'Wimps,' I said, elbowing him gently.

That was the day Max texted, asking if I was free to meet his parents later that week.

Is Friday any good? Morning time. I can always come and get you? he wrote.

Friday perfect and don't worry I'll drive Xxx, I replied, sounding more confident than I felt. What should I wear to meet a viscount? How should I refer to them? And would they think I was a harpy who'd deliberately tried to trap their son?

★

I googled pictures of Little Clench Hall before I went. It was vast, a long Elizabethan house of pale stone and Gothic windows which looked out on to four hundred acres of tufty parkland, grazing for several hundred deer. Plus, it had its very own maze. Queen Victoria had apparently once stayed at the hall while on her way north to Sandringham, and remarked to an ancestor of Max's that she preferred it to all her own houses.

Wikipedia had been useful for stats – the hall had 127 rooms (including 22 bedrooms) and the family owned nine thousand acres of the surrounding Suffolk countryside. The Rushbrookes were one of the Norman families who came over with William the Conqueror and the 8th Viscount Rushbrooke had been a patron of Gainsborough's, so there was also a gallery at the hall with twelve landscapes that the artist had painted of the park, as well as several portraits of the family. Priceless, apparently.

It was only an hour from home, across the Norfolk border, just outside Lowestoft. Dennis offered to drive but I'd decided it would be easier to go on my own and borrow his car. Although as I got nearer, seeing a brown sign for the hall, I wished Dennis was there. He could have wanged on about an obscure naval battle in the 1870s to distract me.

'Here we go, ET,' I said, turning left off the road and pulling through a huge iron gate with stone pillars either side. The drive twisted around trees and parkland for several minutes. I slowed when I spotted a herd of deer on the side of a hill. There were dozens of them clustered together, heads down, chewing grass.

And then, as I drove round a bend and saw Little Clench Hall, I felt like Lizzie Bennet when she sees Pemberley for the first time, albeit slightly less eloquent.

'Jeeeeeeeesus Christ,' I said, taking in the size of the place; its façade was at least as long as Buckingham Palace. It was built from pale yellow stone with several pillars that spanned three floors around what I assumed must be the main entrance. A large fountain was in front of that and even from a distance, I could see a jet of water spouting into the air.

I tried to imagine living in such a place. What if your bedroom was in the top, far left corner, but breakfast was in the bottom, far right? It would take hours to get there. And as soon as you'd sat down with a piece of toast, you'd remember you'd left your phone upstairs. Nightmare.

I pressed down gently on the accelerator and drove on, following the drive until I saw a sign saying 'Visitors', which directed me to a car park behind the house. Then I checked my face in the rear-view mirror. Fine. I was more worried about my outfit. Mum and I had spent last night hunting through her wardrobe because I hadn't brought anything tidy with me from London.

I'd ended up in the least bad option – a floaty, three-quarter length purple dress which I gathered with a thin black belt above my stomach. Then, a pair of black tights and my flat, black ankle boots. I looked like a hippy who'd tried to make herself look respectable for an outing to the theatre.

I parked the car, texted Max – *Here, in car park* – and got out, dusting croissant crumbs from my lap since I'd made a quick Wild Bean café stop for breakfast. Oh good, the purple sack I was wearing had wrinkled during the drive.

I spotted Max approaching from between a stone archway. He waved. I made a final attempt at brushing croissant flakes off my dress and waved back, then started walking towards him.

'Hi,' he said, leaning to kiss me on the cheek. 'How was the drive?'

'Easy.'

'You ready for this?' he said, narrowing his eyes at me and grinning.

'They can't be that bad?'

'Come on, this way,' he said, ignoring my question and walking back towards the archway.

It opened into a big, cobbled courtyard.

'Old stables,' said Max, 'but we don't have horses any more so they're full of furniture that needs mending.'

In front of us, at the top of some stone steps, a brown door suddenly opened and a very ancient woman appeared from behind it. She had a face as brown and wrinkled as a walnut. Yikes, Max's mother was older than I'd expected. About nine hundred years older.

'Nanny, don't come out, it's cold. Stay inside,' said Max, standing back so I could go up the steps first.

I wondered if it was unsexy for a man in his thirties to refer to someone as Nanny, but then I glanced back at Max and figured he was handsome enough to get away with it. Hell, he could call me Nanny if he wanted and I probably wouldn't mind too much.

'Hello,' I said, holding out my hand to the walnut. 'I'm Lil.'

She took my hand with both of hers and beamed. 'Hello, my treasure, very special to meet you.'

'Lil, this is the most important person, who I most wanted you to meet,' said Max. 'She's my old nanny, and my father's nanny, who's lived in this house since, oh, before the war, correct, Nanny?'

She nodded. 'I've seen this one's bare bottom more times than I care to remember.'

'Nanny is a terrible flirt,' Max said, looking at me before turning back to her again. 'Where are Mum and Dad?'

'Lady Rushbrooke is in the drawing room, but I haven't seen your father. Maybe down at the yard.'

'But he knows that Lil was coming?'

'Oh yes, I reminded him this morning.'

Max frowned briefly. 'OK, we'll go to the drawing room.'

I jumped as we walked into a giant hallway because either side of the door was a silver coat of armour. Across the room, hanging on the wall, was a display of old muskets, fanned in a circle. There were shields mounted on either side of another doorway, leading off the hall, and a tattered old flag with a lion on it hung from a pole above that.

'All ancient family stuff,' said Max, seeing my expression, before gesturing that I should follow him through another door with shields on either side. Then down a long, carpeted corridor with mirrors strung along it, facing one another, so if you glanced at yourself on one side you saw dozens of yourself reflected in the mirror opposite. Max stopped and pushed open a big mahogany door to his right.

Behind it was what looked like a state room at Versailles. Red silk wallpaper, paintings of gruesome religious scenes on the walls in gilt frames, a fireplace so big you could have roasted a human being in it and several chandeliers hanging from the ceiling. I was so awed I didn't notice a white-haired woman sitting on a sofa, her back to us.

'Mum, hello, how we doing?' said Max, in the gentle tone of voice I often used on my class.

The white head swivelled.

'Gracious, I'm so sorry, darling, I didn't hear you come in.' Max's mother stood up and turned around. She wasn't how I'd envisaged a viscountess. She looked like a posh gypsy – stooped but elegant, she had on a long grey skirt with a grey jersey tucked into it. Her white hair was loose, shoulder-length, hanging in waves around her face, and she was so thin that it looked like her skin was being stretched over her cheekbones.

'This is Lil,' said Max, and I felt him put a hand on my back as I stepped forward to say hello.

She offered out a fragile hand, her fingers covered in rings. I shook it and smiled nervously at her. 'Hello.'

She smiled briefly back and then looked at Max. 'Darling, we should have some tea. Will you ask Jeremy to bring some?'

'Course. Lil, tea?'

'Yeah, great,' I said, before feeling embarrassed. 'Sorry, I mean yes please.'

Max then went off again which left me and the Viscountess alone.

'Please, do sit down,' she said, gesturing at the sofa on the other side of the fireplace.

We sat and there was an awkward silence, so I glanced at a table on which were several photos of Max when he was younger, a mop of curly dark hair, grinning out from the branches of a tree; from a tractor; sitting on a carpet wearing a fireman's hat that was too big for him.

'Sweet,' I said, looking at them.

She followed my gaze to the photo frames. 'Oh yes, Arundel was such a dear boy.'

Shit. Well done, Lil. You've been here for under two minutes and you've drawn attention to the dead son.

Max, luckily, came back through the door. 'Tea's on its

way.' Then he sat on the sofa next to me. 'Where's Dad?' I didn't sense that this conversation was any easier for him. His mother seemed like she was in a trance, physically here but mentally on holiday. Checked out.

She waved a thin, birdlike hand in the air, rings glinting. 'I don't know, darling. You know your father.'

Then suddenly, from the corridor outside, there was shouting.

'Where the bloody hell is Jeremy? Jeremy! JEREMY!'

A tall man with a beetroot for a head stalked into the drawing room. 'Where is he?' he said, glaring at Max. He was still wearing a coat and wellington boots.

'In the kitchen, I think, making tea,' said Max. 'Why?'

'I can't find my heart pills.'

'Why don't you say hello to Lil and sit down for a minute. That'll be much better for your heart than charging round shouting.'

'I'm NOT shouting,' he shouted.

Max sighed. 'Lil, this is my father.'

I stood up and offered my hand again. The Viscount stomped towards me in his boots and shook it, as if trying to crush my palm into splinters. He had thick grey hair, with a curtain that hung over his forehead and eyebrows that looked like fat slugs. 'How do you do?' he said. But without waiting for a reply, he turned to the Viscountess on the sofa. 'Have you seen Jeremy?'

'Dad, I told you, he's in the kitchen. Look, why don't you go and take your coat off and have tea with us?' said Max.

The Viscount glanced down, as if surprised to find he was still wearing his coat, and then spun and went out of the room again. Max sat back down. I followed. No wonder he'd become a mountaineer so he could travel so far away from home. If I'd been Max I might have considered a career in space.

'Mum, Lil has come here to meet you, and talk about the baby,' Max pressed on.

'Oh yes, the baby,' said the Viscountess, looking at me, her eyes softening. 'Do you know if it's a boy or a girl?'

'Er, no I don't,' I said.

'I always wanted a girl to go with my boys.'

'I think it might be a girl,' I said. 'I felt quite sick, for the first bit anyway, and they say that can be a sign it's a girl.'

'Do they? I can't remember. It was so long ago,' she replied. 'I loved being pregnant, with both of you.' She looked at Max. 'It was such a happy time. I was so worried about you being born, about what Arundel would think, but then you came along and he didn't mind a bit. He was rather pleased he had someone to play with, I think. He used to dress you up, do you remember?'

Max smiled and nodded, as if indulging a small child. 'Yep, I was Del's toy. A soldier one day, or his pet kitten the next.'

The reminiscing was halted by the reappearance of the Viscount, coat and boots now off, and a man in uniform carrying a silver tray of tea things.

'Thanks, Jeremy,' said Max, as he lowered the tray on to a table in front of the sofas.

'Not at all, sir. Will everyone be taking it?'

'I think so. Dad? Tea?'

The Viscount was staring out of a window into the garden.

'Yes,' he snapped. Then he left the window and sat down at the other end of the sofa from the Viscountess. I felt my heartbeat speed up and damp patches spread under my arms. I hoped this hue of purple didn't show up sweat. Keep elbows clamped to sides at all times, I told myself, trying to take a cup of tea from Jeremy without fanning my armpits.

'So,' said the Viscount, taking his tea from Jeremy. 'Lil, where does your family come from?'

'My parents live in Norfolk but I'm in London.'

'Whereabouts?'

'Brixton?'

His eyebrows leapt above the rim of his teacup as he took a sip. 'Brixton. Good God. And that's safe, is it? That's where you'll be living when our grandchild comes along?'

There were so many things that infuriated me about that sentence I didn't know where to start.

'I, er, I...' I looked across at Max. 'I'm kind of working it out as I go along.'

He grunted. 'Where are your parents in Norfolk?'

'It's a tiny village called Castleton, just outside King's Lynn. They've always been there. They're academics, so they both work at Norwich uni and, er, write books and that sort of thing...' The Viscount's glare made me trail off.

'Books!' he exclaimed, as if books were objects of suspicion. 'What kind of books?'

'Military ones mostly.'

'Your father's an army man then?' said the Viscount, his face brightening.

'No.' I shook my head. 'Just a writer.'

'Oh.' His expression fell. 'I wanted Maximilian to carry on with the army, but he refused. So instead he climbs bloody hills all day.'

'Dad,' interrupted Max. 'Lil has very kindly driven here today to meet you both. Is there anything you want to discuss?'

'Well it's a very unfortunate business,' said the Viscount. 'Not the usual way. But we have to make the best of it.'

I clenched my jaw, wondering how much longer I had to sit here.

'It's not unfortunate,' said Max, forcefully

'But if you want to saddle yourself to someone as irresponsible as my son then that's your decision,' went on the Viscount.

'I wouldn't call it saddling,' I said. I was torn between wanting to kick the pompous old windbag in the shins or cry. Couldn't cry. Had to save it for the car.

The Viscountess remained mute, staring into the fireplace.

'In my day, when this sort of thing happened those involved had to marry,' went on the Viscount, glaring at his son. 'Much better for the child.'

'And you would know, would you, what's right or not for a child? Given that you abdicated all responsibilities as a father after Del died?' said Max, raising his voice.

'DO NOT drag your brother into this,' thundered the Viscount, glaring at Max so sternly I wondered if smoke would start pouring from his nostrils. 'At least I understand about responsibility, about one's duty, instead of ignoring it and gallivanting abroad.' His face was now the colour of an aubergine and even I was quite worried about his heart pills.

'Please, no shouting,' whispered the Viscountess, her eyelids fluttering.

'Look,' I said loudly, startling everyone else. 'I know this is a difficult situation. I know it's probably not what you had planned. It's not what I planned. But it's happened and I decided to go ahead with it. I'm not asking anything from you but I would love E— the baby to know its grandparents.' One set of them anyway, I thought. The more normal grandparents.

The Viscount grunted again and stood up. 'I'm going to get my pills and then go down to the yard. Good to meet you,' he said, looking at me, although I was pretty sure he didn't mean it. Then he left.

'Darling, I think I might go outside. The pear trees need pruning,' said the Viscountess, also standing up.

Max sighed. 'Fine.'

'Do look after yourself,' she said, coming over to me and reaching for my hands. She took both of them in hers and looked at me. Max had inherited her blue eyes. 'And look after the baby.'

I nodded. 'Course.' Then she left too, drifting quietly from the room like a ghost.

'I'm sorry,' said Max, sighing and leaning back in his sofa. 'I thought it might help to meet.'

I twisted myself towards him. 'It's all right.' My glance fell on one of the photos of Del again. He must have been about the age of my class, since he was grinning in that rictus way small children do for the camera, and two of his teeth were missing. 'It's all right,' I repeated. 'I can see it from their point of view. It's… different.'

'My family,' he said, shaking his head slowly. 'I can hardly remember when it wasn't like this.'

'Hey, every family has their problems.'

'As bad as this?' he said, looking up at me with such a mournful expression I wanted to reach out and stroke his face.

'Your family seems great,' he added.

I thought about growing up with Mum constantly trying to turn me into a miniature Pankhurst, and Dennis spending hours, whole days, in his shed studying military formations. 'I promise you my parents have their off days.'

Max squinted at me and then suddenly had a question: 'Do you have time for a walk?'

'A walk?'

'Yes, you know, one leg out, then the other, then the first leg again. You'll get the hang of it in no time. There's just something I'd like to show you.'

'Sure,' I said, shrugging.

'Come on then.' He stood up and held out his hand for me to pull myself up. I let it go as soon as I was standing. 'Thanks.'

'Not a problem, madam. This way.'

He led me back down the corridor and into the hallway that looked like a medieval armoury, then glanced at my feet.

'What size are you?' he asked, pointing at a neat line of wellington boots beside the door.

'Don't worry,' I said, self-conscious about my outfit. If there was one thing that would make Mum's Mystic Meg dress look worse, it was a pair of rubber boots. 'These are super old,' I added, looking at my ankle boots. 'They're fine.'

'Try these,' he said, reaching for a pair and holding them out to me. 'Come on, it might be muddy.'

I rolled my eyes and slipped my own boots off, then stepped into the wellies.

'And this,' he said, reaching for a tweed coat and handing it to me.

'Seriously? I'll look ridiculous.'

'It's cold and you look sensational,' he grinned back, before opening the door. 'After you.'

'Where are we going?' I asked, zipping up my coat as we passed through the courtyard and back under the arch again. We turned left through a small iron gate and along a gravel path which ran away from the house, between great expanses of lawn and huge trees that swayed over us.

'It's just a spot that I love,' said Max, as the gravel crunched underfoot. 'And I thought might explain something.'

'What?' I demanded, as the path curved round a hedge and revealed a large lake beneath us. 'Oh wow,' I said, blinking at the sun shining off the murky surface. It was surrounded by fat green clumps of rhododendrons apart from a clearing at one end where space had been made for a pale stone bench.

'That's where,' said Max, nodding towards the bench and

leading me down the path, which twisted between the waxy rhododendrons and skirted alongside the lake. 'Del and I spent hours down here – building dens in the bushes and swimming in the summer.'

It felt unfeeling to answer with an insipid platitude like 'sweet!' or 'adorable!', as if Max had just shown me a picture of a kitten. I wanted to indicate that I was more moved than that whenever he mentioned Del, that I was honoured he'd talk about his brother to me. But before I could phrase some sort of reply, we'd reached the bench and Max stopped.

'This is what I wanted to show you,' he said, pointing up at a huge tree just behind it. 'And I hope you don't think it's too much or too intense but...' He paused. 'As you've made the effort to come here, I wanted you to see it.'

My eyes followed several wooden steps nailed up the trunk to a treehouse that looked like a miniature Swiss chalet, with a small platform that poked out in front of it, overlooking the lake.

It was idyllic, a childhood dream, but I didn't get the significance. Did Max want me to climb it? Was this some sort of initiation test?

'We going up?' I asked nervously. Small boys might have managed but the rotting wooden steps looked less sturdy than matchsticks to me.

'No, no,' said Max, stepping forward to hold out a protective hand between me and the tree trunk. 'Sorry, I'm not explaining it very well. I just still come down here every time I'm home because it's where we sprinkled Del's ashes.'

'Oh,' I said, a hand flying to my cheek, moved that this was why he'd marched me down here.

Mum, Dennis and I had sprinkled her mother, my grandmother, on Holkham beach when I was eight and the wind was belting across the sand dunes. I'd choked on a mouthful of Granny that blew back at me, but I figured it wasn't the moment to mention this.

'Want to sit?' he asked, inclining his head towards the bench.

'Course,' I said.

'My parents are difficult,' he said, once we were sitting down. 'I know that. And I'm sorry this wasn't easier, or more welcoming.'

'Ah, that's all right,' I said. 'I'm a stranger, right?'

'To them, maybe,' he said, giving me a lopsided grin. 'But it wasn't always like that. This is why I wanted to bring you here. We had a perfect childhood, for a time. Until the accident, and then Nanny took over and my parents and I barely ever ate in the same room together.' He twisted his head to look up at the treehouse and then back to me. 'I couldn't bear to be that distant from my own child. Or children. I won't. I can't be that father.'

'So don't be,' I said, gently. 'There's no reason you will be. History doesn't have to repeat itself.'

'Are you always so sure?' he said, frowning at me quizzically.

'About what?'

'Everything,' he replied, which made me laugh so loudly it echoed around the banks of the lake.

'No, I'm really not,' I replied. Roughly three times a week, I wasn't even sure if I had clean knickers for the morning.

We sat in companionable silence for a few minutes, looking out in front of us. Every now and then something twitched on the water which sent ripples across it.

'Thank you,' I said quietly.

'For what?' Max asked, turning towards me.

'For bringing me here.'

He smiled and we held eyes. Spending more time with Max in the past week or so, meeting one another's families and sitting on this bench and chatting had made me soften towards him. I'm not talking heart eyes. I knew I needed to be careful, that I should try to contain any fanciful romantic feelings in case they complicated our situation further. But I liked him more and more. He wasn't just a posh boy with good hair and a ludicrous car. He was smarter than that, funnier, more engaging, more emotionally astute. He was… Oh, for God's sake, get a hold of yourself.

'Right,' I announced, clapping my hands down on my thighs like a sumo wrestler, thereby ruining the moment. 'I'd better be going.'

Max looked momentarily surprised. 'Oh, OK. You going back to Norfolk?'

'Yeah. You?'

'I'm going to drive back to London later.'

'Cool.'

'Come on then, I'll walk you back.'

We strolled up the path again, towards the house. As we

neared it, I could see the Viscountess kneeling on the lawn beside a flower bed, her gardening gloves on. Prince Charles talks to his plants, doesn't he? Perhaps all the aristocracy do, I thought, watching her. Presumably they form closer bonds with inanimate plants than they do the members of their own family.

★

My phone rang as I was filling up with petrol on the drive back. It was a private number which always made me nervous. Was I in trouble? I answered it with my official phone voice. 'Hello?'

'Miss Bailey?' It was Miss Montague. 'Can you hear me?'

'Oh, hello, yes, all clear,' I said. It was never difficult to hear Miss Montague on the phone. She barked down it like a sergeant major.

'I won't keep you,' she shouted. 'But I wanted to update you on the Roman Walker situation.'

'OK,' I replied slowly. Please, please, please could I not be fired.

'It's only that I've spoken to the Walkers, and also to Fergus, and I fear I may have been a bit rash. I gather Fergus was the one who should have been paying more attention. I'm sorry, Miss Bailey, but as you know the security of the boys is my first priority and that is what I was most concerned about.'

'OKKKKK,' I said again, breathing out slightly. Even though she sounded apologetic, I couldn't tell which way this would go.

'So I expect you back at school as soon as possible.'

'Oh right. Er, OK…' I was so surprised, and grateful, and emotionally spent after meeting Max's parents, that I didn't have the energy to be huffy. 'Great.'

'Monday, if possible?'

I knew it wasn't really a question.

'Sure thing,' I said.

'Marvellous,' she said. 'See you on Monday then, Miss Bailey.' She rang off without saying goodbye and I looked at my call list. I immediately wanted to ring Max and tell him. But then I reminded myself I needed to watch it, not let my guard down too far, so I paid for the petrol and decided to call Jess instead. She'd have all sorts of questions about Max's parents, I knew. Did I have to curtsy for them and that sort of nonsense.

CHAPTER TEN

SINCE ST LANCELOT'S WAS run like a military operation by a military leader (sort of), I fell back into place as if I'd never been away. Miss Montague nodded at me in the staffroom as if it was just another morning. The science teachers barely glanced over from their corner, the language department kept on drinking their pretentious coffee in another (they brought fresh coffee in and insisted on making a mess with a cafetière, sprinkling coffee grounds all over the carpet). Mike sat on a chair beside Steph groaning after too many beers the night before. 'I've got Year 4 for their recorder lesson up first. Why me? Why me, God?' he said, reaching his hands towards the ceiling.

Steph rolled her eyes and ignored him. 'How are you feeling?'

I exhaled slowly, glancing around the room. 'All right. I've still got a job. I'm not pregnant and out on the street like a Victorian urchin.'

Steph tutted. 'As if that was ever going to happen. Honestly, all that fuss. Is that boy still in your class?'

She meant Fergus, and he was. Although he looked chastened and tried to talk to me while the boys were practising their vocabulary that morning.

'Er, Miss Bailey,' he said, as I was crouching by Achilles' desk.

'Hang on a minute,' I said. 'OK, Achilles, the what is parked outside the house?' I asked, pointing to a blank space with my pencil.

Achilles thought for a minute and then looked at me. 'Bentley?' he suggested. His face looked so cherubic I had to swallow a laugh.

'Car,' I corrected. 'Look, there, can you manage?'

He nodded and turned back to his sheet, practically sweating with effort.

I sighed and stood up. 'Right, Fergus, you all right?'

'Yes, er, I just wanted to say sorry for everything. For, er, the, er, confusion and the, er, well, for Aunt Venetia, I mean Miss Montague and, er, everything.'

He blushed scarlet while delivering this speech and it occurred to me, yet again, that I really had ten boys in my class, not nine.

'That's all right. I was the one in charge. It was an accident, these things happen.'

'That's awfully good of you,' he said, still puce. 'I won't let anything like that happen again. I've promised Aunt Ve— I mean Miss Montague.'

'Great, shall we start again then?'

Fergus beamed.

If my colleagues and pupils hadn't really noticed I'd been away, the mothers certainly had. It was mostly nannies at pick-up that afternoon, but Hunter's mother, the apple crumble obsessive, shot me an enquiring look.

'Miss Bailey, so glad you're back,' she said as she took Hunter's satchel. She was dressed — as usual — in full lycra and trainers so pristine and white they could blind someone. Although today's highlight were her leggings, which had mesh panels that revealed flashes of thigh.

I smiled as broadly as I could, trying not to goggle at her legs. 'Thank you. Just a few days off with this one.' I put my hands on my stomach. Was I going to hell for using my unborn child to tell a lie? Too late.

'Oh! Congratulations! I had no idea,' she said. 'When are you due?'

'June. Bye, Cosmo!' I said, waving at him and his nanny.

Hunter's mother narrowed her eyes at me. 'Which antenatal classes are you doing?'

NCT classes were on my to-do list. I just hadn't got round to it. Plus, I'd realized they cost £300. Three hundred quid to go to a class on my own and learn to breathe through my vagina, or whatever they taught you. I'd always assumed they were on the NHS and free.

'Er, not sure yet.'

She shook her head. 'You need to get a place on the Happy Baby Class, it's the only class to take. My friend Emily runs them. Leave it with me.'

I tried to remonstrate. 'Oh, no, honestly, it's OK, I don't—'

'I won't hear it,' she said, waving a manicured hand in the air, Barbie-pink nail varnish. 'Consider it a gift from Hunter. Come on, sweetheart,' she said, snatching his hand. 'Your Mandarin tutor will be at home when we get back.'

★

Later that week, I found myself lying on the carpet in the flat, while Grace held her wedding ring, suspended on a piece of cotton, above my stomach. It had been her idea, an old wives' tale which promised to reveal the sex of a baby.

'Are you gonna find out what it is?' she'd asked, when I'd mentioned my twenty-week scan.

'I'm pretty sure it's a baby.'

'You know what I mean, darl. What do you reckon?'

I'd shrugged. 'Honestly not sure, but I just have this feeling it's a girl.'

Which is why I was now lying on my back, on the floor. I rolled my head to the side and looked at the dust and hair under the sofa, pushed back against the door.

'We need to hoover,' I said.

'Concentrate,' said Grace, kneeling beside me.

'I'm not sure it works if it's someone else's ring.'

'Shhhhh, I did this on my cousin once and it totally worked.'

'What did she have?'

'A boy. Declan.'

Lying on my back like this, with ET squatting just above my bladder, made me want to wee.

'So if it goes in circles it's a boy,' said Grace, 'and if it's more side-to-side then it's a girl.'

We both studied the ring as it hung in the air directly above my belly button. It had recently popped out so that whenever

I stood in the shower and glanced down it looked like a nose was protruding from my stomach.

The ring didn't move.

'How long does this take? I need to pee,' I said, arching my upper back.

'Hang on,' ordered Grace, 'look it's moving.'

'You're doing that,' I said, as the ring starting swinging from side-to-side.

'I am not,' she said. 'Look! I think you're right, it's a girl.'

There was a sudden crash which made Grace drop the ring. It was Riley trying to get in the front door.

'What's going on?' he shouted from behind it.

'Two ticks,' she said, getting up and dusting off her shins.

I rolled over and got up too, mostly so that Grace could push the sofa back into place but also because I might otherwise have weed on the carpet.

Grace let him in and explained. 'We were doing a test to see whether she's having a boy or a girl.'

'And?' said Riley.

'We think it's a girl.'

'Great news,' he replied. 'Can you still call her Riley?'

'Maybe,' I said, as I closed the bathroom door.

I googled the test while peeing. Turns out, Grace had got the test wrong anyway. Supposedly if the ring moves in circles it's a girl, and if it's side-to-wide like a pendulum it's a boy. Some witch doctor she was.

★

'And you don't want to find out what sex the baby is having?' said Dr Papadakis, the following Friday evening as I lay in the same, small room where I'd had the twelve-week-scan.

I turned my head and raised my eyebrows at Max, sitting beside me. He shook his head.

'Nope,' I said, turning back to Dr Papadakis. 'Still don't.'

'I'd better not mention that it's a boy then,' he replied.

'WHAT?' chorused Max and I together.

'Ha ha, I am just having a joking with you,' he said. 'The baby has got its leg up so I cannot see anyways.'

I exhaled and relaxed on the bed again, my eyes fixed on the grainy screen.

'All the fingers and toes are correct,' said Dr Papadakis. 'And the art, it looks perfect.'

I looked at one of ET's hands, curled up and poised in front of her chest as if she was bracing herself for a fight. I loved her so completely already. More, maybe, than if she'd been planned and more of an actual, grown-up decision. She seemed more special, more miraculous.

I glanced at Max, sitting forward in his seat, staring at the screen in silence. 'And her vertebrae are all fine? And her kidneys?'

'It is all totally as it should be,' said Dr Papadakis.

'I've been doing some reading,' Max added, looking at my surprised expression.

'Have you now?'

'Yep. And I've downloaded one of those pregnancy apps, so I keep getting daily updates telling me my baby is now the size of a banana.' He leant back and patted his stomach. 'And that I might be terribly constipated. Are you constipated, Lil?' He was joking, but I immediately blushed and put my hands to my cheeks.

'Oh my God, I can't believe you just asked me that.'

'It's very natural,' said Max, still grinning. 'You should be eating more fibre.'

'You are having the constipation?' said Dr Papadakis, swivelling in his seat and looking at me with concern.

'No!' I said, emphatically. 'I'm fine.'

'If you are having the gas,' went on Dr Papadakis, 'this is also very common.'

'Oh my God,' I said, covering my eyes with my hands. If I'd been here with a boyfriend or husband I'd been dating for several years and who knew I farted in bed, I wouldn't have minded. But Max had arrived for the appointment today wearing a plain white T-shirt which stretched against the muscles of his chest and the sight had given me a funny, fluttery feeling somewhere between my belly button and my crotch. How could I lie here, discussing gas, next to that? It was too shameful.

'Lil,' I heard Max say next to me, in a mocking voice. 'Are you having gas problems?'

'No,' I said quietly, although this was a lie. I still felt like a human whoopee cushion. I'd farted so badly the other night I'd repulsed myself, and had to get up and open a window and fan my duvet. The smell could have killed a rhino.

'Sometimes it is just a phase and it passes,' said Dr Papadakis, turning back to the screen. 'But some women have problems with their bowls all the way through their pregnancy.'

'My bowls are fine,' I said. 'Absolutely no problems.'

★

'Thanks for coming,' I said to Max, standing outside the hospital half an hour later.

'Course,' he said. 'So what are we doing next?'

'Er, actually I'm starting antenatal classes soon and there's a fathers' class we all do together, if you want to do that?'

Hunter's mother had handed me an information pack about the antenatal class in the playground that week and told me she'd persuaded Emily to make space for me on a course starting in a few weeks, 'as a special favour'. I tried to protest but she insisted.

'Honey, it's my treat,' she'd said. It made me feel uneasy, like I'd be in her debt for a favour down the line. Extra maths tuition or special dispensation for Hunter to take time out of school so they could go on holiday somewhere like Zanzibar.

'OK, cool,' replied Max. 'When?'

'Not sure. I'll check and text you.'

'Great. Oh and listen, I was thinking, do you need any baby stuff?' Max glanced across at the Houses of Parliament over the river and then back at me. 'I was just thinking I should probably get some... for my place.'

'Like what?' I said, frowning at him.

'Well I should probably get a cot, right? For when she's at

mine. And a pram. And a car seat. And, yeah, just other bits and pieces the books suggest.'

'Course,' I said faintly. It wasn't just the thought of not having ET with me. In just a few words, it was a reminder of what separate lives we'd live once she arrived.

'I know we haven't talked about arrangements,' he added quickly. 'And obviously she'll be with you for the first few weeks at least. But I figured, better to be prepared and all that.' He looked out to the Thames again.

'Sure,' I replied. 'Yeah, we can go shopping whenever.' Mum had been badgering me for weeks about when she could drive down from Norfolk with boxes of old baby clothes. But I'd been putting off buying anything new because I was worried about the expense. I'd been meaning to apply for a new credit card, but it was one of those boring admin chores that had been loitering on my to-do list for weeks.

'Where are you heading now?' he said.

'To my friend's place in Chiswick. Oh, you met her. Jess. At the first scan?' Tonight was Jess and Clem's birthday party, an annual event they threw at home and which Jess always insisted on making fancy dress. This year, after much bickering between the twins, the theme was 'a piece of art'. I'd googled 'pregnant women pieces of art' and decided to go as the Virgin Mary in a blue maxi dress I'd borrowed from Grace with a sheet draped over my head like a cloak.

'Want me to drop you off?' said Max.

'You don't have to do that, it's miles,' I protested (quite feebly). 'I was just going to jump on the Tube.'

'Why don't I just take you? It's not that far. Come on, I've parked the pimp mobile around the corner.'

★

'What are you doing tonight?' I asked him, as we crawled around Hammersmith roundabout.

Max was tapping his fingers on the steering wheel to an Ace of Base song, playing on Magic. He had terrible taste in music, I'd been delighted to learn, because Jake had always pretended that he was deeply into 'the music scene', as he called it, and always played 6 Music. You never hear 'All That She Wants' on 6 Music.

'Not much,' he said simply. 'Going to Wales early tomorrow for a training climb so it'll probably be a takeaway and early night.'

'Want to come in for a quick drink?' I suggested, as he turned the car into Jess and Clem's road.

'Errrr…' Max paused and I felt instantly stupid. Like I'd gone too far. I'd asked him partly because I felt sad at the idea of him going home alone on a Friday night, but also because I thought it might be a good opportunity to normalize our situation. As far as you can normalize a situation at a party when you're dressed as the Virgin Mary.

'You don't have to,' I said. 'Just a thought. I probably won't stay that late. But Jess's new boyfriend is going to be there and I need to chat to him since I haven't really hung out with him and—'

'Lil,' said Max, interrupting me.

I turned my head to look at him. 'Uh-huh?'

'I'd love to, you weirdo. You don't have to gabble,' he said, grinning across at me. 'I probably can't stay that late either, but if… sorry… what's she called again? If your friend doesn't mind a last-minute guest then great.'

'I wasn't gabbling,' I said primly. 'And she's called Jess. She's got a twin brother called Clem. It's their birthday. And Alexi is her new boyfriend.' My stomach suddenly spun with nerves. Was it a good idea to bring Max to a party where everyone was going to be in fancy dress, a party which usually disintegrated into a student night with crusted pots of hummus in the kitchen, fag burns on the carpet and a blocked loo? There was always a blocked loo.

'What number are they?' said Max, slowing down and squinting at the numbers.

'Nineteen,' I squeaked, and then pointed at the rusting railings just ahead of us. 'That one.'

'It says sixteen,' he said, frowning at the little metal '9' which had swung upside down.

'Yeah, don't worry about that. It's just… you'll see,' I replied, wondering what level of pre-party chaos would greet us inside.

★

We were early guests. It was only just seven which meant the house sounded quiet when we stood on the doorstep and knocked. Well, relatively quiet.

'CLEM, CAN YOU GET THAT, PLEASE?' I heard Jess bellow from inside. 'I'M BASICALLY NAKED.'

'My kind of party,' said Max, standing beside me.

'They're quite mad,' I said, feeling increasingly nervous. 'Wonderful, but mad.'

'Good eve—' boomed Clem, sweeping back the front door but stopping as soon as he saw Max. 'Oh my good God.'

'Hello,' I said quickly. 'Clem meet Max, he drove me here so I said he should come in for a drink, right?'

'Of course,' said Clem, still wide-eyed at the sight of Max. 'Step right in and I'll rustle up some beers. Beer, Max? Do you drink beer? You don't have to have beer. We've got other drinks. Wine, spirits, and a punch I've made which tastes a bit sweet but I'm hoping nobody will notice.'

'Beer would be great,' said Max, a bemused expression on his face. 'But can I just ask why you're dressed like that?'

Clem was wearing a big velvet coat, a velvet cap, white tights underneath velvet shorts with a big gold chain swinging around his neck.

'Oh, did Lil not tell you?' said Clem. 'It's fancy dress. Come as a piece of art, so I am Holbein's Henry VIII. Although this kit is bloody hot. Right, come through to the kitchen and I'll get us all a drink.'

'No,' said Max, digging a finger into my back. 'No, Lil did not tell me that.'

Luckily we were all distracted by a blur coming downstairs. It was Jess in a frankly extraordinary outfit. She'd been plotting to come as David for this party, as in Michelangelo's sculpture of the chiselled, naked man. So she'd bought silver body paint and plastered herself in the stuff, including her hair, but was also wearing one of those comedy aprons, which depicted a man's muscled torso with a marble penis.

'Does this look all right? Be honest,' she said, before noticing Max. 'Oh hello, what are you doing here?'

'Hi,' said Max, still looking bemused.

'It's quite confusing, sis,' said Clem, squinting at her apron and then up at her face. 'You look like something from Greek mythology, half man, half woman.'

'Exactly. Funny, no?' she said. 'Not bad for £7.99 from eBay.'

Clem's eyes remained on the apron's cock. It was terrifyingly lifelike.

'Have you got a bare bottom?' I asked Jess. 'What's going on behind?'

'No!' She spun around to reveal a silver pair of pants and a patchy back where she couldn't quite reach with the body paint. 'Lil, can you finish me off?'

'Yeah, sure.'

'I'll just go grab the paint.'

'Why don't I come with you and get dressed? Clem, you sort drinks,' I said.

'Right-o,' said Clem. 'Although technically I am a king and you should all be doing what I say. But come on, Max, let's get these beers going.'

Clem turned and clanked into the kitchen, Max went after him. I followed Jess upstairs.

'How come he's here?' she hissed, once safely in her studio.

'Do you mind? He brought me here from the scan.' I got changed as I talked, peeling off my jeans and jersey and pulling Grace's dress over my head.

'I'm sorry I forgot. How was it? And no, course not, I'm thrilled. So long as you're happy. Is he being nice? Supportive? Look, here's the paint.' Jess waited for me to do up my dress, then handed me a can and turned her back to me, lifting her hair up above the nape of her neck.

'Yeah, all good on the scan front. And he is being nice. I think meeting the parents has helped a bit. It feels more normal.' I shook the can and started spraying between her shoulder blades.

'So what are you guys? Just friends? Ooh, that's cold.'

'I guess? I still don't really know what category "strangers who are having a baby together" falls into.'

'Pregnant fuckbuddies?'

'No! Gross. I hate that expression.'

'So there's no chance of anything romantic?'

I twisted my mouth as I carried on patching up the fleshy bits of her back. 'I don't know. But then I still don't know if I want anything romantic. Maybe it would complicate things? And it feels a bit backwards, in a way, dating someone when you're already knocked up with their baby. Like, say we went on another date and he suggested coming home with me, what would I say, "Oh no, sorry, I think it's a bit early for that?"'

Jess laughed. 'Ha. On the plus side you wouldn't have to worry about condoms.'

'How about you, anyway?' I said, changing the subject. 'Is Alexi here yet?'

'Not sure, he's being a bit mysterious about it all, as usual.'

'You did say ages ago you longed for mystery,' I reminded her.

'When?' She spun round and looked at me.

'Stand still,' I said. 'And when I came over after that date with Max, when you were grumbling about Walt.'

'Oh, yeah. Well, perhaps there can be too much mystery.'

I shook the can a final time and sprayed down her spine. 'Honestly, why are we never happy? But right, you're done.'

'We shall go to the ball,' she said, turning and linking her arm through mine.

'Careful,' I said, brushing silver paint off my dress. 'I don't think the Virgin Mary should get too close to naked men.'

'Too late,' she said, pointing at my stomach.

*

An hour or so later, the first two floors of the house were full of people in strange outfits swigging at beer bottles or drinking wine from plastic cups. There were several Degas ballerinas. A woman I didn't know who was standing in the corner of the kitchen, dressed as a sunflower, with a yellow face and yellow felt petals around her head, talking to a man who'd come as a Campbell's soup tin, two large sheets of painted cardboard hanging either side of him with straps over his shoulders.

Max had proved very game, not seeming to mind that

he was in jeans and a T-shirt while art installations mingled around us. I'd introduced him to the ballerinas and we'd all chatted briefly, before I said I needed to sit down, so he and I retreated to the kitchen, and we both sat on the table, feet on chairs, sharing a bowl of Doritos.

'So these are mostly uni mates?' said Max, holding the bowl out to me.

I nodded. 'Yeah, plus Clem's friends, Jess's art school pals. So a lot of people I don't know. But mostly uni mates.'

'Is your ex-boyfriend here?'

I was so stunned by the question I didn't answer immediately. 'Oh, er, no. He's from a sort of, different uni group.'

'Sorry,' said Max, sensing my hesitation. 'I didn't mean to pry. Was just wondering if he was about to arrive and I'd have to challenge him to a duel.'

He grinned at me so I laughed loudly, then worried that I'd just ejected a mouthful of Dorito-breath directly at his face. 'No. Don't worry. No duelling required.' We sat in silence, our legs nearly touching, while I felt curiously pleased about his chivalrous offer to take on Jake.

'I think it's always difficult to stay friends with them afterwards, right?' I asked him, after a few moments.

'What, exes?'

'Yeah.'

'Er, I think sometimes you can,' said Max, after a brief pause. 'Depending on how complicated the situation was.' He opened his mouth as if about to say something else, then stopped himself.

'What?' I asked. His expression unsettled me and I wanted him to carry on talking, but we were interrupted by Jess coming towards us, pulling Alexi by the hand behind her.

'Lil, Alexi, you remember Lil, from the time we met at that exhibition party?'

'Of course,' said Alexi. 'The famous Lil, how are you?'

He leant forward and kissed me on both cheeks. I'd forgotten he had such a thick Russian accent. Jess loved an accent.

'I'm good. Well, quite tired actually. I'm not sure the Virgin Mary is much of a party animal,' I said. 'And this is Max.'

They shook hands and I asked who Alexi had come as. He was dressed entirely in black, as he had been when I first met him. Long-sleeved black shirt, black jeans, black Converse.

Alexi made a guilty face. 'I forgot about the dress code.'

'Useless,' said Jess, hitting him on the arm.

He shrugged. 'I know, I am sorry. Perhaps I can be The Scream.' He handed Jess his cigarette and put both hands on either side of his face, opening his mouth.

'Stop it, you idiot, that's hideous,' she said, grinning at him, so he leant over and kissed her on the cheek.

'Forgive me, my beautiful David.'

'Cringe,' said Jess, rolling her eyes. 'Not in front of these guys.'

'Hey, don't stop on my account,' said Max. 'I'm just glad there's someone else who's not in fancy dress.'

'Where's your drink, Max?' said Jess.

'I'm good, thanks, driving.'

'OK, I'm going to get another one. Anyone?'

We shook our heads and Jess fought her way past the sunflower to the fridge.

'So good to properly meet you again,' I said to Alexi. 'You travel a lot, right?'

'Yes,' he said, nodding. 'Always on a plane somewhere, everywhere. But I like it. Better than sitting in an office all day.'

'I can imagine.'

'And you are a teacher, yes?'

'Yep. A school in Chelsea called St Lancelot's. Five-year-old terrors. Well, some terrors. But I love them mostly.'

'At where?' he asked, coughing smoke at me.

'It's called St Lancelot's,' I repeated. 'A private school. Mostly the sons of bankers. And celebrities. And I sometimes feel like I should be doing something more worthy, teaching children who need more help.' I rattled through the speech I usually gave when I explained where I worked, as if trying to justify my job. Being apologetic about St Lancelot's was a guilty habit of mine since I knew certain people judged me for teaching in the private sector. Although, to be fair, Alexi bought and sold art for millionaires, so he presumably didn't care.

Alexi clapped himself on the chest and we carried on making small talk. Or rather, Max and I asked Alexi a series of questions while he answered. He wasn't very forthcoming.

I asked where Alexi lived (Kensington), Max asked where

he grew up (St Petersburg), I asked where he went to uni (London), Max asked him what kind of art he liked ('it depends'). I was struggling to think of anything else when Jess reappeared with a glass of red wine. 'Sorry, I got trapped with one of Clem's music friends. Desperate. Budge up, can I squeeze on?' she said, looking at the kitchen table.

'Have my place,' said Max, 'I should get going.'

'Oh no,' said Jess, looking at him and making a sad face. 'I didn't mean to scare you away.'

Max shook his head. 'Not at all, thank you for having me. I've just got an early start in the morning.'

'Thank you for coming,' she said. 'Lil, you're not going, are you?'

'Nope,' I said, although I did feel slightly disappointed that Max was leaving and I quite wanted to head home myself. But I probably had to give it another hour or so. Unsupportive to go home before ten – pregnant or not. 'Hang on, I'll just show Max out, save my seat.'

'Alexi, good to meet you,' said Max, offering his hand again.

'Goodbye,' said Alexi coolly, blowing smoke from another cigarette into the air.

Max and I pushed our way through more artworks to the front door and then stepped outside. I left the door slightly ajar behind me so it didn't lock.

'Let me know about that antenatal class,' he said.

'Course, will do,' I said.

He leant towards me and pulled me into him for a hug.

My face buried in his shoulder, I inhaled while he held me. His smell was becoming familiar. But then I had to clench my bottom because I could feel a fart coming on and if I let that out there'd only be one thing for it: I'd have to fling myself over the wall across the road and into the river.

CHAPTER ELEVEN

I'D GOOGLED 'THE HAPPY Baby Class' before my first session and up came various newspaper articles about it. Turns out it was the 'most exclusive' antenatal class in London, with a waiting list of several months. Rumours were Pippa Middleton had done it, as had Keira Knightley and Carey Mulligan. It made me nervous. What would I have to reveal in front of these perfect pregnant women? I certainly didn't want to ask whether I'd crap myself while in labour.

Needless to say, the classes were held in a private house in Knightsbridge, although this was handy because I could waddle there from school in about twenty minutes.

When I arrived for my first class, that Thursday evening, I triple-checked the address – 5 Drayton Avenue – looking down at my phone and then back up at the enormous white house in front of me, white pillars either side of the white steps.

This was definitely it, I decided, checking the address one more time and looking around me to see if there were any other pregnant women dragging themselves towards me. It was a quiet street and all the other houses looked exactly the same, about five or six levels high, with fat white pillars on either side of the front steps. Range Rovers and flashy sports cars were parked outside most of them.

I climbed the steps and rang a doorbell. A small woman in blue uniform answered it.

'Sorry, I think I have the wrong address,' I said, very confused. Where the hell was this class? Maybe there was a basement underneath here? I peered over the railings to my side.

'No, no,' said the woman in uniform. 'You are here for baby lesson?'

'The Happy Baby Class?' I said hopefully.

'Yes, yes, baby lesson. Please, please.' She ushered me into the house and I stepped into a big hall with grey marble flooring. Then, having taken my coat and as if trying to herd a sheep, she coaxed me along a corridor with her arms towards a doorway behind the stairs. 'Please, please, this way, please.'

I went down into a huge living room. Cream sofas, cream carpet, cream curtains, cream armchairs. The one thing that wasn't beige was an enormous black and white photo of a heavily pregnant woman, entirely naked, hanging on the wall facing me. It was nearly life-sized. I gawped at it for a few moments. She was standing, brown hair cascading in curls down her back, hands on her hips, looking at the camera. But your eye wasn't immediately drawn to her face. Instead it was drawn to her stomach, which looked so engorged I didn't understand how she was even upright, and also to her knockers. The areola on these things had the circumference of a digestive biscuit. I glanced down at my own chest. My areola were still a sensible size at the moment, like 50p pieces. But would they end up looking like that?

'Hello and welcome, can I tick your name off?' trilled a voice behind me and I turned around to find myself eyeballing the woman in the photograph.

'Hello,' I said, surprised. 'I'm Lil Bailey.'

'Lillllll,' she said, smiling at me. 'Of course you are. I'm Emily. Lovely to meet you. Would you like to have a seat? Felicia will take your drinks order. Feliciaaaaa?'

Another woman in uniform appeared from behind a door just off the cream room. 'Yes, madam?'

'Could you see what Lil would like to drink?'

'Oh, er, a tea please,' I said.

'What kind of tea, madam? We have English Breakfast, Earl Grey, Lady Grey, lapsang souchong, green tea, mint, chamomile, fennel and lemon and ginger?'

'English Breakfast is fine, thanks. With a splash of milk?'

She nodded and went back through the door. Meanwhile, I could hear others arriving upstairs where Emily had gone to greet them. She had a theatrical voice, it sounded put on. Breathy and deliberately soft, almost robotic. 'Hellooooo,' she was saying, 'please do come downnnnn.'

I quickly grabbed a seat on the edge of one of the sofas and watched as the other women appeared. I felt anxious, like the first day at school.

'Hello,' I said, waving as, one by one, they arrived and sat down self-consciously on the sofas. We smiled nervously at one another while Felicia bustled around taking drinks orders.

'What alternative milks do you have?' asked a woman perched on the other end of my sofa. She looked like a St Lancelot's mother – jeans, knee-high boots, leather jacket, jet-black hair slicked into a perfect ponytail, not a hair loose. Forehead as smooth as a bowl of custard. I glanced around the room. They mostly looked like that – either in floaty designer dresses which showed off their ball-like stomachs or jeans and jackets which were designed to look casual but probably cost thousands, Chanel bags at their feet. I glanced down at my leggings and yellowing Converse, hoping that we didn't have to take our shoes off. My feet would smell.

Finally, everyone had cups and saucers in their hand and Felicia put a plate of shortbread down on the table in the middle of the room. I stood up and reached for one, and then realized I should maybe offer it around. I picked up the plate and gestured at the others.

They all shook their heads.

I sat back down and tried to eat my shortbread quietly, but the only noise in the room was my crunching. And I was covering my leggings in crumbs.

'Ladiesssss,' said Emily, appearing from upstairs. 'We're nearly all here. Just one to go but,' she looked at her watch, 'I think we'll get started anyway. So what we're going to do is go round the room and introduce ourselves, state our due date, plus…'

And then she said the thing we all dread in an unfamiliar group scenario: 'plus one funny or unusual fact about ourselves.'

Worse, she looked straight at me. 'Why don't we start from this side of the room, Lil, you go first.'

I chuckled nervously. 'OK, er, hello, everyone. I'm Lil. And I'm due on the tenth of June and, um, an unusual fact. I suppose the fact that I'm having this baby after a one-night stand is quite unusual. Ha ha!' I said this in a jokey tone but it met with silence. The other women looked down at their cups.

Emily stepped in, saying in a falsely cheery voice; 'Goodness me, that is unusual. Thank you, Lil. Cecilia, you're next.'

Cecilia was the one with the perfect ponytail. She was due a couple of weeks before me and said her funny fact was that she was 'double-jointed'.

WHAT? That's not funny or unusual.

And so it went, round the room. A woman called Amanda said her funny fact was she was she was scared of jelly. Another called Daisy said she spoke five languages, 'including Swahili.' She looked very pleased with herself about that. We paused when the final woman arrived apologizing loudly and sat in the only spot remaining, on the sofa between me and Cecilia. I was relieved to see she looked flustered and sweaty, less put together than the others. More like me. And she had a rucksack instead of a handbag. I felt instant kinship.

She was the last to go, too. 'Hiya, everyone, I'm Beth and I'm due in early June. And my funny fact is I once touched Prince Harry's arse.'

I burst out laughing.

'Yeah, good, isn't it?' said Beth, turning to grin at me.

Everybody else was smiling uncomfortably.

'Gosh,' said Emily, straight-faced, 'how did that happen?'

'Just a dare at this party years ago.'

'Right, well,' went on Emily. 'On that note I think we should get started. Welcome to the Happy Baby Class, everyone, which will, over the next few weeks, prepare you for the magical adventure of parenthood.' She quacked on like that for a while – the miracle of childbirth, the 'wondrous' first moment you first held your child, even the 'excitement' of the first nappy.

'We can't be coy, ladiessss. We're all going to be best friends by the end of this course, having discussed very intimate details about our bodies. Can you get rid of stretch marks? Not really. Will you poo while giving birth? Probably, yes.'

Bingo, I thought, that's my most urgent question answered.

Emily carried on: 'Am I going to rip my vagina? Again, probably, but today we're going to talk about what you can do to make that less likely.'

She then launched into a discussion about improving the strength of our pelvic floor muscles. 'Imagine you're weeing, then you try and stop. There you go, that's your pelvic floor. Very important for childbirth. Oh well done, Lil, you're doing your exercises now, I can always tell.' She winked at me and I immediately stopped tensing. Then I glanced at the time. It was only twelve minutes past six, which meant we had another hour and forty-eight minutes to go. And this was just class one. Of six. I slumped back against the sofa and made a mental note to tell Max the funny (and less personal) bits of this class on our shopping expedition the next day.

★

The first time Jake and I ever went shopping together was to a sex shop. It must have been our six or seventh date in Edinburgh, and we stumbled into it as a joke, very pissed. We'd cackled at the incredible variety of porn categories available and goggled at the range of dildos before deciding to buy a more modest vibrator, bright pink and the size of a chipolata. It was the same vibrator I used now. Jess said it was bad voodoo to keep a vibrator you used with an ex but that didn't make sense to me. Vibrators were expensive. No point in throwing away a perfectly good one.

The shopping trip I made with Max, to the baby department of Peter Jones in Sloane Square, was quite different. I'd suggested Westfield, but Max said Chelsea was closer to Brixton and he could drive everything over to mine afterwards.

We met on the fourth floor and stood just to the side of the escalator, surveying the sea of buggies in front of us. Before the trip, I spent five minutes scrolling through a Mumsnet forum where users discussed the merits of a Bugaboo buggy versus something called an iCandy with almost religious fervour, but the discussion made me want to stick pins underneath my fingernails, so I'd shut down the page and decided I'd make my mind up on the day. Something with wheels that wasn't four million pounds. That was all I needed.

'Can I help you?' said a doughy, middle-aged lady who approached us as we dithered. The badge told us her name was Marjorie.

'Ah, Marjorie, yes please,' said Max. 'What we'd like to see is the Baby Wagon 4000 with the carrycot.'

'An excellent choice, sir,' said Marjorie, approvingly. 'It's over here, follow me.'

'What?' I hissed in shock to Max, as we started after her. 'How do you know so much about prams?'

'Some of us did our research,' he said, elbowing me gently. 'It's supposed to be the best.'

'Absolute nerd,' I whispered back, feeling secretly pleased, as we stopped in front of a grey buggy. Marjorie ran a manicured hand over it as if it was a racing horse.

'Shhh,' he said, winking at me. 'Listen to Marjorie.'

'It's our most versatile pushchair,' she said. 'Ideal for London, or the country, and incredibly lightweight so it's very easy to lift in and out of the car. And the chassis is very robust.'

'Hear that, Lil? A very robust chassis,' said Max.

'Mmm hmm.' I pressed my lips together to prevent an accidental laugh.

'It takes Baby from newborn to toddler and it comes in a range of colours,' breezed on Marjorie, 'winter grey, berry, summer blue or midnight. As well as a two-year guarantee.'

'Marvellous, I think we should go for it. What colour?' said Max, turning to look at me.

I'd just noticed the price tag hanging from the handlebar: £1,104. Jess said they had an old cot I could use, but I still needed to buy a new mattress, a Moses basket, bottles, muslins, a bath, a sterilizer, a monitor, a changing mat, about sixty million nappies, baby wipes and so on and so on. And these were just the very basics. I couldn't spend over a grand on a buggy.

'Er, it's a bit out of the price range, do you have anything more in the three-hundred-pound area?' I asked, looking hopefully at Marjorie.

'No no, don't worry about that,' interrupted Max, and I felt him put a hand on my back. 'I'm doing all this.'

I turned and tried to protest. 'Max, come on, no way, we're sharing.'

'Absolutely not,' he said. 'I've just agreed to taking a grotesquely rich group of Chinese businessmen up a mountain in Mongolia next month, so this is on them.'

'Max—'

'No arguing. A Baby Wagon 4000, please, Marjorie, and in what colour, Lil?'

I caved pretty quickly. 'OK, well, if you're sure, thank you, then what about midnight?'

'Midnight it is. What next?'

Max, I was astonished to learn, was an enthusiastic shopper. It felt like we whipped around the baby department and ordered so much clobber it was as if he and I were opening a nursery. A hypoallergenic baby mattress, a changing mat decorated with cartoon ducks, a baby monitor with a camera so I could hear and watch ET sleeping, a baby bath that was shaped like a blue whale, dozens of white muslins, babygros, a papoose, a sterilizer and several bottles. Marjorie, it turned out, had grown up in Ipswich so she and Max had a long chat about the merits of Suffolk while we strolled round.

'And will you be needing one of these, madam?' said Marjorie, interrupting their discussion about the Ipswich waterfront and pausing beside a shelf of breast pumps.

Max looked at the boxes and then at my chest, his eyes boggling. 'Jesus, you don't want them to get even bigger?'

It took me a second or so to work out what he meant. Then I almost screamed with laughter.

'No, you muppet,' I said, shaking my head at him. 'They're not to make them bigger. They're for milk, to get milk from here' – I waved my hands vaguely in front of me – 'into a bottle. But thanks for noticing.'

'Oh right,' said Max. 'I see. Blimey.' He leant forward and scrutinized the boxes. 'Weird. They look like gas masks.'

My tits were huge, Max was right. Once a 36B – a dreary size because that meant wide ribcage but unfairly small knockers – I was now a 38E. It was one of the most pleasing things about pregnancy. Sure, they ached. But whenever I'd been lying in the bath recently, I gazed at them with immense pleasure. I'd gone from being one of those women who couldn't manage even a whisper of cleavage unless I forced them together with my hands, to Marilyn Monroe. I used to look wistfully at women on the telly or in the pub with a rolling expanse of chest, great handfuls which made men wolf-whistle in the street. I longed for a wolf whistle. Sorry. I am a let-down to feminists everywhere and my mother would have been appalled. But, until I'd got pregnant, my tits had been the size of two very average tangerines and nobody's going to get very excited over those, are they?

Marjorie interrupted my reverie by advising that electric breast pumps were better than manual ones – 'saves you getting hand ache' – so that was added to our mounting pile of shopping, before we stopped again to look at a little green object, the size of an avocado stone, on display on the next shelf.

'Strengthen your pelvic floor,' said a sign above it.

'Good grief, is that a vibrator?' said Max. To be fair to him, it was shaped a bit like a mini one. Plus, there was a graphic diagram beside it instructing women to place the avocado stone inside their vagina and link it to an app on their phone for their exercises.

'No,' I said quickly, 'it's for, er, tightening things, down there. After labour.'

'It's rechargeable and 100 per cent waterproof,' chipped in Marjorie, standing next to me.

'Honestly, I think we're good,' I said to her quickly. 'I'm sure that's everything.' Since I was almost certainly never having sex again, I didn't think my lady bits needed any personal training. Although I was still laughing (to myself) about Max's confusion as he drove us back, the boot of his car stuffed with our shopping. Turns out there was a parallel to my first shopping trip with Jake after all.

★

After school the following day, Mike, Steph and I went to the Antelope. Steph and I had a stack of mid-term reports to write and Mike was busy going through his programme for the forthcoming concert, St Lancelot's Got Talent.

'Shit. What can I say about Achilles?' I said, tapping my pen on the side of the table, thinking back to last week when I found him pulling the wings off a ladybird at his desk.

'"Delightfully challenging"?' suggested Steph. 'I use that a lot. Or, "remarkably independent". Parents always like that one.'

I bent my head down again and wrote both of Steph's suggestions on Achilles' report, adding that he showed 'keen interest' in the environment.

Then Mike looked up. 'Steph, it says here that Alex Saunders is doing a rap called "Lollipop".'

'Yeah, that's right,' said Steph, not looking up from writing a report.

'I'm just checking you know that's a song about a blow job?' said Mike.

'No, I did not,' said Steph, lifting her head up and rolling her eyes. 'Oh, that boy. I'll talk to him in the morning.'

We carried on like this for a while, Steph and I chipping in the odd word every now and then to help the other out as if we were trying to complete a crossword.

'Exhausting?' I said, looking at Steph.

'"Spirited",' she'd suggest.

'Shouts so loudly in class I sometimes want to walk out and never come back,' she asked, a few minutes later.

'"Energetic"?'

'Is never going to get into Eton. Should be put on a window

sill and watered twice a week instead?' she added, once on to the next report.

'"Tries hard"?' and so on.

'I'm done,' I said, leaning back half an hour later, just as I felt ET kick me right in the ribs. 'Ouuuuch.' I winced and put a hand on my stomach. I loved feeling her roll about inside me, it was like a private party to which only she and I were invited. But occasionally she took it too far with a little foot or fist.

'You all right?' said Steph.

'Yeah, she's just wriggling about a lot at the moment. It's as if I'm housing an acrobat.' I leant forward as I felt her kick again.

'Taking after her dad then?' said Mike.

'What do you mean?'

'All that activity,' he explained. 'I love you but you don't even run for the bus.'

'How is he anyway?' went on Steph, ignoring Mike.

'Max?'

'Mmm.'

'Yeah, good. We went shopping yesterday, actually, for baby kit. Buggies and so on. It was, yeah, nice. Really nice.'

'Uh-oh,' said Steph, looking up at my face.

'What?'

'You're going soppy over him.'

'I am not. Seriously, I'm just glad that we're getting on so well.' This was a teeny-weeny fib. Last night, after our shopping trip, I'd had a sex dream about Max. I'd been straddling him in his car, which was fantastically unrealistic since there was no way ET and I could fit between Max and the steering wheel, but never mind the logistics. As I'd rocked on top of Max, looking at him, inches from his face, my dream had felt so genuine that I'd been on the verge of coming in my sleep, only to wake up at the very moment I was about to explode with my legs thrashing around under the duvet. It was the biggest letdown since I'd found out about Father Christmas in 1991. But Steph didn't need to know this.

'You're such a bad liar,' tutted Steph, before picking up another report. 'Right, Jeremy Parry, you little verruca, what can I say about you?'

*

That was also the week I started flat hunting. I'd put it off for as long as possible because I was so fond of Grace and Riley. Well, I was fond of Grace. But I could no longer pretend that, once ET was born, I could continue living with a pair of sex-crazed Australians. Brixton was out though. Too expensive. As was Streatham. So I'd started looking at places further south.

This quest had put me in touch with an estate agent called Daniel, who was accompanying me round several one-bed flats in Norwood that Tuesday evening after work.

When I was fourteen, Mum, Dennis and I went to San Francisco. Mum was delivering a paper there, so we combined it with our summer holiday. I vividly remembered the small-ness of the cells at Alcatraz, the claustrophobia of the little oblong space, just big enough for a single bed, a loo and a basin.

Some had windows, some didn't. But by the time I looked at my fifth flat that evening after work, those cells were starting to feel roomy.

'And here is the bedroom,' said Daniel, flinging his arm out in front of him as if he was showing me a suite at the Ritz. The room was the size of an airing cupboard.

'Where would the bed go?' I asked.

'Right here,' he said, pointing at a patch of swirling, fudge-coloured carpet.

'A double bed?' I said, frowning at him doubtfully.

'Yes, absolutely.' He nodded. 'This is definitely a double room.'

'OK, you lie down and demonstrate where I'd put the bed.'

Daniel looked uncomfortable.

'Please,' I said, 'just so I can visualize it. You lie on the floor and show me.'

He knelt down on the carpet and then turned over and lay down on his back. 'Sort of here?' he said, looking up at me. His knees were bent, revealing that he was wearing a pair of socks with Minions on them.

'Stretch out your legs,' I said.

But he couldn't because the room was too small.

'Yeah, I didn't think so. You couldn't get a bed in here,' I said, walking out of the airing cupboard as Daniel scrabbled to his feet.

'I've got a lovely one just round the corner,' he said, brushing carpet fibres off his shiny suit.

'Do you promise?' I said.

'I do,' he replied.

'Is it better than all of the other ones we've seen today?'

'It is,' he said, grinning like a village idiot.

'Is it very close?'

'Just round the corner, we can walk.'

'OK, go on then,' I said, resignedly.

I knew I shouldn't have bothered. It was even worse. Up five flights of stairs (no lift) when I'd forewarned Daniel I'd soon have a baby and would struggle with stairs. And there was no actual bathroom, just a shower partitioned off from the kitchen.

'Daniel,' I wanted to say as we trudged down the steps again, 'I have come across earwigs with more intelligence than you. Please take me off your mailing list and never contact me again.'

Except I didn't because I was desperate. 'Could you ring me the second anything new comes up?' I said, before heading to the train station. Daniel promised me and roared off in his car. I could practically see the cloud of Lynx he left behind him.

*

A couple of weeks later, it was the 'Mummies and Daddies class' (barf). This was the only class that 'partners' were allowed to come to. Obviously I dressed more carefully for this class. No leggings and musty Converse. It was one of those bright spring days, crisp but clear blue skies, so I decided on a red dress I'd bought recently from H&M which gathered with a drawstring which I tied just above my bump, and a pair of new, bright white plimsolls. Plus a black Zara jacket. There, I thought, looking in the bathroom mirror at school. I looked fat but neat. Together. Tidy. Almost like a pregnant Middleton.

I'd arranged to meet Max outside 5 Drayton Avenue a few minutes before the class started and there he was, as I walked up, leaning on one of the pillars. Even from a distance, you could tell he was hot. Maybe it was the way he held himself, confidently standing on top of the steps in jeans and a black jacket, not slouching in any way. Or maybe you just really need to get laid, said a little voice in my head.

I silenced the voice and walked up the steps. 'Hello,' I said, waving at him. Why did I wave like a 4-year-old?

He grinned. 'Hello yourself. You look great.' He leant forward and kissed me on the cheeks.

I blushed immediately, obviously.

'Oh, thanks.'

I rang the doorbell. 'Brace yourself,' I said.

'I've seen a few go in already,' he said, smiling. 'I'm intrigued.'

As usual, the woman in uniform showed us in and ushered us downstairs. Today, about half the women had already arrived, together with their partners. More chairs had been added to the circle of sofas so everyone had a seat. I introduced Max to Emily, hoping she wouldn't mention my confession during our first session.

'Emily, hi, this is Max; Max, this is Emily who takes the classes.'

'Maaaaax, hiiiii,' said Emily. 'Heavenly to meet you, please both take a seat.'

I headed for the furthest sofa, still free, and sat down. Max sat in a chair beside it.

'Is that her?' he asked, nodding towards the naked photograph.

'Uh-huh,' I said, quietly.

I felt like several women were staring at Max. It was either because they recognized him, or because they remembered what I'd said about having a one-night stand. Or because he was by far the most attractive man here. I took in the various husbands – mostly in pinstriped suits, as if they'd come straight from their City jobs. Pink noses, with stomachs bulging over their waistbands from expensive work lunches, and balding. All right, I'd only shagged the guy I was here with once, but I'd rather be sitting next to him a million times over than any of the others.

Then Beth arrived and introduced her partner to Emily and everybody lost interest in Max.

'Hiya, Emily, this is my wife, Carmen.'

'Carrrrrmen, lovely to meet you. Please do both take a seat.'

Beth walked straight towards my sofa (we'd become allies in the past couple of weeks) and sat, Beth next to me, Carmen on her other side. I glanced around at the rest of the room. I presumed, from the husbands' delighted expressions, that the closest they'd ever got to a lesbian before now was on the internet. Admittedly, Carmen looked sensational – tanned skin with multiple bangles that jangled up and down both wrists, she was also wearing a black shirt over zebra-print leggings with suede, thigh-high boots and had swept her mass of hair up in a red bandana.

'Now we're all here, let's get started, shall we?' said Emily.

The most poignant moment of that evening, for me, was when Max and I were bathing our fake baby. Each couple had been given a doll and a plastic bath and had to demonstrate to Emily that we could wash the thing without drowning it. Watching Max gently cradle the plastic baby flicked some sort of maternal switch, and I felt myself welling up, so I gritted my teeth and thought about the lecture on mucus plugs we'd just been given (when, literally, a plug of possibly bloody mucus dislodges itself from your cervix ahead of labour), and that sorted me right out again.

'What should we call it?' said Max, still washing the doll in its bath.

'Dunno. I had a dolly I called Ariel when I was little because I was obsessed with *The Little Mermaid.*'

He looked up at me and grinned. 'No, I meant our baby.'

'Oh.' It was the first time he'd referred to ET as 'our' baby and I felt a surge of happiness. It felt more like a conversation a couple in this situation would have, as opposed to two strangers. 'I haven't really thought about boys' names. Only girls.'

'And?'

'OK, don't laugh, but what do you think about Eve?'

He pulled a face.

'Or Iris?'

He scrunched his nose up.

'Oh, OK, Mr Picky, what about Olive?'

He frowned.

'Oh my God, I give up, what names do you—'

'No, I like Olive.'

'Have you thought of any?'

He shook his head. 'No, not really. I mean technically there is this old family rule that Rushbrooke men have to go Randolph, Arundel, Randolph, Arundel and so on, down the generations.'

I raised an eyebrow at him. 'It's lucky we're not married then, isn't it?'

He laughed back. 'Yes, probably. Del used to hate being called Arundel by teachers at school.' Then he looked down and started sloshing the plastic baby again, but within a few moments his shoulders had started shaking. Oh fuck, he was crying.

I bit my lip and looked around the room at everyone else washing their babies. I wondered if I had any tissues in my bag. And I was about to reach for it and have a rummage for anything, even an old napkin, when I realized Max wasn't crying but laughing.

'What's so funny?' I asked, relieved.

He looked up, eyes creased. 'I just haven't thought about Del properly for ages, and I was thinking how mad he'd find this. Me, washing this… plastic doll.' Then I laughed, and we both got the giggles together, as if a release of tension. It was the sort of laughter that makes you double over and gasp for breath. Overheard snippets of other conversations around the room only made us worse.

'No, James, that's not how you hold it.'

'Careful of its head, Harry!'

Max and I carried on in hysterics together for a few moments before Emily came along and asked, in a frosty manner, if we were all right.

'Yep,' I said, trying to regain control of myself as Max caught my eye. 'All good.'

★

'Do you want to grab some food?' he asked, as we walked down the steps outside after the session. It was cold now, in the dark, and my teeth were chattering. My dress and blazer outfit had been optimistic. It was way too early in the year for bare legs.

'Here,' he said, taking off his coat and putting it round my shoulders. 'Have this.'

'No no, I'm fine, honestly, I—'

'Come on. I've been up mountains. I can handle Knightsbridge.'

'Show off. But thank you, and yeah, OK. Where d'you feel like?' I had been planning on going home for a bath and early bed, but weirdly this plan was instantly forgotten.

'I know, this way,' he said. 'Won't take long. There's a place that I used to go with Prim—' He stopped and briefly closed his eyes as if admonishing himself, then grinned sheepishly at me. 'Just a good Italian I know.'

We walked silently down another quiet street of big houses

as I told myself not to brood about Max mentioning her. Don't be that girl, Lil. Don't let that clawing paranoia over an ex into your head. You're not even with him.

'Here we go,' said Max, suddenly stopping outside a restaurant called Da Nonna. 'Pasta? Pizza?' he said.

'Perfect,' I said.

He opened the door and let me go in first. The place was tiny, there were only five tables, none of which were free.

'Looks full,' I said at him, over my shoulder.

'Don't worry,' he said, just as the waiter spotted him and came hurrying over, deftly squeezing himself between tables.

'Signor Maximiliano! It has been too long.' Then he shouted towards the back of the restaurant. 'Francesco? Francesco! Signor Maximiliano is here!'

Another waiter, a stomach almost as big as mine, appeared behind the counter and started shouting in Italian and gesturing at us to come towards him.

I walked between the tables towards the counter, trying not to knock other diners' wine bottles with Max's coat, or ET.

The fat waiter embraced Max and gave us a table which had been hidden, tucked to the side of the counter.

'This OK?' said Max.

I nodded. 'Yeah, great.' Although there then followed an undignified few moments when the thin waiter had to inch the table out slightly, so I could pull the chair out and sit down with enough room for my stomach. Sexy.

I looked around as Max sat down. It was proper Italian

kitsch – red and white tablecloths, dimly lit with candles in bottles, enthusiastic waiters, both with moustaches.

'Signorina, here is a menu for you,' said the fat one, handing it to me and practically bowing. 'And Signor Maximiliano, one for you too.'

'Lil, you want a drink?' Max said, looking at me across the table.

A little bit of me wanted to scream 'YES PLEASE, I'D LIKE A GLASS OF WINE THE SIZE OF A HOUSE BECAUSE THIS FEELS LIKE A DATE AND I'M NERVOUS.'

I didn't. 'No thanks, just water for me.'

Tiresome.

'OK, Francesco, a bottle of water please, and a glass of the Barolo.'

Francesco nodded. He might have even twirled his moustache. It was that kind of place.

'Food's amazing here,' went on Max, opening his menu. 'I always dream about the ragu when I'm away up a hill, stuffing myself with protein bars.'

'What's the worst thing you've ever eaten on a trip?'

'Guinea pig in Ecuador,' he said, instantly. 'Although we'll probably be offered horse in Mongolia. Urgh.' He shuddered.

'Of course, I forgot, your trip.' He'd mentioned his Mongolia expedition while we were shopping and I'd wanted to ask him more about it, but then I'd been distracted by buggies and breast pumps. 'When are you off?' I added, trying to ignore the pang I'd felt at the idea of Max flying across the globe for another climb, wondering if the mountains in Mongolia were as lethal as the ones in Pakistan.

'Week after next,' he said.

'Amazing,' I squeaked, studying the menu in front of me so my face didn't give away any disappointment.

'Lil, don't worry,' he said, reaching his hand across the table and putting it on my menu so I had to look up at him. 'It's an easy climb. I'll be away two weeks, three tops. Depends on the weather. And I have a satellite phone so any dramas, you just ring. Whenever you like.'

I grinned back at him and tried to pretend the relief I felt at Max's reassurance was purely on ET's behalf. Nothing to do with my own feelings, I told myself. I was simply looking out for my child's father.

'You travelled much?' he asked, taking back his hand.

I shook my head. 'Not really. Not like, proper travelling where you go off for several months with a rucksack and come back with multiple tattoos and an STD.'

He glanced up from his menu at me, eyebrows raised.

'What?' I said, laughing at his expression. 'I've just heard that happens.'

I worked in the café of the local sports club in Norfolk during my uni summer holidays, microwaving baked potatoes when others went travelling to India, South America and Indonesia. And Jake was never into going anywhere further than the South of France for his skiing holiday every spring, and back to the South of France for a summer holiday lying by the pool drinking rosé. I'd occasionally suggest going somewhere slightly more adventurous – I wasn't talking Yemen. Somewhere like Sicily, perhaps, or the Greek islands – but Jake would make a face and say how much he was looking forward to going back to the same restaurants. So we always did. I shook my head and smiled to myself thinking about it. I'd been such a wet flannel with him.

'What's funny?' said Max.

'Oh nothing,' I said, 'just… this scenario, I guess.'

Francesco came back with the wine at that exact moment, poured us both glasses and asked if we were ready to order.

'Lil, you know?' said Max.

'Yep,' I said, looking up at Francesco. 'Could I please have a Fiorentina?'

'Absolutely, and Signor Maximiliano?'

'The ragu as usual, please, Francesco, with a salad on the side?'

He nodded and went off again, while I felt briefly unsettled at his order, wondering how many times he and Primrose had come here. Maybe it had been 'their' place? Maybe they'd come here for anniversaries? And Valentine's Day? And maybe the waiters called her Signorina Primrose and they always—

'It is funny,' Max said, interrupting my spasm of insecurity and smiling across the table. 'If someone had said to me a year ago that this is where I'd be now…'

'What, having a baby with someone you barely know?' I joked.

'Ouch,' he said, leaning back in his chair, clapping a hand over his chest and making a face as if he'd just been hit by a sniper. Then he leant forward again and rested his forearms on the tablecloth. 'I know you a bit.'

I rolled my eyes.

'I don't mean like that,' he said. 'Well, I suppose, a bit like that. But no, what I meant was, I admire you. I've realized that, maybe only tonight. For doing this. And I'm grateful too.'

I frowned at him. 'For what?'

'For deciding to do this,' he replied simply. 'All of this. Tonight, when we were laughing, and I was thinking about Del—' He stopped and had a mouthful of wine.

I didn't say anything. I didn't want to blunder in with a joke to lighten the tone.

'I've worried at moments about this. About what's going to happen. But tonight, I was only grateful. I am grateful, I should say. If I could turn the clock back... well, it's sort of unimaginable now. I wouldn't want to change anything. So, thank you, is what I'm trying to say, in a ham-fisted manner. This is a good thing, the greatest thing.'

'You're calling the baby "a thing"?' I said, smiling at him.

'Sorry, I meant Randolph. I beg your pardon.'

'Even worse.'

'You're dissing my dad's name now, are you?' he said.

'No, no, I was joking, it was only a joke,' I said, 'I just—'

Max burst out laughing. 'I was kidding, Lil, it's a ludicrous name. There's no way our baby's being called that.'

I grinned back at him. I knew I needed to watch it. I knew that the only thing Max and I really shared was ET. But I felt my defences drop even lower over dinner as we talked. Not small talk stuff. Big life stuff.

'You know what?' he said at one point. 'I look at my friends, some of my best friends. And they're married and they have children, but they're not happy. They've done it, the whole marriage and babies thing, because they feel like that's what they should do. Find the girlfriend, settle down, buy the house, have the kids, live happily ever after.'

'Rrrrrright,' I said, unsure where this was going.

'But they're really unhappy, some of them, and divorces are starting. Are any of your friends divorced yet?'

I shook my head.

'OK, they'll start soon,' he said confidently. 'And it's hideous and everyone's sad and the children then have to spend every other weekend with their dad, and friends of mine, like tough, old army friends, are broken versions of themselves.'

'I feel like we're veering dangerously into therapy territory again,' I said.

He had a mouthful of ragu so shook his head and smiled. Then swallowed. 'No, we're not, I promise. All I'm trying to say is maybe this is a better way.'

I laughed. 'OK, Sigmund Freud. Maybe.'

We laughed non-stop. Max laughed when I did my impression of Miss Montague. We both laughed when we discussed labour and whether I'd attempt a natural birth.

'No, I want all the drugs,' I said. 'You imagine pushing a garden gnome through your bottom without any pain relief. I don't think so.'

Max smiled across the table. 'It's going to be fine,' he reassured me, 'I'll be there. You can scream and shout as much as you like.'

'It won't be pretty,' I said, suddenly panicked at the thought of buckling on the floor, sweating and potentially shitting myself, while Max stood over me.

'I'm sure I saw worse in the army.'

He also laughed as I ate my pizza with the egg on it, teasing me for eating around the outside first, leaving the yolk in the middle until the very end, which I ate whole in one bite. Again, not a sexy party trick. But that was the relaxing thing about being pregnant and out-for-dinner-but-not-a-date, I could order whatever I wanted, and eat it however I wanted. If I wanted another breadstick I could have one. I could have ten packets of breadsticks if I liked. I ate my pizza with my hands and dipped the crusts into a little pot of garlic sauce. I ordered ice cream for pudding and only agreed to share it with Max on the basis we had an extra scoop of chocolate.

I did try (honestly, I tried a bit) to pay my half of the bill at the end, but he said no.

'No way. Cheapest date I can remember.'

'Thank you,' I said. And then I burped. It was an accident. I hadn't meant to. It just slipped out. And I bit my lower lip and felt mortified for a moment before Max threw his head back and roared so loudly the whole restaurant looked over.

It was the best not-a-date I'd ever been on.

★

He insisted on driving me home to Brixton even though I protested and said I could get the 37 bus which went almost to my door. I blushed as I climbed into the passenger seat, glanced at the steering wheel and remembered my sex dream, although luckily it was dark so Max couldn't see my pink cheeks.

'What's her surname going to be, do you think?' he asked, as we drove over Chelsea Bridge.

'Huh?' I asked. I'd been humming to Simply Red (they were playing 'Stars' on Magic), and looking at the lights on the bridge, thinking how romantic this scene could be if I wasn't seven months pregnant and worried about getting a tiny bit of wee on his leather seats. That couldn't happen, could it?

'ET's surname,' Max clarified. 'What do you want it to be?'

'I haven't really thought about it,' I replied. This wasn't entirely true. I'd assumed initially it was going to be Bailey. But then Max became more involved and I'd briefly wondered whether it should be Bailey-Rushbrooke. But that was a mouthful. I wasn't sure I could saddle an innocent child with that. It sounded like an old-fashioned car. 'Oh look, there goes a Bailey-Rushbrooke.'

'No hurry, I was just thinking about it,' he said, turning into my street. 'But if you want it to be Bailey then I get it.'

'Really?' I said, surprised and turning to look at him. 'You don't want to be included?'

He pulled up outside my flat. 'Course I do, but I don't know the answer here. Maybe two names is too many? And I'm not going to insist she's got my name. So... it's up to you, I guess?'

'OK,' I said, smiling at him and undoing my seatbelt. 'Cool, well, shall we chat about it down the line? I need to go to bed. All that chat about mucus plugs.'

'Ha, I love it when you talk dirty,' he said, as I leant across to kiss him goodnight.

But suddenly it wasn't just a goodnight kiss. It was a proper kiss. On the lips. I'm not sure who started it. OK, I could have slightly missed his cheek and Max might have turned his head a fraction. But neither of us stopped it. It was a soft brush of our mouths against one another that turned into a slow, more probing kiss – with tongues and everything.

After months of nothing but furious masturbating, I felt immediate fireworks in my pants. They say pregnancy either makes you feel as sexy as a lump of Edam, or as erotically charged as Madonna. I was the latter. Just sitting there kissing Max made every cell in my body scream in support like a cheerleader.

Then he pulled back. 'I, er, sorry. I don't want to be a killjoy but, are we sure?'

Instant disappointment. 'Oh, er, no,' I stuttered, 'I'm not sure. But I wouldn't mind, you know, having a go?'

Why did I say THAT? This is sex, Lil, not a game of Scrabble.

Max didn't answer. He just pulled my face back towards him, one hand underneath my chin, and kissed me again, his tongue pressing up against mine. I kissed back, hard, although I worried about my garlicky tongue from the pizza. This was like my sex dream! Except better because it was real. Wasn't it, or was I dreaming again? I half-opened my left eye to check.

Yup, there was Max, his stubble tickling my chin. And there was his arm, reaching around me to pull me closer to him. And there were a couple of men goggling at us from the pavement on the other side of the street.

I pulled back. 'Want to come up?' I suggested, nervous that he'd say no. If Grace and Riley were on the sofa upstairs, I'd just have to kill them. Clock them over the head with our pepper grinder.

'Yes,' he growled, still inches from my face. 'Please.'

'It doesn't have to change anything,' I wittered, as we climbed the stairs to the flat door. 'Not a thing. It's just sex and we've done that before and it's not a big deal and—'

'I might ban conversation,' he said into my ear, as I listened outside my door before opening it. Silence. Hurrah, the hippies were out.

'So this is my flat. Kitchen, sitting room, bathroom over there,' I said, as if I was the world's fastest estate agent. Then I took Max's hand and led him towards my door. 'And this is my room.'

I turned on my bedside lamp so he didn't reach for the main switch. The ceiling light was in no way flattering and I didn't want Max thinking he was about to have sex with Mr Blobby.

Then I threw my blazer on the armchair in the corner, slipped off my plimsolls and turned back to him. We kissed while standing in my room, before he then took my hand and led me to my bed.

You are not at your most flexible when thirty-three weeks pregnant. I wanted to lie back against my pillows in a sexy, come hither way, but I fear I came off like a 94-year-old woman gently lowering herself in the bath. When finally positioned against them, Max straddled me, fully clothed, his knees either side of my hips, while we carried on kissing. He ran a hand down my shoulder, my arm, past my hip and to the hem of my dress, tugging it as he tried to pull it over my stomach.

Ah. This could be awkward. I took over and tried to wiggle the dress from underneath me, then reached behind me to undo my enormous maternity bra. Meanwhile, Max stood up, watching me, and pulled his shirt off in one go before unbuckling his jeans and dropping them to the floor. I remembered him doing the same in his bedroom, the night we first slept together. It seemed so long ago, and so much had happened, that I nearly laughed. But didn't. Couldn't laugh out loud as a man took his jeans off. You'd never hear from him again.

'Oh my lord,' said Max, looking down and seeing my nipples. But not in a bad way. In an admiring way.

'Sit,' he then instructed, nodding at the edge of my bed. I swung my legs to the floor and perched on the edge of the mattress.

Max kneeled in front of me and pushed my knees apart, then moved himself in between my thighs and ran his hands from my shoulders, down over my nipples and around my stomach. I dropped my head back behind me and gasped. I had envisaged a bath and bed. Perhaps a chapter of my book if I could stay awake long enough. This was so much better. So. Much. Better.

So.

Much.

Aaaaaah… Max was still kneeling between my legs but had lowered his head and was now sucking each nipple in turn, flicking them with his tongue. I ran my hands through his hair. 'Fuck,' I whispered. 'Fuck, fuck, fucccccccccck.'

'Can we?' he said, looking up at me. 'I don't know if I can wait much longer.'

'Please,' I said, almost whimpering. 'Do it. Do it now.'

'Begging, are we?' He gently kissed my bump before putting one arm underneath my knees and sweeping them on to the bed.

'Not on my back,' I said, shaking my head. 'I can't. Too much pressure.'

'Uh-uh, I don't want you on your back. I want you on top of me,' he said. 'I want to see every bit of you.'

Max climbed on my bed. His turn to lie back against the pillows and then, with as much elegance as I could (not much), I lifted one leg across him. Truthfully, I never knew I could be so happy to see a penis. I took it in my right hand and then, as both of us moaned, I slid down on top of it.

As I shifted on top of him, I felt like someone who'd been on a very long diet and then let loose in a Krispy Kreme factory. It was the most exquisite sensation I could ever remember, better than the night Max and I met, better than any sex with Jake, certainly better than when I lost my virginity to Andrew Duff in the sand dunes of Norfolk. That was gritty and I chafed. There was no chafing now, and as Max kept running his hands over my stomach, over ET, I tightened myself around him, again and again, to make him groan.

The only trouble with being on top and having a stomach the size of a netball is that you can't move about very much. My bump kept hitting his torso and preventing me from moving any further forward. And so after a few minutes of rocking, while Max was reaching up and pinching my nipples, I told him to get behind me.

Manoeuvring into this position wasn't very dignified either. As Max tried to free himself from underneath me, I felt like a judo champion who'd recently floored her opponent. But then he was up, on his knees and instructing me to put my hands flat against the wall behind my bed.

I felt him push into me again moments later and almost howled with pleasure. This was better than I imagined it the 582 times I'd fantasized about sex with Max because it was actually happening. Granted, I had no idea what was going on with us and I had no idea what co-parenting with Max would look like when ET arrived. But I didn't want to think about any of that right now. I wanted to enjoy the intensely satisfying feeling of Max's skin on mine, his breath on my neck, as he pushed in and out of me, one hand on my hip to steady him, one holding my stomach. Having sex when pregnant felt so different, more animalistic. If humans were biologically impelled to have sex to procreate, then shagging when already pregnant – for a woman – was largely about self-gratification, right? I felt very, very gratified.

Max lowered his hand to my clitoris and slowed down his

thrusts, lightly rubbing me while he pushed just the very tip of himself in and out, in and out, in and out until I felt that heat spread across my hips. I pushed back hard against him and shouted 'FASTER' and came just as Max groaned behind me and then fell forward on to my back, slamming the wall in front of me with one of his hands for support.

We both rested there, heavy breathing, for several moments while I sensed all my anxieties about what we'd just done marshalling like soldiers and about to strike at my brain – what were we thinking? How would this change things? What did this mean? But I willed them to keep away, just for a bit, for a few moments. Or at least while Max was still actually inside me.

★

He stayed with me, although I had to get up to pee four times and he made my bed feel very small so it wasn't a restful night for either of us. When I woke at around eight the next morning to see Max out of bed and standing over me, zipping up his jeans, I felt guilty.

'I'm sorry,' I said, craning myself up on an elbow. 'Did you sleep at all?'

'Of course,' he said. 'Don't worry. I've just got a few things to do today, so was going to slip out.'

I nodded and tried to smile in a cheerful manner, to make this scene feel normal. Just a run-of-the-mill morning, a man with the physique of a lifeguard peeling his clothes from my carpet.

'I'll ring you later,' he said, once his shirt was on. Then he bent down to kiss me on my head, although I turned my face so he ended up planting one on the tip of my bobbly nose.

Brilliant.

'Sorry,' we muttered at the same time. Although we also laughed simultaneously, so it dissipated the tension. It made him feel more like Max again, instead of a stranger in my bedroom.

'I had a good time,' he said.

'Me too.'

'OK, speak in a bit,' he said, from my door, before closing it gently behind him.

I dropped my head back down on to the pillow and the bad thoughts started. This wasn't a good development.

I mean it had been a very, very good development for about half an hour.

But now it was a disaster. It would change things, despite what I'd told him. It was so mad: play a game of squash with a partner and nothing changed. Ditto tennis. Ditto ping-pong. Ditto Connect frigging Four. But take your clothes off and spend twenty minutes doing vigorous physical exercise with someone and it changed everything. And just when I'd got more relaxed about hanging out with Max, too. When I thought we'd got to A Good Place. What was I thinking, letting my hormones take over as if I was a 16-year-old boy? I should be sectioned.

I reached for my phone and started typing a message to Jess. *Slept with Max last night*, I wrote, following by a stream of the screaming face emojis. I added one of the purple aubergines for a bit of balance.

She texted back immediately. All in caps. **YOU KIDDING ME?**

The caps carried on for a while. **I CANNOT GET OVER THIS. HOW DID THIS HAPPEN?**

WHAT WAS IT LIKE?

DID YOU LEAK MILK EVERYWHERE?

YOU FREE TO DISCUSS? I'LL COME TO YOU.

Yes, I replied, glancing at the clock on my bedside table. *Brockwell Park and cake this afternooon, like 2ish?*

DEAL, she said.

I flicked from WhatsApp to my emails. I was being contacted daily by Daniel and assorted other agents with flats which mostly looked like they'd been the scene of a recent and grisly crime, but I still hadn't found anywhere. Too depressing. So I closed my emails and opened my *Mail* Online app, scrolling down the sidebar to try and distract me from thinking about Max. It was the usual stuff. A celebrity papped eating a biscuit. One of the Royals stroking a horse. Another Kardashian had given birth. But then, halfway down, was a headline that made me stop breathing.

'JUST GOOD FRIENDS? Lady Primrose Percy shares happy snap of walk with adventurer ex-boyfriend Max Rushbrooke on Instagram.'

I clicked on the story, still holding my breath, and scrolled down to inspect the photo. The main picture was her Instagram photo of Max, smiling at the camera while her dog strained at the lead he was holding. He was wearing the same coat he'd draped around my shoulders after the class last night.

I gulped for air as I started reading the story. '**Laughing in the spring sunshine, adventurer Max Rushbrooke looks delighted to be hanging out with his it-girl ex, Lady Primrose Percy and her French bulldog, Pumpkin. The pair split early last year but as Lady Primrose revealed in her post, she and her adventurer ex have been spending more time together recently, leading friends to ask whether their relationship is back on.**'

Every word hit me like a wrecking ball in the jugular.

The piece went on to mention Max's disappearance in Pakistan and the interview with Primrose that I'd read while he was missing, in which she'd said how worried she was about him. There were more photos, too. Older ones of Max and Primrose when they were together – an Instagram selfie she'd taken of them on a ski lift together, another at a black tie dinner, Max's arm snaking around her waist.

The last line made me want to throw my phone through my bedroom window.

'**A source close to the couple says they've been trying to patch up their differences. "They both mean the world to one another," the friend told us, "and we're all keeping our fingers crossed that they announce they're officially an item again soon."**'

I sat back against my pillows, numbed with shock, and then, like a masochist intent on cutting deeper, I opened up Instagram and searched for her profile. Here it was. Lady

Primrose Percy. 'Milliner and mischief-maker' read the bio under her name. Oh please. And she had 159k followers. Who were these people?

The photo of Max grinning out at me was her most recent upload, posted at 2.31 p.m. yesterday and tagged to Hampstead Heath. '**My boys back together,**' she'd written underneath. I dropped my phone on my bed as if it had electrocuted me and sat there staring at my duvet. Why hadn't he told me this? Why hadn't he said anything when we were out for dinner – 'Hey, Lil, just so you know my ex and I are "back together", hope that's OK?'

Why had he slept with me?

I was immediately overcome by both rage and desperate sadness. Any high I felt from the sense that Max and I had moved so much closer, any twinge of optimism I had about the future and everything being OK, for ET, for me, for us, instantly dissolved inside me. How could I have been so stupid? Why had I let myself be seduced? The betrayal hurt all the more given the timing. If only I'd seen this yesterday, before last night, it would sting so much less.

I remained frozen for fifteen minutes or so, my mind whirring as if my brain was trying to figure the situation out, attempting to solve it like a crossword. Were there any clues I could have picked up on? I'd tried not to give in to my niggling insecurities about Primrose, but I had often felt uncomfortable whenever Max mentioned her.

In his car when he drove me to Norfolk.

At Jess's party when we sat talking about exes.

Last night on the way to the Italian.

And she'd said publicly that she missed him. Primrose actively wanted him back. Plus, she was everything I wasn't – an old friend of Max's, with the same background, she was glamorous and had thin legs and perfectly flicky hair in all her Instagram photos. Hateful, hateful Instagram.

Plus, hadn't Max occasionally sounded evasive when he'd mentioned her? Hadn't there been a tone I'd picked up on, a hint of unease when her name had come up? I played every scene in my head over and over again, berating myself for not probing further, for not asking questions which would have protected me. And ET.

She gave me a mighty kick, which I took as a sign.

'It's OK, it's OK,' I said out loud, putting a protective hand on my stomach, although it was more for my benefit than hers. 'It's OK,' I repeated again. 'We're fine. Fuck him.' And then I paused. 'You are never to use that word.'

I'd briefly lowered my defences and look where that had got me – weak, susceptible to being hurt. No more, I decided, while sitting in bed. There would be no more hanging out while I was pregnant. It was too painful. I'd tell Max about any hospital appointments and labour, when she decided to arrive, but that would be the limit of our interaction. If he was going to treat me like a mug, then I'd do the same back. He would be nothing more to me than a sperm donor.

★

By that afternoon, I'd almost convinced myself that this decision was freeing. It hurt, but it was liberating in a way. Now I didn't have to wonder whether we could ever be an item. This would stop me fantasizing about the future and whether anything serious could happen between us. There wasn't. That was it.

Why should he keep me informed of his relationship status anyway? I wasn't his mother. I certainly wasn't his girlfriend. What was I? A mate? Not even a mate? An acquaintance who happened to be having his baby? A vessel?

I delivered this speech to Jess later that day as we trudged around Brockwell Park.

'So I'm fine,' I said, 'I'm actually great. This is better. No more confusion.'

Jess looked unconvinced. 'You don't know they're back together,' she said. 'That picture doesn't necessarily mean anything.'

I'd screenshot the Instagram picture and showed it to her, instead of showing her the real thing, such was my paranoia about accidentally liking it.

'Please. It says "my boys". And there's that quote!'

'What quote?'

'In the story, from a friend saying everyone wants them to get back together.' I thought briefly about Max's parents. They'd be thrilled, no doubt, that Lady Primrose Percy was back on the scene and there was no chance of me, a lowly academic's daughter, muscling in on their son after all.

'Hmmm,' murmured Jess. 'Have you heard from him this morning?'

'Nope.'

'Are you going to ring him?'

'Nope. I don't even want to hear his stupid posh voice.'

Jess didn't answer as we trudged up the slope towards the tennis courts.

'I don't want to quiz him. I just want the bare minimum contact,' I added. 'Less confusing. He's going away in a couple of weeks anyway.'

'Where?'

'Mongolia.'

'MONGOLIA?' she replied, as if I'd told her Max was climbing into a spaceship and setting the sat nav for Mars.

'For a climb,' I explained.

'How long's he away?'

I looked up ahead of us, trying to gauge how long we had until we reached the café. 'Not sure. He says it depends on the weather.'

'What about in the hospital?' continued Jess. 'Are you going to have him there?'

I opened my mouth and then closed it again. I wasn't sure. I went through a phase, before I was pregnant, of watching back-to-back episodes of *One Born Every Minute* and fathers always seemed as useful as a bowl of trifle in the delivery room.

'You're doing really well. Keep breathing, keep breathing, keep breathing…'

'I AM FUCKING BREATHING, YOU PILLOCK.'

'Probably not now,' I told her.

'Your mum?'

'Yeah, I don't think I'd be able to keep her away.'

Jess laughed softly and then linked her arm through mine. 'Thing is, you could totally be out there dating too, you know? You're a free agent as well.'

'What, with this?' I said, putting my hand on ET.

Jess shrugged. 'It might be a bit of a surprise on a first date. But some men are into it. Isn't it a fetish for some people?'

'Swollen bellies with stretch marks?' I asked. I was rubbing Neutrogena Winter Berry body moisturizer into my stomach after my shower every morning but it didn't seem to be helping.

'Yes,' Jess replied, loyally.

I hunched my shoulders up as if physically bracing myself against the idea of dating. I'd rather have cartwheeled through Piccadilly Circus naked. That would feel less exposing than opening myself up to someone new again. I'd started trusting Max, but then he'd gone and trampled all over our relationship with his great, galumphing climbing boots. And I couldn't imagine finding anyone else I liked as much for some time, especially not with a vagina like a wind tunnel and a new baby on my hip.

'Thanks, love. But anyway, boring, let's talk about something else.' I was suddenly overwhelmed with exhaustion by that morning's emotional turbulence. 'How are you and Alexi anyway?'

She winced at me.

'What? Why the face?'

Jess winced again. 'I just feel a bit guilty, that's all, because I don't want to bang on about being happy when you—'

'Don't be daft, I'm fine,' I said. 'But how long has it been now? You guys, I mean?'

'About six months.'

'Do you think that's it, then?' I said. 'Do you think you'll marry him?'

It normally annoyed me when people asked this question, especially if you'd only been on two dates with someone. Nobody would ever ask that in your twenties, but – BAM! – hit your thirties and suddenly everyone wants to know if you're going to marry the guy you had a drink with in a pub on a Tuesday night. But because it was Jess, I thought I could get away with it. Plus, I was feeling needy, as if I was in danger of losing everyone today.

Jess shrugged. 'He's super busy with work so I'm not sure he wants to settle down any time soon. But that kind of suits me because I don't really know what I want either. Stay here, move abroad for a bit, go travelling with him. So… I dunno.'

I could sense her being evasive.

'What?' she said, as I narrowed my eyes at her.

'Why does it feel like you're not telling me something?'

She shook her head. 'No, I am. I just feel in limbo at the moment because he's away so much. But it's all great. Promise.'

'OK, good,' I said, as we reached the top of the hill.

We went into the hall for a pot of tea and I ordered two slices of cake. I wasn't in the mood to share.

Later that evening, while I was on the sofa watching *Real*

Housewives of Beverly Hills with Grace, my phone started ringing. Max.

'Answer it, darl, we can pause this,' said Grace. I'd updated her with the latest developments, which is why she'd insisted on making us a tofu stir-fry for a 'cosy' night in.

'It's all right,' I said, ignoring the buzzing in my hand. 'Can't be bothered.'

She shot me a sardonic look. 'You're gonna have to face him sometime,' she said. 'Want some more stir-fry?'

'No, I'm full, thanks,' I said, before turning my phone from vibrate to silent. I'd text him later. But what to say?

CHAPTER TWELVE

I DIDN'T TEXT HIM that night, or for a couple of days in the end. He tried to ring another couple of times but I ignored those, too. It was easier to avoid the conversation. I didn't want to lash out or shout at him. I just wanted to maintain some distance, to put up a boundary. And I had a big distraction, for if you strolled past the menacing black gates of St Lancelot's later that week, you might easily have assumed there was a gala event going on. Some sort of A-list party. Big black cars with drivers idling in the front were pulled up on either side of the road, women wobbled through the gates in heels that chiropodists would frown at, men in slickly tailored suits walked alongside them barking into their mobile phones. There was the odd bodyguard.

Welcome to parents' evening.

After the boys were picked up that afternoon, I'd stayed at school, sitting at my desk, mulling over what to say about each pupil. Normally I went home before parents' evening to shower, change and slap on more make-up. But I had a headache and couldn't face the thought of lumping ET home on the Tube, then trying to find a dress which made me look less like a football, then putting more make-up on before schlepping in again. So I stayed and practised my spiel for each parent in my head.

Phineas. A budding Attenborough, delightful, but could develop better social skills so that he is as comfortable with humans as he is with animals. I'd have to tread carefully with that one.

Cosmo. Will either become prime minister or a mass murderer. Or both. No, I couldn't say that. Hmmm. I'd have to say he had 'clear ambition'.

What the hell could I say about Roman? I hadn't seen the Walkers since coming back to school because he'd always been dropped off or picked up by bodyguards. How did I tactfully suggest to two parents they take more of an interest in their son and less in magazine shoots? I'd make something up when they got here.

We saw the parents for ten minutes each in our classrooms, with the teaching assistants lurking outside in the hallways ready to knock on our doors once the ten minutes were nearly up. Sceptical that Fergus would be able to manage this task, I'd removed the clock from the wall at the front of the classroom, behind my desk, and propped it up on a bookshelf at the back where I could glance at it and speed up the process if needed.

Just before six, when the school hallways suddenly sounded as if they were hosting a cocktail party – 'How was skiing?', 'Gorgeous, Verbier was sensational', 'We went to Klosters this year' and so on – I nipped to the loo for a) a pee since my bladder was now the size of an egg cup, and b) because I thought I should powder my nose, my forehead and maybe go mad and put on a bit of lip gloss.

Steph was already in there, leaning to one side as she manically brushed her hair.

'Ready for it?' I asked.

She stood up straight again, her hair frizzy around her head
like a newborn chick. 'You got any Valium?'

I laughed and shook my head. Steph had it worst because
you could boil all Year 8 parents' questions down into: 'Are
you going to get my son into Oxford?'

'Worth a shot,' she said.

I felt my head throb again and leant on the basin, wincing.

'You all right?' she said, turning to me from the mirror. I
hadn't told her anything about Max yet. I was trying to practise
not thinking about him and I couldn't face admitting that
Steph had been right, and I had indeed been stupidly soppy.

I nodded. 'Mmm. Just tired, I think. And dreading the
Walker parents.'

'You'll be fine, love. They're lucky to have you still looking
after their son.'

I took my hand off the basin and reached into my pocket
for my powder compact. That thing about blooming skin
during pregnancy was total balls. My nose was so shiny I
could practically see my reflection in it.

By 7.25 I'd ticked off five sets of parents (not the Walkers,
they'd been the last to respond to the sign-up email and had
landed the final 8.30 p.m. slot), and was bursting for a pee.
Again.

I was staggering down the hallway, past Steph's classroom,
on the way to the staff bathrooms, when it happened. At first

I only saw a couple standing together. They were hand in hand, laughing at some of the boys' paintings on a pinboard behind them. It was only as the man turned his face to kiss the woman on her head that I saw who it was – Alexi. Alexi, standing there, a woman's hand in his, leaning into her in a protective, familiar manner.

It was as if time slowed down. I saw him before he spotted me, and my brain process went like this: I recognize him, oh, that's Alexi, Jess's boyfriend, but what's he doing here? That's weird. And why's he holding that strange woman's hand? Oh my God. Oh my God. He's a parent. That must be his wife. Oh my God. What do I do?

It took my brain maybe one or two seconds to run through the above as I approached them, and just as it twigged, Alexi looked up and met my eyes.

Fleetingly, very fleetingly, I saw him look panicked, a small ripple of fear running across his face. And then he turned away from me and started inspecting the pinboard again as I walked past.

I reached the bathroom and sat on the loo, my heart beating, as I thought. What was Alexi's surname again? It was something Russian. Volga? Volotov? Volkov! That was it. And Mr Knight looked after Year 7. I tried to think about the clusters of boys in their year groups in the playground. He had a Philip in his class. And a Euripides. But I couldn't think of any surnames.

It was while sitting on the loo, my brain racing from thought to thought like a pinball machine, that it happened.

My headache worsened, as if my brain was expanding like a balloon in my skull and I could suddenly see little white specks floating front of me, like dust particles catching the light. I leant forward on the seat and put my head in my hands. That was the last thing I remembered.

★

It was Fergus who found me after I didn't come back to the classroom, and an ambulance apparently arrived at school within four minutes (a source of great excitement for the parents, Mike later told me). I was at hospital in another ten, where I lay on a bed in the A&E department, staring at my arm as a nurse took my blood pressure. I'd never paid huge attention to these numbers before. They puff the white sausage up around your arm, look at the machine, spout some unintelligible figures and it's generally fine. But this time it was crazy high.

They took some blood. They scanned ET to check her heart rate. They put me on a drip. A different person appeared from behind the curtain every five seconds. Steph arrived at one stage. I don't know how long I'd been there since my headache hadn't shifted and I was lying with my eyes closed, but I heard her voice.

'Oh, petal, how you feeling?'

'I'm OK.' I tried to smile as she took my hand and stood beside my bed holding it. Then I frowned and tried to find the words, ignoring the sharp pain behind my forehead. 'Steph, in Mr Knight's class, do you know if he's got anyone with the surname Volkov?'

She nodded. 'Luka Volkov, yes, pet. Why?'

Another doctor appeared holding a clipboard.

'Hello, Lilian, how are you feeling?' She smiled and I felt instantly soothed by her treacly voice.

'All right,' I said, trying to smile back. 'Do you know what's wrong though?'

'We don't yet,' she said. 'But please don't worry, just try and relax. Easier said than done, I know. Now, can I just ask some questions about your family history?' she asked.

'Course,' I said, still holding Steph's hand.

'Do you have any history of autoimmune diseases?'

I tried to think but I felt like I was wading through a bog, my mind was working so slowly.

'I don't… I can't…' I wanted to say I didn't think so, but then I didn't know anything about Max's medical history, or that of his family. It's one of those questions which doctors ask and I'm never sure how far to go back. What if your grandpa had high cholesterol? Or Great Aunt Elsbeth had heart disease? How far back should you go? What needed to be included – everything from lung cancer to gout? But I suddenly realized I didn't know anything about my real, biological father's medical history either.

I tried to speak again. 'I don't…' but my head felt like it was about to split.

'OK, don't worry for now,' she said.

★

They took my blood pressure every two hours but it fell back to normal overnight. And by the next morning, the blood test came back clear too, so the threat of anything serious had gone, whatever my family history was.

I knew I had to message Max, so I lay on my hospital bed trying to compose it.

Hi, I wrote. That was as far as I got in half an hour as I lay there mumbling sentences to myself. If you'd walked past my hospital bed, I would have looked like I was been admitted with a case of lunacy.

I decided to keep it brief. *Hi, just to say I fainted last night and had some tests done in hospital. But all fine and I'm going home in a bit. L.*

No kiss.

He called me within five seconds of sending the message.

'Lil, what the hell? Are you OK? Is ET OK?'

'Yes,' I said, as calmly as I could, although I could feel my heart thumping underneath the covers. 'We're fine. It was high blood pressure, that's all.'

'But why didn't you call last night?'

'I was having tests. I didn't want to worry you.'

'Didn't want to worry me?' he shouted. 'Are you joking? Why are you being so distant? What the hell's going on, Lil? This isn't fair.'

'FAIR?' I said, loud enough for a nurse to look over from the main station. I waved at her to indicate I was fine and lowered my voice again. 'Fair? You want to talk about fair? OK, why the hell didn't you tell me about Primrose?'

I'll admit, my goal of remaining cool and composed slipped a bit earlier than I expected here. But I was tired.

'What? What on earth do you mean?' he snapped.

'I saw the picture, Max.'

'What? What picture? Whose picture?'

'Primrose's picture, and the story in the *Mail*. Her picture of you on Instagram. Taken that day. The day we slept together again. You and her dog in some park and she'd written "My boys back together" underneath. Can you imagine finding that in the morning, after what we'd just done?'

I hated excruciating conversations like these. Conversations where I sounded rational in my head, but then, as soon as I forced the words out, seemed unhinged.

'So that's why you've been off with me? Why you've been weird?' he said.

'I haven't been weird. I just decided that if you weren't being honest about your personal life with me, then it was best that we keep some distance between us.'

Max exhaled down the line. 'I thought you regretted us... doing what we did. I never thought... I didn't realize—'

'Max, you don't have to explain,' I interrupted. 'It's complicated, I get it. It's totally your business. I haven't really got any right to be cross or interfere. But the last thing I want now is more complication. You understand that, right?'

'There isn't any complication,' he said, before falling silent. I waited for him to go on but he sighed again. 'OK, that's not totally true. Telling Prim about this, about our situation, hasn't been straightforward...'

'Oh my God,' I mumbled, grateful that I was already lying down. My sadness intensified, as if hearing Max admit to this confirmed all my insecurities. He had lied, the story was right. There was still something between them. I swallowed and steeled myself for what I had to say next.

'Listen—' Max went on.

'No,' I said, gripping my phone tightly to my head. 'You listen. It's easier this way. I don't need this. I think it's simpler if we just have a break in these last few weeks.'

'I'm going to Mongolia next week, Lil,' he said, sounding hollow.

'Fine,' I said, 'I hope it goes well. And I'll let you know if anything happens here. But I don't think we work as friends. Or… anything else. We were never friends in the first place and sleeping together again, well, it was stupid.'

'Lil—' Max started again.

'I'm sorry,' I said. 'I just need some space. Good luck with the climb.' I hung up and leant back against the lumpy hospital pillows. They might as well have been stuffed with Weetabix. And then I cried, yet again, only stopping an hour or so later when Jess arrived to take me home in a pair of dungarees covered in red paint, a menacing look on a hospital ward.

She insisted on pushing me out to the front of the hospital for a taxi in a wheelchair and helping me into the back of the cab as if I'd just been in for a hip replacement. She'd also brought an old rug from her house and draped me in it. Pallid and having not washed my hair for a couple of days, I could have been cast as an extra – Peasant 3 – in a period drama.

'Excuse me, driver,' Jess said, just before he pulled out. 'My friend is delicate so could you drive extremely carefully?'

He looked alarmed but nodded at her in the rear-view mirror and we set off for Brixton at such a slow pace I wondered if we'd get home only to have to turn round immediately and head back to the ward because I'd be nine months gone and in labour.

I leant back against the seat and sighed.

'You all right?' said Jess.

'Yeah.' I smiled at her. 'Thank you.'

'Course,' she said, smiling at me so sweetly I felt a fresh wave of guilt at what I had to tell her about Alexi and thought about it the whole way back to my flat.

What should I say? How did I even start having that conversation? Was there any other possible explanation for Alexi being in that corridor? Was it his sister? Did Russians hold hands like that with their sisters? I suspected not. Could it be an ex-wife? Again, I was no expert on relationships, clearly, but I didn't think one should look so friendly with an ex. And even if it was entirely innocent, why had he turned round and ignored me? I recognized the signs. The widened eyes, the tiny inflection of his jaw. The defensive body language. He was guilty. Fuck me, what a soap opera. All I needed now was to arrive home and find the flat on fire and it would be a Christmas special.

Jess helped me upstairs and on to my bed. ET felt quiet, as if she was sleeping. So I lay on my side as Jess sat down on the bed beside me.

'Want a cup of tea?' she said.

'Please,' I said. 'Thanks, Florence Nightingale. Although there's probably only almond milk.'

'Hang on,' she said, getting up again and going next door to flick the kettle on.

I scrolled through the messages on my phone. One from Mum telling me to ring her when home. A get well soon gif from Dennis of a polar bear nuzzling a cub's head (he'd recently learned how to send gifs). A message from Steph, another from Mike.

I couldn't concentrate on polar bear gifs right now. I needed to talk to Jess, so when she came back in carefully carrying two mugs of tea, I heaved myself up.

'Careful,' she said, passing me a mug.

'Got it, thanks,' I said.

'De nada. One day you'll be doing the same for me,' she said, sitting down on the other side of my bed.

I felt my mouth dry up as I tried to think of an opening sentence. I wanted to be composed, calm. I didn't want the words to tumble unthinkingly from my mouth. I was going to start gently, ease in, begin with how I had something I needed to talk to her about.

'Jess,' I said, 'I think Alexi might be married.'

Solid work. I'd blown my careful introduction with one line.

'What?'

'Sorry, love, that's not very clear, but I saw him with a woman at parents' evening. At school. And he was holding

SOPHIA MONEY-COUTTS

hands with her. Outside a classroom. And I think they have
a son there. Called Luka.'

Jess sat frozen, her mug of tea between her hands, staring
at me. 'He has a nephew called Luka. He's on his phone. It's
the picture on his phone.'

'Love, I'm not sure it's his nephew. I think it might be his son.
The woman he was with, it didn't look like his sister. They were…
they looked like they were together.' I said it as softly as I could.

Jess remained quite still for a few moments. Then she shook
her head. 'It can't be. He can't have a son. He travels so much.
He's always away. I'd know. There's no way he could keep…
I just… I'd know. I'd know something like that. He wouldn't
be able to hide, what, a double life? There's no way, there's
no way.' She shook her head again.

'When did you last see him?'

'Last weekend,' she said. 'On Sunday. He went to Hong
Kong the next morning.'

'He wasn't in Hong Kong, love, he can't have been. He
was at school on Thursday night. When was he supposed to
get back?'

'He hasn't,' she whispered. 'I thought he was still there.'
And I watched as a single tear slid down her cheek.

I put a hand on her knee. 'I'm sorry. I'm so sorry, love.' I
kept repeating it. 'I'm so sorry.'

And then she let out a sob, a noise which suggested such
raw, animalistic pain that it set me off too.

It's funny how quickly things can change. Not funny as in
'ha ha'. Funny as in strange, how breathtakingly fast life can

alter and something you thought was safe and permanent is in fact the opposite. One minute you can be with someone, the next they're gone. A death, or a break-up. Or a break-up which feels like a death. Jess was braver than me, so she sent Alexi a message asking if he had a wife and family while still sitting on my bed. He tried to ring her several times and then sent a feeble message just saying 'Sorry'.

By the time her tea had cooled on my bedside table, she was done. It was finished. I took months to wallow over Jake, spending hours listening to sad Passenger songs. True, we went out for eight years while Jess and Alexi dated for six months, but time doesn't dictate the strength of a relationship. The whole of *Romeo and Juliet* takes place over four days. They meet on a Sunday evening, they've kicked it by Thursday morning. Nutters. And so it had proved with Max. One minute it looked rosy; the next we were as distant as we ever had been because I realized he hadn't been honest with me after all.

I hope he did have to eat horse in Mongolia. It would serve him right.

CHAPTER THIRTEEN

IT WAS JESS'S IDEA to go away for the weekend. She surprised me. I got an email from her later that week, while at school, saying that she'd booked us a mini-break and could I please pack a bag with some clean knickers and a toothbrush so she could pick me up from St Lancelot's that Friday.

PS. It's not too far away and the John Radcliffe Hospital is nearby so don't panic. I'm not taking you bungee jumping. It's a treat for both of us.

I wished I was a lesbian, I thought, sliding my phone back into my desk drawer, so I could live with Jess. We'd be so happy. Although try as I might, I just couldn't face the thought of going down on a woman, so that option was sadly out.

She borrowed Clem's car for the weekend, an old, purple Seat that smelled of dog breath, but she refused to tell me where we were going as we crawled through Friday traffic escaping London.

'Wait and see. But you'll like it. I hope. Anyway, how you both feeling?'

My app had told me that morning that, at thirty-four weeks, ET was now the size of a head of celery and I'd sat on the Tube wondering if that included all the frilly leaves at the end or just the sticks. 'We're good,' I said, 'although I'm still not sleeping that well.'

'Uncomfortable?'

'Yeah, and just Grace and Riley are amazing but I still feel like I'm living next to the monkey kingdom at London Zoo.'

No more luck on the flat hunt, either. Daniel had surpassed himself this week by sending me the details of a flat with a police cordon still hanging across the front door.

'I've been thinking about this and come up with a plan,' said Jess. 'You're going to come and live with us.'

'What?'

She nodded and continued staring through the windscreen, focusing on the traffic. 'Yep. We've got all those bedrooms full of crap so Clem can clear one out and that'll be your room. And ET's.'

'Love, you can't—'

'I don't want to hear it. I don't know why I didn't think of it before. Probably because my head was full of that Russian dildo. But it's the perfect solution. Come on, you can't tell me it isn't.'

'What does Clem say?'

'He doesn't know yet.'

I laughed. 'Jess, honestly, you guys don't need a newborn shrieking the house down.'

'Rubbish, it's exactly what we need. And it's a good excuse to try and sort the house out a bit. I was thinking, that room under the attic, it's mostly Gran's old wardrobe and bad paintings. We'll shift them, maybe paint it a bit, get new curtains and it's yours. If you want it?'

I did want it. I wanted it so much. It wouldn't be a normal situation – me, ET, Clem boiling something possibly fatal in the kitchen and Jess playing Nina Simone loudly upstairs. But it would be a modern family. Four of us together. ET with other adults around her, not just me, because I'd been obsessing about whether I was handicapping her from the very start by doing this on my own. The idea that we didn't have to be lonely in a flat with a police cordon around it made my chest feel tight.

'Can I actually?' I said, looking at Jess.

'Yes,' she said, before glancing across at me. 'Although no tears. Shall we try and have a 48-hour period where neither of us cries?'

'Deal,' I nodded. 'But will you check with Clem? I don't want him to feel like he has to say yes.'

She batted a hand in the air as if swatting an imaginary fly. 'He'll be fine. Imagine all the baby food he'll get excited about.'

*

A couple of hours later, we pulled into a gravel drive and crunched along it until we drew up in front of a huge stone house covered with clumps of purple wisteria.

'Welcome to your babymoon,' said Jess, stopping the car.

I laughed. 'Oh my God, no way?'

'Yes, I'm sorry to tell you I've booked something called the "Yummy Mummy Package", but I figured we could both do with massages and facials and not wearing a single item of restrictive clothing all weekend. So here we are.'

'You are the best husband in the world.'

'I know. Come on, let's go in.'

It smelled expensive as soon as Jess opened the door. I spotted several candles burning on different surfaces.

'Welcome to Bluebell Manor,' said a woman standing behind a desk, underneath a sweeping staircase.

'Hello,' said Jess. 'I've got a booking under the name of Russo. Jess Russo?'

The woman tapped at a laptop on the desk. 'Yes, here we are.' She flicked her eyes to my stomach and back to my face again. 'And congratulations! When are you due?'

'Next month,' I said.

'How exciting for you both, do you know what you're having?'

I opened my mouth to explain and say no I didn't. But Jess got there before me.

'We think it's a girl,' she said, draping an arm over my shoulders.

'A little girl, adorable!' said the woman, grinning so widely I could see all her teeth and most of her gums. 'Well, we have you in the Honeysuckle Suite which has a lovely big bath and an emperor sized-bed.'

'Thrilling,' said Jess, so I tried to dig her in the ribs with my elbow but my bag swung off my shoulder.

'Let me carry that, darling,' Jess said, reaching for the bag.

'No no, Marcello will carry it all for you,' said the smiling lady. 'Marcello?'

A thin man with dark hair tied back in a bun appeared through a door behind the desk and looked expectantly at the woman.

'Can you please take this couple's bags to their room, please, Marcello? They're in the Honeysuckle Suite.'

Marcello turned to glance at us, then my stomach, then Jess, then back to the smiling lady again. He looked confused.

'Chop-chop,' she told him.

He nodded and hurried round the desk towards us, taking both our bags. He frowned briefly before opening his mouth, 'Follow me, er, madams.' And then he made for the stairs.

'Thank you so much,' said Jess, to the lady behind the desk. And then, to me, 'After you, sweetheart.'

I rolled my eyes at her and went after Marcello, wondering if she'd keep this up all weekend.

★

The Honeysuckle Suite was insane. Bigger than any of the flats I'd looked at, with a vast bedroom overlooking a lawn in front of the house which dropped down to an outdoor swimming pool. The bed was indeed emperor-sized, although I suspected it could fit several emperors, and it had roughly forty-nine white pillows on it. A soft, cuddly stork with an orange beak sat on top of the pillows like a cherry.

There was also a fruit basket on a table under the window which looked like the sort of Harvest Festival offering a mother at St Lancelot's would pull together. Apples, peaches, grapes, a pineapple, a couple of kiwis, some small, yellow unidentifiable round things I'd never seen in Tesco.

I went to inspect the bathroom. Also gargantuan. A bath big enough for all those emperors, a rain shower, a loo with a little round window next to it that overlooked the pool and another basket beside the basin. I bent over it and inspected the bottles. Something called Lucky Legs with spearmint to help my ankles feel soothed. A cream called Pregnancy Boob Tube which apparently contained antioxidants to help strengthen the skin. Fat chance, I thought. I felt like a forklift truck driver every morning when I put on my bra. It would take more than a layer of cream to lift those puppies.

Plus, a tube of Tummy Rub oil for stretch marks. Again, I feared this was a ship that had sailed. White, wormy lines ran across my hips, either side of my belly button and towards my nipples, arrows pointing in their direction. Finally, a small pot of Perineal Ointment. I thought back to the times Jake and I had come away for romantic mini-breaks at posh hotels. They had been quite different. Certainly no bum cream.

Two white dressing gowns hung on the bathroom door – 'Mum-to-be' in pink and 'Dad-to-be' in blue embroidered on the back of them. I carried both out to Jess, who was picking off the grapes while reading a bit of paper.

'We've got massages tomorrow at eleven and midday, and then facials in the afternoon. Do you want to do a baby yoga class? Not sure I can be arsed,' she said.

'Probably not,' I said. 'But I guess we can tell them tomorrow.'

She nodded, then put the bit of paper down. 'Drink?'

'Yep, good plan.'

★

You can feel exquisitely happy going away with another half for the weekend. It's especially thrilling if it's early days in your relationship, off to a posh hotel, and just the two of you exist, cocooned in Egyptian cotton sheets. Nobody else matters. You roll downstairs for a breakfast of eggs and artisanal sausages before going back upstairs to have sex again, or for a bath, or simply to go back to sleep in one another's arms. The rest of the world could implode, but that would be all right because the other person was there.

But going away with your best friend, even when you're nearly eight months pregnant and as alluring and hairy as a mammoth, can be even better. Jess and I laughed that weekend so much that other couples stared at us in the bar. They frowned at us in the dining room. We laughed so much in the spa, when Jess made fart noises in the jacuzzi, that I thought a bit of wee would run out and maybe a tiny bit of it did.

It was incredibly childish and Jess kept up the pretence that we were a couple throughout, insisting on wearing the 'Dad-to-be' dressing gown down to breakfast both mornings, when she also demanded a copy of the *Financial Times* from poor, baffled Marcello because she said she had to know 'what the markets were up to'. But it was bliss.

Jess texted Clem asking if he minded me moving into the

river house. He called her straight back and said nothing would make him happier. He then set up a new joint WhatsApp group between us called 'ET' with a picture of the alien, and messaged saying he was watching YouTube videos on how to change nappies and the best way to swaddle a baby.

We also howled when I tried the perineal ointment. Not in front of Jess. There were limits. But while she lay on our bed drinking red wine on Saturday night, deciding what film we'd watch, I stood in the bathroom, one foot up on the edge of the bath, trying to follow the instructions on the pot.

The perineum was not an area of my body, or anyone else's, that had ever troubled me much. I vaguely remember once reading an article in *Cosmopolitan* suggesting that it was an erogenous zone for men, and that you could locate this magical area between their balls and their bottom and press gently. This was supposed to have a miraculous effect, but I wasn't convinced. There was enough machinery already down there to get to grips with. Why complicate it further?

As for my own perineum, well, at this stage of pregnancy, I was supposed to hook my thumb into my vagina and tug down towards my bottom, like a small child putting its fingers in the corners of its mouth to pull a face. I was sceptical it would make any difference but Emily had lectured us about ripping and tearing down there in our baby classes, so I decided it was worth a shot. Not that I was ever having sex again after this ordeal anyway, as I kept reminding myself. A week on from finding out about Primrose and Max, the sting of being lied to had receded but I still winced every time I thought of the photo. Which was roughly every other minute. I'd forced myself not to look at her profile again on Instagram, or his to check his progress in Mongolia, but the image of Max laughing with Primrose while walking her dog was imprinted on my brain like a brass rubbing.

I shook my head to try and dispel it again while standing with one foot on the side of the bath, ointment trickling all over my thumb as I tugged down one way with it, and then the next. I had to hold my thumb down for a minute or so before letting it go again.

'*Notting Hill*?' shouted Jess from next door.

'No, she's pregnant and too happy at the end,' I shouted back.

'OK, OK, not happy. Not too happy. Hmmm…' Jess went quiet for a few moments. '*One Day*?'

'Too sad.'

'So you want something where nobody gets married in the end, but nobody dies either?'

'Ideally, yes,' I bellowed at her, releasing my thumb on one side of my vagina and sliding it across.

She went quiet again.

'*Dirty Dancing*?'

'I'm still too upset about Patrick Swayze.'

I heard Jess mumble something unintelligible and then shout again. '*The Jungle Book*?'

'His wolf dad dies.'

And so on and so on while I stretched my vagina like a scrunchie.

We finally settled on *The Way We Were* because neither of us had ever seen a Barbara Streisand film. Turned out it's a story about a pair of mismatched lovers who are doomed, not quite in the way Romeo and Juliet were. But it still made us wail.

'We weren't supposed to cry this weekend,' I said, reaching for a tissue at the end of the film.

'I know, but it's so sad,' sobbed Jess, clutching the cuddly stork. 'Why couldn't she love Robert Redford? He's so beautiful.'

In her defence, she'd finished the bottle of red wine by herself.

It was the next morning, while lying in the spa wearing our dressing gowns, that a message from an unfamiliar number lit up my phone screen.

Lil. I'm at base camp now and switching to my satellite phone before we start our ascent. If you need to get hold me, any time and for any reason, call or email me on this. It gets both. Hope you're both doing well. Mx.

'What is it?' said Jess.

I read it out to her.

'So cool having a satellite phone,' said Jess. 'It's like getting a message from Jason Bourne.'

'Oi.' I reached out and hit her on the arm.

'Sorry,' she said quickly. 'Obviously he's a cad and we hate him.'

'Exactly,' I murmured, still frowning down at my phone screen.

'You going to reply?'

I looked across and wrinkled my nose at her. 'Do I have to?'.

Jess pulled her lips in together and nodded at me. 'Yes. Just to tell him you've got it. You have to be an adult about this, love, it's not just about you.'

'All right, Mum.' I knew she was right, but my anger at Max's dishonesty was still simmering and I wanted to punish him for it.

'I'm not lecturing you,' said Jess. There was an edge to her voice which surprised me. Jess and I never fought, or even bickered. 'I just wonder if—'

'What?' I snapped at her.

She sighed and sat up on her sunbed. 'Look, you don't actually know what the deal is, Lil. You haven't given him a chance to explain. It might be nothing between him and his ex.'

'That's not true,' I shot back. 'He admitted it was complicated.'

'Oh all right, it's complicated. Sue the guy!' said Jess, throwing her hands up in the air. 'Come on, Lil, we're grown-ups, not teenagers. Who doesn't have something tricky with an ex? It doesn't make him a bad person.'

'I just don't need any complications,' I said. It was a mantra I'd told myself a billion times since the morning after Max and I had slept together.

'I know you don't,' said Jess, more soothingly. 'But what are you going to do when she's born? You're going to have to communicate with him. You're going to have to have a relationship of sorts.'

I shrugged. 'We'll work it out then.'

'Fine, all I'm saying is I don't think cutting him out now, when he's thousands of miles away on a dangerous expedition, is very kind. You can be the bigger person here, Lil, set the tone for, well, however you guys handle this in the future.'

'All right, all right,' I muttered, starting to type a reply on my phone. *Thanks for letting me know, and good luck. L*

I read it out to Jess.

'That OK?' I asked.

She nodded and lay back on her bed. I clicked send and slid my phone into my pocket, before resting my hands on my stomach, slick with stretch-mark oil underneath my gown. I'd rubbed in great handfuls of the stuff, feeling ET wriggle underneath it. That week, I'd finally told Steph and Mike about the recent developments with Max, and Mike told me he had a friend who worked in family law if I needed advice. But I didn't want to think about the legal implications of what might happen when she was born. Other people spent the last few weeks of pregnancy decorating nurseries and planning hospital routes with their other half. I didn't want to spend mine talking to a lawyer.

*

Luckily, like sisters who squabble but embrace one another minutes later, Jess and I were back to laughing about perineums by the time we drove back to London that evening. She dropped me outside the flat, and I staggered upstairs to tell Grace and Riley about my moving plans.

Riley looked visibly relieved. I don't think he'd been relishing the prospect of a mewling baby in the adjacent bedroom. 'Oh no, we'll miss you, darl,' he said, not wholly convincingly, while he stood at the cooker fluffing their quinoa.

Grace was sadder. 'Can I come visit you guys?'

'Course,' I said. 'Who else is going to tell me what I should and shouldn't be feeding her?'

Grace's face suddenly brightened. 'Can I throw you a baby shower before you go?'

'You don't have to do that,' I said. 'That's a load of faff.'

She shook her head. 'No it isn't. I'd like to. Like a leaving party. Just tell me who to ask and I'll sort it.'

'Really?'

'Yes, really,' she insisted.

'OK, thank you, but honestly nothing crazy,' I said. 'A bit of cake and, er, some tea would be ace.' I glanced over at the cupboards behind me, wondering how alternative Grace could make a baby shower.

Cupcakes made from shiitake mushrooms?

Nettle tea?

Hemp brownies?

We sat on the sofa later, Grace sitting cross-legged with her notebook in her lap, dutifully jotting down the names that I gave her. Jess, Clem, my old uni mates Nats, Luce and Bells, Steph, Mum, Dennis.

'What about the baby daddy?' Riley asked, turning from

the telly to look at me. I'd explained the situation to them both too and while Grace had made sympathetic sounds, Riley had merely whistled and referred to Max as 'a stud'.

'Uh-uh,' I said, shaking my head. 'No way.'

Grace bent her head back down to her notepad and carried on scribbling, biting the end of her pen from time to time and mumbling cryptically, 'I know', before writing something else.

I was touched. I'd spent the weekend laughing with my best friend and then, this evening, being looked after by these two chickpea obsessives.

'See?' I said to ET as I pulled back my duvet and fell into bed that night, reaching for my other pillow to prop it under my stomach as a bolster. 'We're doing perfectly all right without him.' Although I checked the weather in Mongolia on my phone before I went to sleep, just in case.

★

The following week was my last at school before going on maternity leave. Sitting behind my desk in the classroom, I struggled to reach my laptop and standing for too long while doing words on the whiteboard made my swollen ankles feel like they would explode with pressure.

Steph said I shouldn't be in school at all by this point but I wanted to make sure the handover to my maternity cover went smoothly. She was an owlish-looking woman with a neat bun and spectacles called Mrs Gimson who'd been poached from our rival school in Knightsbridge, Barnaby's Prep. She seemed nice enough but I was anxious about handing over my boys.

Leaving a teaching job isn't like taking a break from accountancy. You can't just set an out-of-office and chuck away all little packets of ketchup from your desk drawer. I wouldn't see these boys until next year, by which time they'd be in Mrs Peers's class and not the same shape. Bigger, rougher, even noisier, their small, hot hands wouldn't slip into mine in the playground. I wouldn't know if Cosmo had got better with his 'r' words. Achilles would have grown out of dinosaur stories. They might remember a nursery rhyme I taught them, they might not. But that's the deal with being a teacher. You have to remember they're borrowed, never yours in the first place. Maybe it was the pregnancy hormones charging round my system, but I teared up as I gazed at the splotchy paintings on the classroom walls one afternoon that week.

Miss Montague called me into her office on Friday. My last day. Across her desk, she pushed me a present wrapped in paper with a card stuck to it.

'That's so kind, er, thank you,' I said, stuttering because the gesture – and the bright pink floral paper – seemed so out of character.

She looked embarrassed. 'It's a small thing,' she said, stiffly. 'And I expect you back next year.'

I nodded as I unwrapped it. 'Course.' And then I clapped my hand to my mouth. 'Oh, Miss Montague!'

It was a knitted bear wearing a St Lancelot's blazer. His mouth was curved slightly, so it looked like he was smiling, and he had small black eyes like little currants. 'This is… I'm so touched… thank you.' I propped the bear on her desk and grinned back at him, before looking at her. 'I didn't know you knitted.'

Miss Montague's cheeks had turned pink. 'I don't knit very well, I'm afraid, but I thought it would remind you of us.'

'I promise I'm coming back.'

Miss Montague nodded as if this was never in doubt. 'I'm full of admiration, you know,' she went on. 'You're brave.' Then she turned in her seat and glanced out at the playground through her window, which was letting in the shouts of Year 6 charging about like small barbarians. 'It was different, in my day and…' She stopped and looked back to me. 'Well, never mind. We'll all be thinking of you. Jolly good luck.'

I stood, holding the bear, unsure suddenly how to say goodbye properly. A hug? I must have shaken Miss Montague's hand when I first met her, for my interview. But we'd never touched another since. It would be like touching the Queen. Forbidden. So I just smiled and moved towards the door. 'Thank you, Miss Montague,' I said. 'For everything. I'll bring her in as soon as I've mastered how to get on the Tube with a buggy.'

The bear wasn't the only present that day. Unbeknownst to me, Fergus had organized a send-off in the classroom just before the boys went for the weekend.

'Boys,' said Fergus, suddenly, while they were all sitting

in front of me listening as I finished the last page of *There's a Wocket in my Pocket*. 'We have something for Miss Bailey, don't we?'

Ten blank faces looked back at him, then Phineas shot his hand in the air.

'Yes, Phineas,' said Fergus.

'A card because she's poorly?'

'Not poorly,' said Fergus. 'Miss Bailey is having a…'

'BABY!' shouted Oscar.

'Not so loud, but exactly,' said Fergus. 'So who wants to give Miss Bailey this?'

He turned in his chair and picked up a huge card and a present from behind him. Achilles and Dmitri immediately got up and started squabbling over who gave me what.

'Achilles, why don't you do the card first, and then Dmitri you give Miss Bailey the book?' said Fergus.

I wasn't sure quite how Fergus had suddenly developed these diplomacy skills but I felt oddly proud. Apparently we'd all been learning things in the past few months.

Achilles walked towards me with the card, holding it as carefully as if he was an approaching waiter with a tray of martinis. 'Thank you, Achilles,' I said, taking it from him. Glitter cascaded from inside the card on to my lap.

'Good luck, Miss Bailey,' it said on the front, over an alarming drawing of a baby in a pram. It looked like the pig baby in *Alice's Adventures in Wonderland*.

'Thank you,' I said, smiling out at them. 'Who did the baby?'

'That was me,' said Fergus, proudly.

Inside the card, it said 'WE WILL MISS YOU' in glittery letters and everyone had signed it. Some in large wobbly letters – HUNTER, ARTHUR. Some in tiny wobbly letters. 'Phineas', and 'Oscar'.

'I'll take this home and frame it,' I said, gently laying it down on my desk and taking the present from Dmitri.

Inside the wrapping was a thin booklet made from several pages of A4 paper stapled together. The cover had a picture of me with the class around me on stage, taken just after their nativity play. And the title said 'We love Miss Bailey because…'

Each boy had decorated a page and written (with Fergus's help), a reason they loved me with a drawing. George wrote, 'I love Miss Bailey because she reads to us', with a ropy drawing of the Gruffalo underneath it.

Phineas's page said, 'I love Miss Bailey because she smells nice,' illustrated with a drawing of a flower.

Roman's page was the one that got me most of all. 'I love Miss Bailey because she looks after us,' it said, beside a dinosaur he'd drawn with yellow fangs. So I welled up yet again, although I was momentarily distracted from tears when I reached the end of the booklet and found an envelope tucked into the back page.

'That's from the mothers,' said Fergus.

'Oh, amazing.' My heart skipped. A big cheque? I opened it to find a voucher for a package of hot stone massages at a Knightsbridge spa.

'That's incredibly generous of them,' I said, smiling grate-fully at Fergus, whose cheeks turned quite as pink as his aunt's had earlier. Must run in the family.

I slid the voucher into my book and looked at my boys. 'I'll miss you all too, so much. Can I come back and visit? And bring my baby to meet you all and say hello?'

'Yes but, Miss Bailey,' piped up Phineas, his face severe, 'I still think you should get a puppy.'

★

Mum drove down from Norfolk that weekend to drop off old baby clothes, so we met at the river house since I didn't see much point in schlepping them across town when I moved from Brixton.

'Mrs B, what a treat, come in, come in!' said Clem, opening the door to us both in jeans and a faded red T-shirt that had a hole in one armpit.

He kissed Mum hello and then leant forward to me. 'Hello, darling, how you feeling?'

'Fat.'

'Cup of tea?'

'No, Clem, you need to help me unload the car first,' said Mum.

'Right-o,' said Clem, saluting and then grinning at me before following her back down the garden path – bare feet – to where she'd parked.

'Lil, put the kettle on,' he said over his shoulder.

I went inside to the kitchen and stood at the sink filling it up, then heard the thuds of Jess coming downstairs.

'Morning, roomie,' she said, sleepily, stretching in the doorway.

'Hi, love.' I flicked the kettle on and went over to give her a hug, although I was so enormous that physical greetings were becoming awkward. It felt extremely intimate to kiss someone hello while my stomach ground into their pelvis.

'Wait until you see what Clem's done to the room,' she said, sitting down at the kitchen table.

'Actually?' I spun round from the mug cupboard and smiled at her.

She nodded. 'Yeah, all cleared out and painted. Floorboards sanded. You might need a rug of some sort but there are loads rolled up in the room next to Clem's, so we can have a rummage later.'

There was a sudden commotion outside the kitchen and Clem burst through the door with three boxes piled on top of one another in his arms. I couldn't see his face.

'Careful, Clem, some of that is very fragile,' barked Mum, behind him, several blankets stacked in her arms.

He edged the boxes on to the table and stood back, panting.

'Blimey, Mum, how come there's all this?' I waved my arm at the table.

'Oh, you know, just bits I've kept from when you were little. And toys. And a few books.' She put the blankets down on a free chair. 'Where's this tea?'

'I didn't know you kept so much,' I said, opening up the

box closest to me. It was mostly clothes – babygros of varying sizes and colours, a few with pale yellow stains on them (I didn't want to complain), vests, thinning muslins and, right at the bottom, a tiny pair of red patent shoes with a little buckle, so small they were the kind of thing a woodland sprite might wear if he was off to a party.

'Your first shoes,' said Mum, as I pulled them out. 'For a Christmas party. You could hardly walk. It was silly really. I think you only wore them the once.'

While I was rifling through the box, Clem had taken over tea duty.

'Here we go,' he said, putting a mug down in front of Mum and me.

'Where's mine?' said Jess.

'Right here, bossy boots.' He handed her a mug. 'Crumpet, anyone?'

'Yes please,' said Jess, as she opened another box. 'Oh my God, I remember this.' She lifted out a book and turned it round to face us. '*I Want My Potty!*'

Mum laughed. 'I used to read that to you while you were on yours,' she said, nodding her head towards me, 'and every now and then you'd get up to inspect your potty, waving your bum in the air. I used to give you a Smartie if you did something.'

'I wish I still got a Smartie for doing that,' said Clem, putting butter and various jams on the table.

'Don't be disgusting,' said Jess.

'Can we see upstairs?' I said, putting my miniature shoes

carefully back into the box. 'Mum, Clem's apparently been hard at work all week on my room.'

'Well, it's not like I have anything better to be doing,' said Clem. 'Although can I just nip up first and check it's all perfect?'

'Course.'

He bounded upstairs like a greyhound – thud, thud, thud – so we gave him a couple of minutes before following. Mum first, then me, then Jess trailing behind in her dressing gown.

It was on the second floor, overlooking the river. I'd never stepped into this room before because it was so full of junk. Occasionally a dusty chest of drawers would be pushed back from the door and an artist friend of Jess's would camp on the floorboards for a few weeks, but both Jess and Clem had been against letting anyone stay permanently, even though they could have done with the cash. They were like an old married couple – they bickered from morning until night but they needed one another too. I just hoped ET and I wouldn't disrupt the balance.

'Clem,' I said, walking into it and gazing around me. 'This is amazing.'

He'd painted the walls pale yellow and the bay window, several panes high, was letting in the morning light from across the Thames so the room glowed. The floorboards were pale and smooth, newly sanded and varnished, and there was a double bed pushed up against the far corner.

'I thought there's enough space here for a cot,' said Clem, standing beside the bed and waving his hands in front of him like an air traffic controller. 'And then there's this cupboard and the chest of drawers but if there isn't enough space you can always use one of my cupboards.'

I shook my head. 'It's wonderful.'

'What a view,' said Mum, walking towards the window and looking out. The sun was glinting off the river.

'You don't mind the curtains?' said Jess. A pair of blue silk curtains ran from the ceiling to the floor either side of the window. 'They're ancient.'

'No no, they're great.' The chain on the blind was broken in my Brixton bedroom so I just left it permanently down. Having so much natural light, and a view of something other than McDonald's, made me feel like I was checking into the most luxurious hotel in the world.

'Let's have breakfast and then we can unpack,' said Jess. 'Although when are you moving the rest of your stuff?'

'I thought next weekend, if that's all right? Grace is throwing this baby shower on Saturday. She's invited you all, right?'

'Yup,' said Jess and Clem simultaneously.

'And Dennis,' said Mum.

'OK, cool, so I thought maybe move all my stuff on Sunday. If that works for you guys?'

'Perfect,' said Clem, 'and then I expect you'll want to do lots of nesting.'

'How do you know about nesting, you freak?' said Jess.

'Because I've read a book. Some of us are being responsible about having a newborn moving in.'

'It's a baby, not the Hadron Collider,' said Jess. 'They can't be that complicated.'

'Thanks, guys,' I said, interrupting before they got going. 'I'm very excited about our new dysfunctional family.'

'Modern, not dysfunctional,' corrected Jess.

'Have you told his Lordship where you'll be living?' asked Mum, as we traipsed back downstairs in formation.

Since updating her about the situation with Max – the picture, our subsequent phone call, his latest expedition – Mum had taken an even dimmer view of the aristocracy.

'No,' I told her firmly. Max and I hadn't messaged since our exchange about his satellite phone the weekend before. All right, I'd given in once and looked at his Instagram profile, but he hadn't posted anything since arriving in Mongolia so I didn't know whether he was due back tomorrow or not for another week or so. But I sure as hell wasn't going to give in and send my new address as an excuse for getting in touch. I was staying firm on this one. If Max wanted an update, he'd have to message me.

CHAPTER FOURTEEN

HAVE YOU EVER BEEN to a baby shower? Imagine a baby-themed hen party with baby bunting and baby napkins but no drinking. That's the level of fun we're talking about. Nobody ever got roaringly pissed and twirled their knickers above their head at a baby shower, alas. Although I'm being unfair on the drinking front since Grace had bought two bottles of organic Prosecco and I managed to have one sip before she said, pointedly, that she'd made the rhubarb cordial especially for me.

Gathered in the sitting room in the flat were Mum, Dennis, Jess, Clem, Grace, Nats, Lucy, Bells, Steph and me, sitting on the sofa surrounded by presents as if it was my fifth birthday party.

'Forgive me if I don't come on Saturday, but I'd rather have a prostate examination than go to a baby shower,' Mike had told me, earlier in the week.

'You and me both,' I'd replied.

'You don't have a prostate, darling,' he said.

The truth was, ever since Grace mentioned the baby shower, I'd had a small voice in my head whispering, 'You don't deserve a baby shower.' The whispery voice told me it was strange, almost inappropriate, to have a party to celebrate

ET, given the circumstances. That accidentally knocked-up 31-year-olds should get on with things quietly, no showing-off.

But for all this worrying and self-chastisement, I was genu-inely touched at the effort Grace had gone to. She'd made a special baby-shower playlist on Spotify which included Michael Bublé's 'Haven't Met You Yet' and Sonny and Cher's 'I Got You Babe'. Pink and blue helium balloons bobbed above our heads. On the kitchen counter, a stack of paper plates saying 'Girl or boy?' sat next to a mound of cucumber and egg mayonnaise sandwiches (organic), the rhubarb cordial and a cake-stand of mini beetroot muffins.

I was less into the frosted carrot cake with a gold sign stuck in it which said 'Happy Pushing!' And she also made me wear a cream and pink sash that read 'Mummy-to-be'. Pulling the sash over my stomach was like rolling an elastic band over an apple. At my last antenatal appointment, my blood pressure was just in the acceptable range but I felt as swollen as the marshmallow man. And my ankles were as thick as telegraph poles, so I'd taken to sleeping with my feet elevated on a pillow. Who were those women bouncing round Brockwell Park in lycra looking as heavily pregnant as me and yet so perky? I'd spent the past few days lying on the sofa alternating between *Homes Under the Hammer* and *Masterchef* reruns, and even watching them felt like an effort.

'Is your bag packed for hospital?' asked Nats.

I nodded. 'Yup, all done. Victorian nightie for easy access down there, check. Nappies, check. Sanitary pads so thick they could block the Hoover Dam, check. Sorry, Dennis. And Clem.'

'Not to worry,' said Dennis. 'Clem and I can sit here and talk about the football, can't we, Clem.'

Clem's eyebrows jumped in alarm. He knew precisely nothing about football.

'Is Max going to be back in time for it?' asked Steph.

'Hope so,' I said breezily, even though there hadn't been any further messaging. He'd now been away for just over two weeks (although I was trying not to count the days like a fretful girlfriend), and he'd said it could take up to three weeks. But I didn't want to get into the timings with everyone there. Discussing him today would only make me feel his absence more.

'Talking of nappies, we've got a game to play,' said Grace, clapping her hands together and diverting the conversation. She disappeared into her bedroom and came back out carrying a cardboard box. 'Everyone listening? It's called the Dirty Diaper game and I'm going to pass round several nappies, and you have to sniff and guess what's in them.'

Dennis cleared his throat. 'Grace, forgive me, I'm very old and I fear I'm being very slow. You're going to hand us some dirty nappies and we have to smell them?'

Grace cackled. 'Yes, but sorry, I should have explained. I've rubbed various products into these nappies and you have to guess what they are. It's nothing bad.'

'Like what?' asked Jess.

'That's the game! You have to guess,' said Grace, passing

Bells the first nappy from her box. Bells opened it as if handling a bomb. I could see something brown rubbed in the gusset and sniggered. Playing Mr and Mrs at a hen party and coyly 'ooooooh-ing' at your friend's favourite position is bad. But this, the nappy game, was another level of bad. What sicko even invented this?

Bells slowly lifted the nappy to her face and wrinkled her nose, as if she'd just smelled someone else's fart. Then she frowned. 'Is it Snickers?'

'Maybe,' said Grace. 'Pass it along, darl.'

Bells passed the nappy to Mum and Grace handed another one to Dennis. 'Here you go, Den, I think you'll like this.'

Dennis didn't look convinced but lifted up the nappy, smeared with something darker, and frowned as he sniffed it. 'Oh no, I'm not sure about this at all.'

Mum snatched the nappy from him and stuck her nose straight in.

'Oh, come on, don't be silly, that's Marmite.'

'Mars bar?'

'Barbecue sauce?'

'Balsamic vinegar!'

Everyone shouted suggestions as the nappies kept circulating like a game of pass the parcel. I stopped for a moment to take it all in, my best people, gathered here, smelling revolting brown stains rubbed into multiple Pampers and yelling at one another. Mum had doubled over with laughter, Dennis was frowning at another nappy in his hand, Jess was barking at Clem to hurry up and pass his nappy along. Grace was standing behind the sofa, grinning while shaking her head or nodding at the guesses.

I caught her eye. 'Thank you,' I mouthed, because despite my worries about having a baby shower, about making a big deal about ET, about whether a baby shower was even justified, I felt more love for my family and friends that day than I could remember. And that wasn't just because they gave me presents. Nats, Lucy and Bells had clubbed together to give me a vibrating baby bouncer. Grace, on top of the party, had bought me an eco-friendly Moses basket made in Ghana from 'sustainable dried elephant grass'. Steph gave me a collection of Peter Rabbit books. Clem had found a packet of muslins with dogs all over them. Jess cryptically told me my present was waiting 'at home', for when I moved in the following day. Dennis slid me an envelope once I'd opened all the presents. I opened it and welled up immediately. It was a cheque for £1,000 with a card. 'To our grandbaby, this is so your mum can buy you whatever bits and pieces you need. We love you so much already. Grandpa Dennis and Granny Jackie.'

'I love you both,' I said, my voice wobbling, as I hugged them in turn and wiped an index finger under each eye.

'You haven't finished,' said Grace, holding out a parcel wrapped in white tissue paper. 'There's one more.'

'Thanks,' I said, taking it from her and glancing round the room from face to face. 'Who's this one from?'

'Open it and see,' chided Grace, nodding at the parcel.

The paper crinkled in my hands as I unwrapped it to find

a cream woollen blanket with small heart patterns stitched across it. It felt old and delicate, worn soft like a comforter.

'How beautiful,' I murmured, running my fingers across it.

'There's a note,' added Grace, as an envelope fell from between the blanket's folds to the carpet.

I groaned as I bent over to pick it up again, still just about able to reach the floor, and opened it to find a card written in spidery ink.

'Dear Lil, I wanted you to have this. I made it for Arundel when he was born and later wrapped Maximilian in it when he came along, although he hated being swaddled and would kick and scream. Always an independent spirit, it seems. I will be thinking of you over the next few weeks and look forward to meeting my grandchild. With affection, Eleanor Rushbrooke.'

'Max's mother?' I asked, frowning up at Grace. 'How did she know?'

Grace sighed and held her palms up in front of her chest as if to ward off any protests from me. 'I know you said not to, darl, but I thought it was only right that Max know about today. Just in case he wanted to send something.'

'Huh?' I said, squinting at her in confusion. 'How did you get hold of him? And how did you get this? He's a million miles away.'

'There's this thing called the internet,' Grace said, rolling her eyes as if I was 900-years-old. 'So I found his blog and emailed him and then, bingo, this arrived in the post a few days ago.'

I sighed and looked down at the blanket in front of me. 'Thank you,' I said softly, squeezing the wool again, overcome with a simultaneous sense of joy and intense sadness. Max had organized this from abroad and Eleanor Rushbrooke had called ET her grandchild, but if he and I couldn't work ourselves out, I had no idea what their relationship would look like. I suspected there probably wouldn't be cosy family Christmases at Little Clench Hall. But there'd always be Granny Jackie and Grandpa Dennis, I thought, glancing across to the other sofa where Mum was sniffing a beetroot muffin with suspicion.

★

Clem drove across in his purple Seat early the next morning to pick me up from Brixton. He'd already pushed the seats flat in the back and insisted that I could carry nothing more arduous than a pot plant Grace and Riley had given me as a leaving present. It was a Hawaiian ti plant, Grace told me, which was supposed to bring luck and love to everyone living near it. Worth a shot, right?

I cried, obviously, and gave them back a selfie I'd framed of all three of us taken the previous summer in the park. Then Riley squatted down in front of me.

'Take care of your mum, kiddo,' he said, before putting his ear to my stomach. He looked back up at me. 'She says she will and she still wants to be called Riley.'

'Get up, you idiot,' said Grace, cuffing him over the head.

'Bye, guys,' I said, having lowered myself into the car as carefully as a limbo dancer. 'See you soon. I'll text as soon as there's any news.'

Then Clem pulled out and we were off to Chiswick, although we stopped at a petrol station in Hammersmith because I needed a wee.

Once parked outside the house, Clem then made a great show of helping me inside the house and helping me upstairs to my new room where I found Jess's present – a mural painted across one whole side of the wall.

A huge tree, with a thick brown trunk and branches that stretched across the wall like fingers, it was painted with bright green leaves and animals sitting in it. A barn owl on one branch, a red squirrel on another. A monkey swung by its tail from another sprig, a pink parrot sat above him. And at the bottom of the tree sat a fox, its small cub curled up beside it.

'You like it?' said Clem, standing behind me.

I nodded. 'I love it,' I said, choked. 'You have both been so, so kind. I don't know how... I don't know what... It's just, I don't know how I could ever repay you for any of this.'

'Nonsense,' said Clem, 'although there is something I want to ask you.'

'What?' I said, spinning round to see him on one knee, looking up at me.

'Clem...'

He shook his head and a curtain of hair fell into his eyes, so he had to sweep it back with his hand. 'No,' he said firmly. 'Listen, I've thought about this. It's the right thing to do and I want to look after you properly. Lilian Bailey, would you do me the enormous honour of marrying me?'

I burst out laughing. Not kind when a man has been brave enough to kneel down and ask this question, but the scenario was mad. Clem was mad. Lovely but mad. I'd sooner have married Gerald the tortoise.

'Why are you laughing?' he asked, still wobbling on one knee, looking offended.

'I'm sorry, Clem, I don't mean to. I love you for this, I really do, but… what on earth is that?' He had pulled something small and red from his pocket and was picking lint off it.

'Haribo,' he said. 'It's a cherry one. Can't afford a ring but I figured this would do in the meantime. Symbolic.' He held the Haribo ring out to me.

I bit my lower lip and smiled at him. 'Clem, this is the sweetest and most generous thing anyone has ever asked me. And I do love you. But not like that. Come on, get up.'

I held out my hand to pull him up from the floor.

'Well all right,' he said, leaning over to dust off his knee. 'But I wanted to offer.'

I laughed again. 'It's all right. I don't need a husband. I've got you and Jess anyway. But thank you for asking, I'm touched.'

'Are you?' Clem looked pleased.

'Yes, course. But honestly, can you imagine waking up next to me every morning?'

He blushed and pushed his hair back again. 'Well no, no perhaps not.'

'Exactly. Better as friends. And you're basically going to be ET's surrogate father anyway.'

'Am I really?' he said, incredulously.

'Yes. But shall we not tell Jess about this proposal?' She'd be mean to Clem, I knew. She'd tease him about it for ever.

'No, good idea. Our secret.'

'Our secret,' I agreed. 'Right, come on, shall we get the bags inside?'

He nodded. 'Absolutely. Yes, ma'am.'

Jess came back an hour or so later, having dropped a portrait off at a client's house in Kensington.

'Did you see the wall?' she asked, as soon as she shut the front door and I came downstairs.

'I did, it's amazing. You're amazing.'

'Oh good,' she said, hugging me. 'And you all settled in? Has Clem been useless?'

I shook my head. 'Nope, he's been brilliant.'

'Where is he?'

'Upstairs, stashing my suitcases away.'

There was then a sudden crash upstairs which made the floorboards shake, as if several pieces of furniture in the spare room had toppled over on top of him.

'You all right?' Jess bellowed up the stairs.

'All fine, no need to panic,' he shouted back, although he sounded muffled.

'Tea?' said Jess, looking back to me.

'Why not?' I said, following her to the kitchen.

★

Jess announced we were ordering takeaway that night to celebrate me moving in.

'Why don't I just cook?' said Clem, looking forlorn.

'Nope,' Jess replied firmly. 'Holy Cow. Come on, what do you want? I'm ringing them in two seconds. Lil, you know what you're having?'

I was lying across one of the yellow sofas in the sitting room, head propped up by a cushion, watching *Take Me Out*. 'Chicken jalfrezi please. And can we get lots of poppadoms?'

'Yup. Clem?'

'Hang on, I'm looking.'

'Oh God, you're so slow,' said Jess, exasperated.

I laughed quietly to myself at the bickering, feeling content, relaxed, lazily chuffed that I wouldn't have to get on the Tube back to Brixton after supper because I was home already. Bliss. I lifted my arms above my head to stretch and felt a sudden shooting pain that ran like a lightning bolt down the length of my body to my socks.

I winced and leant forward.

'Clem, hurry up, we'll all die of old age otherwise. Or starvation.'

'I can't decide between the spicy chicken with cumin or the biryani. What did I have last time?'

'How am I supposed to remember what you had last time? I can't remember what I had last time. Just pick one. Or go for the biryani and you can have some of my spicy chicken.'

I hunched over my stomach as the shooting pain ran down my body again and I felt a gush of warm water between my thighs. This couldn't be happening. I spent my life telling five-year-olds off for peeing themselves, I couldn't have gone on Granny Blanche's sofa, could I? On the first night I'd moved in? Some flatmate I was. But as I leant back against the sofa arm again and felt another spasm ripple around my belly, I realized it had to be labour. Goes to show how greedy I am that my first thought was, 'But what about my chicken jalfrezi?'

'Guys,' I said, loudly, because I needed to immediately interrupt them. 'I'm sorry but I think my waters have broken on the sofa.'

'Don't worry,' said Clem, cheerfully. 'I'm going downstairs to get a top-up so I'll get you another one.'

'Clem, stop being so thick,' said Jess, scrabbling to her feet from where she'd been sitting on the floor. 'She's in labour.'

'WHAT?' said Clem, glancing at my stomach with horror, as if ET was about to burst from it. 'But it's not supposed to be yet, it's not supposed to be for another, what, three weeks?'

'Yeah.' I nodded, hands clenched around my torso, trying not to freak out. I winced at the contraction tightening like a belt. Fuck. I wanted the drugs already. They promised me drugs. WHERE WERE THE DRUGS?

'OK, OK, no panicking,' Jess said. 'Clem, is your car outside?'

He frowned and manically scratched his head. 'Er, yes, I think so.'

'Go and get the keys. Lil, where's your bag?'

'Upstairs, on my bed. And can someone grab a pair of tracksuit bottoms from my room? Not sure where I put them, maybe in a drawer.'

'OK, Clem, you need to get them too.' Then she turned back to me. 'You all right?'

I nodded, but felt terrified. The damp patch between my thighs was already turning cold.

'It'll be all right. We've got this.'

I listened as Clem clattered upstairs, into my room and then back downstairs again. 'Bag, bottoms, keys,' he said, panting in the doorway. 'Let's go.'

'Get the car started,' said Jess, before helping me up. 'Come on, you heffalump, let's go to hospital.'

If I hadn't been so worried, the car journey would be up there with my all-time great road trips. Clem drove and Jess sat beside him in the front, but spent most of the journey turned towards me, lying along the back seat.

'Do you know where you're going, Clem?'

'Yes,' he said emphatically, nodding at the wheel. 'The Chelsea and Westminster.'

'No, it's St Thomas's,' I said weakly from the back as another contraction hit and I screwed my eyes shut. It felt like ET was wringing out my womb with her hands.

'St Thomas's, you moron,' shouted Jess. 'Look, I'll put it in my phone. Here you go, just follow this.'

The bickering continued for the half hour it took for us to wind our way across London. Not that way, this way, let's have some music, no, turn the music off, overtake that bus, mind that cyclist, never mind that red light, Clem, just GO, and so on.

'Jess, can you ring the hospital and tell them we're coming in. It's in there under maternity unit, I think. And then text Mum and Dennis?' I said, passing her my phone. 'Don't panic them, just say it's fine and we're on the way to hospital.'

'Sure,' she said, taking my mobile. 'What about Max?'

'He's still away,' I said, panicked, feeling a wave of emotional pain that outdid any physical discomfort I felt on the back seat of Clem's car. Max wasn't here. ET and I were going to have to do this without him after all.

'It's OK,' said Jess, reaching for my hand to squeeze it. 'What about that satellite number? Can I text that?'

I nodded. 'Yeah, think so. Look in my message inbox, it's still in therrrrrrrrrrarrrrrgh,' I groaned, as my stomach tightened again.

A few minutes later, Clem dropped Jess and me off at the entrance to the maternity unit and I waddled in.

'Hello, I'm Lil Bailey. I think my friend Jess rang ahead. I'm thirty-seven weeks and my waters have broken.' I slid my notes across the desk to the man behind it who took them wordlessly and tapped at his computer.

I looked around me at the waiting area where a handful of other pregnant women sat – some looking bored, some looking pained. One was slugging on a bottle of Lucozade. Another was leaning with her hands up against the wall, her back to us, making noises like a mating whale. A man who I presumed was her partner was standing awkwardly next to her, occasionally rubbing her back in a limp, circular manner, as if dusting a precious piece of porcelain. It didn't look remotely soothing.

'How far apart are your contractions?' asked the man, looking up from his computer.

Fuck. I'd forgotten to time them. How long were we in the car for? 'Maybe fifteen minutes?'

He frowned briefly. 'OK, let's get you into an assessment room.'

That was where we met my midwife, a large woman with bright yellow hair called Buzzy.

'Buzzy by name, Buzzy by nature,' she said cheerfully, wheeling a blood pressure machine up to the bed.

'Can I have some drugs?' I asked, pleading like a junkie on a comedown. My stomach was pulsing with extreme period pains.

'Hang on, my darling,' said Buzzy, snapping on a pair of gloves as I lay back on the bed. 'We need to have a look and see where you are first.'

Just as I settled my feet in the stirrups, there was a knock on the door and Clem's face appeared from behind it. His mouth fell open and gaped at the sight of me lying back on the bed.

'Not now!' shouted Jess, sitting beside me. Clem's head vanished again.

I tried to relax as Buzzy slid her fingers inside me. I turned my head and inspected a poster on the wall. 'Positions for labouring out of bed,' it said at the top, above several drawings of a pregnant woman in different contortions. Kneeling with her bottom in the air, one leg up on a chair, squatting in front of someone with her arms hanging around his neck. It was like a much less sexy version of Position of the Month.

I caught my breath at the back of my throat suddenly as I felt Buzzy's finger's right up there.

'Sorry, my darling, you're only two centimetres,' she said, retrieving them and peeling off her gloves. 'But I think given your blood pressure we need to keep you in here and monitor.'

'I can't have any drugs?' I asked, increasingly desperate.

'Yes, you can,' she said. 'I can give you a couple of paracetamol.'

'OK,' I mumbled, disappointed. I took paracetamol for headaches. Where was the gas and air? Where was the lovely numbing anaesthetic?

'You all right, love?' said Jess, squeezing my hand.

I nodded, but in truth I was properly frightened. It was happening, I was here, ET was on her way and I was in pain. I'd tried to imagine childbirth. At the Happy Baby Class we'd all been told to try and envisage it in order to practise our breathing. We'd all been encouraged to listen to Emily's mindfulness recording at home, although I'd found it so irritating I'd flicked it off after three minutes. But until the body is there, until the body is actually going through it, you can't know the process, the strange and punishing way your body starts operating by itself as if totally independent from your brain.

'Yeah,' I said to Jess. 'It's OK. You texted Max?'

She nodded. 'Course. I'll keep your phone on me, don't worry.' She squeezed my hand again. 'We've got this.'

I squeezed back as I felt my belly spasm.

★

Whenever I'd tried to envisage my own labour, I'd thought it might be like a romcom, with a comedy doctor who made jokes about pushing and me screaming that I didn't even want this baby any more and could someone please put it back in.

In truth, it was awful, hardly any jokes, and it went on for so long that, at three or four junctures, I lay on the floor and cried, exhausted. I moaned to Jess and Buzzy that I couldn't do it any more, that I didn't have the physical or mental energy to go on. I went into hospital just after 9 p.m. that Sunday and it wasn't until Tuesday lunchtime that I had dilated enough and was told to push.

Birth, Emily had told us in the Happy Baby Class, was a beautiful process. But nothing about this birth was beautiful. It was brutal, like something you see on a nature documentary. Bloody, sweaty, sweary, debilitating.

Gas and air didn't help me much, so at first I'd kept moving around my room, restless in agony. I stood up for a while and leant on the wall like the woman I'd seen in the waiting area, I kneeled on the floor like a cat, I sat on a birthing ball and screamed, then got back into bed, got out again and tried a shower in the hope that the warm jets of water would help distract my brain from the aching.

One benefit of this marathon – kind of – was that it gave Mum and Dennis enough time to get down from Norfolk, although as soon as they arrived Mum kept trying to take pictures of me on her phone. 'Smile, darling, try a little smile!' This made me so enraged I'd said could they go home to Chiswick and Jess would text them once I was close.

Clem, bless him, remained in the waiting room like Lassie for the duration, darting back and forth to a nearby Pret when told to by Jess for sugary drinks and packets of their chocolate biscuit cake.

The highlight was the appearance of the anaesthetist, when I was 5 cm. He set up the epidural and numbed everything below my belly button (Jess later told me I proposed to him. I have no recollection of this), but it was still another twelve hours until ET started wriggling down. If I ever hear a man complain about a long day in the office again, I'm going to tell him to imagine pushing a small human being through his penis for two days.

'OK, Lil, we're in business,' Buzzy eventually said, on Tuesday afternoon. She'd had enough time since my admission to clock off after a shift and then come back on duty again. 'This is when I really need you to work.'

'I can't,' I mumbled pathetically. I was back in bed again because I felt so drained, so depleted I wasn't even sure if I could stand.

'Well I can't go in there and get this baby out for you, so it's the only option, I'm afraid,' said Buzzy, from between my legs. 'Come on, we've got this far. Don't give up on me now.'

'If you insist,' I mumbled weakly, closing my eyes, reaching for Jess's hand. I found it and tried to breathe with the convulsions I felt. The pain wasn't as intense as it had been because of the epidural, but it was summoning the energy that felt almost impossible.

'That's good, that's good, that's good,' I heard Buzzy say. 'OK and breathe, breathe, breathe.'

'I AM BREATHING I'M NOT DEAD AM I,' I suddenly screamed. Ah, I was in transition. I didn't know about this before reading my pregnancy books, but it's the moment where the baby's head presses up against your cervix, releasing a stream of hormones which essentially sends you slightly mad. Very shouty, in some cases.

'It's all right, love, you're doing amazingly. Imagine the drink you can have after this,' said Jess, in an attempt to be placatory.

'I DON'T WANT A DRINK I WANT TO GO HOME.'

'I know, love, and we will. Just a bit left to go,' she said, her fingers over mine.

'OK, Lil, and again, I'm going to need you to push,' said Buzzy. 'OK, push, push, breathe into it, push.'

'I can't do it any more,' I said, whimpering.

'I know, sweetheart, but you're going to have your baby very soon,' said Buzzy. 'Come on, big deep breath, chin on chest, let's go, Lil, let's go.'

I gripped on to the side of my bed and tried to push, roaring with the effort. I rocked up and down on my back, screaming.

'Oh my God, her head,' I heard Jess say. 'Her head, her head, Lil, her head.'

'WHAT'S WRONG WITH HER HEAD?'

'No no, nothing, but I can see it, I can see her, Lil. I can see your baby!'

And then, suddenly, after I gasped for another lungful of air, I could see my baby too. She was out, she was here, Buzzy having lifted her on to my bare chest.

'Well done, Lil, well done,' said Buzzy, beaming at me. 'It's a boy.'

It was like the world's most extravagant fireworks display was going off inside me, and within less than a second my heart swelled to make room for him. He lay on me roaring for life while Buzzy wiped him down. 'You were brilliant, congratulations. Welcome, little man.'

The overwhelming and instant rush of love almost physically hurt. I studied his wrinkled little face, wanting to commit every detail to memory. His tiny nostrils, his mouth, his damp, matted head. Apart from getting his sex wrong, it was like I'd known him all along. He felt familiar, as if he was coming back to me after a long trip. Did he look like Max? I squinted down and tried to imagine my new baby with a beard. Nope, couldn't. He looked pretty baby-shaped to me. Not like ET at all, it turned out. He was the most beautiful, most delicate, most entrancing baby I'd ever met.

'Hello, you,' I said, gazing down at him and stroking his cheek with my finger. Then I glanced across at Jess. 'Jess, look, he's here.'

'I know, love,' she said, through tears. And we stayed like that for a while, both crying, looking at him with astonishment. I mean, I'm sure the Pyramids and the Taj Mahal are great, but they haven't got anything on your own, new little person, roaring in your arms.

It was a few moments before I had any thought other than for him. But then, suddenly, something else popped into my head: 'Thank CHRIST that's over.'

★

Back on the postnatal ward some hours later, things down there were throbbing. 'Second-degree tear,' Buzzy had said, inspecting me while I was still on the delivery bed. She said this casually, as if she was talking about a paper cut, but what it actually meant was that I'd ripped from my vagina into my perineum. Fat lot of good all that finger stretching had been in the Cotswolds. She'd stitched me up and injected the area with local anaesthetic but a dull pain was still making itself felt. I tried to shift in my hospital bed without taking my eyes off the little, wrinkly person in my arms. He was asleep, a fist the size of a prawn curled under his chin. It was like holding a very small, very old man, damp licks of hair sticking up from his head. It presumably looked like a warzone inside my knickers but that didn't matter now because I didn't need anybody else. It was going to be me and him. And Mum and Dennis from time to time. And Jess and Clem. But that was all I needed. Nobody else. My vagina was shutting up shop. Taking voluntary redundancy and retiring. It might take a little holiday and start playing golf. I snorted slightly at my own, bad joke and instantly winced. Laughing and contracting my stomach muscles, or the few that were left, made the stitches bite.

While being stitched up, to distract myself I'd thought about names. I'd mostly been thinking girls' names for the past few months – Olive remaining the front runner. But I figured Olive didn't quite work for a boy and if I called him Oliver, he'd go through life taunted by musical songs. In my head, I'd settled tentatively on Finlay, or Finn for short. Plus, it was Dennis's middle name. But I figured I couldn't officially christen him without Max.

Max.

Jess had told me at some point during labour, it felt like days ago, that he was on his way, that he was trying to get back to London. I remembered nodding and then being distracted by the need to gear up for another physical push. But Max still wasn't here and nor was Jess, so I couldn't check if she'd heard from him again.

The curtain round my bed was still partially drawn but I looked across the ward to a man sitting in an armchair beside another hospital bed. One of his arms stretched from his side to the hand of the woman lying asleep in the bed; his other arm was cradling a bundle swaddled in a blanket. Another wrinkly little person. The man was gazing at it with the sort of adoration that I guessed could only come from a father. I frowned down at Finn – I was trying it out on him – and then at the man across the room again. Did it matter? Would it matter?

My baby was five hours old, but was he already a few steps

behind in life because he was fatherless? Well, not fatherless. He had a father, cramponing his way back down a Mongolian hill. It was just going to be a different kind of relationship.

I sighed and then caught my breath. Sighing hurt too. Physical activity of any sort was clearly going to be curtailed for a while. Apart from breast-feeding. It had taken me nearly an hour earlier poking at my frankly enormous nipple with a finger, trying to get Finn – did he look like a Finn? – to take it while he wailed, the scratchy, high-pitched mewl of a newborn. I'd cried with frustration and then, as if his miniature brain had suddenly clicked, on he went. He sucked at my nipple (honestly, the thing was the size of a thimble), as if he had a hangover and needed water, and then his head fell back again and he went to sleep. Typical man. A nurse had offered to put him down in his plastic tray beside my bed but I wanted to keep hold. I worried this boded badly, that it meant I'd be the sort of clingy mum who was still dabbing at his face with a spit-soaked hankie when he was nineteen. But then a head popped round the curtain to distract me: it was Dennis.

'Hi, love, how you feeling?' he said in a loud whisper, stepping towards us and leaning down to kiss me on the head.

'I'm good, this one's been out for a while,' I said, smiling up at him. 'Here, have a seat. Move all that stuff.' I wiggled my right arm free and waved vaguely at the regulation armchair by my bed, where there was my box of sanitary towels.

'Just… shove them in my bag,' I said, pointing towards my case on the floor.

Dennis picked up the sanitary towels as carefully as if he

was handling a newborn and stowed them in my bag. Then he sat down and lifted a Tesco bag on to his lap.

'I wasn't sure what you'd feel like so I bought a few things.' He lifted out a punnet of mixed grapes, a big bag of Twiglets and a bottle of chocolate Yop, which had been my favourite as a kid. If Dennis picked me up from school instead of Mum, he always brought one from the newsagent and we'd walk home again, me swigging from the bottle and holding his hand, Dennis carrying my backpack over his shoulder, discussing our mutual days. I generally talked of spelling tests and the ancient Greeks; Dennis talked of historic battles and why the German offensive into Russia in 1941 was such a disaster for the Nazis.

He held the bottle up in front of him. 'Thought you could do with the sugar. Want me to open it?'

I felt them coming, but I couldn't do anything about it. More tears. They made my vision go blurry and then spilled out and down my cheeks. I reached to wipe my face as one dropped from my chin to Finn's head. Christ, only a few hours in this world and already being wept on by a woman.

'Oh, love,' said Dennis, putting the Yop down and reaching for my hand. 'You're doing fine.'

I nodded, tears still running down my face. 'I know. I think I'm just tired. And emotional. And…' I trailed off and looked across the room again at the other father across the ward, still holding his baby, still gazing at it. Was my love enough? Would Finn manage with just my love most of the time, 50 per cent of the love that the other babies in here would get?

Or would I just have to love him twice as much? I felt a wave of panic and looked at Dennis again. 'I just…' I went on, my voice constricted, 'is it going to be all right?'

'Yes,' he growled, fiercer than I could remember hearing him sound before. 'It's going to be better than all right. And do you know why?'

I shook my head and sniffed. I felt pathetic.

'Because that baby has you as his mum,' said Dennis, nodding his head at Finn. 'And I don't know anyone more capable, more talented, more… brilliant. You're going to be a super mum, Lil, and he's the luckiest little chap in the world. And you've got us too. Every step of the way.' Dennis grinned at me. 'It's going to be great.'

I smiled at him, eyes still blurry, just as Finn made a small grunt.

'I'm so proud of you, my girl. Of you both,' said Dennis. 'Look, have some of this.' He reached for the Yop again and twisted off the cap. 'It'll help. Always did.'

I took it from him and drank. It was the best bottle of Yop I'd ever had, the gloopy sweetness felt like a fairy-tale potion. If only it could knit my vagina back together, I thought, but its powers probably weren't that strong.

'Where's Mum?' I asked, putting the bottle down and wiping my mouth with the back of my hand.

'In the chemist, she said she wanted to get you something but told me to come up and find you. Said she'd text when she was on her way.' He reached into his pocket for his phone and squinted at it.

'Oh, she's coming up now, brace yourself.' He grinned at me just as I heard Mum's voice from across the ward, talking loudly enough to wake all the babies in this ward and possibly all the maternity wards across London.

'She's in bed eleven. Which is just along here… not this one, not this one, goodness me it smells in here… I hope they're cleaning it properly… Oh look, here we are. Bed eleven.' The curtain was partially pulled back and Mum appeared with Jess and Clem behind her. Mum was holding a plastic bag; Jess had a huge bunch of white roses wrapped in cellophane lying in her arms as if it was her own baby.

'How are we feeling?' said Mum.

'Good, I got him to feed in the end.'

'Well done. He'll be like you, I expect,' she replied briskly. 'Some days it was like having a piranha attached to my breast.'

'Gross.'

'Hi, little man,' said Jess, kissing me on the head before looking down at Finn. 'He's got your nose.'

'Oh no, poor boy. Don't say that.'

'Honestly, he's a mini you. I love him so much already, Lil.'

I smiled at her and then looked at Clem, hovering awkwardly at the end of my bed. 'How you doing, Clem?'

'Good,' he said. 'You? Have you slept?'

I nodded. 'Yeah, a couple of hours.'

'Get used to it, darling, because that's all it'll be for the next few weeks,' said Mum, ever helpful, rifling in her bag.

'Do you want to hold him?' I said, seeing Clem gazing at Finn with an awed look on his face.

'Oh, could I?'

'Course,' I said, 'look, come here.' Clem shuffled up to the edge of my bed and I leant forwards, lifting Finn gently up towards him.

'Clem, careful of his head,' said Jess, wincing from the other side of my bed. 'You're going to drop him, I know you're going to drop him, please be careful. Can you just—'

'It's all right,' I said, 'he's got him.' And I nearly welled up again at the sight of Clem, giant Clem, cradling Finn in the nook of his arm and staring down at him as if hypnotized. It made me momentarily think about his proposal again. Could I? Nah, sorry, I couldn't. Couldn't have sex with Clem.

Mum finally pulled a small metal pot out of her bag. 'Here you go, this is what I wanted to find. It's shea butter. For your nipples. I'm telling you, you went at mine as if they were wine gums and it was only this that helped.'

'Thanks, Mum,' I said, taking the pot from her. 'I'm so glad that everyone's here to join in with these intimate conversations.' I caught Dennis's eye and gave him a quick half-smile.

'Clem, can I have a go?' said Jess, staring jealously at Finn sleeping in his arms.

'I've only had him for two seconds.'

'Pleeeeeease can I, I'm desperate.'

'Guys, we're coming home later. I promise you're both going to have plenty of time with him. No squabbling.'

Jess looked at me and burst out laughing.

'What?'

'Look at you already playing mum, you're a natural!'

'Course she is,' said Dennis. I grinned and had another mouthful of Yop but I slightly missed my mouth so it dribbled down my chin and dripped on to my new M&S pyjamas.

'Oh shit, Dennis. can you chuck me a tissue?'

He leant forward and the tissues were mid-air when the curtain rippled again and another person appeared from behind it. Max.

I snatched a tissue and quickly wiped my chin.

'Hi,' I said, momentarily stupefied and hoping I'd caught all the Yop.

'Hi,' Max said back, hovering awkwardly with one hand still holding the curtain. He looked as if he'd been stranded on a desert island for a couple of weeks. His hair was a tangled mop, his beard tangled and even more bleached, his cheeks and forehead were chestnut brown. And he was still in what looked like explorer kit – big black coat, khaki trousers and boots that laced halfway up his calves.

'Sorry,' he added, self-consciously glancing down as I stared at him. 'I went home briefly from the airport to drop my stuff but then came straight here.'

I shook my head. 'No, no, it's just a surprise.' And then I remembered why he was here. 'Oh, yeah, Max, meet, er, our baby.'

I gestured at Clem from my bed. Finn was still asleep in his arms, blissfully unaware of his parents' stilted conversation and general awkwardness. Long may that last, I thought quickly.

Max glanced at Finn, then up to Clem's face, then back to Finn again. He stepped tentatively towards Clem, who looked stricken by this point, as if he'd rather not be holding another man's precious baby.

'Hi,' said Clem, trying to free one hand from underneath Finn.

'Clem, DON'T! You're going to drop him,' screeched Jess, from the other side of my bed.

'Can I…?' Max said quietly, gesturing at the bundle in Clem's arms.

'Of course,' replied Clem, practically flinging Finn at him like a hot potato. 'Here you go.'

Max took Finn gently, as if he was a glass ornament that could shatter in his big explorer hands, and then, with Clem's help, edged him up his arms until Finn was cocooned in them.

'Sorry,' said Max, looking anxiously at me. 'I haven't done this before.'

'I think we'll go and get a coffee,' said Dennis.

'You've just had a coffee,' said Mum. 'You know what too much coffee does to your insides, Den.'

'A tea then,' said Dennis, looking pointedly at her. 'Come on, Jacks, there's a shop downstairs. Jess? Clem? Fancy a tea?'

'Good idea,' said Jess, winking at me. 'Clem, come on, you too.'

'I'm all right for tea, thanks,' said Clem, before Jess glared at him. 'Oh right, yes, I see, course.'

Max didn't seem to hear any of this because he was staring so hard at Finn.

They left, Mum's voice floating down the ward as they went. 'He does have nice eyes. I wonder if he'll get his eyes…

Of course, all babies tend to look like their fathers to start with but...'

She faded and Max glanced up at me. 'I could never have imagined this. What it feels like. It's... extraordinary.'

'Sit down if you like,' I said, nodding at the armchair, silently thanking Dennis for having removed the box of sanitary towels.

He walked slowly and lowered himself on the chair. Then he looked up at me, shaking his head. 'I'm so sorry, I should have asked, how are you?'

'I'm all right. It's true what they say. It's worth all the pain.' I didn't think I needed to go into details about my vagina with Max.

'Good, I'm glad.' His eyes stayed on Finn. 'I'm sorry I wasn't here,' he added, after a few minutes. 'I got the message from Jess when I was in Ulaanbaatar.'

'Huh?' I frowned at him.

'The capital,' he explained. 'Of Mongolia.'

'Ah.'

'I got the next flight home. You have to go via Moscow and the flight was looking delayed at one point and I felt like I was going to be trapped there for ever. But it was all right in the end. Sorry,' he repeated, making a guilty face at me. 'I probably stink.'

I shook my head. 'No no, you don't.' I went on, nervously, 'I've been thinking about names, by the way, and I was thinking Finlay, Finn for short. I know we didn't discuss it. But I like it, although if you don't then we can...'

'No,' said Max, still staring at Finn. 'I like it.'

'And maybe Arundel as his middle name?'

Max looked up at me. 'Actually?'

'Yeah, course,' I said, and we sat quietly, both staring at our son.

'Did you get the blanket, by the way?' Max asked, a few moments later.

'Oh, yes, thank you, so kind of your mum.'

'Not at all,' he said, shaking his head. 'I called her from Mongolia. I so hated the thought that I wasn't there. I'm sorry. And I'm sorry to miss you having him and just, well, I'm so sorry, Lil.' He sounded almost as emotionally strung out as I felt.

'It's all right,' I said, shrugging and then flinching as my stitches dug into me again.

'You all right?' said Max, shifting forward in his seat.

'Yeah yeah, fine. Don't worry.' I waved a hand at him. 'All fine, just a bit, er, tender.'

'Listen,' said Max, his tone suddenly more urgent. 'While I was away, I was thinking. About you. About us.'

'Max—' I started. I was physically and emotionally in pieces. I didn't have the energy for a big talk on the maternity ward.

'I know we've had difficult moments,' he went on, ignoring me, 'but I realized after that night, when we ended up at your place and we, well, you know, but I realized how much you mean to me. Not just because of him,' he said, nodding down at Finn, before glancing back up, 'but because I like you and I admire you and I couldn't imagine not having you now. Not having either of you.'

'Max...' I said again, trying from somewhere deep inside me to find the words to articulate my feelings sensibly. 'You weren't honest with me, that's what it comes down to,' I said, after a few seconds. 'After everything. After I thought we were getting closer.'

'We were getting closer,' Max said, fiercely, 'and that's all that I've thought about while I was away. How to explain to you, how to justify it, how to tell you that Prim—'

'I don't want to know,' I said, another tear breaking free and falling down my cheek. 'Please don't, Max, not now. Not here.'

'She lost a baby, Lil,' said Max, looking at me almost pleadingly.

I'd put a hand to my face to catch the tear, but my fingers froze at this revelation. 'What?'

'Not recently,' he added. 'A few years ago. When we were together.' He stopped and exhaled in his seat. I glanced at Finn, mercifully still asleep while this episode of *EastEnders* went on above his head.

'It was an accident,' said Max. 'We'd been going out for a while and it just happened. And I reacted badly because I was getting somewhere with climbing and I wasn't ready for a child. But Prim, well, she wanted to keep it. But then she miscarried, and it broke her. It really broke her.'

Max's voice had dropped lower than I'd ever heard it and my eyes slid to Finn in his arms. Now that he was here, safely three feet away from me, I couldn't imagine losing him.

'I knew at this point that we weren't made for one another,' went on Max, dropping his head and shaking it as if in a confession box. 'I knew that it wasn't right. But she picked me up after my bad patch; I couldn't leave her then. That would have been too cruel.'

'How long was it,' I asked softly, 'before you guys broke up?'

'Another three years,' said Max, anguish in his eyes. 'Too long. But I didn't know what else to do. So I started spending more time climbing. It was selfish. But I thought abandoning her entirely would be worse.'

I nodded again but didn't reply. What was the right answer? Was there a right answer? The hot, prickling jealousy I'd felt towards Primrose had turned to pity.

'I didn't know when to tell you,' he said, his gaze sliding to the floor. 'There were moments when I nearly did, but I didn't want to worry you when you were pregnant. And I suppose I felt disloyal to Prim.' He met my eyes again. 'But I've been rehearsing this speech since I've been away. I'm sorry I haven't told you until now. I'm sorry I wasn't straight from the very start. But this is it, there's nothing you don't know now.'

I remained quite still in bed as Max inched his armchair towards me, freed one of his arms from underneath Finn and reached out for my hand. 'Lil, listen. Primrose and I are friends now, nothing more. That's why I was with her that day. I hadn't seen her for months but I wanted to tell her about you. About us. About our baby.'

I ignored his hand, lying on top of mine on the blanket, and sighed, looking up at the plastic panels of the hospital ceiling.

'We were over a long time ago, long before we actually broke up, if I'm honest,' he said. 'She didn't mean we were back together that day. She meant me and Pumpkin.'

I looked down and frowned at him.

'Her dog,' Max explained, with a sheepish expression.

I paused and thought to myself for a moment. Every bit of me was drained, but I wanted to get to the end of this conversation.

'So you're not together?'

'I promise you. I'm sorry. I can see how that photo looks. I know how the papers work. But if you even asked her, Lil, she'd tell you.'

'How do I believe you?' I whispered, my vision blurring again.

'You have to trust me,' he said. 'I know that's asking a lot, but you've got to believe this is where my priorities are now. Here. With him. With you.'

Part of me wanted to give in immediately to his supportive, seductive pleas. I had little fight left. But my more rational sensibilities were on guard, primed like night watchmen. How did I know he meant this? How did I trust again?

'Lil, please,' said Max. 'What I wanted to say before this picture fiasco, before I even went to Mongolia, was would you even consider starting again with me?' He paused and looked at the speckled hospital lino. 'If I wasn't holding our son, I'd beg you. I would honestly get on my knees and beg.'

'Please don't,' I said, wiping my cheek with my knuckles.

'In fact,' he said, standing up and carefully holding Finn out to me.

'Max, stop…' I said, taking Finn back into my arms and watching as Max lowered himself down to the floor. 'I'm not sure it's that clean. You don't know what's been on that floor.'

'Shhhh,' he instructed. 'I'm sure I'm covered in worse. Yak shit, mostly.'

Then he looked up at me, one hand clamped around the rail running alongside my bed.

'Lilian Bailey, I am now begging you. Please can we start again?'

I stared at Max on the floor, looking so sincere that I sighed again. My brain felt like it needed to shut down and reboot. What did starting again even mean?

'Do you mean like dating?' I asked.

Max nodded. 'Yes, I mean like dating. If you want to.'

I leant my head back on my pillow, wondering if you could 'date' someone if you've already had their baby. It all felt backwards. And my vagina really wasn't in any sort of state to go out in public. Probably not for several months, at least.

'Or not dating exactly,' carried on Max, filling the silence. 'But not not dating. Just… seeing.'

I couldn't help smiling, and then as if in support, a tiny cheerleader, Finn mewled and waved a fist in the air.

'Is he all right?' said Max, peering over the bed at him.

'Yeah,' I said. 'Think so. He might need feeding again soon.'

'Oh, OK. I've got so much to learn,' he said, shaking his head, still kneeling on the floor.

'We've got so much to learn,' I corrected him.

He grinned up at me. 'Yes,' he said. 'Yes, we probably have. But I want to do it with you. That's all I want.'

I swallowed. Here I was, lying in bed, my undercarriage throbbing, while Max knelt beside me, asking me something that, until very recently, I'd dreamt of him asking. For months I'd fantasized about it, while simultaneously trying to persuade myself that if it didn't work out, I could manage on my own. But here he was, asking me the very question, suggesting that we give it a go, and my overwhelming emotion was fear. My head was full of what ifs. What if it was a disaster? What if we fell out? What if we weren't compatible after all?

Ah, but what if it was all fine, chimed another little voice. Or even better than fine. What if it was wonderful?

What if it was everything?

'Lil, I might have to get up in a second,' said Max, interrupting my thoughts. 'This floor is hellish hard. I'm starting to feel as if I've been kneecapped.'

'Serves you right,' I said, but laughing as I did.

'All right, I asked for that,' he said, holding his hands in the air, 'but before I do get up, Lilian Bailey, would you consider going on another date with me?'

I must have looked alarmed because he quickly added, 'I don't mean tomorrow, but at some point?'

I lowered my head to kiss Finn, and then smiled shyly at Max.

'Oh go on then,' I said.

And even though I've insisted multiple times that I was never going to have sex again, even though it felt like my internal organs could all tumble out from behind my stitches down there at any second and milk was leaking into my bra from my nipples, which were now the colour and size of Rolos, I felt a surge of optimism as I said yes. I had no idea what would happen now. But I felt peaceful. Calmer than I'd felt for a long time. Maybe everything wouldn't be such a disaster, after all?

ACKNOWLEDGEMENTS

Did you know the average person says thank you five times a day? Admittedly this is according to a random survey I just found on the internet, but it doesn't seem that many to me. I reckon I say it roughly 54 million times every day – to the nice (and quite handsome) man in my coffee shop where I write, to the woman behind the till at the Co-Op next door who never rolls her eyes when I tell her I forgot my plastic bag again, to bus drivers, to Uber drivers, to my flatmate when I fail to water my plants and he remembers, to the woman in the call centre when I have to ring them and admit I've mistyped my password and been locked out of my bank account for the 98th time, and so on and so on. Loads of thank yous. But there are small thank yous and big thank yous, and the ones I'm about to make here are bloody enormous.

Firstly, to my agent Rebecca Ritchie for continuing to be my support, dispenser of excellent advice and the reason I write books in the first place. Without your email some years ago asking if I'd ever considered writing a book, I wouldn't be thanking anyone for anything at all and the only words I'd ever write would be 'loo roll' and 'milk' on the back of my hand. Saying that I feel lucky because I get to write every day doesn't even come close. I am absurdly fortunate and you started it.

Secondly, a whopping thank you to my editor Charlotte Mursell. I am grateful for your many talents – for your discerning and light-fingered way with copy, for your constant reassurance, for your sense of humour and unflappable calm. But I'm also grateful that you offer me cake whenever I come into your office and there we sit, gossiping about the Royal family, before doing the odd bit of work. Thank you, too, to Joe Thomas, Lisa Milton and Janet Aspey for making visits into the HQ office such a joy. If I can continue to come and eat cake with you all until I'm 97 I'd be delighted. You're the best in so many ways.

To the various people I have spoken to for this book, thank you as well. These include all of my friends who have actually had babies. I'm so sorry for asking questions like 'Do your nipples leak if you have sex when you're pregnant?' and 'How horny were you at seven months?', but I'm thankful that you gave me such detailed answers and the good news is I've finally stopped having nightmares about mucus plugs. More seriously, thank you to the friends I've talked to who've helped shape the main storyline of *What Happens Now*?. You know who you are. I am full of admiration for your strength.

A huge thank you to the Tulloch family who lent me their cottage in North Yorkshire for a few months where I went to drag this book out from my head and get it down in actual words. It was a proper haven and I miss the cake shop in Helmsley every day. (Look how obsessed with cake I am, it's tragic.)

Penultimately, thank you to my family even though you deserve much bigger words. To my parents, to my siblings, to uncles and aunts, to nieces and cousins, I know we constantly grumble about one another on multiple WhatsApp groups and try hard not to send the wrong message to the wrong person, but I love you all and would be rudderless without you.

Lastly, and I'm just going to optimistically chuck this out here, thank you to the handsome man in the coffee shop. You're the one with the beard. Some mornings, I worried that you'd looked over my shoulder at my laptop screen while I was writing scenes from this book and I'd shocked you. Hope not. Thanks for all the perfect Americanos. You're my kind of superhero.

If you loved *What Happens Now?* then turn the page for a sneak peek at the laugh–out–loud debut from Sophia Money-Coutts, *The Plus One.*

Available now!

I BLAME SENSE AND SENSIBILITY. I saw the film when I was twelve. A very impressionable age. And more specifically, I blame Kate Winslet. She, Marianne, the second sister, nearly dies for love. That bit where she goes walking in a storm to look at Willoughby's house and is rescued by Colonel Brandon but spends the next few days sweating with a life-threatening fever? That, I decided, was the appropriate level of drama in a relationship.

I consequently set about trying to be as like Marianne as I could. She was into poetry, which seemed a sign because I also liked reading. I bought a little book of Shakespeare's sonnets in homage, which I carried in my school bag at all times in case I had a moment between lessons when I could whip it out and whisper lines to myself in a suitably dramatic manner. I also learned Sonnet 116, Marianne and Willoughby's favourite, off by heart.

'Let me not to the marriage of true minds admit impediments. Love is not love, which alters when it alteration finds…'

Imagine a tubby 12-year-old wandering the streets of Battersea in rainbow-coloured leggings muttering that to herself. I was ripe for a kicking. So, yes, I blame *Sense and Sensibility* for making me think I had to find someone. It set me on the wrong path entirely.

I

IF I'D KNOWN THAT the week was going to end in such disaster, I might not have bothered with it. I might just have stayed in bed and slept like some sort of hibernating bear for the rest of the winter.

Not that it started terribly well either. It was Tuesday, 2nd January, the most depressing day of the year, when everyone trudges back to work feeling depressed, overweight and broke. It also just happened to be my birthday. My *thirtieth* birthday. So, I was gloomier than anyone else that morning. Not only had I turned a decade older overnight, but I was still single, living with Joe, a gay oboist, in a damp flat in Shepherd's Bush and starting to think that those terrifying *Daily Mail* articles about dwindling fertility levels were aimed directly at me.

I cycled from my flat to the *Posh!* magazine offices in Notting Hill trying not to be sick. The hangover was entirely my own fault; I'd stayed up late the night before drinking red wine on the sofa with Joe. Dry January could get stuffed. Joe had called it an early birthday celebration; I'd called it a wake for my youth. Either way, we'd made our way through three bottles of wine from the corner shop underneath our flat and I'd woken up feeling like my brain had been replaced with jelly.

Wobbling along Notting Hill Gate, I locked my bike beside the *Posh!* office, then dipped into Pret to order: one white Americano, one egg and bacon breakfast baguette and one berry muffin. According to Pret's nutritional page (book-marked on my work computer), this came to 950 calories, but as I hadn't actually eaten anything with Joe the night before I decided the calories could get stuffed too.

★

'Morning, Enid,' I said over my computer screen, putting the Pret bag on my desk. Enid was the PA to Peregrine Monmouth, the editor for *Posh!* magazine, and a woman as wide as she was tall. She was loved in the office on the basis that she put through everyone's expenses and approved holidays.

'Polly, my angel! Happy Birthday!' She waddled around the desk and enveloped me in a hug. 'And Happy New Year,' she said, crushing my face to her gigantic bosom. Her breath smelled of coffee.

'Happy New Year,' I mumbled into Enid's cardigan, before pulling back and standing up straight again, putting a hand to my forehead as it throbbed. I needed some painkillers.

'Did you have a nice break?' she asked.

'Mmm,' I replied vaguely, leaning to turn on my computer. What was my password again?

'Were you with your mum then?' Enid returned to her desk and started rustling in a bag beside it.

'Mmmm.' It was some variation of my mum's dog's name and a number. *Bertie123*? It didn't work. Shit. I'd have to call that woman in IT whose name I could never remember.

'And did you get any nice presents?'

Bertie19. That was it. Bingo.

Emails started spilling into my inbox and disappearing off the screen. I watched as the counter spiralled up to 632. They were mostly press releases about diets, I observed, scrolling through them. Sugar-free, gluten-free, dairy-free, fat-free. Something new designed by a Californian doctor called the 'Raisin Diet', on which you were only allowed to eat thirty raisins a day.

'Sorry, Enid,' I said, shaking my head and reaching for my baguette. 'I'm concentrating. Any nice presents? You know, some books from Mum. How was your Christmas?'

'Lovely, thanks. Just me and Dave and the kids at home. And Dave's mum, who's losing her marbles a bit, but we managed. I overdid it on the Baileys though so I'm on a new diet I read about.'

'Oh yeah?'

'It's called the Raisin Diet, it's supposed to be ever so good. You eat ten raisins for breakfast, ten raisins for lunch and ten raisins for supper and they say you can lose a stone in a week.'

I watched over my computer screen as Enid counted out raisins from a little Tupperware box.

'Morning, all, Happy New Year and all that nonsense.

Meeting in my office in fifteen minutes please,' boomed Peregrine's voice, as he swept through the door in a navy overcoat and trilby.

Peregrine was a 55-year-old social climber who launched *Posh!* in the Nineties in an attempt to mix with the sort of people he thought should be his friends. Dukes, earls, lords, the odd Ukrainian oligarch. He applied the same principal to his wives. First, an Italian jewellery heiress. Second, the daughter of a Venezuelan oil baron. He was currently married to a French stick insect who was, as Peregrine told anyone he ever met, a distant relation to the Monaco Royals.

'Where is everyone?' he said, reappearing from his office, coat and hat now removed.

I looked around at the empty desks. 'Not sure. It's just me and Enid so far.'

'Well, I want a meeting with you and Lala as soon as she's in. I've got a major story we need to get going with.'

'Sure. What is it?'

'Top secret. Just us three in the meeting. Need-to-know basis,' he said, glancing at Enid. 'You all right?' he added.

Enid was poking the inside of her mouth with a finger. 'Just got a bit of raisin stuck,' she replied.

Peregrine grimaced, then looked back at me. 'Right. Well. Will you let me know as soon as Lala is in?'

I nodded.

'Got it,' said Enid, waving a finger.

★

An hour later, Lala, the magazine's party editor, and I were sitting in Peregrine's office. I'd drunk my coffee and eaten both the baguette and the muffin but still felt perilously close to death.

'So, there's yet another Royal baby on the way,' said Peregrine, 'the Countess of Hartlepool told me at lunch yesterday. They have the same gynaecologist, apparently.'

'Due when?' I asked.

'July,' he said. 'So I want us to get cracking with a quick piece which we can squeeze into the next issue.'

I wondered if I'd live as far as July given how I felt today. Some birthday this was. 'What about something on the Royal playmates?' I said.

Peregrine nodded while scratching his belly, which rolled over his waistband and rested on the tops of his legs. 'Yes. That sort of thing. The Fotheringham–Montagues are having their second too, I think.'

'And my friend Octavia de Flamingo is having her first baby,' said Lala, chewing on her pen. 'They've already reserved a place at Eton in case it's a boy.'

'Well, we need at least ten others so can you both ask around and find more posh babies,' said Peregrine. 'I want it on my desk first thing on Friday, Polly. And can you get the pictures of them all too.'

'Of the parents?' I checked.

'No, no, no!' he roared. 'Of the babies! I want all the women's scan pictures. The sort of thing that no one else will have seen. You know, real, insidery stuff.'

I sighed as I walked back to my desk. *Posh!* was now so insidery it was going to print pictures of the aristocracy's wombs.

★

My Tuesday evenings were traditionally spent having supper with my mum in her Battersea flat and tonight, as a birthday treat, I was doing exactly the same thing.

It was a chaotic and mummified flat. Mum had lived there for nearly twenty years, ever since Dad died and we'd moved to London from Surrey. She worked in a curtain shop nearby because her boss allowed her to bring her 9-year-old Jack Russell to the shop so long as he stayed behind the counter and didn't wee on any of the damask that lay around the place in giant rolls. Bertie largely obliged, only cocking his leg discreetly on the very darkest rolls he could find if Mum got distracted by talking to a customer for too long.

It was the curtain shop that had landed me a job at *Posh!*. Peregrine's second wife – the Venezuelan one – had come in to discuss pelmets for their new house in Chelsea while I was in there talking to Mum one Saturday. And even though Alejandra had all the charm and warmth of a South American despot, I plucked up the courage to mention that I wanted to be a journalist. So, because I was desperate and Peregrine was miserly, he offered me the job as his assistant a few months later. I started by replying to his party invitations and buying his coffees, but after a year or so I'd started writing small pieces for the magazine. Nothing serious. Short articles I mostly made up about the latest trend in fancy dress or the most fashionable canapé to serve at a drinks party. But I worked my way up from there until Peregrine let me write a few longer pieces and interviews with various mad members of the British aristocracy. It wasn't the dream role. I was hardly Kate Adie reporting from the Gaza Strip in a flak jacket. But it was a writing job, and, even though back when I started I didn't know anything about the upper classes (I thought a viscount was a type of biscuit), it seemed a good start.

'Happy birthday, darling, kick my boots out of the way,' Mum shouted from upstairs when I pushed her front door open that night to the sound of Bertie barking. There was a pile of brown envelopes on the radiator grille in the hall, two marked 'Urgent'.

'Mums, do you ever open your post?' I asked, walking upstairs and into the sitting room.

'Oh yes, yes, yes, don't fuss,' she said, taking the envelopes and putting them down on her desk, where magazines and old papers covered every spare chink of surface. 'I've made a cake for pudding,' she went on, 'but I've got some prawns in the fridge that need eating, so we're having them first. I thought I might make a risotto?'

'Mmm, lovely, thank you,' I replied, wondering whether Peregrine would believe me if I called in sick because my mother had poisoned me with prawns so old they had tap-danced their way into the risotto.

'Have you had a nice birthday?' Mum asked. 'How was work?'

'Oh, you know, Peregrine's Napoleonic tendencies are as rampant as ever. I've got to write a piece on Royal babies and their playmates.'

'Oh dear,' said Mum vaguely, as she walked towards the kitchen, opened the fridge and took out a bottle of wine. In the four years I'd worked at *Posh!*, I'd learned more about the upper classes than I'd ever expected to. A duke was higher than an earl in the pecking order and they were all obsessed with their Labradors. But Mum, a librarian's daughter from Surrey, while supportive of my job, wasn't much interested in the details.

She poured two glasses of white wine and handed me one. 'Now, let's sit down and then I can give you your present.'

I collapsed on the sofa whereupon Bertie instantly jumped on my lap and white wine sloshed over the rim of my glass and into my crotch.

'Bertie, get down,' said Mum, handing me a small jewellery box and sitting down beside me. She stared at Bertie and pointed at the floor, as he slowly and reluctantly climbed off the sofa. I opened the box. It was a ring. A thin, delicate gold band with a knot twisted into the metal.

'Your dad gave it to me when you were born. So, I thought, to mark a big birthday, you should have it.'

'Oh, Mum…' I felt choked. She hardly ever mentioned Dad. He'd had a heart attack and died at forty-five when I was just ten years old. Our lives changed forever in that moment. We had to sell our pretty, Victorian house in Surrey and Mum and I moved to this flat in Battersea. We were both in shock. But we got on with our new life in London because there was no alternative. And we'd been a small, but intensely close, unit ever since. Just us two. And then Bertie, when I left for university and Mum decided she needed a small, hairy substitute child.

I slipped the ring on my finger. It was a bit tight over the knuckle, but it went on easily enough. 'I love it,' I said, looking at my hand, then looking up at Mum. 'Thank you.'

'Good, I'm glad it fits. And now, listen, I have something I need to chat to you about.'

'Hmmm?' I was trying to turn the ring on my finger. A bout of dysentery from prawn-related food poisoning might not be the worst thing, actually. I could probably lose half a stone.

'Polly?'

'Yes, yes, sorry, am listening.' I stopped fiddling with the ring and sat back against the sofa.

'So,' started Mum. 'I went to see Dr Young last week. You know this chest pain that's been worrying me? Well, I've been taking my blood pressure pills but they haven't been doing any good so I went back on Thursday. Terrible this week because the place was full of people sneezing everywhere. But I went back and, well, he wants me to have a scan.'

'A scan?' I frowned at her.

'Yes. And he says it may be nothing but it's just to be sure that it is nothing.'

'OK… But what would it be if it wasn't nothing?'

'Well, you know, it could be a little something,' said Mum, breezily. 'But he wants me to have a scan to check.'

'When is it?' I felt sick. Panicky. Only two minutes ago I'd been worrying about the sell-by date on a packet of prawns. It suddenly seemed very silly.

'I'm waiting for the letter to confirm the date. Dr Young said I'll hear in the next couple of weeks but the post is so slow these days, so we'll see.'

'It might help if you looked at the pile of post downstairs every now and then, Mum,' I said, as gently as I could. 'You don't want to miss it.'

'No. No, I know.'

I'd always told myself that Mum and I had done all right on our own over the years. Better, even, than all right. We were way closer than some of my friends were with their parents. But every now and then I wished Mum had a husband to look after her. This was one of those moments. For support. For help. For another person to talk to. She could hardly discuss the appointment with Bertie.

'Well, will you let me know when you get the letter and I'll come with you? Where will it be?' I asked.

'Oh there's no need, darling. You've got work. Don't fuss.'

'Don't be silly, obviously I'm coming. I work for a magazine, not MI6. No one will mind if I take a few hours off.'

'What about Peregrine?'

'He'll manage.'

'OK. If you're sure, that would be lovely. The appointment will be at St Thomas'.'

'Good, that's sorted,' I said, trying to sound confident, as if the scan was a routine check-up and there was nothing to worry about. 'Now let's have a sniff of those prawns.'

★

By Friday afternoon, I had six posh babies and their scan pictures. Where the hell were another four going to come from? My phone vibrated beside my keyboard and a text popped up from Bill, an old friend who always threw a dinner party at the end of the first week of January to celebrate the fact the most cheerless week of the year was over.

Come over any time from 7! X

I looked back at my screen full of baby scans. Jesus. A baby. That seemed a long way off. I hadn't had a proper boyfriend since university when I went out with a law student called Harry for a year, but then Harry decided to move to Dubai and I cried for about a week before my best friend, Lex, told me I needed to 'get back out there'. My love life, ever since, had been drier than a Weetabix. The odd date, the odd fumble, the odd shag which I'd get overexcited about before realizing that, actually, the shag had been terrible and what was I getting so overexcited about anyway?

Last year, I'd had sex twice, both times with a Norwegian banker called Fred who I met through a mutual friend at a picnic in Green Park in the summer. If you can call several bottles of rosé and some olives from M&S a picnic. Lex and I drank so much wine that we decided to pee under a low-hanging tree in the park as it got dark. This had apparently impressed Fred, who moved to sit closer to me when Lex and I returned to the circle.

We'd all ended up in the Tiki bar of the London Hilton on Park Lane, where Fred ordered me a drink which came served in a coconut. He'd lunged in the car park and then I'd waited until I was safely inside my cab home before wiping off the wetness around my mouth with the back of my hand. We'd gone on a couple of dates and I'd slept with him on both those dates – possibly a mistake – and then he'd gone quiet. After a week, I texted him breezily asking if he was around for a drink. He replied a few days later.

Oh, sorry been travelling so much for work and not sure that's going to change any time soon. F

'F for fucking nobody, that's who,' said Lex, loyally, when I told her.

So, that, for me, was the total of last year's romantic adventures. Depressing. Other people seemed to have sex all the time. And yet here I was, sitting in my office like an asexual plant, hunting for scan pictures, evidence that other people had had sex.

I squinted through the window up the alleyway towards Notting Hill Gate. It was the kind of grey January day that couldn't be bothered to get properly light, when people hurried along pavements with their shoulders hunched, as if warding off the gloom.

Whatever. It would be six o' clock soon and I could escape it all for Bill's flat and a delicious glass of wine. Or several delicious glasses of wine, if I was honest.

★

At one second past six, I left the office, winding my way through the hordes of tourists at Notting Hill Gate Tube station. They were dribbling along at that special tourist pace which makes you want to kick them all in the shins. Then, emerging at Brixton, I walked to the corner shop at the end of Bill's street to buy wine. And a big bag of Kettle Chips. 'Let's go mad, it's Friday, isn't it?' I said to the man behind the till, who ignored me.

Bill lived in the ground-floor flat on a street of white terraced houses. He'd bought it while working as a programmer at Google, though he'd left them recently to concentrate on developing an app for the NHS. Something to do with making appointments. Bill said that it was putting his nerd skills to good use, finally. He'd never tried to hide his dorkiness. It was one of the reasons we became friends at a party when we were teenagers.

Lex had been off snogging some boy upstairs in the bathroom (she was always snogging or being fingered, there was a lot of fingering back then) and I'd been sitting on a sofa in the basement, tapping my foot along to Blue so it looked like I was having a good time when, actually, I was having a perfectly miserable time because no boy ever wanted to snog me. And if no boy ever wanted to snog me then how would I ever be fingered? And if I was never fingered how would I ever get to have actual sex? It seemed hopeless. And, just at the moment when I decided I might go all *Sound of Music* and enter a convent – were there convents in South London? – a boy had sat down on the other end of the sofa. He had messy black hair and glasses that were so thick they looked double-glazed.

'I hate parties,' he'd said, squinting at me from behind his double-glazing. 'Do you hate parties too?'

I'd nodded shyly at him and he'd grinned back.

'They're awful, aren't they? I'm Bill by the way.' He'd stuck out a hand for me to shake, so I shook it. And then we'd started talking over the music about our GCSEs. It was only when Lex surfaced for air an hour or so later, gasping for breath, mouth rubbed as red as a strawberry, that I realized I'd made a friend who was a boy. Not a boyfriend. I didn't want to snog Bill. His glasses really were shocking. But he became a friend who was a boy all the same. And we'd been friends ever since.

'Come in, come in,' Bill said when I arrived. He opened the front door with one hand and held a pair of jeans in the other. 'Sorry, I haven't changed yet.' He grinned. 'You're the first.'

'Go change,' I said. 'Is there anything I can do?'

'No. Leave those bottles on the side and open whatever you want. I'll be two minutes,' he said, walking towards his bedroom.

I opened the fridge. It was rammed. Sausages, packets of bacon, some steaks. Something that might once have been a tomato and would now be of considerable interest to a research scientist. No other discernible vegetables. I reached for a bottle of white wine and fished in a drawer for a corkscrew.

Bill appeared back in the kitchen in his jeans and a t-shirt that said 'I am a computer whisperer' on it. In the years since

I'd met him, he'd discovered contact lenses but developed a questionable line of t-shirts. 'I'll have one of those please. Actually, no I won't. I'll have a beer first. So, how's tricks?' he asked, opening a bottle. 'How was Christmas? How was your birthday and so on? I've got you a card actually.' He picked up an envelope from his kitchen table and gave it to me. 'Here you go.'

'Being single at 30 isn't as bad as it used to be,' the front of the card read. I smiled, 'Thanks, dude. Really helpful.' I put the card down on the side and had a sip of wine. 'And Christmas was lovely, thanks. Quiet, but kind of perfect. I ate, I slept. You know, the usual.' I'd been worrying about Mum and her scan all week, but I didn't want to mention it to anyone else yet. If I didn't talk about it, I could keep a lid on the panic I felt when I woke in the middle of the night and lay in bed thinking about the appointment. I had decided to wait for the results of the scan and then we could go from there. 'Anyway, how was yours?'

'Terrible,' Bill replied. 'I was working for most of it, trying to sort out some investors.' He took a swig of beer and leant on the kitchen counter. 'So, I haven't left the office before midnight this week and I'm doing no exercise apart from walking from my desk to have a pee four times a day. But that's how start-up life is,' he sighed and had another slug of his beer.

'Love life?' I asked.

'I'm still seeing that girl, Willow. I told you about her before Christmas, right?'

I nodded. 'The Tinder one? Who works in… ?' I couldn't

actually remember much about her. I was always, selfishly, slightly peeved when Bill was dating someone because it meant he was less available for cinema trips and pizza.

'Interior design, yeah. She's cool. But everything's so busy at the moment that I keep having to cancel on any plans we make in favour of a "chicken chow mein for one" at my desk.'

'Have you invited her tonight?'

'Yeah. But she couldn't make it.'

'OK. So, who's coming?'

Normally, Lex would be here too, and she and I would spend the night drinking wine while discussing our New Year's resolutions. But Lex had gone away to Italy with her boyfriend, Hamish, this year. So, I was slightly nervous about who Bill had invited. Or not nervous exactly. Just apprehensive about having to talk to strangers all night.

'Er, there's Robin and Sal, who you know. Then a couple I don't think you've met who are friends from home who've just got engaged – Jonny and Olivia. Two friends from business school you haven't met either. Lou, who's in town for a bit from America, who you'll love, she's amazing. And a guy called Callum I haven't seen for years but who knows Lou, too.' He looked at his phone as it buzzed. 'Oh, that's her now,' he said.

'Lou, hi,' he said, answering it. 'No, no, don't worry, just a bottle of something would be great… number fifty-three, yep? Blue door, just ring the bell. See you in a tick.'

★

By 11 p.m., everyone was still sitting around Bill's kitchen table, their wine glasses smeary from sticky fingers. I'd drunk a lot of red wine and was sitting at one end of the table, holed up like a hostage, while Sal and Olivia, sitting either side of me, discussed their weddings. How was it physically possible for two fully grown women to care so much about what font their wedding invitations should be written in? I thought about the countless weddings I'd been to in the past couple of years. Lace dress after lace dress (since these days everyone wanted to look as demure as Kate Middleton on her wedding day), fistfuls of confetti outside the church, a race back to the reception for ninety-four glasses of champagne and three canapés. Dinner was usually a bit of a blur if I was honest. Some sort of dry chicken, probably. Then thirty-eight cocktails after dinner, which I typically spilled all over myself and the dance floor. Bed shortly after midnight with a blistered foot from the inappropriate heels I'd worn. I couldn't recall what font any of the invitations were written in.

'Polly,' they said simply at the top. Just 'Polly' on its own. Never 'Polly and so-and-so' since I never had a boyfriend. Sometimes an invitation said 'Polly and plus one'. But that was similarly hopeless since I never had one of those either. I reached for the wine bottle, telling myself to stop being so morose.

'Who's for coffee?' asked Bill, standing up.

'I'm OK on red.'

'You're not on your bike tonight?' asked Bill.

'Nope, I'll Uber. But touched by your concern.'

'Just checking. Right, everyone next door. I'm going to put the kettle on.'

There were murmurs of approval and everyone stood and started to gather up plates and paper napkins from the floor. 'Don't do any of that,' said Bill. 'I'll do it later.'

I picked up the wine bottle and my glass and walked through the doors into the sitting room, collapsing onto a sofa and yawning. Definitely a bit pissed.

Sal and Olivia followed after me and sat on the opposite sofa, still quacking on about weddings. 'We're having a photo booth but not a cheese table because I don't think it ever gets eaten. What do you think?' I heard Sal say.

As if she'd been asked her opinion on Palestine, Olivia solemnly replied, 'It's so hard, isn't it? We're not having a photo booth but we are going to have a videographer there all day, so...'

I yawned again. I'd been at uni with Sal. She once stripped naked and ran across a football pitch to protest against tuition fees. But here, discussing cheese tables and photo booths, she seemed a different person. An alien from Planet Wedding.

'So, you're a fellow cyclist?' said Bill's friend from business school, sitting down beside me on the sofa.

'Yup. Most of the time. Just not when I've drunk ten bottles of wine.'

'Very sensible. Sorry, I'm Callum by the way.' He stuck his hand out for me to shake.

Stuck, as I had been, between two wedding fetishists, I hadn't noticed Callum much. He had a shaved head and was wearing a light grey t-shirt, which showed off a pair of muscly upper arms, and excellent trainers. Navy blue Nike Airs. I always looked at men's shoes. Pointy black lace-ups: bad. The correct pair of trainers: aphrodisiac. Lex always criticized me for being too picky about men's shoes. But what if you started dating someone who wore pointy black lace-ups, or, worse, shiny brown shoes with square ends, and then fell in love with them? You'd be looking at spending the rest of your life with someone who wore bad shoes.

'I'm Polly,' I replied, looking up from Callum's trainers.

'So you're an old mate of Bill's?'

'Yep, for years. Since we were teenagers.'

He nodded.

'And you met him at business school?'

He nodded again. 'Yeah, at LBS.'

'So what do you do now?' I asked.

'Deeply boring. I work in insurance, although I'm trying to move into K&R.'

'What's that?'

'Kidnap and ransom. So more the security world really.' He leant back against the sofa and propped one of his muscly arms on it.

'How very James Bond.'

He laughed. 'We'll see.'

'Do you travel a lot?'

'A bit. I'd like to do more. To see more. What about you?'

'I work for a magazine. It's called *Posh!*' I said, as if it was a question, wondering if he'd heard of it.

He laughed again and nodded. 'I know. Sort of… society stuff?'

'Exactly. Castles. Labradors. That sort of thing.'

He grinned at me. 'I like Labradors. Fun?'

'Yup. Mad, but fun.'

'Do you get to travel much?'

'Sometimes. To cold, draughty piles in Scotland if I'm very lucky.'

'How glamorous,' he said, grinning again.

Was this flirting? I wasn't sure. I was never sure. At school, we'd learned about flirting by reading *Cosmopolitan*, which said that it meant brushing the other person with your hand lightly. Also, that girls should bite their lips in front of boys, or was it lick their lips? They should do something to attract attention to their mouths, anyway. My flirting skills hadn't progressed much since and, sometimes, when trying to cack-handedly flirt with someone, I'd simultaneously touch a man's arm or knee *and* lick my lips and end up looking like I was having some kind of stroke.

'Hang on, hold your glass for a moment,' he said, leaning across me.

My stomach flipped. Was he lunging? Here? Already? In Bill's flat? Blimey. Maybe I didn't give myself enough credit. Maybe I was better at flirting than I realized.

He wasn't lunging. He was reaching for a book. Underneath my glass, on the coffee table, was a huge, heavy coffee table book. Callum picked it up and laid it across both our laps.

He leant back and started flicking through the pages. They

were exquisite travel photos – reindeer in the snow around a Swedish lake, an old man washing himself on some steps in Delhi, a volcano in Indonesia belching out great clouds of orange smoke.

'I want to go here,' he said, pointing at a photo of a chalky landscape, a salt flat in Ethiopia.

'Go on then. And then... let's go here,' I replied, turning the page. It was Venice.

'Venice? Have you ever been?' He turned to look at me.

'No.' Was now a good moment to touch his arm? I quite wanted to touch his arm.

'Then I will take you.'

'Ha!' I laughed nervously and clapped my hand on his forearm.

We carried on turning the pages and laughing for a while, discussing where we wanted to go until the photos were becoming quite blurry. I wasn't really concentrating anyway, because Callum had moved his leg underneath the book so it was touching mine. I glanced across at him. How tall was he? Hard to tell sitting down.

'Right, team,' said Bill, sometime later from across the room, draining his coffee cup. 'I think it might be home time. Sorry to end the party but I've got to go into the office tomorrow.'

Callum closed the book and moved his leg, stretching out on the sofa and yawning. 'Fun sponge.'

'I know, mate, but some of us can't just drink for a living. We've got real jobs.'

'Talk to me when I'm in Peshawar.' He stood up and clapped Bill on the back in a man hug. 'Good to see you after so long, mate. Thanks for dinner.' He was the same height as Bill, I noted. Sort of six foot-ish. A good height. The size I always wanted a man to be so I didn't feel like a giraffe in bed next to him. That thing about everybody being the same size lying down is rubbish.

Around us, everyone else was saying goodbye to one another. 'Thanks, love,' I said, hugging Bill. 'Don't work too hard tomorrow.'

'Welcome,' he said back, into my shoulder. 'And I won't. I should be around on Sunday if you are? Cinema or something? Is Lex back?'

'Yup, she gets back tomorrow so said I'd see her for lunch on Sunday. Wanna join?'

'Maybe, speak tomorrow?'

I nodded and Bill turned to say goodbye to Lou behind us.

'Where you heading back to?' Callum asked as we stood by the open front door. I was squinting at my phone, trying to find Uber.

'Shepherd's Bush.'

'Perfect. As you're not cycling I will escort you home.'

'Why, where are you?'

'Nearby,' he replied. 'What's your postcode?'

This never happened. Sightings of the Loch Ness Monster were more common than me going home with anyone. I frowned as I tried to remember what state my bikini line was in. I probably shouldn't sleep with him; I had an awful feeling it looked like the Hanging Gardens of Babylon.

'What's wrong?' he said, looking at my face.

'Nothing, all good,' I replied quickly. Also, I knew I hadn't shaved my legs for weeks. Or months, maybe. So, a few minutes later, in the back of the Uber, I reached down and tried to surreptitiously stick two fingers underneath the ankle of my jeans to check how bristly my legs were. They felt like a scouring brush.

'What you doing?' asked Callum, looking at me quizzically.

'Just an itch.' I sat back in the taxi.

'You're not coming in,' I said, in my sternest voice, when the car pulled up outside my flat.

''Course I am. I need to make sure you get in safely,' he replied, opening his door and getting out.

So, as alarmed as I was about my ape-like levels of hairiness, I let him in, whereupon he immediately started looking through my kitchen cupboards. I kicked off my shoes and sat at the kitchen table, watching him, still hiccupping.

'Shhhhhh, my flatmate's asleep,' I said to his back, as he inspected the labels of five or six half-empty bottles he'd discovered in one cupboard.

'This'll do.' It was a bottle of cheap vodka, the sort that turns you blind. 'Where are your glasses?'

I pointed at a cupboard above his head.

'I can't drink all that,' I said, as he handed me a glass.

'Yes you can, just knock it back.' He swallowed his in one and looked at me expectantly.

I lifted my glass, nearly gagged at the vapours, then opened my mouth and took three slugs.

'Good work.' He took the glass back as I shivered and put it down on the table. 'I mean, why do the Russians like this so much? It's disgusting, swallowing it makes me—'

He interrupted me by cupping my face with his hands and kissing me. His tongue tasted of vodka.

'Which one's your room?'

I pointed at a door, and he took my hand, pulled me off the kitchen table and into my room, where I froze. There were two embarrassing things I needed to hide: my slightly shrivelled, browning earplugs on the bedside table, and my ancient bunny rabbit, a childhood comforter, which was lying between the pillows, his glass eyes glaring at me with an accusatory air.

I reached for both, opened my knicker drawer and stuffed them in there. I felt briefly guilty about my rabbit and then thought, *You are about to have sex for the first time in five hundred months, Polly, now is not the time to be sentimental about your stuffed toy.*

Callum sat down at the end of the bed and started unlacing his shoes.

'Hang on, I'm just going to do something.' I picked up a box of matches on the bedside table and lit a candle next to it.

And here is a list of the things that happened next, which illustrates why I should never, ever be allowed to even think about having sex with anyone.

Having lit the candle, I sat next to Callum and he started unbuttoning my shirt. But then I panicked about him doing this while I was sitting because of the fat rolls on my stomach, so I lay down instead, pulling him back onto the bed. He then undid the rest of my shirt buttons and there were a few undignified moments where I flailed around like a beached seal trying to get my arms out of it.

The tussle of the bra strap. Callum reached for it, clearly wanting to be one of those nimble-fingered men who just have to blink at a bra strap – any bra strap – for it to ping free. 'I've nearly got it,' he said, after several seconds of fiddling while I arched my back.

Getting my knickers off. This required me to waggle my legs in the air like an upturned beetle.

Callum then moved his way down my stomach until he was kneeling on the floor, his head between my legs. I wondered whether to make a joke about needing some sort of Black & Decker machinery to get through the hair and then decided it would kill the vibe. So, I started worrying about my breathing instead. It's awkward to just lie there in silence, so I decided to start panting a bit as he used his tongue on me. But it's quite hard to pant when, after a promising beginning, Callum – perhaps encouraged by my erratic breathing – started working harder with his tongue, like a dog at a water bowl. So, then it started hurting, as opposed to feeling remotely pleasurable, and I decided I'd lost sensation in my entire vagina and instead lay there wondering when to suggest that he came back up again. And how do you do that, anyway, without causing offence?

The worst bit of all. I tapped him on the head and he looked up. 'Come up,' I said, in what I hoped was a seductive, come-hither way.

He looked up from between my legs and frowned. 'Why? Aren't you enjoying it?'

Oh, GOD, why is sex this embarrassing? Does it always have to be this embarrassing?

'No, no, I just want to, erm, return the favour.'

CRINGE. I thought I might die. I might actually die from cringing.

So Callum crawled back up and rolled over, lying on his back, still with his boxers on. I then climbed on top of him, trying not to slouch again so that my stomach didn't crease into rolls of fat. Then I noticed that I hadn't plucked my nipple hairs recently either. Too late. I wriggled backwards so that I was kneeling between his legs and started pulling his boxers off. Another difficult move because I had to stand up to pull them out from underneath him.

Callum's penis wasn't quite hard, so I opened my mouth and gently started sucking the head of it. He groaned. I ran my mouth slowly down it, trying to ignore the musty smell. After a few minutes, my thigh muscles started to burn. For God's sake. How much longer was this going to go on for? I wriggled my knees in a bit closer, then opened one eye and squinted at his penis. Why do they look like giant earthworms? Then his moaning started getting louder and I felt one of his hands on my head, pressing my mouth down. I'd read magazine articles before that said you should suck their balls as well, but I'd never been sure I could fit everything in my mouth at once. It would be like tackling a foot-long Subway. Or were you supposed to suck just one ball at a time?

I gagged as his penis hit the back of my throat, then he gave a sudden shout and my mouth filled with warm semen. Slightly salty, slightly sweet. I swallowed as quickly as possible. The thought of that swimming around in my stomach with the vodka was ungodly.

'Just going to get a glass of water,' I said through a sticky mouth, climbing over him and picking up an empty glass from the bedside table. In the bathroom, I wiped my mouth with some tissue and looked in the mirror. Well, that bit's done so that's something. And it's always quite gratifying to get there, isn't it? Mostly because then your thighs get a break, but also because it means that you've done something right and your teeth didn't get in the way. And anyway, I decided, filling up the glass from the tap again in case he wanted a drink, it's my turn. That's the rule. He should possibly have tried harder to sort me out first. But never mind. He could make up for it now.

'D'you want some water?' I whispered, walking back into the bedroom and holding out the glass. Callum was standing up with his jeans back on and his phone in his hand.

'No, I'm good, thanks. I'm actually going to get an Uber. Got golf in the morning so I need to get home.'

'Oh. OK. Cool. No problem,' I stuttered.

WHAT?

'Thanks though, that was great.' He reached down for his t-shirt, pulled it over his head, patted his jean pockets, then – while I was still standing there, naked, cold, holding the glass of water – leant in and kissed me on the cheek.

'Good to meet you.'

'Er, yeah. You too. Hang on, I'll let you out.'

'Nah, don't worry. I can let myself out. See you soon.'

'Oh… Sure. OK… Bye,' I said, still holding the glass of water, as he walked out.

I heard the front door close, put the glass down and stood naked in my bedroom thinking. Was that now a thing? Can men just Uber at – I looked at my phone – 2.54 a.m. after a blow job, having not returned the favour, and think that's acceptable?

He's perfect ... on paper

If you loved *What Happens Now?* don't miss the new laugh-out-loud novel from Sophia Money-Coutts

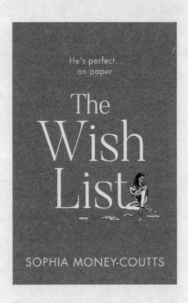

Florence Fairfax *isn't* lonely. She loves her job at the little bookshop in Chelsea and her cat, Marmalade, keeps her company at night. But everything changes after Florence meets Irish love coach, Gwendolyn.

When Gwendolyn makes Florence write a wish list describing her perfect man, Florence refuses to take it seriously. Finding someone who likes cats, doesn't wear pointy shoes and can overlook her 'counting habit'? Impossible!

Until, later that week, a handsome man asks for help in the bookshop... But is Rory the one, or is he simply too good to be true? Florence is about to find out that her criteria for finding Mr Right aren't as important as she thought...